SUA SPONTE:
THE MINNEAPOLIS ADOZ

-- A WATCHTOWER PREQUEL--

MIKAEL CARLSON

DANBURY, CONNECTICUT

Sua Sponte: The Minneapolis ADOZ
Copyright © 2025 by Mikael Carlson

Published by Warrington Publishing
Danbury, CT
www.warringtonpublishing.com

Printed in the United States of America
First Edition
ISBN: 978-1-944972-64-6 (paperback)
          978-1-944972-65-3 (hardcover)
          978-1-944972-63-9 (ebook)

Cover designed by JD&J
Edited by Mike Waitz at Sticks & Stones

Novels by Mikael Carlson:

– The Michael Bennit Series –
The iCandidate
The iCongressman
The iSpeaker
The iAmerican

– Tierra Campos Thrillers –
Justifiable Deceit
Devious Measures
Vital Targets
Revealed Secrets
Decisive Endgame

– Tierra Campos Thrillers Prequels –
Narrow Escape: The Summerville Massacre

– Watchtower Thrillers –
The Eyes of Others
The Eyes of Innocents
The Eyes of Victims
The Eyes of Addicts

– Watchtower Prequels –
Sua Sponte: The Minneapolis ADOZ

– The America, Inc. Saga –
The Black Swan Event
Bounded Rationality
Boiling the Ocean
Caveat Emptor

– The Santa Trilogy –
Banning Santa
Delivering Santa

For the proud men and women who serve this great country in uniform and place service to it above all else.

FOUR YEARS PRIOR TO THE EVENTS DEPICTED IN
THE EYES OF ADDICTS

PROLOGUE

SSG EMMIT "CHICAGO" HASKINS

NEAR THE IRAQ BORDER
SYRIA

This place is the armpit of the world. Sure, that can be said about a lot of backwater countries and inhospitable landscapes. Many of the soldiers Emmit knows say that about the Army posts they live on. Hell, Fayetteville, North Carolina, used to be called "Fayettenam" because of all the violence in the city outside of Fort Bragg. But this is different.

Al-Tanf Garrison is a key U.S. military outpost near the borders of Iraq and Jordan in southeastern Syria. Originally set up to train and support anti-ISIS fighters, its location on a major highway makes it strategically important in the campaign against the Iranian-backed militias. They need an established land corridor from Tehran to Damascus and Beirut to conduct and support their operations. The Rangers are posted here to deny them use of that route.

Not that anyone back home cares. The Syrian mission is all but unknown to the American public. Emmit is fairly certain the politicians want it that way. There are only around nine hundred U.S. soldiers, not counting contractors, operating in all of Syria. Most are in the North to support Syrian Democratic Forces, while his unit of Rangers holds down the South with a few coalition troops and the Maghawir al-Thawra rebel group.

Most of Staff Sergeant Haskins's time here has been pretty boring. It's a lot of downtime spent with the guys in his squad. Sure, there are missions, but nothing like a lot of the veterans of this unit saw in Iraq and Afghanistan. The end of their deployment is growing closer. In a couple of short weeks, they will be on a plane home. To a man, all of them hoped things would stay quiet. Then, ISIS got frisky.

An Iranian suicide drone flew low over fencing into the base and struck a maintenance facility, killing a contractor and wounding several Rangers. It was a coordinated attack that targeted a number of bases in the country. It deserved a response.

Two platoons are convoying to a nearby village where Reaper drones surveilling the area reported the ISIS fighters fled after launching the attack. It smells like a trap, but the commander decided to press forward with the mission anyway. About two clicks from the village, their worst fears are realized.

IEDs eviscerate the road, and the center of the convoy is rocked by RPG fire. Movies do a great job with visual effects, but the reality is far more brutal. Films can't capture the feeling of the concussion from a blast wave and what it does to your insides.

A screen can't fully convey the assault on the senses – sight, sound, smell…it's a fight to keep your senses and think clearly. That's what good soldiers in combat are trained for and mentally condition themselves to do – fight through all that to make decisions.

"Ho-ly shit!" one of his men shouts. It sounded like Tulsa up in the turret.

The MRAP in front of them gets hit by an RPG after the IED takes out the vehicle in front of it. There are almost a hundred meters between the convoy vehicles, meaning there is more than a kilometer of separation between the lead and trail vehicles.

Two guys in the heavily armored vehicle are thrown more than twenty feet from the road. Fire is pouring down on them from small rises on either side of the road. It's a classic ambush, and they drove right into it. Why they didn't have a drone reporting what lay ahead is anyone's guess. It's a good question for the after-action report.

"Floor it. Get to that MRAP," Haskins orders as he reaches for the mic on his SINCGARS. The Single Channel Ground and Airborne Radio System is a VHF combat net radio his unit is using for voice and data communications.

"Blackjack One-Six, This is Blackjack One-One," he barks. "Two men are down and in the open! Need suppression and CASEVAC!"

"This is One Actual, roger," his platoon leader acknowledges.

Private First Class O'Leary, whom the team has come to call "Nashville" after his hometown, stops their up-armored Humvee short of the burning MRAP. His remaining squad members pour out of their vehicles, identifying and suppressing enemy fire while maintaining defensive positions.

The enemy fire is withering. Emmit looks around. This is a bad place to be. They're stopped in the kill zone and are easy targets for the ISIS fighters. Dust and smoke choke the air as Emmit ducks behind his HMMWV to dodge the bullets whizzing past him.

"Blackjack One-One, this is Blackjack Six Actual. Get out of that kill zone. Now!"

"Did he just order us to leave men behind?" Specialist Hibbard asks. Emmit just calls him "Tulsa" for brevity.

Emmit shakes his head in disgust. "Blackjack Six, negative. I have men down."

"You can't help them, One-One. You're going to get your men killed. Air support is en route. Now, get out of there before you're cut to pieces!"

"Not without my men, sir!"

"It's an order, Staff Sergeant!"

Emmit drops the radio. His commander isn't wrong. The SOP is to move out of the kill zone as quickly as possible. He stares over the hood of the Hummer and sees Missoula clutching his bleeding leg as he tries dragging Gamecock with one arm to a defilade to his rear. It's drawing a lot of enemy attention. Puffs of dirt are kicked up with every bullet strike, and they are uncomfortably close to them.

"Chicago, we can't leave them!" one of his team leaders shouts.

"Yeah, no shit," Emmit retorts. "How good's that pitcher arm of yours, Atlanta?"

He yanks a smoke grenade from his vest, pulls the pin, and lobs it between the downed soldiers and the enemy. "Nolan Ryan ain't got shit on me."

Atlanta repeats the throws to the left and right of his first. The thick gray cloud belching out of the canisters buys precious seconds. ISIS can't hit what they can't see, not that it has stopped them from trying.

Emmit slaps a fresh mag into his M4 and fires controlled bursts toward the enemy positions. Most of his Rangers, including Nica, Nashville, Tulsa, Bronx, Hollywood, and Atlanta, join him. Their accurate fire suppresses the enemy marksmen on bluffs to both sides of the road.

His heart is pounding out of his chest. He sprints through the open ground, sliding next to Missoula, who is in serious pain, having reached the shallow defilade with Gamecock. The Montanan is as tough as nails. Hailing from a long list of ranchers, he's no-nonsense.

"Fancy meeting you here. I told you to keep your arms and legs in the train car at all times. See what happens when you don't listen?"

"Ha, ha."

"All right, let's get you out of here."

He hoists Missoula onto his shoulder in a fireman's carry, gritting his teeth against the weight. The volume of fire picks up from both sides. Frustrated, two ISIS fighters rush down from the small rise, their AK-47s raised. Emmit's squad fires controlled bursts and drops both of them. That was dumb.

"Take care of him," Emmit says, laying Missoula down next to their Humvee. I'll be right back."

"Chicago!" Nashville shouts. "Aw, hell…."

This isn't suicide, but it's close. The ISIS fighters have figured out what's going on and are intent on stopping Emmit from retrieving their trophies. The covering fire is the only thing keeping them at bay…and him alive.

He checks on Gamecock. The Ranger is unconscious and has blood trickling from his mouth. It looks like he's breathing, but there's no time to ensure that. Not that it matters. He isn't leaving anyone behind, alive or dead.

Chicago grabs him by his body armor and drags him back to the road. It's slower than the carry but presents a smaller target for the terrorists to shoot at. Most of them are firing in his direction. Countless rounds slam into the dirt beside him.

Gamecock gets hoisted into the vehicle as Chicago climbs into the front. The rest of his squad mounts their vehicles while the combat lifesaver works on applying a tourniquet to Missoula's leg. He isn't paying any attention to Gamecock. That isn't a good sign.

"Get us out of here!" Emmit commands.

The vehicle lurches backward just as two RPGs scream past them to the front.

"Oh, shit! I could read the serial number on that thing!" Tulsa screeches.

That was close. Chicago sees three more men pop up on the bluff and pull launchers up to their shoulders. He's about to shout at his men to engage them when they evaporate into pink mist. He saw the results before he heard the sound.

The AC-130J "Ghostrider" is a heavily armed, long-endurance, ground-attack Air Force aircraft designed for close air support, air interdiction, and armed reconnaissance. It has a 25mm GAU-12 Equalizer Gatling gun, a 40mm Bofors cannon, and a 105mm howitzer. The Gatling gun took out the guys with the RPGs, and now the "Angel of Death" is pounding both sides of the road with the cannon and howitzer.

Chicago leans out, firing his last rounds to cover the retreat. Not that he needs to. The ISIS terrorists not already wiped out by the Ghostrider will run, and they will only die tired. Air dominance is a beautiful thing, and he wouldn't be surprised if the F-22 Raptors, which technically aren't in-country, are flying cover for the gunship.

"You're a crazy bastard, Chicago," Bronx says from the back. "You must have really wanted that Silver Star before you get out of here."

He doesn't answer. The Silver Star Medal is the third-highest military combat decoration. It's awarded to members of the U.S. military who display exceptional gallantry in enemy action. That's not at all why he did it.

This squad is his family, outside of his little sister. He doesn't want to see a video uploaded of them parading around the body of a fellow Ranger and then desecrating it. He's sure that the families of these men wouldn't want to see that either. "Leave no man behind" isn't just a phrase. It's part of the warrior ethos. If nothing else, Emmit satisfied that pledge.

The convoy is going to return to base. Chicago isn't looking forward to what happens next. This mission is over, and the Army will have to report the casualties to the American people. Worse, he disobeyed a direct order from his commanding officer. There are going to be consequences for that. Forget a medal…he will be lucky to avoid a court-martial when the dust settles on this debacle.

A YEAR LATER

CHAPTER ONE
CHIEF VANESSA CAMPBELL

CITY HALL CONFERENCE ROOM
MINNEAPOLIS, MINNESOTA

The police chief enters the impressive pink granite structure that occupies an entire city block between Third and Fourth Avenues and Fourth and Fifth Streets. Vanessa Campbell has always admired the massive five-story building and its soaring clock chime tower that was once heralded as the largest public timepiece in the world.

The exterior, with its arched entryways, turrets, and steep roof pavilions, exhibits Romanesque design features. The Fourth Street entrance leads her into a five-story atrium with a stained-glass window skylight illuminating marble walls and a ceremonial staircase. At its center is the massive "Father of the Waters" statue. The building has been remodeled and expanded several times since its opening, but it has never managed to lose its charm. The same cannot be said for some of the people who work here.

She enters the conference room just as she does every Monday morning. This weekly meeting has been on the calendar at the mayor's insistence since he took office. You would think the man would show up on time for it. It looks like today isn't that day.

"Good morning, everyone."

"Chief," they all say in unison.

Following the fallout from the death of George Floyd in 2020, the department was reorganized into three administrative bureaus: Patrol, Investigations, and Professional Standards. Each is led by a deputy chief, with the Patrol Bureau further divided into five precincts with a commander given the rank of inspector. The revamped structure was designed to be decentralized, giving each precinct and bureau a degree of independence with policing. The jury is still out on whether it's a net benefit to the community.

"We all know what the hot topic is for today's meeting, so we might as well get it out of the way."

"Should we wait for the mayor?" one of the deputy chiefs asks.

"We're already five minutes past the start. The mayor can catch up."

Vanessa would wait for most people, but their "fearless" leader is a different story. He hates cops and doesn't hold back in showing his resentment about the department. The chief is convinced she would have been sacked long ago if she weren't a minority woman. Her merits aren't saving her job in this city. Her skin color is. At least, that's her belief.

Everyone around the table knows the story of the incident at this point, but the recap does fill in some details. A black man held up a convenience store in the downtown area and assaulted the clerk when he tried to fight back. The man is okay, but he did get a serious laceration to his scalp. A 9-1-1 call came in, and officers responded. The first patrolman to arrive on the scene shouted commands that were naturally disobeyed.

The subject fled the area on foot, knocking an older woman to the ground as he fled. She required hospitalization, and the man was finally tackled a couple of blocks from the robbery scene. After a struggle, the officer disengaged and drew his taser. The man was armed with a knife and was threatening the officer and other bystanders. After the subject failed to heed commands, the patrolman fired his taser when the suspect lunged for him.

In the grand scheme of things, it was a textbook way to handle the situation. The officer didn't use deadly or excessive force on a noncompliant criminal. Unfortunately, there are entire groups of people who only see a white cop tasing a black man. Since the video the news is playing is completely without context, she can almost understand why people are upset.

"The wall-to-wall national media coverage isn't helping," Otto Goldberg moans. "They relish dragging old skeletons out of the closet, and we have a lot of them. Perhaps if you embrace the community policing model more, unfortunate incidents like this wouldn't happen."

The assistant chief of community trust is a new position, and the man who is filling it is the bane of Vanessa's existence. Goldberg commands the Constitutional Policing Bureau, the Internal Affairs Bureau, and the restructured Professional Standards Bureau. Among his duties are serving as a community liaison to implement and achieve compliance with the state settlement agreement. While she understands the mandate, he interprets his role as someone who sides with criminals and demonizes the officers on the force. He isn't overly popular with the officers in the ranks.

"Yes, perhaps we should have given him the key to the city for robbing a convenience store, assaulting the clerk, and knocking an old woman to the ground during the pursuit."

"There's no need to be glib, Chief," Inspector Wilma Sillyere warns. "We need to evaluate whether there was a better way for the officer to handle the situation."

"Yeah, he could have shot him," one of the other inspectors mumbles.

"Because shooting an unarmed man would solve our PR problem with the media."

"He was armed. You'd know that if you had bothered reading the report, Wilma."

Wilma and Otto are partners in crime, if such a thing can exist on a police force. They both have radically different ideas on how to keep the people of this city safe than suit Vanessa's tastes. Unfortunately, both are protected by the mayor. The three of them together are the trifecta from hell when it comes to protecting and serving. She needs to move this conversation along before it devolves into something she can no longer control.

"What about the officer in question? What's his service record like?" Vanessa asks, nodding at the 1st Precinct boss. He opens a file folder and picks up a sheet of paper.

"Impeccable. Officer Eirik Ohlsen was a top graduate of the academy and is a veteran with almost seven years on the force. He is well-regarded by the community and volunteers for a program that mentors disadvantaged children. Most of them are minorities."

"That doesn't sound like someone they will easily paint as a closet racist," Vanessa concludes.

"Like that will stop people," Inspector Sillyere argues. "The truth is, because of his actions, we're sitting on a powder keg…again."

"That's the reason we reorganized this department, as I recall," Mayor Elliott Thurlow says, walking into the room and taking his seat. "Apparently, we haven't learned our lesson after what happened with George Floyd. Isn't that right, Chief Campbell? Or do you not remember?"

Her eyes narrow. "I was on the *front* line for those riots."

The mayor wags his chubby finger at her. "I would be careful calling them riots or characterize the protests of our citizens as anything related to warfare. Don't you agree?"

Whether they were protests or riots depends on which side of the prevailing narrative someone falls. Either way, the demonstrations and civil unrest that erupted following George Floyd's death rocked the city and the nation. Video footage showed Floyd repeatedly saying, "I can't breathe," which became a rallying cry. While the mayor is correct in saying that many protests were peaceful, the ones here were not. There were a number of reports of looting, property damage, confrontations between protesters and law enforcement, and arsons, including the torching of the 3rd Precinct police station.

"It was a poor choice of words, sir," Vanessa says, choosing to bite her tongue. Riots are what they were, and anyone with two eyes would attest to that.

"I would think so. What administrative actions have been taken against Officer Ohlsen?"

"Administrative actions?"

"Yes. You're the chief of police, Vanessa, so I know you are aware of what those are. What is the expected punishment for this incident? Suspension? Dismissal?"

"I don't think either would be appropriate at this time. We have bodycam footage and are still looking at video from other devices. We are still investigating the incident, but it doesn't appear that Officer Ohlsen is in the wrong in this case."

"I see," the mayor says, checking the length of his fingernails. "I remember that being the department's position with the officers involved in the Floyd murder as well. Protesters wanted real change in response to systemic racism and police brutality. Is this your idea of delivering that?"

"What about justice for Officer Ohlsen?"

"What about justice for the man he tased?"

In the mayor's eyes, it doesn't matter whether the man who was arrested is a criminal. It doesn't matter that Ohlsen was protecting the city's citizens. It doesn't matter that most people would think his actions were justified. There is no chance of Vanessa winning this argument.

The mayor stands, signaling this meeting is over. Or, at a minimum, his participation in it.

"Fire him. Today. Then, send out a press release condemning his actions and apologizing to the community. I want the local news reading it on air tonight."

CHAPTER TWO

DAVID BRASS

CONSTITUTION AVENUE NW
WASHINGTON, D.C.

Washington is the hub of the federal government and the epicenter of the American political universe. Congressional sessions, Supreme Court cases, the churning bureaucracy, constant protests and rallies, and the millions of tourists who visit the monuments and museums make the city feel active and alive. Those are among the reasons David Brass hates this place so much.

The National Mall is moderately busy, but the arrival of fall means fewer crowds compared to spring and summer. The popular area, with its iconic landmarks and museums, is about the last place he wants to be. But orders are orders, and the one summoning him to the corner of Constitution Avenue and Seventeenth Street was unambiguous.

He is a stone's throw from The Ellipse, which is a stone's throw from the White House. It is the center of rot in a decaying society. Little of worth escapes the walls of that complex. Like so much in society, it's a showpiece while the dirty work is done elsewhere. In that respect, it's the world's greatest magic trick. Washington is the nucleus of deceit and lies. He prefers to avoid this city while he engages in his own.

That's the sandbox that CIA operatives play in. New agents see working for the world's premier intelligence agency as a way to contribute to national security and protect U.S. interests. Others are fascinated with geopolitics and international relations. The die-hards in the ranks that you have to be concerned with are drawn to the high-stakes missions and the challenging work. David Brass joined because it suits him.

The limelight is for suckers. Despite what the American public believes, power is not concentrated with their elected representatives or even the president of the United States. The real levers of power hide in the shadows and away from the scrutiny of the press and showboats in office. There is no operation on Earth more secretive than the CIA, and there is nobody in the agency more off the grid than he is.

A Lincoln Town Car rounds the corner and pulls over to the curb. Black sedans are ubiquitous in this city, but they don't stop on random corners without reason. His ride is here, and Brass slips into the back seat before closing the door. The tall, gaunt, bespectacled man with the salt and pepper hair doesn't bother acknowledging him.

"I could have met you in the office. It would have saved me the descent with Virgil into the depths of hell."

The CIA director continues looking out his window toward the WWII Memorial. "Which circle do you think this is?"

"The Fourth, Fifth, or Ninth, depending on which part of the government you're meeting with."

The first part of Dante Alighieri's 14th-century epic poem, *The Divine Comedy*, envisions hell as a vast, funnel-shaped structure with nine concentric circles representing increasing levels of sin and punishment. Guided by the Roman poet Virgil, Dante journeys through these circles, each of which corresponds to specific sins. In the work, the Fourth Circle is greed, the Eighth is fraud, and the Ninth is treachery.

Alistair Lancaster smirks, the *Inferno* reference not being lost on him. The man should have come to age in a British boarding school. From a wealthy and politically connected family, the man has been a fixture in political circles for three decades. Getting named as the director of the Central Intelligence Agency is only his most recent conquest and one that he looks like he's regretting.

"The White House should have been the Tenth Circle that contains all the previous ones. I just got done being verbally flayed by the DNI and president in the Oval Office. It's not how I wanted to start my week. Do you want to guess why?"

There is only one reason that Brass can think of. "Railspike."

"When I find out who leaked the details of that operation, there isn't a hole dark or deep enough for them to hide in."

That's not an idle threat. There is no love lost between Director Lancaster and the director of national intelligence. The two men are constantly at odds, and the political battles between them have become the stuff of legend within the Beltway.

The DNI serves as the principal advisor to the president and the National Security Council on intelligence matters. Born from the 9/11 Commission report, the role oversees and coordinates the eighteen agencies and organizations that comprise America's intelligence community, including the best-known three-letter ones such as the CIA, NSA, and FBI. This DNI will use anything he can to make Alistair's life miserable.

"What do you need me to do?" Brass asks, making the question as matter-of-fact as possible.

"What makes you think I want you to do anything?"

"I wouldn't be here otherwise."

The director nods. "Put Pendulum in motion."

Brass stares out the window as the driver makes a lazy loop around the Lincoln Memorial. "Are you sure? That's a 'break glass in case of emergency' operation. If the details of it ever see the light of day, the DNI will be the least of your problems. You won't survive the congressional hearings…or prison."

"I'm aware of the stakes. That's why I rely on you. You're a man who can be relied upon in high-risk, high-reward operations."

The corner of Brass's mouth curls. "And I'm expendable."

"You are. Every person who rises to the top ranks of the federal government was expendable at some point in their lives, myself included. But I persevered because I realized that was the price. So do you, and that's what makes you indispensable. I'm counting on you to get me results. If you do, there is a good chance you will have my office someday."

"That's the carrot. What's the stick?"

"Railspike became a reality out of necessity. If it fails, or the details make it into the public's view, what do you think will happen to Watchtower?"

It's the fallacy of false equivalency. The two programs have absolutely nothing to do with each other. They have different aims and priorities. They also require different resources. The only reason for the director to bring it up is leverage. He knows all about Brass's pet project.

"It isn't even a program yet. Even if it was operational, there is a distinct difference."

"Do you really think Congress will care after they finish dragging me through the mud? You can fool people all you want, but I know full well what Watchtower will mean for surveillance in this country and who it will target. Pendulum is a go. Fix my problem, David, and I will make your pet project a reality."

The driver pulls to the side of the road. This conversation is over. It looks like David will be hopping the Metro back to Virginia. That suits him fine. He hasn't stepped foot in Langley in half a decade.

"Consider it done."

CHAPTER THREE
EMMIT "CHICAGO" HASKINS

THE FIFTH STREET HOUSE
MINNEAPOLIS, MINNESOTA

Emmit bounds forward and stops. Fire seems like it's coming from everywhere. Off to his right, one of his teammates goes down. Figures. Cover and concealment are not the same thing. Just because you are hiding behind something doesn't mean that something stops bullets. That moron just learned that the hard way.

After a quick magazine change, Emmit is back in action. They are almost at the objective. He takes a deep breath and races forward. If he can make it to the corner of the building, he can flank the five or so assholes firing at his squad. He reaches it and peeks around the pillar, almost getting his head shot off for the effort. He grabs a grenade from his vest and pulls the pin. He's about to throw it when the television goes dark.

"What the hell?"

Emmit turns to see his sister standing behind him, her arms folded with a remote in her right hand, giving him the same disapproving face she did as a kid when he hung her dolls from the fire escape of their fourth-floor Chicago apartment.

"Was that really necessary?"

"It's the only way I can get your attention. I've said good morning to you a half dozen times. Do you want me to turn it back on?"

Emmit drops the remote next to him. "No, I'm sure I'm already dead."

"Is this how you plan on spending the rest of your life? Playing video games from dawn to dusk every day?"

"I don't play every day."

"You know, I missed my brother while you were in Georgia. I was thrilled when you said you were coming up here to stay for a couple of weeks."

"Good, I'm glad—"

"It's been six months."

Emmit furrows his brow. Has it been that long?

"Are you trying to get rid of me?"

Kenyala crashes into the sofa and hugs a throw pillow. "No. I like having my big brother around, especially after what happened."

The Haskins family story is nothing if not tragic. Emmit and Kenyala lost their father as children when he got drunk at a bar and wandered into the street in front of a sanitation truck. Their mother was never the same after that.

She did just enough to get them through high school and then found her final solace at the bottom of a pill bottle. With both parents gone, it fell to Emmit to look after his sister. He thought that responsibility was finally relinquished to the sound of wedding bells and "I dos."

Clayton Brown was a good man. He doted on Kenyala and treated her with love and respect. As if he had a choice. Emmit was in the military at that point and making friends. He promised to bring them all with him if Clayton ever mistreated or stepped out on his wife. Not that he would have.

Unfortunately, like all tragedies, their marriage was cut short. Clayton was in construction and had an accident due to his employer's negligence. Kenyala received a generous settlement, but she can never be made entirely whole. Emmit isn't trying to fill the void, but he is trying to lessen its depth.

"But…?"

"But, Emmit, you need to move on with your life."

"Are you my therapist?"

Kenyala bops him in the head with the pillow. "No, but I will kick your ass if you sass me like that."

"You know that I was well-trained in hand-to-hand combat, right?"

"And I'm your little sister who learned how to fight dirty growing up. Look, Emmit, I know how much the Rangers meant to you. It wasn't just your job. I get it."

He shakes his head. "No, you don't."

"Yes, I do. I may not be able to relate, but I have eyes…and ears. I've heard you say, 'Suey Spaghetti' a thousand times since you joined the Rangers."

"Sua Sponte."

"Whatever," Kenyala says, waving her hand dismissively.

"It's Latin."

"I don't care."

"It's the Ranger motto that means—"

"Of their own accord. I know. You've told me a thousand times. Have you heard back from the security company?"

"Yeah."

"And?"

"Do you really think I'm going to be happy acting as a rent-a-cop?"

"Emmit, nobody is saying that you have to stay in the job until you retire. Go to work and make some money until you find something more permanent."

She's right. And he can't hide from the world in her house forever. Sooner or later, she will start dating again. She will get engaged and then married. All of that will be awkward with her overprotective brother waiting for her to get home like a parent making sure a child makes curfew.

Still, he can't imagine himself as a security guard. It's not that he would suck at it. Well, maybe he would. Rangers use small-group tactics to provide the maximum opportunity for America's enemies to die for their country. Somehow, Emmit doesn't think that will play well in a suburban shopping mall.

"I miss my guys," Emmit mumbles.

"Call them."

"I have," he says, staring at the television as if it were still on.

"Then invite them over."

"Kenyala, it's the military. It's not like taking a vacation. It doesn't work that way. The Army doesn't just let its soldiers come up to Minnesota for a weekend. They need to fill out a DA Form 31 Request Authority for Leave and get it approved by the entire chain of command, up through the company commander. It only gets approved if there is no training."

"And?"

Emmit smirks. "Rangers are always training."

"Okay…what about the ones who were discharged?" she asks, cocking her head. "Not all of your squad are still in, right? Why don't you have them over for a barbecue or something? There's plenty of room in this house for them to crash."

He's not so sure about that. Yes, there is an extra bedroom, and yes, his guys have spent a lifetime sleeping in the woods, mountains, desert, and even swamps. But his sister's house isn't *that* big.

"Do you think you can handle a bunch of stone-cold killers in this place? They'll tear it apart."

Kenyala tightens her jaw. "Do you think they can handle my wrath if they don't leave *my* house exactly as they found it? I will start ripping arms off if they so much as forget to use a coaster."

Emmit cracks a smile. It's the first time he's had a reason to wear one in a while. His sister has no idea what door she just opened.

"Okay, I'll call them. Maybe some magic will happen. Now, hand me the remote. I have more bad guys to kill."

CHAPTER FOUR

KAI Z

COFFEE BEANS & CAVIAR DREAMS CAFE
HOLLYWOOD, CALIFORNIA

Kai checks his watch for what feels like the hundredth time. She's late, not that it's unexpected. His assistant-turned-girlfriend has never been known for her punctuality. Add to that the traffic jams and long commute times Los Angeles is notorious for, and it's a recipe for wasted time. He should have known not to bother getting here early.

He's on his second latte as he ponders what the draw to this city is. The metro system lacks destination and convenience, the city offers no walkability, the cost of living is high, there are homeless everywhere, and the smog deprives residents of anything resembling fresh air. What makes that funny is how many of the rich elite here lend their voices to the climate change agenda.

L.A. has stark divides between wealthier areas like Beverly Hills and Santa Monica and poorer neighborhoods such as South Los Angeles. The latter is just trying to make ends meet. The former shapes Hollywood's perception of promoting shallow, consumer-driven values and being image-focused. Most of the wealthy celebrities living in their gated communities prioritize appearance over substance. At least, that's been Kai's experience.

Babs O'Leary breezes in, her blonde ponytail swaying back and forth with her hips. L.A. may be a fashion mecca, but you wouldn't know it with her attire. It hasn't changed much since the riots in Portland. She's wearing her usual olive drab army jacket and jeans. The clothes suit her personality, but they are more 1980s retro than current fashion trends allow. He would never think about pointing that out. She is also his on-again, off-again girlfriend, although he isn't sure what that status is at the moment.

"I'm sorry I'm late. You look miserable."

"I am miserable," Kai admits.

"Yeah, being the most renowned independent journalist in the country must be sooooo taxing," she says, placing the back of her hand against her forehead before throwing her head back in her typical dramatic flair. "Kai, your stories are blowing up on social media. Your last video has over two million views!"

He leans back in his chair. "Have you ever asked yourself why Americans care so much about celebrities?"

"They don't. You know that better than anyone. The public likes to build people up, and when they get too big, watch them fall. It's entertaining. That's what you're helping to facilitate here, in case you needed a reminder."

That's why he likes Babs. Despite having to live with the blonde stereotype all her life, she is as sharp as they come. She doesn't let anything characterize her other than her wit, sass, and sometimes brutal honesty. And she has no problem speaking her mind. Those traits are absent in most of his generation. It's why he's drawn to her…professionally and personally.

"I don't need a reminder, thank you. And just because I'm reporting on it to my millions of followers doesn't make it right."

"But it is necessary. Kai, these people are scumbags. The public should know exactly how the people they put on golden pedestals act when they aren't in front of a camera."

Babs is one of those unique people who are completely apolitical. Her ideology is her own, and she resents anyone who tries to manipulate her line of thinking. If the deepest depths of hell are reserved for politicians, she thinks that celebrities have an adjoining room. She considers them phonies who parrot whatever movement is trending in a shallow effort to stay relevant in Hollywood elitist circles and the like-minded sheep who follow them on social media.

"Okay….fine. Necessary doesn't mean exciting."

"Ah, yes, I almost forgot about your unhealthy obsession with needing an adrenaline rush. I thought you said you wanted to play it safe after what you've been through."

Kai made a name for himself while covering protests, civil unrest, and left-wing movements as an independent journalist. Instead of peddling his stories to mainstream media, he documented anti-fascist protests, clashes, and riots and posted them to video streaming services like YouTube and Rumble. His reporting quickly caught national attention when he highlighted the violence by left-wing groups. It made him a target for disciples of that movement.

"I was getting tired of getting death threats."

Babs rolls her eyes. "Yeah, that comes with the territory when you become a highly regarded independent journalist who redefines reporting and builds a massive following in the process."

"Should it?"

"No, but you're effective because you're more than a camera-wielding journalist. You embed yourself in the heart of the action, and you've become part of the culture because of it. The Kai X brand of reporting has been woven into the fabric of society."

The journalist presses his lips together tightly and stares out the window at the uneventful comings and goings of people on the sidewalk. Culture. If he's shaping it, then that explains the arguments from critics that his reporting lacks balance. How much balance are they looking for in riots? Yes, he focuses on their far-left, but they are the ones torching cities. The far-right has its violent tendencies, but nothing on the order of what he has seen from groups like Antifa.

Kai is aware of the accusations of selective editing levied against him by his detractors. He's watched as the talking heads accuse him of amplifying tensions or misrepresenting events to fit his narrative. Like he's the one throwing Molotov cocktails and carrying shields made of carved up large plastic trash cans. And he has paid a physical price to get the story.

"Well, it wasn't worth getting my ass kicked."

"Then why are we having this conversation? Tracking down celebrities who attended rape parties isn't as dangerous as covering Antifa clashes, but here you are, whining about it."

"I'm not whining."

Kai has been physically attacked at protests, even suffering a serious brain injury after being assaulted while covering an Antifa clash in Portland. A PleaseHelpMe page was set up by supporters to cover the medical bills, as they saw him as a victim of political violence. Detractors just accused him of being provocative and said he deserved it.

"You absolutely are whining. Look, if this isn't fulfilling for you, say the word. You have become a beacon of free speech, freedom of the press, and ethics in journalism. Your work matters. It influences political discussions and guides the contemporary media discourse. I happen to think this is important, but if you want to do more, then let's find something."

He nods. "I heard Minneapolis is having some issues again."

"You want to go there?" Babs says. Again, she's agnostic about the direction he wants to go in. It's rare to meet someone who will support whichever direction you decide to go.

"Not yet. Let's keep an eye on it, though. The story in L.A. is played out. A lot of journalists are poking around now, so there isn't much more for me to do. If things go south in Minnesota, we should be ready to catch a flight."

Babs offers a smile. "It's going to be tough trading SoCal for the Land of 10,000 Lakes, even in summer. Do you think it will get bad there?"

Kai shrugs. "It depends on whether someone up there wants to stir the pot."

CHAPTER FIVE

LANDON TAYSON

LANDON'S APARTMENT
ARTS DISTRICT, MINNEAPOLIS, MINNESOTA

Landon quietly inserts the key in the lock. He twists it and turns the handle, slowly edging the door open. The apartment is pitch-black outside of the glow of LEDs on a smattering of gadgets and appliances. Navigating the hardwood floors will be like tiptoeing through a minefield. Boards creak, and the noise will sound like a backfiring muffler in the still night air.

He unties and removes his shoes, quietly setting them on the mat near the door. He takes a step…and then another. So far, so good. Emboldened, he passes the small kitchenette on his right and heads deeper into the living area.

The creak announces his presence with all the subtlety of a marching band comprising nothing but trumpets and tubas. He freezes in place, listening for any stirring. There isn't any. Landon takes three more steps forward and stops, scanning for any telltale signs of life. Then he hears a click.

"You can kiss your career as a cat burglar goodbye," Raven says as the room is bathed in soft white light. She's sitting on the end of the couch wearing pajamas and sipping whatever she has latched onto as the cocktail of the month.

He hangs his head, knowing he's busted. Sneaking into his own apartment should have been easier than it turned out to be. Of course, he wouldn't need to had he told her he was going out in the first place.

"What are you still doing up?"

"I couldn't sleep, so I came down here to think."

Landon stretches out his arms. "In the dark?"

"Can you think of a better way to avoid distractions?"

No, he can't. He's a firm believer that television has made society more informed and dumber at the same time. He prefers books, and Raven prefers getting lost in her thoughts.

Landon plops down on the sofa next to her. Raven Crusoe is a force of nature. He would have wooed her like it was 15th-century Europe if that's what it took to win her heart. Instead, she pursued him relentlessly. It was his first experience in a notable series of examples that illustrated an unwavering truth: Nothing gets between Raven and what she wants.

"What are you thinking about?"

"Me first. Where were you?"

"Out having hot sex with triplets on the UM cheerleading squad." That earns him a slap across the chest that was harder than he was expecting. "I had a meeting."

"At two in the morning?"

Landon sighs heavily. "Do the guys we usually meet with seem like morning people to you?"

"No, I'm pretty sure they're vampires. Why didn't you bring me? Did you think I wouldn't notice you sneaking out?"

"I agreed to keep this meeting small. It was just the three of us, and I knew you would be upset that you weren't included." She nods. "See? You're mad."

"I'm not mad. At least, not about that. I'm…what are we doing here, Landon?"

"What do you mean?"

"That's what I was thinking about while you were gone, to answer your previous question. All we do is talk, talk, talk. There's never any action behind all those words. That's why we aren't moving the needle. People don't care about what we say. They care about results, and we aren't delivering any."

"You're right," Landon says with a nod.

"I am?"

Landon cocks his head at her. "Don't sound so surprised, my love. You're right about a lot of things."

"I'm not. I mean, I am, but what do you mean?"

"That's what the meeting was about. We're going to take our cause to the next level."

Raven shakes her head. "You can't plan this like you're taking a trip to the Mall of America. It has to be organic…otherwise, it's as fake as everything else in this country."

She isn't wrong about that. Much like a Hollywood movie set, this country is nothing but a façade filled with set props. The people in it are shallow actors with little intelligence and fewer morals. If the American people could only be shown that….

"Did you know MLK wasn't even known when the first bus boycotts happened in Montgomery? Claudette Colvin refused to give up her seat to a white passenger on a segregated bus nine months before Rosa Parks. Colvin was arrested, but there were no protests. Why? She was a teenager and later became pregnant, which some civil rights leaders believed made her less suitable to be the face of the movement. By the time Rosa Parks did the same thing, Martin Luther King Junior was ready to lead the boycott."

"What's your point?"

"Timing is everything. The pieces have to be in place to make change happen. What would the civil rights movement have been without King? Would it have succeeded? Failed? Who knows? But he was the catalyst needed for the reaction to start. Now, we have the catalyst that is going to start our reaction, and it's going to change the country."

"What is it?"

Landon smirks. "And spoil the surprise?"

"I hate surprises," Raven moans.

That's why he said it. Surprises are the bane of Miss Crusoe's existence. Her mother threw her a surprise birthday party once and Raven didn't talk to her for two weeks. On their second date, she warned him of the ramifications of keeping things from her. Or maybe their first date. He can't remember.

"Then you're just going to have to trust me."

"Tell me."

"No."

She turns her back to him and folds her arms. The silent treatment. It's how she shows her displeasure, but he has tried and true workarounds to it. Raven Crusoe has a weakness, and he's going to exploit it. Landon sits up on the couch and kisses the back of her neck.

She shrugs him off, so he does it again, getting the same reaction. Hardball it is. Landon reaches around her body, sliding his hands under her arms, and cups her breasts.

"Oh, you think so, eh? Not tonight, buddy."

"Your stiff nipples say otherwise."

Nothing gets her engine purring like kissing her neck and caressing her breasts. She moans a few times before turning and kissing him passionately. He yanks her shirt over her head as she undoes his belt and goes to work on his pants. It's going to be a great day of significant change that will usher in a new era. Might as well start it with a bang.

CHAPTER SIX

CHIEF VANESSA CAMPBELL

NORTH STAR MEDICAL CENTER
MINNEAPOLIS, MINNESOTA

The reports came in fast and furious. There are already scene commanders on-site, so there's no point rushing to where her officers were gunned down. Instead, Vanessa hops in a squad car and floors it to the emergency room a block or two away.

She's seen utter chaos in this ER before, and this sight is no different. The chief still doesn't have the full story of what happened. Details are sketchy, but they don't paint a pretty picture. If anyone will know, it's the 1st Precinct's top cop. There is little doubt in Vanessa's mind that he is here with his men.

The emergency room is packed. Uniformed officers are everywhere, and nurses are weaving around them as they hurry around the room. The deputy chief of constitutional policing is already in a heated conversation with the 1st Precinct inspector. Vanessa moans. What is that clown doing here other than causing trouble?

"They walked into an ambush!" the inspector says, his voice a dozen decibels higher.

"Let's not jump to conclusions," Otto Goldberg says, a snide smirk on his face like he's enjoying this.

"Are you serious? What other conclusion is there?"

"Eyewitnesses say that your men were acting aggressively. From what I have seen, they may be right. What gives them the right to discharge their firearms like that?"

The inspector tenses up and looks ready to explode. "My men were responding to a bogus call and ended up getting shot at from five directions!"

"Face it, Inspector, your men acted inappropriately and will likely face charges if they live!"

The comment was enough for the inspector to lose what little composure he had left. He doesn't telegraph his next move. The punch lands on the deputy chief's face before he can even register what's happening. It was as quick as it was violent. Goldberg's knees buckle as the force of the haymaker snaps his head back. The combination of backward momentum and the unrelenting force of gravity all but guarantees his hard impact with the ground.

The inspector lurches at the prone man before being intercepted by three of his men. The emergency room erupts with cops and hospital staff trying to create some separation between them. If bedlam had a picture in the dictionary next to the term, this would be it.

"Get out!" an ER doctor shouts as several beefy orderlies take position next to him. "All of you! Get out of my ER!"

"I'm not leaving my men," the inspector says, pointing at the triage where his officers are being worked on.

"There is nothing you can do for them here! You're in our way. Leave now!"

The precinct leader sticks a finger in the man's face. "I'm not letting an ER doctor tell me what to do."

Vanessa weaves her way through the mass of humanity that's watching the interaction. Nurses have stopped what they're doing. Orderlies look like they're ready for a rumble. There is nothing about this situation that is making the department look good. More importantly, the medical professionals in this room need to be focused on the patients.

She inserts herself between the two men, pushing the inspector backward before speaking over her shoulder. "Get back to work, Doc."

"Calm down, Inspector. This is his building. Let's not make a bad situation worse. He has a job to do, and so do you. Move your men outside."

"What about that asshole Goldberg?" the inspector says, pointing.

"I will deal with the deputy chief. You have your orders. Go."

I hope you're going to do something about this," he warns. "That man is a disgrace to the force and needs to be fired."

Vanessa doesn't disagree. Otto Goldberg is the living definition of the word "scumbag." He's a charlatan more interested in currying favor with the mayor than he is in helping the force mend its fractured relationship with the city. His title doesn't fool her. His idea of constitutional policing is handing every criminal in the city a popsicle and a gift card.

"And you need to return to duty."

"He struck me!" Goldberg says, slinking over. "You saw it. Fire him right now, or I will have the mayor fire you!"

Vanessa grabs a handful of his shirt and puts her finger centimeters from his face. "The mayor won't do anything until this crisis is over. However, if I hear you went around me…if I even think you intend to…I will fire you immediately. You will follow the chain of command or you will be collecting unemployment. Do you understand?"

He nods.

"I asked if you understand, Assistant Chief Goldberg. Use your words."

"I understand," he says after scoffing.

"Good. Get your ass back to City Hall and stay there. That's an order, and I dare you not to follow it."

He reluctantly leaves, and Vanessa searches for the ER doctor so she can issue an official apology. Hopefully, that will smooth things over and keep them out of the news.

"Chief!" a lieutenant with the 1st Precinct shouts as he rushes over to her.

"What is it?"

"We have a serious problem with the crowd gathering at Gold Medal Park. Apparently, they think the police started the firefight in Midtown Phillips."

"What? They were ambushed!"

"I saw the same video, but the one circulating on social media has been manipulated or something. It makes us look like the aggressors."

Vanessa rubs the bridge of her nose. She shouldn't be surprised in the era of deepfakes and easy access to video editing applications. It used to be that you couldn't believe anything you heard. Now, in their new reality, that extends to not believing what you see, either.

"Has there been any violence?"

"There's been a few scuffles, but otherwise, it's peaceful. My sources on the ground are telling me they're planning to march on City Hall. If they make it there and decide to storm the building, it will be too late for us to stop them. It's only blocks away."

"Contain the gathering to the park. If they start marching, it needs to be in any direction other than toward City Hall. Divert them, but don't be heavy-handed, or we'll be holding this whole city back."

"I'm not sure I have the resources."

"We need all hands on deck. Men are already reporting to their precincts after hearing what happened. Borrow heavily from the 2nd Precinct and ready SWAT, just in case. Get them in position, but nobody makes a move until we learn what the crowd's intent is."

The lieutenant nods and moves off in a hurry. There's no reason to panic yet. At least, that's what Vanessa keeps telling herself. People have a right to voice their frustration, even if it is based on bad information. It's not a protest that bothers her. It's what it could turn into. With all the violence this great city has seen, it's the last thing anyone needs.

CHAPTER SEVEN

KAI Z

GOLD MEDAL PARK
MINNEAPOLIS, MINNESOTA

This place is already getting packed with people. He came here straight from the airport and joined the hundreds of people streaming in. Kai stands off to the side as he checks the map application on the phone. He already knows about this place. Gold Medal Park is a seven-and-a-half-acre public green space located on the Mississippi Riverfront in downtown Minneapolis. He thought it was to honor some Olympian, but he was wrong. The park is named for the Gold Medal Flour brand as an homage to the area's storied history as a flour milling hub.

What Kai doesn't know is the layout of the place. The central feature is a gentle, spiraling pathway leading to a mound that offers a panoramic view of the area. That's where the protest leaders will be.

The park has arranged rows of trees, large open spaces, and public art. None of that is interesting to him. The proximity to landmarks like the Guthrie Theater, Stone Arch Bridge, and Mill Ruins Park will make this easy to get to for protestors. It will also attract a substantial police presence, which he is already seeing signs of.

Kai contemplates meandering with the crowd toward the mound at the center of the park but decides to stay on the periphery. It's the result of another lesson learned the hard way. Protest leaders who pay attention to YouTube and Rumble probably know who he is and will be quick to turn the crowd against him. Despite his growing popularity and resulting notoriety, the rank-and-file protesters likely don't.

It gives him a chance to people-watch. The crowd is diverse, both in skin color and dress. Many are in plain street clothes. This is not Antifa's black block. Nobody is dressed for combat and equipped with masks and helmets. People are armed with signs, not makeshift shields and weapons. However, he is certain that anti-fascists are here or somewhere nearby.

"All right," Kai mumbles to himself as he scans the gathering crowd. "What are you going to be?"

The terms protest and riot are often used interchangeably in the American lexicon when describing civil unrest. In reality, they differ significantly. Protests are peaceful, planned to spotlight a message, and lawful. They are deliberate, organized events where people gather to express grievances or demands about a specific issue or cause.

Riots are violent, and Kai has the wounds to prove it. They erupt spontaneously and are usually spurred on by agitators intent on creating disruption and destruction.

Even a small fracas can exponentially grow when people see others looting stores, vandalizing cars and buildings, and attacking other people.

The small group of people entering the park is shouting obscenities at a pair of cops standing nearby. Heightened emotions are a primary cause for a protest to turn into something violent. Provocations from law enforcement are another. Tear gas and rubber bullets naturally escalate tensions. Much of what happens here will depend on the police response.

Kai nonchalantly does a full turn, looking like he's searching for someone. He only pulls out his phone to use the camera if those around him are. It stems from the need to blend in. His body camera will take care of capturing footage.

It's a useful device since it's hands-free and always recording. Kai can capture the misdeeds of protesters or police without looking obvious. His model is compact, unobtrusive, easily attaches to his clothing, and features a wide-angle lens. It's also weatherproof and, as he has learned, pepper spray resistant. Since he hates swapping batteries and memory cards, this has plenty of capacity for both.

It can also be targeted by people who notice it. Rioters hate video, so he also has a redundant camera hidden in his clothing in case the body camera gets torn off. He learned that the hard way. It's why he didn't have good footage of getting assaulted in Portland.

He feels his phone vibrate in his pocket and checks the caller ID before answering. "Hey, Babs."

"Where are you?"

"Standing in the corner of the park off 2nd Street near one of the sculptures. Where are you?"

"The Commons. It's a small park a couple of blocks southeast of City Hall. The police are mobilizing here."

That's interesting. What does law enforcement know that he doesn't? This crowd doesn't appear to be aggressive. Maybe it's a precautionary move considering what happened in this city in 2020. Or, maybe they have intel that something is brewing. That would validate the feeling he is getting.

"Are they wearing riot gear?"

"Most aren't, but they have it with them. Some of them are donning it like they're expecting trouble. Should they be?"

Kai surveys the crowd. "I'm not sure yet."

"Have you identified any leaders?"

"No. So far, it looks like a gathering of upset residents. But…."

"But what?"

"I don't know. This somehow feels…organized. Not that I've seen any evidence of it."

Not that he needs to. He's been to hundreds of protests and experienced countless riots. Kai has developed instincts that have made him a media celebrity and managed to keep him alive. Those instincts and his eyes are currently at odds with each other.

"Well, there is all kinds of misinformation about what happened during the shootout, and it's spreading rapidly. From what I saw on the video, the police were ambushed. Unfortunately, social media is intent on painting them as the aggressors."

"That will lead more people to show up and fuel the crowd's anger. All they need is someone to channel it. I'll keep you informed of any developments here."

"Be careful, Kai," Babs says, a healthy dose of worry in her tone.

"You too."

He pockets his phone and returns to scanning the crowd, looking for leaders. They will be the ones with the megaphones. He knows there are probably plain-clothed police here doing the same.

CHAPTER EIGHT

LANDON TAYSON

GOLD MEDAL PARK
MINNEAPOLIS, MINNESOTA

The mound in Gold Medal Park is the perfect place for speaking. First, it's smack in the middle of the greenspace. Second, it is prominent with a stand of trees and a small walkway around it. The walkway isn't important, except that it provides a firm foundation for Landon to build his stage.

There is nothing fancy about this, and it doesn't need to be. He only needs to elevate himself high enough so people can see him. Milk crates are the perfect tool for what he needs. They are cheap, disposable, lightweight, and sturdy. His disciples carry two each to the center, and a minute later, he has a nice pedestal that's three crates high to stand on.

There are enough people in the park to make a difference. Raven and the rest of his organization did a fantastic job getting the word out on social media. He may hate Twitter…or X, but it is useful in relaying information. The same goes for other social media sites and message boards. Most shockingly, local news reported the gathering as it began. Many who arrived in the park learned of the protest from their televisions and alerts on their phones.

Most of the people here are ordinary citizens upset with the actions of their police force. They aren't agitators, and that is by design. His sizable group of malcontents and anarchists have their own assignments, and most of them don't need to be here.

"It's time," Raven says, tugging on Landon's shirt to get his attention.

"Is everything in place?"

She winks. "Right on schedule."

"What about the Minneapolis PD?"

Raven glances at the text messages on her phone. "They're mustering in The Commons, Government Center Park, and Federal Courthouse Plaza. Apparently, municipal trucks with mobile barricades have shown up around City Hall and have started unloading."

Landon smiles. It's a sensible precaution but one that plays right into his hands. "Perfect. You're right, it's time. Watch my back?"

"You know I will."

The feedback from the megaphone when he activates it hurts his ears. Fortunately, the shrill sound commands the attention of those around Landon without his needing to bellow to demand their attentiveness. These people are looking for a speaker. They are waiting for a leader to arrive to address them. Now, they have one.

"I would say it's a good morning, but we're all here because it isn't," he shouts into the megaphone, waiting for the crowd's response to die down before continuing. "For too long, we have trusted the men and women in the Minneapolis Police Department to learn from the mistakes of the past. We gave them time to correct their deficiencies and make good on their promises to clean up their act. We stood by and listened as they promised us change. We patiently waited for results. They have failed, and the shootings this morning are all the proof we need of that!

"This city can no longer be patient while police indiscriminately gun down citizens in the street. We deserve better than that. We need to *demand* better than that. Because if the department isn't capable of changing, we will force it to change ourselves. That, my friends, starts today. That starts right now!

"We tried it their way, but our elected leaders don't hear our voices at the ballot box. They don't read the op-eds in the paper or the comments on the city's social media sites. They can't be bothered with any of that. They can't be bothered with us!"

The angry roar of the crowd is satisfying. Landon has never fancied himself a public speaker. Addressing the masses isn't the same as rallying the revolutionaries in his group of dedicated change agents. They are much easier to convince of the righteousness of the cause. These are average citizens. He doesn't expect them to be as angry as he is, but they are.

"We are blocks away from City Hall. Anything we say here will fall on deaf ears because that's always how it is. We are the little guys. We are the critters the people running this city step on and don't give a second thought to. They think we will hem and haw and then go back home and brood while the citizens of this city live under the thumbs of jackbooted thugs that call themselves police."

Using that level of rhetoric is a risk. Landon doesn't want to lose this crowd by being too inflammatory too soon. People here may be unhappy with the police, but essentially calling them Nazis could backfire if they still broadly respect the department. From their response, they don't. Or, at least, they don't respect them right now.

"I say to hell with that. Let's take this protest to the steps of City Hall and make our voices heard loud and clear. Insist that our leaders address our concerns. If they don't want to talk…if they don't want to listen, then we'll burn the place down because what good is it?"

The crowd cheers their support for the plan. That was a better reaction than Landon anticipated. The wounds from the riots in 2020 are still raw, and much of the city doesn't want to return to those days. Maybe they thought he was speaking metaphorically. He wasn't, but they don't need to know that. At least, not yet.

"The time for change is now! The time to be heard is now. If the police try to stop us, then you'll know what this city's leaders think about you! Let's go, and I will be honored to lead the way."

He jumps off the milk crates and catches Raven's wry smile. He's getting good at this. The last part of his impromptu speech accomplished two important things. The first is that he made this protest personal for attendees. They now have a mission and a vested interest in carrying it out. The second is that he is demonstrating that he is willing to risk everything to lead them. People love that kind of thing. Of course, the downside is that a target gets painted on your back.

Landon spotted the three men now moving toward him when he was standing on the makeshift dais. Raven did, too, and now she's issuing instructions over a walkie-talkie. It's good to have friends and better to have a crowd behind you. Each of the men gets intercepted by a pair from Landon's group. Panicking, they pull out their badges as if they will make a difference. Fists immediately fly. All three are brought to the ground as people around them kick and shout obscenities.

Raven grabs the megaphone from Landon, screaming at the top of her lungs that the police are trying to silence them already. That gets people worked up. They may be citizens, but emotions are running high, and this adds fuel to the fire.

Landon knows he's making himself a target for arrest. Every cop in this park will have him pegged as the leader. When things begin to go south, they will isolate him and place him under arrest. It doesn't matter. He knows what is going to happen, regardless of whether he's leading the charge or sitting on a cold metal bench in a jail cell. Nothing will stop this movement now.

CHAPTER NINE

EMMIT "CHICAGO" HASKINS

THE FIFTH STREET HOUSE
MINNEAPOLIS, MINNESOTA

Combat in video games is fun, but it's far different than what soldiers experience in real life. There are no health bars, hitboxes, or power-ups on a battlefield. Dodging fire and executing an attack is more than pressing buttons, and you're dead if your timing is bad. There is no respawn.

Warfare is unpredictable and chaotic, and deciding factors are often training, endurance, and situational awareness. A soldier needs to overcome physical pain, fatigue, and psychological impacts that can last a lifetime. Video game combat is relatively stress-free by comparison because of its low stakes.

Emmit has seen it for real. Combat is terrifying. Adrenaline spikes trigger fight-or-flight responses. Everyone reacts differently, even Army Rangers. He's seen fear, hesitation, and confusion when the shit hits the fan. Strategy in games revolves around exploiting game mechanics. On a battlefield, soldiers must adapt to dynamic situations. It's stressful as hell.

That's why soldiers become brothers when faced with the trials and tribulations of combat. He misses that element, and there is nothing in this game that can recreate it. Frustrated, he powers down the console and switches the HDMI source on the television back to the cable box.

He's about to change the channel when he sees the breaking news chyron with "Protests Erupt after Minneapolis Shooting" emblazoned across it. Emmit sits up on the couch when he hears a reporter coming live from a park just on the other side of the river.

"Thank you, Scott. Thousands of people are descending on this small park in the downtown area. The protest has been peaceful so far, but emotions are high following a police shooting early this morning in the Midtown Phillips neighborhood, only a stone's throw from North Star Medical Center.

"A police spokesman claims officers responding to a 9-1-1 call of an armed robbery in progress were ambushed when they arrived on the scene. Witnesses confirm that shots were fired at the police. However, the return fire was indiscriminate, hitting multiple innocent bystanders. Cell phone video of the incident is inconclusive. Here is some of that footage."

Emmit narrows his eyes as he pauses and rewinds the report after the footage plays. He knows what he saw. He hits play, and the street-level recording of the firefight starts again. One leg of gunfire stops the police from entering what looks like a storefront. They all seek cover behind their vehicles as they return fire.

The other leg engages the exposed police from the opposite direction. They were caught in a crossfire, and a pair of cops dropped instantly. Emmit can see the frantic looks on their faces as they scream into their radios before the anchor reappears on the television.

"Textbook L-shaped ambush," he mumbles.

In a tactical sense, an ambush is designed to surprise and overwhelm an enemy by attacking from a concealed position. It's common in combat, but he's watching this in an American city. Success relies on detailed planning, including understanding movement patterns, reactions, and vulnerabilities. Someone studied the Minneapolis Police, scouted the location, called in the crime, and organized the attack. This is not something gangs or random thugs are capable of. He hits the live button on the remote.

"As of this report, no arrests have been made in the shootings. Reporting live from Gold Medal Park for Channel 3 News, I'm —"

Emmit rewinds and watches it again. The timing was perfect. The gunfire immediately disoriented the cops. The element of surprise creates confusion, thus reducing an enemy's ability to effectively respond. That's what happened here.

And then there is the exit strategy. Ambush forces usually have a clear, pre-planned exit strategy to safely retreat after the action. There was mention of no arrests, so that's what this group must have done. Group. What group would attack police and why? Emmit has some ideas, and none of them are pleasant.

He picks up his phone and selects his sister's number from recent calls. She picks up on the second ring.

"Emmit?"

"Are you watching the news?"

"We all are. Every television in this place has it on, and there's a small group huddled around each of them."

"Good. Then you know what's going on. You need to leave the office."

"Uh, I don't know if I can. It's going to be a banner day for defense attorneys. I'm probably going to be here late."

The MK Law Group isn't the biggest or most prestigious firm in Minneapolis, but they are among the best-known. They offer diverse legal services for defendants accused of everything from drug-related crimes to traffic accidents to sex crimes and domestic disputes. Defending thugs rioting in the streets is right up their alley.

Kenyala is studying to become a paralegal and is working as an administrative assistant to one of the partners until she completes her coursework. It's not the career path Emmit would have picked for his sister, but she enjoys it and, God forbid, likes the people she works with. Happiness is all he can wish for her, considering the trajectory their lives have been on.

Emmit sighs. "How late?"

"I don't know. The news is talking about the police shutting down the downtown area."

The office is only about three miles away on the other side of the Mississippi River from his sister's house in the Arts District. For her, it's a ten-minute drive. He can make it in forty minutes if he's walking briskly and faster if he runs. He could use the exercise anyway.

"I'll come and drive you home in your car."

"Emmit, it's a protest," his sister insists. "There's no reason to get jumpy."

"I don't think that's what this is. I need to get you home."

"All right…is this my overprotective brother talking? The one who scared off a date once because he owned an SUV that had a pillow and blanket in the back?"

It's an honest question. What Kenyala doesn't know is what happened after Emmit thwarted that date. He happened to run into the same guy at a bar a week later just as he was trying to slip a roofie into a girl's drink. Rohypnol, also known as flunitrazepam, is a potent sedative-hypnotic medication primarily used for the treatment of severe insomnia. In the U.S., it gained notoriety as a date rape drug that incapacitates and causes memory loss in unsuspecting victims. Needless to say, he beat the guy to a bloody pulp in the back of the bar. He left for basic training five days later.

"Yeah. It's also the well-trained Army Ranger who recognizes tactics and can sense trouble. That instinct kept me alive in the desert. I'll be there at five. We'll leave the office when you're ready, but tell your bosses that I'm not waiting forever. They should consider calling it an earlier night and having Zoom calls if they need to talk."

"Okay. See you at five."

His sister disconnects, and Emmit tosses the phone on the cushion next to him. The news has switched gears. Apparently, several bystanders were struck by bullets meant for other targets. People are saying the cops were gunning people down at random. That has changed the tone and tenor of the reporting. It didn't look to Emmit like they were firing indiscriminately, but this incident will put the police force on the defensive. He was hoping he was overreacting to this incident. Now, he knows he isn't. Something serious is going down in Minneapolis.

CHAPTER TEN
FIELD OFFICER DAVID BRASS

Reston is a planned community nestled in northern Virginia, about twenty miles west of Washington. Part of the Dulles Technology Corridor, it's home to countless tech companies and an obscene number of government contractors and employees. Despite its access to mass transit, shopping centers, restaurants, and entertainment venues, Brass has never enjoyed living in this area. For him, it's a means to an end.

That's what brings him to this bar to meet one of his best contacts. When people think of spies, James Bond instantly comes to mind. He was a loner, sipped martinis, and looked dapper in a tuxedo. The real experience couldn't be further from the truth. That's why David is dressed in jeans, sipping a beer at the bar, and networking. He has developed a promising source in FBI Counterintelligence, and now it's time to put him to the test.

"I see the Department of Agriculture is keeping you busy, Dave," Matt Remsen says as he slides onto the adjacent bar stool.

"There's never a dull moment in the apple export business."

To ensure the safety and effectiveness of covert activities, the CIA equips its operatives with covers to conceal their identity and purpose. Often, it's under the guise of being employees of other government agencies, like David's job with the Agriculture Department. Foreign assets are usually given diplomatic credentials, but non-official covers mean posing as private citizens like businesspeople, journalists, or aid workers. Regardless of the cover, looking and acting the part to blend in is critical.

"There are worse places to be posted," Brass says with a half smile.

"I'm sure. So, I know you didn't ask me here to talk about whether the Nationals will make the playoffs this year."

"No, I hate baseball. I just wanted to check in and see what was new in counterintelligence."

Matt smirks. "Nothing on our end. You guys are another matter. I've heard the chatter about some clandestine op called 'Railspike.'"

One of the most dangerous things to do in the intelligence world is underestimate your opponents. Wars start that way. Governments fail that way. Operatives get killed that way. Remsen knew exactly why he was asked here. David has to remember that the man isn't stupid. Failing to recognize that could lead to his downfall someday.

"Yeah, I read about that. I'm familiar with the operation. It's an innocent program being painted as something nefarious by people who want to knock the CIA down a peg or two."

"Innocent?"

Brass shrugs slightly. "Mostly innocent. Langley has been receiving field reports that foreign actors are infiltrating lobbying groups to help steer American foreign policy. You can see the problem with that."

"Clearly."

Lobbying groups wield significant power in American politics. Their combination of resources, relationships, and strategies has helped shape public policy for decades. Each comes to the game with their own agenda to promote, and because of their deep pockets, politicians listen.

If foreign agents are infiltrating domestic lobbying groups, it's a cause for concern. The FBI may normally be involved in such intrusions, but they have turned a blind eye. When it comes to dealing with foreign intelligence agencies, the CIA is unsurpassed. Of course, there are side benefits to the operation as well, but those aren't worth discussing.

"So, the reports that the CIA is meddling in domestic affairs?"

"Misrepresented. We aren't spying on these groups. We're protecting them."

Matt nods. Brass isn't sure Remsen buys that, but it doesn't matter. This is as much a test to see if he's a team player as an actual request. Brass can probably find out the information on his own. But if he is going to realize his vision, he needs to know whom he can trust and whom he can't.

"Now I know why I'm here. You want to know where the leak came from and are wondering if the Bureau knows anything."

Brass taps his nose and points at Matt.

"Why?"

"Leverage. Let's say that it would be used for me to know before the director finds out."

Matt straightens on his stool. "You're going to blackmail the head of the CIA to get Watchtower authorized."

Watchtower is an idea Brass got after reading too many spy novels. *Tom Clancy's Op-Center* is a series of military and political thrillers written with co-author Steve Pieczenik. The series focuses on a covert U.S. government organization identified as the "National Crisis Management Center." Known to its members as Op-Center, it was an elite group tasked with identifying and responding to critical national security threats. They were part intelligence-gathering entity and part operational unit capable of deploying field teams to combat terrorism, cyber warfare, and even rogue nations. It's something right up Brass's alley.

"Blackmail is an ugly word, but something like that." It's a lie, but the FBI doesn't need to know that.

"The FBI isn't investigating the leak. It's a CIA problem."

"I know. But I also know you have the resources with the expertise to do some sniffing around. If anyone can uncover who leaked the details of Railspike, it's you and the FBI Counterintelligence team."

"And if I say no? Will you think differently about my joining Watchtower?"

The answer is "yes," but Brass doesn't want to say that. "The project won't exist if details about Railspike make it to the eyes and ears of the American public."

"It already has."

"Seriously, Matt? Half the country can't name a Supreme Court justice. Far fewer than half watch the news regularly. So long as this doesn't get widely reported, most of the country will never know."

"All right. I'll dig into it and let you know if I come up with something."

Matt leaves without ordering a drink. That's good because it means Brass can finish his beer in peace. It's good having friends, even if the man is nothing more than a useful idiot. That could make him useful if Watchtower ever does come to fruition. For the first time in a long time, it feels like it will. All he needs to do is work the right levers of power.

CHAPTER ELEVEN
CHIEF VANESSA CAMPBELL

OUTSIDE CITY HALL
MINNEAPOLIS, MINNESOTA

This is turning into a complete shit show. Most people believe law enforcement acts as a single, unified entity during a crisis. Sometimes, that's true, but not always. It certainly isn't the case here.

Vanessa's arrival outside of City Hall will likely do little to change that in the short term, but she might have time to introduce a smidgeon of order to the chaos. None of the officers posted outside the city's primary municipal building have any clue what to do. They have orders to stop protestors from entering the area but aren't being provided with any guidance on how to do that.

Moveable metal barriers have been erected and now ring the building, but that will do next to nothing to deter the motivated, angry mob descending on this part of the city. Her "all hands on deck" order was followed, but manpower doesn't always equal effectiveness. These officers need rules of engagement, and they need them fast.

"What the hell is going on?" Vanessa asks a 1st Precinct sergeant, shouting over the growing din so he can hear her.

"Nothing according to plan, Chief, that's for sure. We weren't able to divert the march. Protesters were determined to come here, and nothing was going to stop them."

"We're going to need backup. Has anyone contacted the state patrol?"

A division of the Minnesota Department of Public Safety, the Minnesota State Patrol is primarily tasked with ensuring highway safety. Their responsibilities have evolved beyond traffic safety in the last few years. Now, they help deal with emergency response during large events or natural disasters. This is a little of both.

The sergeant shrugs and shakes his head. "I doubt it. I can barely stay in contact with our own people. The inspector is trying to get everyone organized. The MSP is here, somewhere, but they are on a different frequency."

"Wonderful. What about the protest leaders? Have they been identified?"

"I haven't heard anything. I got a report that three plain-clothes officers in the park are down. They were beaten pretty badly."

Vanessa frowns. Maybe this protest isn't as nonviolent as it appears. "We need to disperse this crowd. The last thing we want is the mayor watching a standoff out his office window."

"Lieutenant Burke and his SWAT team are on standby in Government Plaza," the sergeant advises her. "That much I know for sure."

"Let's hope it doesn't come to that."

Vanessa stares at the approaching tsunami of humanity. They are a mix of ages and races, and most of them don't look dressed for brawling. These are angry citizens. There are most certainly agitators in the crowd, but they may be able to avert violence and restore order. That starts with removing the leaders and diverting the crowd away from City Hall.

"Sergeant, have our guys order them to disperse. Tell them that they are free to protest in Gold Medal Park but not on the street. Also, tell our guys that nobody acts against the crowd without my authorization. Understood?"

He nods and starts barking into his radio. The crowd stops at the hasty barrier the police erected. Words are being exchanged with officers on the other side, but the crowd isn't pushing to breach the barrier. With the march halting, people are pooling on 4th Street and spilling onto 4th Avenue. It doesn't look like they are looking to occupy Federal Courthouse Plaza. At least, not yet.

Orders to disperse are being shouted over a squad car's PA system and are being ignored. While the barrier isn't being challenged, this crowd has no intention of going anywhere. This is a standoff and will stay that way until one side yields. It won't be hers.

A sudden burst of screaming gets Vanessa's attention. She jerks her head around to see a white cloud erupt from near the center of the crowd. People rub their eyes and gasp for air as they try to put distance between themselves and the gas. Then, another cloud unleashes more screams. Then, a third.

There is no place for people to run. The street is tightly packed with protesters, and efforts to get away from the clouds of noxious gas are starting to cause panic. The desperation may begin to cause injuries, which is why Vanessa didn't want these measures used in the first place.

The chief grabs the sergeant's shoulder and spins him to face her. "Who is using tear gas?"

"Nobody!"

She points at the clouds of smoke erupting from canisters in the middle of the crowd. "Then tell me what those are!"

The sergeant doesn't get the chance to respond, even if he wants to articulate an answer. A gunshot rings out, followed by two or three more. People scream and duck. Her officers raise weapons from behind the barrier. With the sound of the shots reverberating off the surrounding buildings, it's difficult to know where they came from. She can't imagine it was from any of her people, but some protesters are pointing in her direction.

"Where did those shots come from?"

It was a rhetorical question. Maybe someone got eyes on the shooter, but in this mayhem, identifying who it was will be done through scouring video from the overhead drones and checking to see what the surrounding buildings caught on closed-circuit surveillance.

That's going to be a secondary concern. The popping of firearms starts small and then picks up in volume. More tear gas canisters are launched from somewhere behind the police line. People begin to scream. Some fall, and others are pushed to the ground as people become desperate to escape the riot countermeasures. Vanessa's worst nightmare is playing out before her eyes.

Rubber bullets sound harmless enough. Varying in size and shape and fired from standard firearms or specialized riot guns at lower velocities than live ammunition, they are intended to cause pain or incapacitation to prompt immediate compliance with police commands. The fact is that rubber bullets can cause serious injuries at close range and if employed improperly.

Her force is trained to aim at the lower body to minimize the risk of severe injury. Hitting a sensitive area like the head, neck, or chest can lead to blunt force trauma, vision loss, head injuries, and, in rare cases, fatalities. That's what she's trying to avoid.

The media is here. Even if they weren't, every cell phone has a camera. Dozens, if not hundreds, of videos are being filmed of people panicking because the police are firing at them. Nobody will see what happened leading up to it. That's not how things work in today's era of selective editing.

"Tell them to cease fire, Sergeant! Cease firing!" Vanessa screams.

It takes a while for word to travel through the ranks. By the time it does, the damage is already done. This is more than a public relations nightmare. It's a safety issue. People are trampling each other to get away from the choking smoke, tear gas, and the police causing both. They are moving in every direction, but most seem to be fleeing north toward the river.

"We need EMTs here to render aid to anyone who needs it."

"Yes, ma'am," the sergeant says, getting back on the radio.

Vanessa watches a pair of officers approach a man down on his knee and bleeding from his forehead. He shoves them away as they bend down to offer first aid. Instinctively, the men back off. It's a smart move. It's also symbolic. Her men are supposed to be protectors of the city. Now, they look like oppressors.

"Chief, we have a problem!"

"You think?"

"Not this one. A different one. Dispatch received a 9-1-1 call from a café on University Avenue Northeast. A squad car was dispatched from the 2nd Precinct but couldn't get there."

"Why not?"

"The streets leading there have been blocked with makeshift barricades."

This is the last thing Vanessa needs right now. With downtown erupting into chaos, she doesn't have the time or manpower to deal with idiots taking advantage of this situation to make their jobs more difficult.

She sighs heavily. "Which ones?"

"All of them."

CHAPTER TWELVE

LANDON TAYSON

OUTSIDE CITY HALL
MINNEAPOLIS, MINNESOTA

This is almost too easy. The police have a playbook that they run for situations like this. Unfortunately for them, Landon has already read it. It's like having the offensive coordinator's play card on the sidelines of a football game. If you know what the other team is going to do, it's easy to use that knowledge to your advantage to stop them.

A balance of effective crowd management, de-escalation strategies, and minimal use of force is how law enforcement ensures a protest doesn't turn into a riot. Considering what happened here in 2020, the Minneapolis PD will go above and beyond to respect human rights. That starts with communication, and they have already used loudspeakers to encourage dispersal. The police posture wasn't as nonconfrontational as he expected, and outside of a few scuffles, they were exhibiting patience.

That's not surprising. In fact, Landon was counting on the police to avoid getting into clashes. They are gun-shy. The leadership is more worried about public perception than doing their jobs. Any action they take will be to isolate aggressive individuals or agitators to reduce crowd momentum. That means they are looking for him, and many are dressed for the festivities.

Riot police are equipped with shields, batons, and helmets. SWAT teams are posted nearby. Vehicles with water cannons are parked just up the street, and drones buzz overhead to monitor the movements and actions of the protesters. All that's left to do is get this shindig started.

When you throw a party, you need to bring the music to get people dancing. Nothing gets people moving like tear gas. That's why he had members of his group deploy it on those protesting with them. Nobody would ever expect that. All they had to do was ensure that there were no drones overhead when the pins were pulled. Even if cameras did catch the act, Landon could easily pass it off as police infiltrators. A convincing lie is better than a questionable truth. Just ask any politician.

The tear gas caused distress and movement but not the panic he needed. His team was instructed to read the crowd and the police response. When they didn't see the reaction they needed, one of them was instructed to fire his weapon. That worked, which was a relief to Landon. The third and final phase was to start gunning down protesters. He's thankful it didn't come to that. Too many things could have gone wrong.

The shots fired were enough to create the needed panic. The lead ranks of the protesters surged toward the barriers separating the street from City Hall, and the police took action. Maybe they felt fear and thought it was justified. That will give something for the talking heads on television to debate. Excessive force and indiscriminate use of even nonlethal riot control methods can be viewed as heavy-handed. The tactic inflames tensions and can cause casualties. Both have happened. The chief of police will have a lot to answer for about her officers responding with tear gas and riot suppression.

Raven tugs on his shirt, dragging him back into the chaos of the moment. "Landon, we need to go! The crowd is thinning."

He looks back to see if the police have begun firing their water cannons at anyone who gets too close to City Hall. Unfortunately, they have restrained themselves from using them. That's too bad. He was looking forward to seeing that on tonight's news.

"Is everything set for us in the district?"

"They are ready and waiting."

"All right. Then let's go."

Landon jogs after Raven as she guides them down a side street. Their escape route is preordained. This road will turn hard left into South 1st Street. His people have already opened the access gate to the construction area of the city's newest bridge over the Mississippi River. Vehicles won't be able to use it, but there is nothing to stop a stream of protesters from flowing over it. It's just a matter of getting the panicked sheep moving in that direction.

The members of his group, embedded in the crowd, know what to do. As the crowd scatters, they will encourage people to flee north to safety. On the other side of the river, more members will direct them up to the Arts District and a promise of refuge from an aggressive police department. The only question that remains is how many will take them up on the offer.

The more who head north, the better. Not everyone will, but he needs manpower in the short term. Even if only one in ten decides to stay, it's hundreds more added to the ranks of his group. Every addition will make a difference and increase his chances for success. By the time they call it quits and go home, reinforcements that Landon knows are on the way from all over the country will be arriving.

Raven stops and smiles as she reaches the bridge. People are already walking or jogging across it.

"You couldn't have planned this any better."

"Yeah, so far, so good."

Part of him is surprised things have worked out this well. No plan ever survives first contact with the enemy intact. That is Murphy's most important law. Landon had a hundred contingencies swirling in the back of his mind, but he didn't need to act on any of them. He wonders how long that trend will last.

"I just heard from Muzzie. He's on the other side and says people are willingly heading up to Broadway."

"Good."

Raven throws her arms in the air. "Try to be a little more excited. This is a huge victory!"

Victory. How many leaders have fallen into that trap? One battle doesn't win a war, and only a fool believes otherwise. Things are going according to plan, but they have accomplished nothing yet. This was nothing more than the first few steps on their journey.

Landon presses his lips together and shakes his head. "No, my love, this is just the beginning."

CHAPTER THIRTEEN

CHIEF VANESSA CAMPBELL

BROADWAY STREET BARRICADE
MINNEAPOLIS, MINNESOTA

In all her time in Minneapolis, she has never seen this street empty. Broadway may not be as iconic as its namesake in New York City, but it is a major thoroughfare that denotes the southern border of the Arts District. There are always cars on it, making this a first.

She couldn't believe the reports that people were cordoning off the area, and she decided to check on things herself. Apparently, they were spot on. Every street is closed off, and her officers have done the same on the other side using their squad cars. The one attempt made to force their way in was violently turned away. It's a miracle nobody was hurt or killed.

"Jesus."

"Yeah, they aren't screwing around," Inspector Sillyere says, coming up alongside her. "The barricades are manned with heavily armed guards. Every intersection is blocked from the river to Logan Park."

"What about the east and north sides?"

"Same deal. I have some people out determining the boundaries now. It isn't quite the whole Arts District, but it's most of it."

"Have you tried talking to them?"

"I got on the megaphone a half hour ago. All we got was middle fingers in return. When I tried a second time, they raised their rifles at me. They're not interested in talking right now, and I didn't want to put anyone in harm's way by forcing the issue."

The chief doesn't usually dress in tactical gear. On most days, she doesn't need her gun at her side. There isn't much use for a firearm while pushing papers and meeting with municipal and community leaders. Today is not one of those days. She strips off her gun belt, laying it on a squad car's trunk.

"What are you doing, Chief?"

"Forcing the issue."

"Vanessa, they shot at our people. There has been random gunfire all over the area. They almost shot at me, and there's no guarantee they won't shoot you. Or, at least, shoot at you."

"At least we'll know their intentions."

The chief takes a deep breath and strides confidently across the road. Broadway Street Northeast has four lanes and doesn't offer parallel parking on either side. She gets to within fifteen feet of the barricade before she notices a rifle trained on her.

"Stop right there," a voice from behind the barricade orders. Vanessa complies, showing she is unarmed. "What do you want?"

"To talk."

"Find a shrink."

She smirks. "To talk to *you*."

"I'm not in the mood for a conversation, thanks."

"I understand. You're probably tired from lugging all this crap into the street. Let me talk to your leader."

There's a long pause, and she begins to wonder if he heard her.

"He's indisposed."

She takes a couple of steps forward. Several other men behind the barricade raise their rifles, causing her officers to do the same. Vanessa pats the air with her hands to calm everyone.

"If you pull your triggers, my men *will* return fire."

"Then we'll all die together," the man deadpans. "When I said stop, I meant it. Take another step forward, and you'll see how serious I am."

It's almost tempting to challenge him. Vanessa doesn't appreciate taking orders at gunpoint in her own city. Unfortunately, these men are likely serious. If they're willing to seize a district and shoot at her officers, they won't shy away from violence now. It's best not to press her luck and risk becoming a casualty.

"You're blocking people from reaching their homes with your illegal barricades."

"It may be illegal according to your laws, but we call this border security. And our citizens are free to come and go through the perimeter, providing they show proof of citizenship."

"Citizenship?" Vanessa asks, confusion dripping from her voice.

"Yeah, I'm sure you're aware of the concept."

The chief looks up and down the vacant street. "It doesn't look like you're letting people in. There is no way for cars to get in."

"Vehicular traffic is forbidden without a permit from leadership. Our residents have two functioning legs. They can walk. Accommodations will be made for those who can't."

"I see. What about emergency services?"

"We have that covered. Anything else?"

A person's rhetoric says a lot about their opinions and mindset. Terms like citizenship indicate a level of indoctrination, and his ability to relay plans of action means there is a sophisticated level of organization behind this. These men are trained on what to do and how to respond. This isn't something that was pieced together this morning. Everything about this points to months of planning, at a minimum.

"Yes. Can you pass a message on to your leader for me? Tell him that maintaining the safety of his citizens and ours is a priority. We can't be pointing guns at each other across this street. Someone is bound to get hurt."

"I'll relay the message. Until then, consider Broadway and the other surrounding streets a DMZ. The moment one of your officers crosses it armed, they're fair game. Stay on your side, and we'll stay on ours."

Vanessa has never served in the armed forces, but she understands the term. A demilitarized zone is an area where military activity is prohibited. One of the most well-known is the Korean Demilitarized Zone, established after the war as a buffer between North and South Korea. It helps opposing forces avoid direct confrontation. That's something she can get behind, at least for now.

Vanessa nods, takes two steps backward, and pivots on her heels. She walks back behind the squad car, and her officers relax. Inspector Sillyere is waiting for her with her arms crossed. She clearly doesn't approve of the action. There isn't much the chief does that the head of the 2nd Precinct does approve of.

"What did that accomplish?"

It wasn't a question so much as a sarcastic critique of her decision to walk across the street unarmed. "Keep everyone south of Broadway. Do the same for Monroe Street and wherever they established their northern boundary. Nobody challenges their perimeter under any circumstances."

"What if they shoot at us first?"

Vanessa looks back at the barricade. "They're under orders not to unless they're provoked."

"Orders? Chief? Chief?" the inspector shouts as Vanessa walks south. "What did you learn? What's going on here?"

Vanessa stops and turns. "They think they're in a foreign country."

"What are we going to do?"

"Make plans to invade it before they have time to erect their version of the Berlin Wall."

CHAPTER FOURTEEN

KAI Z

Kai has seen this movie before. In 2020, protesters in Seattle set up the Capitol Hill Autonomous Zone, later known as the Capitol Hill Occupied Protest. The CHAZ, or CHOP, was a six-block expanse declared an autonomous area established in the Capitol Hill neighborhood following the murder of George Floyd. The zone was created as a place to safely protest police violence and systemic racism.

That's not what this is, at least on the surface. There were power and passion behind the Floyd protests, and there is little of either here. Sure, people are angry at what they perceive to be more police violence, but it's not a movement that will sweep the nation. This is acute anger, not long-term angst.

Despite the lack of motivation, there are striking similarities between the original and this sequel. Barricades were a defining feature of Seattle's autonomous zone. They demarcated and protected its boundaries and also played a symbolic role. Anyone who has ever seen *Les Misérables* on Broadway or in the movies knows that the barricade is central to the story's plot.

They are used to block streets to prevent vehicle traffic from entering an area, effectively creating a pedestrian-only area. That's all fine, but to what end are they setting up one here? Volunteers are manning these barricades being erected in the streets along Broadway. One won't accomplish anything. That means there must be dozens.

The Seattle CHAZ was six blocks. Kai doesn't know the extent of the area these guys are cordoning off, but it must be dozens. That means they have a lot of manpower – a thought that is confirmed when he sees three men carrying an old sofa down the street to add to the barricade. These people couldn't have been at the protest downtown. There would have been no time to accomplish this much if they were.

A white panel van pulls up behind the men. The driver talks to one of them before the side door opens, and someone hands out two rifles and a few boxes of ammunition. These aren't your grandfather's Remington, and those rifles won't be used to drop deer. They are what the media likes to call "military-style assault rifles."

Kai slides to the side to see if he can see into the van through his monocular. There is a full arsenal in there. He takes a sharp breath. This is something he would expect to see from a right-wing militia. This crew means business. They are even handing out some body armor, and that stuff isn't cheap. Someone with deep pockets is funding this endeavor.

A throng of people hustles diagonally across Broadway Street. This may be his best chance. Kai takes off at a jog and joins in behind them. He isn't sure if the people don't notice or just don't care. Maybe a little of both.

"Stop right there," one of the sentries behind the barricade orders.

The group complies, but one of the guys in his mid-twenties steps forward. "We were told to be here. We were at the protest downtown, and a guy said we'd be safe up here."

"The police attacked us!"

Kai doesn't expect the excuse to work, but to his surprise, the armed man's face softens, and he gestures them forward. "This is a safe space. You can come in. We'll protect you."

It's not like they have to open a gate. The barricade is nothing more than some old furniture, tires, and a junker car. There is plenty of room on both sides for foot traffic, and an armored vehicle would make quick work plowing through this if the police opted to do so. It doesn't look like anyone will be challenging them anytime soon. There is very little police presence here, at least so far.

"Head over that way to Logan Park," the armed man says, pointing east. "We have people there who can make accommodations for you. Relax. You're safe here."

This group believes that. Kai doubts they were ever in danger, but his perception doesn't matter. Theirs does. If they feel like they're in danger, countless hundreds more making the sojourn up here likely feel the same. That means the ranks of this movement, or whatever this can be characterized as, are about to swell.

Kai follows the group, now understanding that they don't know each other. He is blending right in with them. This is a bad idea on many levels, but he's curious. The answers are in the park, and he wants to know what is going on. That doesn't mean he's going to be overly talkative and friendly with this group. One of them may recognize him or connect the dots if he begins asking questions. As a result, he lags a few yards behind them and retrieves his phone to call Babs.

"Kai! Where the hell are you!"

He looks around before answering. "I'm in the Arts District."

"What? I heard rumors that armed protesters are blocking it off. How did you get in?"

"I joined a group of people that were downtown and the men at one of the barricades let us pass. Apparently, they're providing a safe haven for anyone who was near City Hall when all hell broke loose."

"Kai, that's all well and good for them, but if they catch you there…."

"I know the risks. I'll keep a low profile. It'll be fine."

Does he believe that, or is it wishful thinking? That's a question Kai will ponder later. He is, quite literally, behind enemy lines. If he's caught, it will be like an American spy being identified in the heart of Red Square and will end just as badly. A sensible man would leave this place now, but Kai didn't get to where he is in life by being "sensible."

"Okay. Just be careful. This feels like Seattle all over again."

Kai hears a couple of gunshots in the distance. Everyone's head turns in that direction. They weren't close, but they weren't far away either. Whatever is going on here, it's serious. It may be up to him to show the world what's happening.

"No, this isn't the CHAZ, Babs. This is going to be much, much worse."

CHAPTER FIFTEEN
EMMIT "CHICAGO" HASKINS

Patience has never been one of Emmit's virtues. As a child, when he wanted something, he wanted it at that moment – not five minutes from then, but more like five minutes ago. It used to drive his mother crazy. From what his sister tells him, he hasn't improved much with age.

That could be why she's making him wait in this foyer. They were supposed to leave a half hour ago, but she is still nowhere to be found. The lawyers who are coming and going have been friendly enough, but he doesn't like them. It's not personal, and he understands the importance of the accused having representation, but most of their clients are guilty as hell. They deserve to be in prison for their crimes.

Emmit couldn't get out of there fast enough. His sister seems oblivious to what's going on as they retrieve her car. Situational awareness isn't her thing. He is the one who always had good instincts for danger. The Rangers didn't beat that skill into him – they honed what was already there. Right now, he senses it all around him.

The streets are eerily quiet. The few cars Emmit sees are heading mostly north and west, but far fewer than there should be at this hour. He'll feel better about things when they get back to his sister's house. "RTB" are the three best letters in the English language. Return to base means you can come off high alert and relax, if only a little.

"I told you it wasn't necessary to come here. Nothing's happening."

Emmit doesn't look over at her. "Something is *definitely* happening."

"You're overreacting…again," Kenyala moans. "There are barely any cars on the streets!"

"It's after five in the heart of downtown. Does that seem like a good sign to you?" Emmit asks, steering his sister's car toward the Hennepin Avenue river crossing.

"Whatever."

Kenyala stares out the window and perks up when she sees the unfinished river crossing doing its best impression of a pedestrian footbridge. People are flooding north across it like they are heading into one of the entrances of U.S. Bank Stadium for a Vikings game.

"What are they doing? Migrating?"

Emmit doesn't respond to the quip. He turns onto Fifth Street. The road is a straight shot northeast until Broadway Street, when it runs due north. They are only a few minutes from Kenyala's house, but getting there isn't going to be as simple as he thought. He idles at the intersection before rolling forward to a makeshift barricade blocking the street. The old furniture in front isn't the problem and wouldn't deter him if he tried to run it. The junk cars behind it would be a little tougher to move unless he was driving a tank or Bradley fighting vehicle.

"You can't come this way, buddy," a kid shouts from the side of the road after Emmit rolls down his window.

"We live here."

"Then park your car and walk home. This road is closed to vehicular traffic. The whole area is."

Emmit stares at the man. He isn't wearing a day-glow safety vest. Even the Army wears PT belts, even when they aren't doing physical training. The practice has spawned a gallery of memes on the Internet from soldiers who think wearing the reflective strap while cutting the grass is a sick joke.

His eyes shift to the barricade blocking the road. There are no municipal trucks or traffic cones present. The barrier is ad-hoc, comprised of old furniture and beater cars. Whoever this jackass is, he has no authority to stop the free passage of anyone.

"What's going on?" Kenyala asks from the passenger seat.

The kid smirks. "You'll find out soon enough."

"I'd rather you tell me now," Emmit says, challenging him with his eyes.

"Move along."

The kid has swagger. How much of that is youthful exuberance versus blissful ignorance remains to be seen. There is one thing Emmit knows for sure, and that's this kid has no idea who he is dealing with.

"Yeah, I'm not going anywhere until you remove the crap from the street and let me through."

The kid doesn't have a witty comeback. He doesn't say anything as he draws a pistol from his back and sticks it in Emmit's face. Kenyala doesn't scream, but she does recoil at the sight of the weapon and pushes deeper into her seat.

The Ranger doesn't flinch. He's been shot at before, even if it wasn't by someone holding a gun inches from his face. That isn't his primary concern. Emmit eyes a slightly older guy, maybe in his late twenties, readying a rifle a dozen meters away. If one guy is covering this kid, it's a safe bet there is one or two more who have eyes on this car.

"You ain't giving the orders here," the kid says. "I said move along, and I ain't askin' again."

"All right," Emmit says. "I'm moving."

He shifts the car into reverse, backs up, and turns the wheel to head down Broadway. It looks like the street is about to be shut down. Police are lining up, and some are even shouting at him to make a right turn. He ignores them as he speeds up.

"Emmit, what's going on?" Kenyala asks, her voice cracking mid-question.

"I don't know."

"How are we going to get home?"

"We're going to find another way in, that's how."

Every street north of Broadway is blocked off. Sixth, Washington, and Adams Streets are all barricaded. Every road all the way to Logan Park is closed off with obstructions manned by armed men. Emmit turns north up Monroe. It's much of the same thing here.

"Ho-ly shit!" his sister exclaims. "They've blocked off most of the Arts District. Who are they?"

"No idea," Emmit answers, stomping down on the accelerator and sending his sister's car hurtling up Monroe Street.

"What are you doing?"

"Making my way to the back door."

It takes a lot of manpower to pull something like this off in such a short time span. They are sealing off the area, but their focus appears to be on the approaches from the south and choking off the major arteries. It's how he would have planned this. If they come in from the north down one of the side streets, they'll have a fighting chance. He hates basing that plan on an assumption, but that's all he can do. It's not like he has a Predator drone at his disposal.

"What makes you think there is one? A back door, I mean."

"Hasty perimeters are bound to have soft spots. It takes a lot of manpower and organization to close off an area this size. We need to find a hole before they plug it."

Emmit turns onto Lowry Avenue. It's much of the same, only the barricades aren't as large, and fewer people are manning them. University Avenue and Third Street are blocked by dump trucks. It appears they are building a serpentine, so maybe they plan on letting certain vehicles into the area.

A serpentine road barrier is designed to force vehicles to navigate through an S-shaped path to slow them down. The military used them extensively outside of their bases in Iraq and Afghanistan. They were instrumental in defending against high-speed vehicular bomb threats. Emmit half wonders if this one will be covered with machine guns. It wouldn't surprise him. Someone in this group has military experience.

"There's my huckleberry," Emmit says, spotting an access driveway they either forgot about or haven't had the time to block off.

He yanks the wheel to the left. Kenyala grabs the handle above her window and braces herself against the dash as the car turns hard. Emmit thinks they're home-free when several shots ring out. Worse, she heard them, too.

"Were they shooting at us?"

Emmit shrugs, not to alarm his sister. They were absolutely shooting at them. The shots were way off the mark, but they were the target. That brings whatever this is to a whole new level. It also begins to make him question whether returning here was the right move.

He accelerates and careens down the alley, only slowing to cross Twenty-Fourth and Twenty-Third Avenues. It's quiet now, so he slows down and drives casually. They can make it home. Whatever the plans are for the Arts District, the focus is on the perimeter, not the interior.

Emmit's cell rings, and he connects it after glancing at the caller ID. "Hey, Nashville."

"Hey, Brother! We still on for this weekend? I've got coolers full of steaks, ribs, and beer. All I need to do is load them in the truck and hit the road."

"Yeah, about that. I'm still game, but you may have some problems getting here."

"What do you mean?"

"You should turn on the news. I know I need to."

CHAPTER SIXTEEN

CHIEF VANESSA CAMPBELL

CITY HALL CONFERENCE ROOM
MINNEAPOLIS, MINNESOTA

The mayor convened this crisis meeting when it became clear that the situation in the Arts District would only continue to deteriorate. Vanessa could have told him that. In fact, she did, not that he listened. Now, with national media flooding into the city and ready to share the next chapter of unrest in Minneapolis with the world, it may be too late.

It's nine o'clock, and none of the senior police officials or prominent members of the city government gathered in this City Hall conference room will be going home anytime soon. The mayor is actually on time for this meeting. Apparently, it takes a crisis of this magnitude for him to be punctual.

"Take your seats, everyone," he announces, silencing the room. Everyone who has a chair plants themselves in it. "We all know why we're here. Where are we going to start?"

"We need to talk about what happened today," Deputy Chief Goldberg says.

Vanessa scowls. "Information is still being—"

"You attacked a peaceful protest, Chief Campbell! As the man in charge of constitutional policing—"

"I did no such thing, you slimy son of a bitch! And neither did any of the officers on this force! If you want to say otherwise without evidence, I will rip your tongue out of your lying mouth!"

"Enough! It's already been a long day, and there will be plenty of time to litigate what happened outside these walls later. I need to know what's happening in the Arts District."

"I can speak to that, Mr. Mayor," Inspector Sillyere interjects, straightening in her seat. "Can you put the map up on the television?"

The lieutenant sitting behind her goes to work on screencasting his display.

"Barricades have been erected in every intersection north of Broadway Street, west of Monroe up to the train tracks. At that point, the tracks serve as the divider until reaching Lowry. The barricades were constructed south of that street all the way to the river. We assume they will use the Mississippi as their western border. In total, they have seized and cordoned off about seventy percent of the Arts District."

The map comes up on the television, showing the extent of the area. The mayor stares at the map impassively as the slide transitions to show the locations of the barricade and some photos showing what they are comprised of.

"Each barricade is manned by no fewer than three people. We have seen a mix of men and women, multiple ethnicities, and ages that range from teenagers to middle age. This is not a racial or youth movement. From our estimates, more than eight hundred people are involved, and that number is steadily growing. There is representation across the spectrum, and they are armed. We've seen everything from hunting rifles to semi-automatic AR-15s. My officers even spotted an AK-47. That's a fully automatic weapon."

The mayor removes his glass and rubs his eyes. "It's hard to believe they could have thrown this together because of a protest gone bad."

"They didn't, Mayor Thurlow," Vanessa interjects. "This is a well-thought-out operation. We worked out the timeline and corroborated it with video from the area. The barricades were being constructed even before the crowd began to march on City Hall. This was planned, no matter what happened outside the doors of this building."

"You mean before you dispersed them with tear gas and rubber—"

"I meant what I said, Deputy Goldberg. *All* of it."

"I said knock it off!" the mayor shouts, slamming his hand down on the table. "We can discuss the constitutionality of those actions later. I want to know what we plan on doing about a mob cordoning off more than half of the Arts District."

"Disperse it. We find the weakest barricade and punch a SWAT team through it using armored vehicles. Once we are inside their perimeter, they will scramble to react, and it will collapse."

The mayor narrows his eyes at Vanessa. "You're advising direct action?"

"The longer we wait, the harder it will be to restore order. Eight hundred now could be double that by this time tomorrow. People *will* come to support them. You can count on that."

"Whatever happened to negotiating? Is that no longer an option for this department?" Goldberg asks.

"They aren't interested in negotiating, Otto," Vanessa says, refusing to look at him or anyone else in the room.

She has pleaded her case, and most of the men and women around this table think she's insane. They are entitled to their opinions. Her recommendation is based on what happened in Seattle when they occupied a neighborhood. This is different, and the faster they understand that, the less blood will be spilled.

"How do you know?"

"Because I spoke with one of the men manning a barricade on Broadway Street."

Mayor Thurlow leans back in his chair and rubs his chin. "You spoke to one of the foot soldiers. Got it. Did you talk to their leader?"

"I asked the sentry to relay a message."

"Have you heard back?"

Vanessa shakes her head. "No, not yet. To my knowledge, this group has not communicated any demands to us, posted anything online, or spoken to the media. We don't know what they want."

Mayor Thurlow steeples his hands in front of his face, making a show of being reflective and measured. It's an act. This man is neither of those things, so she just waits for the theater to end.

"So, you want to breach their perimeter, terrify the citizens already in their area more than they are, and risk countless lives by engaging in what is likely to be a prolonged firefight in the middle of my city?"

"We're going to ensure it doesn't come to that. But the longer we wait, the deadlier any action will be. All this group managed to do today was erect barricades. If they decide to dig in, or their numbers swell, it will take the military to dislodge them. If that happens, sir, I promise you that the casualties will be *much* higher."

"Perhaps. If the estimates of eight hundred armed protesters are correct, a four- or eight-man SWAT team might not punch through. Even if it does manage to pierce it, they have a small army that can mount a resistance."

"Once their perimeter is breached, they will stand down," Vanessa concludes.

"And you can guarantee that? Because I don't think they will. They already have shot at the police, so we need to take their intention seriously. I am not going to let this become a massacre. Blood will not be allowed to run in this city's streets again."

"Then, ask the governor to send in the National Guard. That will give the leaders of this separatist movement a moment of pause."

"Oh, yes, escalate things," Otto mumbles. "Is that all you think about, Chief Campbell?"

"It beats surrendering, which I'm sure you're advocating."

"These people have a legitimate point of view and freedom to get their grievances addressed. I support their right to do that."

"So do I, until they deprive the citizens in those neighborhoods of *their* rights in the process. They are not airing grievances. They are engaged in a paramilitary takeover of a major American city. Our duty is to protect—"

"I've heard enough," the mayor says, standing and buttoning his suit jacket. "I'm going to hold a press conference warning all residents to avoid the Arts District. Nobody makes a move against that area until we understand what the protesters' demands are. Stand your people down, Chief. Those are my orders."

The mayor leaves, and many of the municipal leaders join him. Vanessa isn't sure if they agree with his decision, but God has spoken. He's not God, but he thinks he is in this city. If he's proven correct, they get rewarded for their support. If he fails, they can claim they were against him all along and turn the issue into a political football.

None of that matters to the chief. She has a job to do. That starts with issuing orders to stand fast and having her inspectors come up with a manpower rotation. The entire force has been working today, and they need to start getting some rest. Vanessa has a feeling this crisis is going to last a while.

CHAPTER SEVENTEEN

LANDON TAYSON

LOGAN PARK
ARTS DISTRICT, MINNEAPOLIS, MINNESOTA

As energized as Landon is, he can feel the fatigue down to his bones. He's simultaneously wide awake and yet still groggy like he hasn't slept. Then, he remembers he actually hasn't. Who could sleep on this momentous occasion?

That's what he told himself last night as he directed his group to set up the command center. He needed a place to receive communications and coordinate a response when the police finally made their move. Only, it never came. There was no attempt to ram a barricade, nor were any officers apprehended trying to sneak in.

Landon was surprised but not as surprised as Captain Muzzie was. In all their war-gaming exercises, not once did his loyal commander assume that law enforcement wouldn't test them at least once. The leadership of this city must be okay with armed vigilantes holding an entire district hostage. The mayor is weaker than he thought.

At least the inaction gave them a chance to reinforce the barricades and build an interior line. The major intersections are heavily reinforced, thanks to a trucking company that was deprived of their vehicles. The smaller streets needed a lot of work. Nothing they do will stop a determined assault, but that's what guns are for…and they have a *lot* of those thanks to their generous benefactor.

They also needed to organize the protesters who had joined the cause. Landon, Muzzie, and Raven planned for zero additional help until reinforcements arrive a few days from now. They were pleasantly surprised when hundreds of people who witnessed the police assault downtown enlisted their services. It's a fraction of the thousands at the protest, but still more than he expected.

The best part is the rumors he is hearing from downtown. The number of people who joined his small army from the protesters who fled north may be small, but that doesn't mean they aren't supporting the effort. Chatter on social media is pointing to another protest in Gold Medal Park against the impending police action against the ADOZ.

Landon didn't expect that. It doesn't matter if they are native Minnesotans or professional protesters. Any gathering will further deplete police manpower outside the perimeter. Once his own reinforcements arrive, it will truly be "game on."

Logan Park is a hive of activity. It has played host to countless neighborhood events, seasonal celebrations, art shows, and community clean-up days. Now, the family-friendly recreational area is ground zero for one of the greatest political movements of the decade.

Most of his core team is here, performing various functions. They have centered most operations on the basketball and tennis courts, although some of them have taken breaks to screw around on the modern playground that kids must absolutely love. It's a shame they'll have to relocate their administration center. This park is way too close to the perimeter to be sustainable.

"Here they come," Raven says, pointing at the large group of people being escorted into the park.

"Okay…I wasn't nervous until now."

His group has a public relations guy who is second to none. Landon expected a handful of reporters to show up for this press conference. The number is several dozen, not counting another third carrying cameras.

"Bryce invited every news organization worth a damn. It looks like most of them answered the call," Raven says, satisfaction oozing from her voice.

She has a right to be impressed. Every major news outlet in the country is represented. They are guided over to the stage, and the cameramen go to work setting up. Raven and Landon watch them, mesmerized. He's never in his life been the center of attention. That's about to change.

This stage is as temporary as the one in Gold Medal Park was, except it's constructed with plywood and two-by-fours instead of milk crates. It doesn't have to be pretty, just functional. Landon wants to be able to look down on the horde of reporters crowding the platform. And he wants them to look up at him. Symbolism is more powerful than most people realize.

"It's almost showtime, boss. You ready for this?"

Bryce Cronkite is Landon's most unexpected and welcome supporter, not counting Raven. Cronkite isn't his real family name, but it doesn't matter. In his apartment, the man has a shrine built to the venerable news anchor, and he's a dedicated journalism student at UM. What he lacks in real-world experience, he more than makes up for in untempered zeal.

"Yeah, I think so. Any last-minute advice?"

Bryce looks out at the gathered press corps. "Reporters aren't your friends. Some of them will be sympathetic. Others won't. When they try to get under your skin, and trust me, they will, be sure to channel your anger at the police, not back at them. As insufferable as the media is, we need them on our side."

"Good tip. Anything else?"

"Yeah. Don't screw it up. We've been waiting a long time for this."

Landon smirks and nods. He isn't the only one. Years of planning have all come down to this moment. They succeeded beyond his wildest expectations yesterday. Whether that trend continues partly lies in what happens in the next fifteen minutes.

"Where's Muzzie?" Landon asks, wondering where his most faithful commander is hiding.

"The captain is walking the barricades. He said handling the media is your job. Keeping the police on their side of the border is his. He wants to ensure the sentries understand and are following their instructions to the letter. You're on your own."

Landon nods. Muzzie is a good man, and this whole exercise would be futile without his expertise. He belongs on this stage to soak up the moment, but rallying the troops is more important. There's no reason to think the police won't seize this opportunity to end this occupation. They may have a sniper set up to do precisely that. On that wonderful thought, Landon steps up to the podium on their makeshift stage.

"Good morning, ladies and gentlemen. My name is Landon Tayson. I've lived in Minneapolis for most of my life and have seen the good times…and the bad. I was here for the 2020 protests and listened to the empty promises made in their aftermath."

Landon stares at the reporters in front to gauge their reaction. Most stare back at him impassively. Bryce's warning about them not being friends rattles around his brain. He needs to focus. This message isn't meant for reporters but for the people watching.

"We all want the same things – safe streets, a government that isn't mired in corruption, and a police force that protects and serves the people, not its own self-interest. Sadly, we have none of those things. They have taken our patience for granted. They have ignored our pleas. They have betrayed their own citizens…and now, they have done it for the final time.

"Yesterday, we took matters into our own hands. A peaceful protest in Gold Medal Park turned into a march…a march for our rights…a march to make our voices heard in City Hall. What was that message greeted with? Pledges for discussions with the community and honest change? No. We were met with tear gas and rubber bullets. That's what the Minneapolis Police Department thinks about its citizens.

"People deserve a safe space, not just from criminals but from the law enforcement officers and government officials responsible for our welfare. Their repeated failures have left our streets violent and our citizens with no recourse to correct that. In this city, calling the police is just as deadly as facing the criminals.

"Therefore, I hereby declare this area the Arts District Occupied Zone until a formal resolution declaring our independence from the City of Minneapolis, the State of Minnesota, and the United States of America can be drafted."

Murmurs between reporters turn to shouts from the assembled media. That may be known forever as the line that launched a thousand questions. Landon tries to silence them with his hands, contemplating how many interview requests Bryce will have to deal with. This isn't the time for that, although he knows it's an eventual requirement. People need to understand this action, and he's the best person to explain why they are here.

"What are your demands?" a female reporter shouts from his direct front.

Landon smiles. "We have no demands. We do not want an audience with state or local authorities to air our grievances with the futile hope that it will change anything. We know that it won't. The time for talk is over. This is our home, and living with it is their new reality."

CHAPTER EIGHTEEN
CHIEF VANESSA CAMPBELL

Vanessa hates this place. It's not because of the short fifteen-minute drive on I-94 and certainly not because the Beaux-Arts architecture of the Minnesota State Capitol building isn't beautiful. It's because she is rarely here in St. Paul for a good reason, and today is no different.

"Therefore, I hereby declare this area the Arts District Occupied Zone until a formal resolution declaring our independence from the City of Minneapolis, the State of Minnesota, and the United States of America can be drafted."

She can almost hear the reporters asking themselves if this is real. Apparently, this Landon character hears them, too, and he tries to silence them with his hands.

"What are your demands?" a female reporter asks. It's a damn good question because Vanessa hasn't heard them make any.

"We have no demands. We do not want an audience with state or local authorities to air our grievances with the futile hope that it will change anything. We know that it won't. The time for talk is over. This is our home, and living with it is their new reality."

An aide turns the television off, bathing the room in a tense silence. The governor's office is located on the capitol's ground floor and is the perfect blend of grandeur and functionality. It has intricate woodwork and hand-carved panels, large windows, murals, and historic furniture. It's typically a warm place to conduct official state business. The mood here today is anything but warm.

"I desperately try to stay out of city business," Governor Prescott St. James says, rubbing his hands together as he addresses the four people at the table. "Unfortunately, this protest has become my business."

"We're handling it," Mayor Thurlow says, a knife-like edge to his voice.

Vanessa fakes scratching an itch on her upper lip to hide her grin. Despite these two men serving the same political party, there is no love lost between them. Actually, they despise each other. She isn't sure why that is, other than they are both political. Thurlow has his eye on the governor's mansion, and St. James is likely to run for the United States Senate as a stepping stone to fulfill his presidential aspirations. With both men dreaming of higher stations in life, neither wants to make a mistake now.

"This is you handling it, Elliott? Damn, I would hate to see what happens when you ignore a crisis."

"It's our problem, and we will take care of it, Governor."

St. James leans back in his chair and rests his hands on his chest. "No politician likes the media. We need them, and we love facetime with cameras, but they are encouraged by their editors and producers to make our lives miserable. Do you know what happens when I step outside this office? I'm going to be bombarded with questions asking how I feel about my state being a couple of square miles smaller."

"Their proclamation is meaningless," the mayor says, flicking his hand.

"I agree. Will the rest of America?" he asks, leaning forward. "How long before every nonconformist revolutionary in the country pours in to join their cause? How was this allowed to get this far to begin with?"

Vanessa fights the urge to speak. It's a golden opportunity to throw the mayor under the proverbial bus, but that could create long-term complications. Like it or not, she needs the man's support, and he's going to need hers. The old adage is true — politics does make for strange bedfellows.

"The men at the barricades were armed. We didn't want the aftermath of the downtown protest to turn into a bloodbath."

"And you agreed with this approach, Chief Campbell?"

"Not initially, no. I was ready to send SWAT in last night. I was dissuaded by the mayor, and I believe, in hindsight, that he made the right choice in doing so."

That tasted nasty coming out of her mouth. She can almost feel the mayor relax across the table. There is a time to be the hard-charging law enforcement officer, and there is time for diplomacy. She doesn't really mean that, but there is a bigger point to be made here, and it's better if Thurlow is on her side.

"You do?"

"Governor, I think there may be something more to this ADOZ than a reaction to the ambush or what happened downtown. There is a level of organization here that leads me to believe this was pre-planned."

"Pre-planned? That's a hell of an assertion."

"Yes, sir, it is. However, my people have confirmed that the barricades along the perimeter of this ADOZ were being erected *before* the downtown march. And these sentries are *heavily* armed and fairly well-trained. This came together too quickly and with too much effectiveness to have been random."

"Mayor?"

"I'm not completely convinced," Thurlow says, glancing at his top law enforcement official. "But Chief Campbell is neither an alarmist nor a conspiracy theorist. It requires further analysis, but she makes a strong argument, and I'm compelled to believe her."

Now, it's Vanessa's turn to relax. Thurlow is an opportunist, and there was no guarantee that he wouldn't take the bone she tossed him and chew on it in the corner. He could have just as easily embarrassed her. They will never see eye-to-eye, but there may be some hope that they can successfully weather this crisis together.

More importantly, there could be a détente between the governor and mayor. Whether Thurlow realizes it or not, he gave the governor a much-needed political out.

"If that's true, then this likely becomes a federal problem," Governor St. James concludes. Bingo.

"It does."

"Find out, and quickly. Do you need anything from me?"

"Are you offering?"

"I am here to support you, Mayor Thurlow. If you have a request for state resources, make it."

So, it was a short-lived détente. The two men are back to jockeying for position. That will become important when the three of them address the media in fifteen minutes. Politics doesn't stop during a crisis – if anything, the game gets played harder. It's almost like the last two minutes of a football game.

"Governor, bringing in the National Guard right now may only serve to inflame the situation. Would it be possible for you to draft a mobilization order but not execute it yet?"

"It can be arranged, but it will leak. I can promise that."

"And if it does, it may lead to the escalation of tension we are looking to avoid."

"Talk it over and let me know. There's one more thing. Handle this. The moment you ask for the National Guard, you make this my problem. I urge you *not* to make this my problem. It's better for all of us that way."

The threat isn't lost on Vanessa, and she doubts the mayor missed it, either. If the most dangerous place on Earth is between a politician and a camera, then the second most dangerous place to be is in the way of one realizing their aspirations. The governor doesn't want to get his hands dirty. It doesn't take much imagination for Vanessa to know what will happen if they force his hand.

The governor stands and buttons his jacket. "Let's go meet the press, shall we?"

CHAPTER NINETEEN
FIELD OFFICER DAVID BRASS

Brass settles into his sofa with a glass of scotch. The breaking news chyron has been at the bottom of the screen all day. News of the happenings in Minneapolis is absolutely dominating the airwaves.

The anchor finishes a recap of the ADOZ announcement. The smug smile he's wearing betrays the stoic demeanor this crisis calls for. He's enjoying this. In his mind, this is another American underdog story. The country loves those. Only this one involves a possible secession from the Union. The vote is out as to whether the country will support that action.

She introduces a guest who is a bigwig around Beltway circles. Brass knows the guy, and his "expert" opinion is only respected in media studios. To the rest of the men and women who work in and around the federal government, the man is a complete moron.

"This isn't a noble cause…it's a blatant violation of the Constitution," he says after the anchor poses a loaded question. "It doesn't matter *why* these protesters are setting up barricades. It's an illegal act, and the police should have begun tearing them down the moment they started going up."

"Some people are arguing that the protesters have a voice and are using it. Are you saying that they shouldn't express their disgust with the city government? The police? Doesn't this protest have merit?"

"What merit?" the guest asks. "I've seen the video of the police ambush that started all this…the *whole* video. I still fail to see how law enforcement acted inappropriately."

"People got shot by the police!"

"And the police walked into an ambush based on a false 9-1-1 call."

"That hasn't been proven," the anchor maintains. "What about the march to City Hall? Do you think they should have used tear gas against that crowd?"

"Are you sure we were watching the same video? Police fire tear gas from a distance. I haven't seen any evidence of that happening until shots were fired."

"By…the…police."

"There is no conclusive proof of that, either. Unless you have seen something that I haven't. Those shots easily could have come from someone in the crowd and probably did."

"Yes, I'm sure the protesters were shooting at each other," the anchor says with a sneer.

Brass smirks. The media can always be counted on to take a stance. The days of objective journalism are over. This anchor will argue his point with any guest who dares challenge the narrative. He changes the channel to see what one of the other networks is saying.

The field reporter on camera is behind the police line on the opposite side of the street from the occupied area. Brass doesn't know where – he isn't that familiar with Minneapolis.

"Our newsroom has learned that there are reports of shots fired on the perimeter of this ADOZ, as their leaders call it," the anchor relays. "Can you confirm that?"

"There was at least one incident with police yesterday afternoon. That much I can confirm. There were no injuries, but several shots were fired at law enforcement. There has been the occasional sound of gunfire since then, but no casualties have been reported."

"Have the police provided any information about their intentions? Are they planning on storming in?"

"They seem to be holding their positions outside the ADOZ perimeter since the barricades went up. They could be waiting for nightfall, or maybe they are looking to negotiate now that the movement's leader has been identified. We'll have to wait and see what their intentions are."

Brass smirks. He was counting on inaction, even when he was told the likely result would be otherwise. Field operatives may be closer to the action, but they lack the ten-thousand-foot view of the world. No elected leader wants to preside over a bloodbath when there are options to avoid one. At least, that's the logic, even if the most prudent measure is to put a stop to the nascent movement while it's in its infancy.

His secure phone rings, and he checks the caller, even knowing who it likely is. Brass's work with the CIA doesn't require him to have much contact with the mothership. He likes it that way. Unfortunately, in an operation of this magnitude, there is likely to be a degree of micromanagement.

"Yeah?"

"It looks like you're off to a good start," Director Lancaster says. Alistair has always had a flair for understatement.

"You expected less?"

"I expected not to see our own citizens bleeding on the national news."

"Director, eleven men died building the Golden Gate Bridge. It's the cost of progress. You knew that when you gave the green light."

Alistair exhales. "Do you have control of this situation?"

That's a funny question coming from the director of the Central Intelligence Agency. He knows better. Situations are managed, not controlled. Operations are planned, and contingencies are developed when the plans go to hell. That it turns out the way you want it to can never be assured, only guided.

"I have someone on the inside to manage things."

"That's not what I asked."

"It's what you asked when you gave the order to activate Pendulum. It was always designed to be a last resort because of the risks and the consequences of something going wrong. We have taken every precaution to avoid both, but not all risks can be mitigated."

Brass sips his drink as he waits for a response. Lancaster is a typical politician. He wants results but isn't willing to pay the price for them. As a presidential appointee who didn't come up through the CIA's ranks, he only tangentially knows how they operate. In the real world, progress comes with a price tag.

"What about the other cities?"

"I'm keeping those in our back pocket for now. If we need to expand the program, we will. For now, what's happening in Minneapolis is accomplishing your goal. Railspike will be forgotten by the time this is over. If the movement spreads, we can rest knowing our fingerprints aren't on it."

"David, don't make promises you can't keep," Alistair warns.

"I could say the same to you, Director."

He's right. Something could leak, but Brass doesn't think so. The Pendulum operation is unknown within the CIA outside of a handful of people. The same applies to Watchtower. If David pulls this operation off for the director, he expects to get his wish fulfilled as a reward. Everything has a cost. This isn't one the director can afford *not* to pay.

"Keep me informed of any developments. Tell your man on the inside not to cross lines he can't come back from."

Brass chuckles. "Who says it's a man?"

Alistair hangs up without responding. Brass stares at his phone to ensure the call is gone. Typical. He sets it down and unmutes the television before taking another long sip of his drink. It's late, and he should get some rest, but this is too entertaining not to watch. The best part is that this operation has only just started. David stares at the remaining amber liquid in his glass and contemplates getting a refill. He can catch up on his sleep when this is over.

CHAPTER TWENTY
EMMIT "CHICAGO" HASKINS

THE FIFTH STREET HOUSE
MINNEAPOLIS, MINNESOTA

The press conference was all he needed to see. Not only did it offend his sensibilities, it was a personal affront to everything he believes in. This is the United States of America, and he is a Ranger who swore an oath to defend the Constitution against all enemies, *foreign* and *domestic*. This may be some of both.

Emmit retreats upstairs and grabs the shotgun from under his sister's bed and a box of shells from her nightstand. She eyes him coming back down with the weapon and cocks her head.

"Really?" his sister asks, hugging her cup of coffee.

"Yeah, really. I don't know what the hell's going on, but I'm going to be prepared," Emmit says, inspecting the chamber. "I'm half surprised you kept this thing."

"Are you kidding? That's the most inappropriate housewarming gift you could have given me." The sound of a gunshot startles her. "Okay, maybe not so inappropriate. How close was that?"

"A couple of blocks over. Don't worry, if anyone comes here, nothing screams 'go away' like a Benelli twelve gauge."

The thought causes Emmit to smile. The Italian company Benelli Armi is god-tier when it comes to semi-automatic and pump-action shotguns. The M4 model is his personal favorite. The reliable, semi-automatic tactical shotgun is widely used in the Marine Corps and is the only reason he would have ever considered becoming a jarhead. That, and he never developed a taste for crayons.

The doorbell chimes, and Emmit looks at his sister. "Are you expecting anyone?"

Kenyala shakes her head slowly. "No."

Emmit racks a round and moves toward the door. Nothing is more intimidating than watching someone perform that simple action. It's the last warning people get before it gets real, but that's in the movies. In real life, you want to be ready to rock if the barbarians at the gate have bad intentions.

He quickly glances out the side window. Emmit smirks, knowing he won't be shooting anybody today, before yanking the door open. The two men grin at him like a pair of boarding school students watching the headmaster drink his morning coffee after they pissed in it.

"Helmet. So, at last, we meet for the first time for the last time."

"*Spaceballs*. I see you're still up to your old tricks, Hollywood."

Specialist Felix Ramone is one of the quirkiest soldiers he served with. A physical specimen with looks only a mother could love, he outperformed everybody on PT tests and was an excellent soldier. His only downside is that he can quote almost any movie ever made, and he usually does. Outside of the occasional "yes, sir, no, sir, and here, sergeant," that's the extent of his linguistic repertoire. No wonder he's still single.

"Don't encourage him, Chicago. He was insufferable on the way here."

Specialist Buddy O'Leary is Hollywood's polar opposite. A country boy through and through, his world revolves around beer, honkytonks, and four-wheeling in his truck. Pudgy, especially by Ranger standards, he has added on more than a few pounds since he left the Army. It doesn't matter. There was no soldier he could depend on more when things went to hell.

"Nashville. How you doin'?"

"Outstanding. Sorry we're late. I'd have been here sooner if I didn't have to pick this clown up at O'Hare Airport."

Emmit does the mental math. Nashville to Minneapolis is a twelve-and-a-half-hour drive, not counting stops to take a piss, eat, and fuel up. He made pretty good time considering having to detour through Chicago.

"Please tell me you still brought the steaks and beer."

"Are you kiddin'?" Nashville says, turning to show the oversized rucksack on his back. Hollywood does the same. "We spent our days in the Rangers haulin' a hundred pounds of ammo and water through the desert, woods, and jungle. This was way more satisfying."

"In that case, come on in."

The two men lug their rucksacks and duffle bags in and set them down. Emmit introduces Kenyala, whom neither man has ever met. They've only heard stories about her. Nashville is the polite one. Hollywood's tongue is dragging on the ground behind him as he eyes her like a teenage kid who got a hold of his first *Playboy* magazine.

"How did you guys even get here? We've heard on the news that every road leading here is blocked."

"And witnessed it firsthand," Kenyala adds.

"Aw, hell, Chicago…that perimeter ain't worth shit. No OPs, sleepy, undisciplined yahoos watching the barricade, if you can call it that. I can't understand why the police haven't just streamed in here."

"I can," Emmit mumbles. "Politics. We all know how much fun that can be."

"Yeah, but that's really not the important point. A bunch of anarchist wack-a-doos decide to set up the Federated States of Crazyland in *your* neighborhood and have no idea that a highly decorated, kick-ass Ranger is behind their lines?"

"Technically, it's my sister's neighborhood…but, yeah. And, don't make a thing of it, or we'll get a steady diet of *Die Hard* quotes all weekend."

"Pay no attention to that man behind the curtain!" Hollywood shouts, opting for the *Wizard of Oz* reference.

"Nah, I don't plan on starting trouble. The police will do their thing, and this will all be over soon enough."

"That's a nice wish," Nashville says, his lips creasing into a sly smile.

"I'm serious, bro."

"Chicago…you're smack in the middle of a bunch of spoiled morons whose parents didn't give them enough attention trying to secede from the United States. You can't be naïve enough to think you won't end up involved."

"My fighting days are over. I did my part for 'God and country,' same as you. Look, I didn't ask you guys up here to wage war. We're gonna have a barbecue. But, if something does go down, I can't think of anyone I would rather have at my side. That is, if you're in."

"You don't even need to ask, Brother," Nashville says, clapping him on the shoulder. *"Sua Sponte."*

Emmit turns to the other former Ranger. "Hollywood?"

"Shut up — you had me at 'hello.'"

"All right. The guest room is upstairs and to the left. Grilling operations begin at 1300. Get your gear stowed, and I'll make a pot of coffee."

"Outstanding. I could use some."

"Coffee's for closers only," Hollywood decrees, uttering the famous line from *Glengarry Glen Ross.*

"What the hell do you know about closing, Hollywood?" Nashville says, climbing the stairs with their buddy right behind him. "I've been to the club with you, remember? You couldn't close a prostitute with a wad of Franklins in your pocket."

The men disappear upstairs, but he can still hear the faint murmur of their voices in the colloquial back-and-forth soldiers engage in daily. He misses it. Having them around almost makes it feel like old times.

"Are they always like this, or was it for my benefit?" Kenyala asks.

Emmit chuckles. "Actually, they were on their best behavior in front of you."

"All righty then, I'll make the coffee. Yours is strong enough to keep an elephant awake for three days," his sister says, moving into the kitchen. "Do you think there's going to be trouble?"

"I think this is going to blow over quickly. But if there is, we have two really good men watching our backs."

CHAPTER TWENTY-ONE
KAI Z

He may be in a self-proclaimed foreign country now, but the Internet still works here. And the American dollar is still almighty. Kai wonders how long it will be before the leaders of this movement try to change both of those things. Good luck. The people who live in this district may be hiding in their homes for the moment, but that won't last forever.

As promised, the key is in the lockbox. It took only a few minutes of searching the app to procure this place, even if the price was a little steep. Then again, it is huge, and it sure as hell beats sleeping on the street or whatever arrangements the weirdos in the park are making for protesters who wandered up here.

The newly built modern house has five bedrooms and four-and-a-half baths. Maybe that will be useful if he ends up having houseguests, not that any are expected. Then again, you never know who may need refuge from the craziness going on outside the front door.

Real estate is about location, location, location. The house also has a porch, patio, and a balcony that overlooks the ADOZ's northern border of Lowry Street. The rental is only a block or so south of it, and he can see one of the barricades from the top floor. It's a great spot to quietly keep an eye on things. The only downside is that most of the action is happening to the south. That's a problem for tomorrow.

Kai needs to procure groceries, which are likely going to be in short supply very soon. There are small markets in the district, but none of the ones he passed were open. Even if any of them unlock their doors, there are easily thousands of people who rush to hoard food. It's a safe bet that the organizers have a plan for that. Rationing and doling out sustenance is a great way to apply leverage to gain compliance.

He slides his phone out of his pocket, unlocks it, and taps Babs's number under recent calls. This is his fourth try. The first three resulted in no answer, and now he's beginning to worry. It's not like her to fail to stay in contact.

A knock at the door causes him to jerk his head so hard he nearly pulls a muscle. Nobody knows he's here. The house's owners are in California and certainly wouldn't return during this mess. They have a maid and a guy who tends to the small yard, but what are the odds either would be working on a day like today?

Kai quietly moves to the door and leans his head next to it. "Yes?"

"Open the door, Kai, and you won't have to keep calling me."

He does as instructed and swings it open to see her standing there in jeans, a T-shirt, and a baseball cap with her ponytail looped through the back. Best of all, she is holding two large paper sacks filled with all manner of groceries.

"Babs! What the hell are you doing here?"

"Looking for you, idiot. I come bearing gifts."

He takes one from her and peers at its contents after closing the door. She knows what he likes.

"You went shopping?"

"I know you well enough to conclude you haven't thought about how you're going to feed yourself while you're trying to save the city."

She places her bag on the kitchen counter and gives him a hug.

"How the hell did you find me?"

"All right…I might as well come clean. I Lojacked you a long time ago. I put a tracking app on your phone that tells me where you are at all times."

"Seriously?"

"Your unlock code should be a little more complicated than the combination on Skroob's luggage."

It's an old *Spaceballs* joke. The code to planet Druidia's air shield was one, two, three, four, five…and that happened to be the code for the president of planet Spaceball's luggage. He's always liked that movie, and he never expected anyone to try to hack into his phone.

"We'll talk about this later. How did you get through the barricade?"

Babs rests her chin on the top of her hands and bats her eyelashes. "What can I say? I'm cute."

He shakes his head. "You shouldn't have come here."

"And you shouldn't have either, yet here we are. Nice digs."

He won't argue with that. The house is spacious, with modern furniture and oak floors stained in three or four different shades of brown. It also will likely be assumed that the owner has money and won't cause trouble. Security forces in the ADOZ may eventually pay a visit, but they'll focus on problem areas first. Or so Kai hopes.

"I like my base camp to be comfortable. I could use someone on the outside to make sure my stories get reported."

"We have friends who can do that. You need someone on the inside to watch your back because you get tunnel vision and don't pay attention to your surroundings. It's going to be the death of you, and I kinda like having you around. So, what's the plan?"

"I was just thinking about that."

Kai pulls out a bag of potato chips. Breakfast can wait. He needs a snack, and the chips will work. Who cares if it's seven in the morning? He's eaten far worse at this hour.

"We need to show people what's going on behind enemy lines."

Babs frowns. "Yeah, that'll make you popular with the thousand or so armed men who took over this neighborhood. When I came through the barricade, the guy after me made the mistake of taking a video with his phone."

"What happened?"

"Let's just say he doesn't have a phone anymore. When he got upset and protested, he got thumped. These people aren't screwing around. Apparently, they have a set of new laws or something."

Kai presses his lips together. He is a veteran of dozens of protests, half that number in riots, and even the Seattle CHAZ. The one thing they all had in common was chaos. This is anything but. If they are drafting laws to govern the swath of neighborhoods they control in this part of Minneapolis, then there is an unprecedented level of organization at work. And planning.

"I haven't heard anything about that."

"Me neither," she says with a shrug. "Then again, I just immigrated here."

"I'm assuming the First Amendment isn't one of them."

"Safe bet. You're going to need this. I swiped an extra one when I went through customs."

"Customs?" Kai asks, cocking his head.

"They have quite the operation set up. You need to have either an ID that has an address on it that proves you live here or one of these on your person at all times. If you're going to walk around, you'll stick out like a sore thumb without one."

"Well, we don't want that," he says, tossing the laminated badge on the table. "It will be easier and safer to move around at night. Let's lie low here until sundown. We can make breakfast and watch the news while we come up with a plan."

"Ohh! I love playing house!"

Babs goes to work on making breakfast. She brought eggs, sausage, and bread for toast. The woman thinks of everything.

He makes his way to the living room and turns on the television. News of the ADOZ is dominating the cable networks, as one would expect. There will be a long lineup of experts weighing in today, and none of them will have anything important to say. The only two groups that matter are the leaders of this armed rebellion and the police squaring off with them opposite the barricades. It's a high-stakes game of chicken, and the side that flinches first loses.

CHAPTER TWENTY-TWO

LANDON TAYSON

The small two-story red brick building isn't much to look at. Landon climbs out of the SUV and frowns. He was hoping for a building that was a little more impressive. The building isn't wide, but the ADOZ leader knows why Muzzie chose it. He looks at the world and judges it in terms of functionality. The structure runs the length of a fenced-in parking area, complete with a security gate. That could come in handy.

"Who owned this place?" Landon asks, getting a grin from Raven in return.

"The Police Officers Federation of Minneapolis. It's the labor union representing police officers up to the rank of captain employed in the city."

Now, it's Landon's turn to grin. Functional, with a side order of symbolism. He likes it, even if it's not the most attractive building to house his new government.

"This will do nicely."

They walk through the door and into a small foyer area with a receptionist desk. He has some people who can staff this, but it's far more building than he currently needs. Most of his group are performing their functions, ranging from security to food preparation to citizen in-processing. That piece can likely move here, using the rooms on the first floor. That leaves the entire second floor for him and his closest advisors.

"Take an office upstairs, Muzzie," Landon orders. "I'm sure there's plenty to choose from."

"No need," he says, readjusting his grip on the rifle slung across his chest. "I don't plan on being here much."

"What if I need you?"

The captain unclips a walkie-talkie from his tactical vest and wags it. "You know how to find me."

It dawns on Landon that, for as many preparations as he made to be ready for this day, there's a lot that slipped through the cracks. Who would be with him versus out in the field is one of those things.

"You're ADOZ leadership. We call you captain, but you're really the commanding general. I need you here."

Muzzie shakes his head. "I'm leadership, not staff. I need to be with my troops. You're the administrator. Administrate. We can post a liaison here for communications and coordination. I need to be out on that perimeter to prepare our guys for the inevitable. The police may be racked with indecisiveness and inaction now, but someone will grow a backbone sooner or later."

Landon is about to protest when Raven places her hand on his arm. "He's right."

The ADOZ leader nods. "Fair enough."

"Speaking of administrating," Raven says. "It's day two."

"I know. I half expected the police to challenge you at least once by now, Muzzie."

The captain strokes his AR-15, kitted out with a red-dot aimpoint. "Only if they have a death wish."

"The media might have something to do with that inaction," Bryce adds. "They're keeping the cops and politicians on their toes. Did you see the press conference at the capitol yesterday?"

"You mean the dog and pony show where they said little and meant none of it?" Landon asks. "Wouldn't have missed it. Let's make the most of it. What's the status of the perimeter?"

"Secure enough. We are continuing to reinforce the barricades in case SWAT tries to barrel through one of them. I have some teams patrolling the interior of the district now. So far, there haven't been any issues. Other groups are readying the areas for meetings, food distribution, and such. We are also looking for generators in case authorities decide to cut the power."

"They won't, but it's a prudent move. You've done a great job. Both of you."

"If you boys are done thumping your chests like cavemen, we have work to do," Raven decrees.

"I didn't mean to leave you out of that. You're indispensable, my love."

"Yeah, yeah, yeah...."

She riffles through her satchel and hands them each a sheet of paper. Landon scans the top and isn't quite registering what he's reading.

"What's this?"

"The first laws of our new ADOZ."

"Laws?" Muzzie asks.

"Yeah, those pesky things that define an organized society. Our fighters know the rules, but you have a few thousand terrified people huddling in their houses. That's bound to change, and soon. When they emerge, they need to understand a few things about where they're living now."

"All right. Let me look this over and then start spreading these around."

"I've already started distributing them." Landon joins his captain and public affairs representative in staring at her. "What? I'm not here for my looks."

Landon cocks his head at her, eliciting a heavy sigh.

"I knew you would be okay with everything written on that page, so don't look at me like that."

He quickly scans the page. She's right. There's nothing objectionable. If anything, Landon knows that he should have done this already.

"Anything else?"

"Yeah, you're a founding father, Landon. Act like one. You can start by giving this place a name?"

His brow crinkles. "I thought I did."

"Yeah, 'Arts District Autonomous Zone' is a bit of a mouthful for a country. Keep it simple – like Italy or Greece. Short and sweet."

"How about Muzzieland?"

Landon's mouth curls in amusement as he shakes his head. "We want people to take us seriously, Captain."

"Oh, shots fired."

"We're going to refer to this place as the ADOZ for now. We can think of a better name later, assuming that doesn't stick."

After all the planning, he never considered giving their occupied area a formal name. He was too worried about all the things that could go wrong and never dreamed that everything could go right. Fortunately, Raven is on it. He doesn't know what he would do without her.

CHAPTER TWENTY-THREE
EMMIT "CHICAGO" HASKINS

THE FIFTH STREET HOUSE
MINNEAPOLIS ARTS DISTRICT OCCUPIED ZONE

Military men have some of the best senses of humor. Much of it is inappropriate gallows humor, but laughing is what helps soldiers cope with stressful situations. Then there are the stories. Soldiers, and especially veterans, have some of the best. Gathered in the back yard with beers in their hands, they are reliving the glory days.

Everyone is laughing at the safety brief stories except Kenyala. She doesn't understand why these three find any of this funny. Not that Emmit expected her to. Most civilians don't understand the military mindset, and vice versa.

"I have no idea what you guys are talking about," Kenyala confesses.

"Have you ever heard of the Darwin Awards?"

Her eyes shift upward for a moment before returning to Nashville. "I'm assuming it's not like the Emmys or Oscars."

"Kinda," Emmit confirms. "Darwin Awards are given to individuals who improve the human gene pool by accidentally removing themselves from it in a spectacular manner."

"Our safety briefs were the result of somebody doing something stupid somewhere," Nashville adds. "Every Friday at final formation, one of our senior leaders would stand in front of the company and dole out sage advice on why Rangers shouldn't 'drink and insert poor life choice here.'"

"It was a list of what *not* to do if we want to remain happy, healthy, and out of trouble. One of my favorites was when we were ordered not to burn off frays. They're threads sticking out from our uniforms. Apparently, a Ranger in another company suffered second- and third-degree burns because he mistakenly lit his uniform on fire trying to remove them with a Zippo."

"I remember that one," Nashville confirms as Hollywood nods.

"I'm beginning to think my brother served with a bunch of idiots," Kenyala decrees, standing and placing her hand on Hollywood's shoulder. "Can I get you anything from the kitchen?"

A smile creases his lips. "Mrs. Robinson, you're trying to seduce me. Aren't you?"

She smacks the top of his head. "Like I said…idiots."

Emmit watches her disappear inside. He couldn't be prouder of the woman she's become. Strength and confidence are things to be respected. He loves that Kenyala has both in spades.

"You know, I'd like to say my sister is wrong, but…who was the guy who got shocked riding the buffer?"

"PFC Duffy," Nashville says, cracking up. "He was doing pretty well riding that bull until he ran over the electrical cord."

"That briefing was hysterical. How did Top keep a straight face when he decreed that we were forbidden from riding floor buffers?"

The first sergeant in the U.S. Army is a company's senior noncommissioned officer. The man occupying that role, at least in the infantry and Rangers, is often referred to as the "top sergeant" or "top." Not all of them like the moniker, with some retorting that they don't spin on their heads. Despite the best efforts to eliminate the term, it was still widely used in his Ranger company.

"Hey, Emmit," Kenyala says with a concerned tone from the back door as she cocks a thumb over her shoulder. "Some guys are at the front door."

"I'll be right back," Emmit says to his buddies, quietly leaving the back yard and moving along the side of the house.

The five men at the door exhibit no situational awareness. Two of them are on the stoop, with the other three at the bottom of the stairs. If he were armed, he could drop all of them in less than two seconds. It would be faster if he had a grenade. That's why professional soldiers don't bunch up. War is hard enough. Never make it easier for your enemy.

The man next to the head honcho keeps banging on the door before turning to his boss.

"Screw it."

The leader of the group starts to yank the American flag out of the bracket that's screwed into the side of the house on the left side of the front stoop. The short flagpole is held in place only with a single thumbscrew, so he shouldn't be having this much difficulty. It's like watching a toddler try to open a sealed cookie container.

"You really don't want to do that," Emmit warns, causing all five men to jump and turn to face him.

"Are you the owner of this residence?"

Emmit takes measure of the men. The oldest is a few years younger than him. They are dressed in tactical clothing, likely bought on Amazon. All of them are armed with handguns, most in hip holsters typically used when a pistol is a secondary weapon to a rifle. They don't look or act like soldiers, meaning they are untrained clowns posing as warfighters.

"Who are you?"

"I'm Lieutenant Artie Stein, ADOZ Security Forces."

"How official," Emmit muses. "What can I do for you, Artie?"

The kid thrusts his chin out. "Per order of the president, this flag must be removed."

"President…of the United States?"

Emmit isn't an idiot. He knows full well that the kid wasn't referring to the commander-in-chief. He just wants to hear him say the words.

"Of the ADOZ. You don't live in the United States anymore."

"Is that so?"

"Yeah, that's so. Take it down, or we will."

Emmit has never responded well to threats. He dealt with them in basic, AIT, and Ranger School. The men issuing them were far more experienced and competent than any of these five posers could be in a dozen lifetimes. As much as he would like to teach them an important life lesson about what happens when you don't know who you're screwing with, it isn't worth burning the calories.

"Tell me, *Artie*, is there a hospital in your ADOZ?"

"We have a medical clinic. Why?"

"Touch that flag, and you'll be spending some quality time in it."

The lieutenant rotates his body so Emmit can see the gun in his hip holster. "I don't think you're in a position to make threats."

Nashville racks a round into the Benelli. The intimidating clacking sound gets everyone's attention. Emmit didn't know he was standing in the doorway, but he probably should have. Back in the day, he knew what each of his guys would do when bullets started flying.

None of the five men move. They are frozen in place like statues. One of them looks like he's about to piss himself.

"What we've got here is…a failure to communicate," Hollywood says in his best Southern accent as he comes up beside his old squad leader. "Some men you just can't reach."

Emmit smirks. That was actually a decent impression of the captain in *Cool Hand Luke*. Artie doesn't seem to be impressed…or amused.

"You don't know who you're dealing with."

"We can say the same thing, buddy," Nashville announces.

"Last chance. Remove the flag."

Emmit crosses his arms. "Or else? You want it down so bad, go ahead. Make your move, and let's see what happens."

Hollywood leans over to Emmit. "I see dead people."

The lieutenant eyes the three men before signaling his guys to return to the van. "This isn't over."

"No, I figure that it probably isn't. You do your thing, butter bar. My advice is that you leave us alone to do ours."

Artie strides back to the white panel van and climbs into the passenger seat. The driver fires up the vehicle. The lieutenant extends his arm out the window, forming his index finger and thumb into the shape of a gun. Then, he drops the hammer a second before the van drives off. The message is received loud and clear.

"You know, Chicago, they'll be back," Nashville concludes, stepping out onto the stoop.

"No doubt."

"Keep your friends close and your enemies closer," Hollywood says in a passable Sicilian accent.

"I'd prefer if they stay away altogether, buddy," Nashville says. "We're going to need more than a shotgun if things get ugly."

Emmit can't do anything but agree with that statement. The question is, what to do about it?

CHAPTER TWENTY-FOUR

CHIEF VANESSA CAMPBELL

SOUTH OF THE BROADWAY ST. BARRICADE
MINNEAPOLIS, MINNESOTA

The life of a police chief isn't what Vanessa thought it would be. For her entire career, she dreamed about being the top dog. Every decision, incident, and crisis she experienced during her climb up the ladder came with a mental note of what she would do the same and differently when it was her turn to call the shots.

Only once she was appointed to run a department did she realize how little she actually controlled. Precinct inspectors have a lot of sway in this city. The mayor holds most of the good cards. The people have their say, some of it constructive and some of it destructive. The bureaucracy is stifling.

All of those competing interests have left her with an uneasy truth about the job – she has all the responsibility of policing in Minneapolis and very little authority to ensure it's done effectively.

On top of that, there is dealing with personality conflicts. The mayor despises her, but that's because of conflicting ideologies. She understands that much. The 2nd Precinct's inspector is another issue entirely. She's ambitious to the point of being cutthroat, and she's a kiss-ass on top of it. There is little doubt that Wilma Sillyere is gunning for her job and will probably get it when the mayor blames her for…well, everything when this is over.

"What's the status?" Vanessa asks her as she comes up from behind the police cars opposite one of the Broadway Street barricades.

"Same as an hour ago. Other than some mean glares and the occasional taunt, the sentries show no signs of aggression."

Unless you count taking over dozens of square blocks of a major Northern Midwestern city and all but holding its residents hostage. Sentries. She makes it sound like they are guarding the Tomb of the Unknown Soldier in Arlington. Wilma Sillyere is at least somewhat sympathetic toward the insurrectionists. Vanessa wonders whether she would have joined them had she not been a member of law enforcement.

"You need to talk to Burke. He wants to go in and isn't keen on taking no for an answer."

"What did you tell him?"

"That decision is above his pay grade…and mine."

"That's all?" Vanessa knows there was much more to the conversation than that. The commander of the SWAT team and the 2nd Precinct inspector hate each other with a burning passion.

"I may have mentioned that violent action against the protesters by a militarized police force only proves their point."

As much as the chief would love to argue with that, she isn't wrong. Of course, there is also a cost of doing nothing, which Sillyere isn't considering. She'd be willing to surrender the whole district to them if it meant currying favor with the mayor to advance her career. Who gives a damn about the people living in the Arts District?

"Where is he?"

"He walked back south, whining to every officer he could find."

Vanessa sets off after him without any parting words for Wilma. She has things under control here, and the chief is going to lose it if she has to deal with her inspector for a moment longer.

Unfortunately, the leader of the SWAT team is doing what Wilma said he was. He is pleading his case to a young officer who barely looks like he's out of high school, much less the academy.

"Lieutenant Burke? A word?"

The SWAT leader slaps the relieved kid on the shoulder before walking over. "So long as that word is that we're going in and that I should prep the men."

"Aren't you the eager beaver?"

Those words to a civilian would make him sound like a war-mongering adrenaline junkie traveling down a reckless path of violence just to scratch an itch on his trigger finger. The truth is far more complicated. Burke is one of the most measured tacticians she knows. He never unnecessarily risks his men's lives and always looks for ways to de-escalate before resorting to violence.

"Not really," Burke moans. "I wouldn't have let these jackasses set up their barricades in the first place. If Sillyere were even half-observant and at all competent, she would have flooded her entire precinct into this area before they could close it off."

He's also not entirely wrong. The inspector had limited manpower at her disposal because of the protest downtown, but there were enough officers up this way to disrupt the takeover attempt. It's water under the bridge, as they say.

"Well, she didn't. So, here we are."

"Yeah, here we are. Chief, we need to go in, and I mean *now*."

Vanessa shakes her head. "Not gonna happen."

"Every minute we sit on our asses, they use that time to fortify their barricades. And I don't mean just with old sofas and car tires. They're blocking some streets with dump trucks now. They're already well-armed and have decent manpower that's bound to swell when all the crazies driving here to join them arrive. How long are you planning to wait?"

"It's not up to me."

"It is up to you! You're the damn chief of police!"

Responsibility without authority. It's a curse that nobody understands until they walk in these shoes.

"And I serve at the pleasure of the mayor. I've been arguing to end this from the beginning. Thurlow has explicitly forbidden any direct action against the protesters."

"Protesters?" Burke asks, throwing his arms in the air. "Protesters are people carrying signs and shouting catchy slogans that rhyme. These people are insurgents who dare to think they can set up their own country!"

"And I agree, but the solution isn't an assault that will result in a body bag shortage. We need to negotiate a way out of this. Period."

"Only, they don't care to negotiate. So, what's the plan? Let them carve out a piece of this city to call their own and hope they get bored with it at some point? Do you have any idea what that will do? It will embolden groups like this across the country. Civil wars start that way."

"Burke, every avenue will be explored before violence. Those are the mayor's orders. Get some rest. Understood?"

"So, the mayor is willing to let this drag on? You know he won't ask for the National Guard. He and the governor hate each other. That means my guys will be forced to go in after they have doubled their numbers and firepower, and this will turn into Fallujah 2003. Great plan."

"It won't come to that," Vanessa assures him, not at all believing her own words. Unfortunately, Burke doesn't either.

"Right. Chief, when this is over, I want to be able to go home to my family. I don't want my wife and two boys dressed in black at my funeral because we waited too long. If I don't make it home, my death is on you as much as it is on Thurlow."

Vanessa balls her fists as she fights the surge of anger. Responsibility without authority. That dynamic is not going to work. Something is going to need to change, and soon. If the mayor doesn't listen to reason, there is only one avenue of recourse left, as unattractive as it is.

CHAPTER TWENTY-FIVE
FIELD OFFICER DAVID BRASS

SMITHSONIAN NATIONAL ZOO
WASHINGTON, D.C.

There are a lot of other things Brass could be doing on a Thursday afternoon. Lord knows there are a lot of things he should be doing. Unfortunately, part of his job is keeping people in line. It's not what he wants to spend his time doing, but it's part of the job. Or, at least, the job as he likes to do it.

The Smithsonian's National Zoo is one of the oldest in the United States. Admission is free, making it a popular destination for locals and tourists eager to see the giant pandas on loan from China. They also have various trails featuring animals from nearly every continent. The only animal Brass wants to see happens to be human.

He took the metro to Woodley Park-Zoo /Adams Morgan station and walked to the zoo in Rock Creek Park. It's not huge, but it isn't small, either. Fortunately, the man he's looking for sticks out like a sore thumb. He spots him on the Elephant Trail and nods when he finds a spot ten feet away, pretending to have any interest in the gigantic pachyderms.

"Honey? Why don't you take the kids to see the pandas? I'll join you in a few minutes."

"Yay! Pandas!" his daughter says, grabbing her brother's hand as they run back down the trail.

"Don't be too long," she says, eyeing David before hustling after her energetic offspring.

Christopher Byrnes may work for the CIA, but he's the last person anyone would expect to work for such a morally ambiguous group. He's a devout Christian, a dedicated family man, and an overall good guy. How a thirty-something spook found himself involved in one of the Agency's most questionable and sensitive operations is anyone's guess. Fortunately, everyone would instantly think that he's too pure a soul to do what he did.

"Your wife isn't wondering who I am?"

"We've been married for a while now. Bree knows not to ask too many questions. What are you doing here, David?"

"I had a burning desire to see the chimpanzees."

Byrnes looks around and cocks a thumb. "You're in the wrong part of the zoo. They're back over there. Are you wondering whether they were the smart ones for not evolving with us humans?"

Brass laughs at the fair question. "I didn't expect to find you here."

"Yeah, well, I was told to run a low profile and not be home. It's hard to subpoena someone when they aren't there."

"So I've learned. The director is being cautious."

"Or paranoid," Chris corrects. "Unless, of course, he isn't."

Alistair Lancaster is not the most popular director the Agency has ever had. He's despised by politicians, loathed by bureaucrats in Langley, and not trusted by the rank and file. He is viewed as being protective of his position at the expense of nearly everything else, including the CIA's mission.

"Congress can hold all the hearings they want. Nothing will come of them if that's what you're worried about."

"You sound like you know that's a certainty. Remind me to borrow your crystal ball for the next lottery drawing."

"I'd tell you to trust me, but I know you won't."

"You've been in the CIA for more than thirty seconds. You never should have told me to leak the details about Railspike, and I never should have let you talk me into it."

Brass knows a thing or two about human nature. Chris Byrnes wouldn't have agreed to anything he didn't want to. Especially something that dangerous. Leaking details about a highly classified CIA operation is treason, and the penalty for treason is death. He wanted to be talked into it, and Brass was happy to oblige.

"Railspike's a dead-end program."

Chris scoffs. "Says you."

"Yes, says me. I think you believe that, too. Otherwise, you wouldn't have leaked the details about it. We both know there are more efficient ways to gather the intelligence that Railspike was collecting. It's a shame that leadership is too short-sighted to realize that."

"More efficient ways," Chris says, kicking a clump of dirt. "I think we may not agree on what those ways are. You going to share yours?"

"It's better that you don't know mine."

"Yeah, I get it. I should simply trust you…with my future, my family's welfare, and even my life. Right."

"Nothing is going to happen to you or your family. Railspike won't last another five minutes in the news cycle with all the BS happening in Minnesota."

At least, that's the plan. So far, it's working like a charm. The longer this drags on, the more optimistic David is that Railspike will become nothing more than a faint memory. The American public will be too caught up in a takeover of part of Minneapolis, and the news coverage will reflect that. There won't be oxygen for any other story, no matter how underhanded and nefarious.

"What do you know about that business?"

Brass shrugs. "Not much, other than I've heard they're very organized. It sounds more planned than officials are admitting."

Chris nods slowly. "I thought the same thing."

"Their ADOZ, or whatever the hell it's called, won't last. The only thing left to be determined is how many casualties there will be before order is restored."

"It sounds like you're rooting for that."

"Nah, I don't want people to die, but there is a benefit to the media looking at the North Star State and not filing articles or foaming at the mouth over what they think they know about Railspike."

"Then why have me leak it at all?"

It's a question best left unanswered. "A means to an end."

"All right. I'm wasting my time here, and my family is waiting for me. I've done my part. You had better come through on yours."

"If I had any reason not to, I'd be ducking you, not interrupting family time at the National Zoo."

Chris shakes his head and starts to walk away before stopping. "I heard FBI Counterintelligence is looking for the leaker."

"They won't trace it back to you. I have it handled." Brass almost says, "Trust me," and forces the words back down his throat.

"See that you do."

If that was a threat, it's a hollow one. Byrnes has just as much or even more to lose than David does. Brass has plausible deniability. The same can't be said for the man he convinced to leak information about an illegal CIA operation to start putting some wheels in motion.

It's not like Byrnes's asking price was high, considering the potential benefits to the outcome. He craves stability and job security – two things that Brass happens to be in a position to offer. If he can pull this off, the road leads to the proverbial pot of gold at the end of the rainbow. Until then, he's going to be spending his days juggling anvils.

CHAPTER TWENTY-SIX

EMMIT "CHICAGO" HASKINS

THE FIFTH STREET HOUSE
MINNEAPOLIS ARTS DISTRICT OCCUPIED ZONE

Now he gets it. For years, Emmit could never understand why the German people were so indifferent to the atrocities their soldiers were committing. War is hell, but exterminating millions of people for their religious beliefs is a different kind of disgusting.

He was doing the same thing by turning a blind eye to this takeover. Granted, the leaders of this "ADOZ" aren't putting people in gas chambers, but Emmit was content to let them go about their business. The whole thing is a farce, and that's how he was treating it. The run-in with Lieutenant Moonbeam and his misfit toys has changed his perspective. A fight is coming, and it's coming fast.

And therein lies the problem. They're walking into a war without any effective guns or bullets. That's a tough way to fight. And while the three men are capable of relieving some of these "soldiers" of their arms, it will draw unnecessary attention. The separatists have the numbers.

Nashville and Hollywood agree, but they are advocating for a more aggressive approach, as true Rangers would. Under any other circumstances, Emmit would be right there with them. Unfortunately, this is his sister's house, and her life is in just as much danger. They may not be able to put the genie back in the bottle, but they can de-escalate things. Maybe.

"All five of those guys were armed, fellas," Emmit says. "Every news report says the men manning the barricades are heavily armed. There ain't shit we're gonna do with a shotgun and a single box of shells."

"Why don't you all get dressed up, put a knife between your teeth, and hide in the bushes to wait for them to return."

"Whatever possessed God in Heaven to make a man like Rambo?" Hollywood mumbles. He thinks it's a viable suggestion.

"I have a better idea," Nashville says. "What do we need? Besides a miracle."

Hollywood smiles. "Guns. Lots of guns."

Chicago smiles at *The Matrix* reference. Nashville walked right into that one. He even set it up perfectly. As annoying as Hollywood can sometimes be, he actually has kinda missed his constant barrage of timely quips.

"Before I make a call or two, there's one more thing we need to discuss."

Emmit and Hollywood follow his eyes to Kenyala.

"What?"

"He's right, sis. You shouldn't be here."

Kenyala recoils slightly. "I shouldn't…you aren't saying what I think you're saying, are you?"

"It's not safe here."

"Emmit, I don't know who you think you are, but this is my *home*. My home! The one that my late husband and I bought with *our* own money," she says, tearing up.

"I understand."

"Do you? Because you were willing to defend a Syrian village with your life once, and that wasn't your home. Are you really asking me to abandon mine?"

Emmit stares hard at his hand before looking up. "Yes."

"Wow! You have some nerve!"

"Kenyala, this isn't a game," he says, standing and pointing at the door. "Those lunatics are dangerous, and they mean business."

"Then, let them have the stupid flag! Who cares?"

"Who has the nerve now?" Emmit fires back.

She shows him the hand. It's the universal symbol for "stop talking to me," but it has a special significance in the Haskins family. The last time his sister did that, he almost broke her wrist and was grounded for months. Chicago is still bitter about that. Fortunately, the gesture isn't a thing in the military. He can imagine how his platoon sergeant would have reacted to that.

"You guys…you're just three macho assholes looking for a fight."

"They call me *Mister* Tibbs!"

"Now's not the time, Hollywood," Emmit scolds before turning to glare at his sister.

"I get why you don't want to leave, Kenyala," Nashville says, his Tennessee accent almost soothing in the otherwise tense atmosphere. "I wouldn't want to leave, either. But you have to understand that some things are worth fighting for. You're right to say a flag isn't…but what it represents is. A lot of people in this country don't believe that anymore. We do."

"What does that have to do with me leaving?"

Nashville wrings his hands. "Chicago is one of the best leaders I ever served under. He always took care of his men, and right now, that's us. He can't do that if he's terrified about what could happen to his little sister."

"What could happen?" she challenges.

"We don't want to find out. The three of us saw some horrific shit in Syria – stuff that your brother has never told you and never will. There are no limits to human depravity, especially when it comes to women. If something were to happen to us…."

Emmit wants to say something but doesn't. The truth is, he hasn't told his sister much about his experiences in Syria. He convinced himself that she didn't need to know. What he witnessed…it was traumatic in ways only soldiers who experienced it would understand. It's also why civilians wonder why the veteran suicide rate is so high. They can never comprehend what was seen, and once it was, it can never be unseen.

On some level, Kenyala does understand. She gets a thousand-yard stare of her own before snapping out of it.

"Will they even let me through the barricade?"

"They will, or I will sneak you out," Nashville assures her. "Nothing will happen to you."

"Where do you want me to go?"

"A hotel outside of the city," Emmit advises. "Anywhere safe."

"I don't have the money for that."

Hollywood reaches into his back pocket and pulls out his wallet. He hands Kenyala his credit card with the nonchalance that Richard Gere had while handing Julia Roberts his card in *Pretty Woman*. Only Hollywood isn't a billionaire.

"Since when do you have money?"

Hollywood shrugs. "Greed, for lack of a better word, is good."

"Are you kidding? He has more money than all of us combined," Nashville asserts.

"I can't take your money," Kenyala says, trying to hand the card back. "You earned it, and I barely know you."

Nashville shakes his head. "That defense won't work. Chicago isn't just an Army buddy…he's our brother, and that makes us family. You're his sister, so that makes you family. And family takes care of each other. We'll leave you two to talk."

The two men make their way through the house and retreat into the back yard.

"Did I just hear a white boy from Tennessee call you 'family?'"

"Yeah. The blood of the covenant is thicker than the water of the womb. Those guys are more my brothers than if we had a sibling. When you're getting shot at, the skin color of the man next to you don't mean shit."

"More your family than your own sister?"

"Because you're my sister and because I love you is why I'm asking."

Kenyala closes her eyes before opening them and looking around the living room. "Okay. I'll pack a bag. Just promise me you'll take care of the place. Besides you, it's all I have. I want both in one piece when I return."

CHAPTER TWENTY-SEVEN

LANDON TAYSON

UNIVERSITY AVENUE COMMAND CENTER
MINNEAPOLIS ARTS DISTRICT OCCUPIED ZONE

The large office on the second floor was the obvious pick for the ADOZ president. He should have had a flag designed and made to put in the stand next to his desk. It would have completed the picture. This is starting to feel like a leader's office.

Landon knows he needs to rest. There hasn't been much time to sleep since he put the wheels in motion for this takeover. Unfortunately, there's no rest for the weary. His eyes are tired, and stress has given him a wicked headache, but Landon is too amped up to force himself to sleep.

Raven gives a couple of quick knocks on the door before breezing in. The woman is a bundle of energy, even at this ridiculous hour. She isn't exuding cheerleader energy – she's way too nonconformist for that. Instead, it's a quiet confidence that comes from sheer determination. The yearning for success is fueling her more than the coffee she no doubt has made downstairs.

"Give me some good news, Raven."

"Okay," she says, staring at one of the framed pictures on the wall. "The police haven't challenged any of the barricades."

"That's something," Landon says, moving around his desk and collapsing into a swivel chair. "It's the end of day three. Are they trying to wear us down?"

She shrugs. "It's not a bad approach. You're worn down."

"It's almost two in the morning."

"And you're a night owl. Everyone manning the barricades is on an adrenaline high that's bound to wear off sooner or later. Maybe the police think they'll get bored and abandon their posts. You have to admit that we're going to suffer from attrition at some point."

"That's why we need our reinforcements to get here. They'll be here in another day or so. Until then, we have one of our people on most of them."

During the day, the command center is a cacophony. People come and go, and a dozen conversations are happening at once. Things die down at night. The people are fewer, and the conversations are quieter. That's why Landon's ears perk up when he hears someone's raised voice on the other end of the long corridor. Whoever is on the receiving end of this dressing down isn't having a good day.

"What's going on?"

"I don't know," Raven says with a quick shrug. "It sounds like Muzzie is pissed at somebody about something. Do you want me to find out what's going on?"

"No, I need to get coffee anyway. Unless you want to get it for me."

If a picture tells a thousand words, a good withering glare writes a novel. "Keep dreaming."

The corner of Landon's mouth curls as he steps out of his office and quietly skulks down the long hallway that runs almost the full length of the building. Raven is behind him, moving equally stealthily. They both stop before the door and listen.

"You need to learn to report incidents like this," the captain says from the office. "If you can't handle it, escalate to me. That's why I'm here. People who don't want to follow the rules need to be made an example of. Especially that rule. Understood?"

"Yes, sir."

Landon has heard enough and pivots around the door jamb. Three men are in the office. He knows the captain and one of the others, but the third guy who looks like he's the one receiving this tongue-lashing isn't someone he recognizes.

"What's the problem, Muzzie?"

"Nothing we can't handle, Mr. President," he says, standing at attention.

The two men with him follow suit. Landon may never get used to hearing that, but he does like it. He can almost hear Raven rolling her eyes behind him.

"I'm sure you can. Now, tell me, what's the problem?"

"Go ahead. Tell him," Muzzie orders, gesturing one of his underlings to speak.

The young officer explains how they spotted the flag while on patrol and what happened when they demanded the homeowner take it down. The man in the front door with a shotgun was an interesting revelation. He knew at least some of the residents here would be armed and likely not to abide by the laws Raven drafted. In addition to a ban on flying or displaying an American flag, all firearms were to be turned in to security forces.

"Where is this place?"

"It's over on Fifth Street...Mr. Pres...Mr. President."

"All right. Let's go."

"To where?"

Landon smiles. "To take care of business."

The small crew files out of the command center and piles into an SUV they "reappropriated" from one of the area's residents. Muzzie drives as the lieutenant directs them to the house. It's not that far away, not that the Arts District is *that* big to begin with.

The captain slams the SUV into park but doesn't kill the engine. He opens the door and studies the houses on the street. They are all dark, including the one with Old Glory affixed to the left side of the front door.

"Well...that's tough to miss, isn't it?" Landon asks as he climbs out of the vehicle.

He sticks his hands in his pockets, watching the house intently. There is no obvious sign of movement. They could be lying in wait, but the bushes in front aren't that big. Part of him is almost disappointed. He's itching for a confrontation to spice things up.

"FYI, they have a shotgun."

"Yeah, and we have an arsenal," Muzzie counters.

That doesn't seem to console the lieutenant. "These guys…they may be military. Or they were."

"Do you think I care?" Landon asks.

Raven slides up next to him before checking over her shoulder. He may want some action, but she prefers things quiet.

"You don't need to be involved in this," she says, keeping her voice low. "Muzzie can take care of the flag. You have other pressing things to worry about."

"Not at two in the morning, I don't."

Landon walks across the street and climbs the three stairs on the stoop. He stops and listens for the sound of any footsteps. Nothing. He reaches for the flag.

"Careful," the lieutenant calls out. "These assholes could have electrified it."

Landon looks back and smirks. He won't give anyone the satisfaction of checking for wires hooked up to a car battery. He twists the screw out of the bracket, slaps his hand around the pole, and pulls the stars and stripes affixed to it out.

He walks back to the SUV, twirling the banner like a flag bearer at the head of a parade. It amazes Landon that so many people still believe this piece of cloth stands for anything important. The dream of America died long ago. He stops and pulls out his lighter, rolling the wheel against his jeans to spark the flint.

"What are you doing?" his girlfriend asks.

"Making a point."

"That's right. Burn that thing!" Muzzie urges.

"Just take the flag, Landon," Raven pleads. "Take it back with us. You don't need to burn it to enforce our laws."

He holds the lighter near the edge and grins. "Yeah, I really do."

Fire races up the cheap fabric. The group watches with satisfaction as it burns, and their leader only drops the pole it's attached to when the flame gets too hot. The show lasts only another thirty seconds until nothing is left but ash and scorched material.

"Muzzie, have your roving patrols keep an eye on this place. If they replace this flag, let me know."

"Mr. President, who would have multiple American flags in their house?" the lieutenant asks.

He turns and scowls. "Patriots."

CHAPTER TWENTY-EIGHT

KAI Z

Life comes down to a series of moments. Those moments often come down to being in the right place at the right time. It's how Justin Bieber got discovered. It was the stars aligning and a fair share of luck.

Kai doesn't know what he did in a previous life to deserve to stumble on this by happenstance, but it must have been good. The odds of seeing anyone other than a roving patrol in this ADOZ were slim. For the last four hours, he thought he was wasting his time. Then he turned and walked south on Fifth Street, and Lady Luck smiled at him.

Kai stares at the LED screen as the Stars and Stripes go up in flames. He can see the man holding it, and it looks like the guy from the press conference. The light from the fire illuminates the street, but Kai's far enough away that it doesn't dent the inky darkness. He just needs to stay silent…and not move a muscle.

The fire burns out, and the five people attending this flag-burning party climb into their vehicle and leave. It disappears around the corner, and Kai waits a couple of minutes to ensure they don't return. Satisfied, he steps out from the side of the house a few doors down.

The street is quiet again, but Kai still takes measures to quietly walk over to the pole and the charred remains of Old Glory attached to it. He presses record on his camera and gets some up-close video. He walks around, getting footage from every angle. Once he has what he needs, he hits stop and looks at the destroyed flag.

A light comes on in a house a couple of doors down. It's time to go. He slinks away, getting out of the street and making ready to duck into cover if needed. He makes a left at the cross street and checks the map on his phone to confirm that he's going in the right direction. When he notices the time, he curses under his breath.

Kai keys his walkie-talkie three times. This thing has more than enough range to reach their home base from anywhere in the ADOZ. He checks the volume and turns it down. It's a good thing she waited for him to make contact. Had she radioed while he was that close to the lost boys, he would be having a very uncomfortable conversation with them right now…assuming they were in the mood to talk instead of settling for kicking his ass.

"Hey, Babs," Kai whispers, checking up and down the road to ensure nobody is coming.

"It's about time you called! You're late for your check-in!"

"Sorry, I was too close to the baddies to talk."

Kai closes his eyes. That was a mistake. He should have said he was busy rescuing a kitten out of a tree.

"Baddies? Kai...."

"I know...I know. You don't need to say it."

"Tough. I'm going to say it anyway," Babs says in an exasperated voice. "You promised to run a low profile tonight."

"I did!" Kai protests, knowing it's not going to do anything to defuse the lecture he'll get when he returns to home base.

"Oh, really? Getting close enough to smell their chewing gum isn't running a low profile. It's begging to get caught."

"I got some footage."

That pacifies her. Or it piques her curiosity enough to shift Kai's breaking a promise to the back burner for the moment. "Of what?"

"Going dark!"

Headlights announce the presence of a vehicle turning onto the street. Kai hightails it over and hides behind a short azalea bush. Thank God these guys aren't using searchlights. The bush won't do much to conceal him. Only his black clothes and the shadows are obscuring him from being seen.

The white panel van creeps by, and its engine noise fades in the distance. Kai stands and brushes himself off before tentatively continuing his trek north.

"I'm back. Sorry."

"Patrol?" she concludes.

"Yeah, there are a few of them roving around."

If there is anything good about the "no cars in the ADOZ" edict, it's that roving patrols are easy to spot. They drive with headlights on, and the journalist doesn't need to guess whether it's the bad guys or a young professional coming home late from happy hour with the girls.

"What did you get a video of? And this had better be good."

"Only five asshats burning an American flag. I think the one who torched it is the self-proclaimed leader of the ADOZ."

"What? Are you kidding me? That's gold!"

He's not going to argue. Someone will run with it, and the other news organizations will clamor to catch up, not wanting to miss out on their share of clicks, likes, and comments. It doesn't matter if they believe in the reasons behind this movement. Content is king. That's the beauty of capturing the burning on unaltered video. It will get replayed a million times, and nobody can claim with a straight face that it's fake.

"I'm heading back to the nest now. Fire up the laptop, Babs. We're about to put this online and shock the country."

CHAPTER TWENTY-NINE
FIELD OFFICER DAVID BRASS

OFFICES OF THE U.S. DEPARTMENT OF AGRICULTURE
MCLEAN, VIRGINIA

There is a time for anger, and there is a time to reach for the antacids you keep stashed in your desk drawer. Brass feels the former but does the latter. It's going to be one of those days.

McLean is home to America's premier intelligence agency, which is located in the Langley section of town. Why any other function of government would bother locating here is anyone's guess. It is close to the capital, so it makes sense on some level. Maybe Agriculture moved some operations here because Tysons Corner is home to the Farm Credit Administration. That's his best guess.

The U.S. Department of Agriculture is a real government entity, but Brass's job here is a front. It allows him to travel, and the proximity to Langley is convenient. He is a deep cover operative, and anyone who pokes around will learn that the surly apple export expert has worked here for a while.

One of the beautiful things about this job is that most of the bureaucrats in this building leave him alone. He doesn't have any direct reports or colleagues that he has to collaborate with. That means he can spend whole days in his office without being bothered. Today was not one of those days.

What's happening in Minneapolis is being discussed and debated over coffee at every cubicle in this place. For some reason, a couple of people here have made it their mission to ensure everyone has seen it. Thus, the knock on the door fifteen minutes ago.

All the news channels are running the video on a near loop as talking heads tell viewers what they should be thinking about it. The favorable coverage the protest has been receiving is morphing into something far less understanding.

The footage didn't come from a news camera. An anchor explains it was posted to YouTube by renowned independent journalist Kai Z. More like troublemaker Kai Z. If being a self-serving egotist were a sport, he'd be a gold medalist. His videos are meant to divide, shock, and exploit, and he's good at doing all three.

"Shit."

Brass closes his eyes and shakes his head. What the hell are they thinking? Life is complicated enough without going through it making unforced errors. Drinking and driving, taking too many drugs, and making stupid comments on social media are expressways to ruin. There are countless examples of each in this country. You can add burning an American flag to that list.

He pulls out his phone and selects contacts. Brass is old-school and despises SMS messages. Why kids today are so enamored with them is beyond him. Unfortunately, his contact isn't likely to pick up a call from him. He doubts he will even get a response to this text anytime soon.

> **Brass**
> *I thought you said that you have things there under control.*

> **Nightshade**
> *We do.*

The response comes quicker than he thought it would. He doesn't know what goes on in the ADOZ during the day. They must be more concerned about the police breaching the perimeter at night, so maybe daylight is downtime. Not that it matters. At least he'll get some answers.

> **Brass**
> *Watching the news. Doesn't look like it.*

> **Nightshade**
> *We're handling it.*

"My ass, you're handling it," he mumbles.

He shouldn't expect a high level of operational competency. His contact is young and inexperienced. Still, even a fool would know that what he's watching on television isn't going to help their cause.

> **Brass**
> *How did that punk Kai get through your perimeter?*

> **Nightshade**
> *Don't know. We're looking for him. Kai has a reputation for being slippery.*

> **Brass**
> *Find him quickly.*

> **Nightshade**
> *Anything else?*

He can almost feel the impatience and arrogance. That won't do as he puts his thumbs back to work. He has never and will never use the speech-to-text function on this thing.

Brass
Yeah. Remember who you work for.

Nightshade
As if you would let me forget.

"Insolent little bitch," Brass says, tossing the phone on his desk.

He turns his attention to the news before turning it off. He's seen enough. Politics is perception. Facts don't exist in this world – only truth matters. And the truth can be fluid. It takes on a different meaning for each individual once washed through the laundry of their adopted ideology and preconceived notion of the world.

Movements need to grow beyond their initial confines to survive. Actions and words attract supporters swayed by their plight, causing numbers to swell. Once a critical mass is reached, a movement can change the direction of a country and the trajectory of the world. Nothing halts that faster than burning an American flag.

People are sensitive to the act. Individuals who may have otherwise been interested in the message will tune it out. The far left won't care, but the middle and right of the ideological spectrum are going to throw a fit. The ADOZ is only quasi-supported by a third of the nation. Brass needs that to grow. These morons have all but assured that it won't.

The Minneapolis ADOZ has surpassed his wildest expectations. Nightshade has done a good job herding the sheep, but it may be time to bring in the big guns. With that thought, Brass picks up his office phone and places a call.

"Harvest Moon Orchard. Kurt speaking."

"It's David Brass. How's business?"

"David! It's good to hear from you. We've had our difficulties, but I think we're in store for a great harvest. We have a lot of apples on the trees ready to go."

Despite the high-tech gadgets and encrypted communication the Agency has at its disposal, much of its business is still conducted over unsecured telecommunications networks. It draws less attention. All the participants need to do is speak in code. In this case, his contact has plenty of manpower and is ready for his part of the operation if needed.

"That's good to hear. Listen, do you remember that export program we were talking about last week?"

"Of course. It sounded very exciting. We're looking forward to it getting off the ground."

"Things are moving pretty fast here. We may be moving it up, but there's a catch. This may not be a local deal. You'll need to meet the distributor in the Midwest."

The man sighs. "We were hoping to bring some revenue to the local economy."

Apples are an economic driver in Washington state. That's why Brass used the office line for this interaction. Considering his cover, it's perfectly in line with the business he's expected to conduct. Not that there is any government program available for apples. At least, not until the representatives in that state stash a line item in some pork-filled omnibus spending bill.

"I understand, but investments are needed elsewhere."

"When is the meeting with the distributor?"

Brass leans back in his chair. "Let me find out his schedule, and I'll get back to you."

"Sounds good, David. I'll be waiting for your call."

He sets the receiver back on the cradle and grins. Pendulum was meant to span several cities, but that's a logistical challenge. If the ADOZ can get their act together, this movement will expand naturally. You can always count on the sheep to bleat when they're being herded. All he needs is the right shepherd to ensure Railspike is never mentioned in media circles again. If Nightshade can't get it done, he has people who can.

CHAPTER THIRTY
EMMIT "CHICAGO" HASKINS

Most Americans are not morning people. Even if their jobs or family life compels them to be up before dawn, they don't necessarily like it. Emmit has never been one of those people. Even before joining the military, where you have to be assembled in the unit area at 0630 for morning physical training, he liked being up early. There's something peaceful about mornings that he's always enjoyed.

Unlike most people, his first action isn't pouring coffee or brushing his teeth. Emmit immediately drops to the floor and knocks out seventy-five push-ups. These aren't the civilian variety that would never get counted in an Army physical fitness test. His back is straight, his head is up, and he goes down until his arms are at a ninety-degree angle before fully extending them until his elbows lock.

Once those repetitions are complete, he does a hundred sit-ups, coming up to a ninety-degree angle before returning to the floor where the bottoms of his shoulder blades touch the hardwood. Once those are finished, his engine is running. It's time to get on with the day.

Emmit dispenses with his morning bathroom routine and heads downstairs for a cup of liquid energy. The aroma of fresh-brewed coffee is already wafting up the stairs, and that means his fellow Rangers beat him down here. They are huddled over Nashville's phone at the kitchen island before turning their attention to him. They don't say anything, but the look on their faces is enough to raise the alarm.

"What?"

"Houston, we have a problem."

Nashville scowls at Hollywood as he hands Emmit his phone. He has YouTube on the screen with a video paused.

"What is this?"

"Just press play."

He does as instructed and watches the video of the flag burning. He's seen footage like this before, but…it dawns on him where this was filmed. It also marks the revelation of whose flag just went up in flames. His face flushes, and his jaw tightens as he tosses the phone back to Nashville.

"It's good to meet you, Dr. Banner," Hollywood sings out as Emmit storms toward the front door. "And I'm a huge fan of the way you lose control and turn into an enormous green rage monster."

"Let's hope not," Nashville says, turning to follow him.

Emmit swings the front door open and steps onto the stoop. The bracket is still affixed to the house, but the flag and pole are no longer attached. The video wasn't a spoof or a sick joke. He sees the white pole in the street and walks over to it, taking a knee and picking up a piece of the charred material. He feels the surge of adrenaline, and his head begins beating like a bass drum.

The guys come out and stand a respectful distance away. Emmit looks up and down the street, searching for the likely spot where the video was taken from. His eyes fixate on the side of the house a couple of doors down. That looks about right.

"Who the hell is Kai Z?"

"You don't get out much, do you, Chicago? He's a journalist…sorta. His YouTube channel is huge. He made a name for himself back during the 2020 riots and reporting on Antifa protesters."

Emmit nods slowly. "He watched them burn this flag and did nothing."

"What did you expect him to do, call them names?"

He's right. Kai is a civilian, and Emmit shouldn't expect anything more. Emmit has always been a patriot…and a fighter. Even before he became an Army Ranger, he would have throttled anyone burning a flag in front of him. Then again, these guys were armed, and the YouTuber likely wasn't. He probably couldn't have done anything. Emmit knows he can.

"Oh, hell…I know that look in your eye, Chicago."

Hollywood puts his hand on his former sergeant's shoulder. "Forget it, Jake, it's Chinatown."

"This country seems dead-set on tearing itself apart. We are being divided by race, religion, and political ideology…the only thing left that unites us is this flag. We are Americans. That should mean something. This flag has watched the best of us stand together, and it has watched us fall short of the ideals it represents. But this is a symbol that 'We the People' can endure. The moment we let them burn it and set up an autonomous zone is the moment we lose what it means to be American."

You don't spend time in the military and not learn the meaning behind the flag. Men have died for it. They have given "the last full measure of devotion" to ensure that the nation it represents "does not perish from the Earth." The leader of this ADOZ just made things personal.

"All right. So, what do you wanna do?"

"Follow me."

The guys help Emmit haul two-by-fours, rope, paint, an eyebolt, and tools up from the basement. Kenyala's house was beginning to fall into disrepair after her husband died. When Emmit got here following his discharge, he spent two months fixing up the place. These materials are the leftovers, and now he's happy he saved them for a rainy day. That day has come.

After securing a legal pad from the junk drawer, Emmit drafts a quick sketch on the paper as Hollywood watches. Nashville pours another cup of coffee as his squad leader feverishly scribbles on the pad. He nods when he's done. He eyeballed the measurements, but they have plenty of material for this.

"What are we doing? Building a dollhouse?"

Emmit walks over to the mantel and lifts the encased flag from its place of honor in the house. The two men watch as he opens the tabs on the back and retrieves a folded American flag from the case. He closes his eyes as he holds and whispers a prayer before placing it on the counter with a sense of reverence.

"Is that Gamecock's flag?"

"His widow gave it to me. She wanted me to have it," Emmit nearly whispers. "I don't think she wanted to be constantly reminded that he was killed for a mission she never understood or agreed with."

Gamecock was from Charleston, South Carolina, and was killed in Syria during the ambush on their convoy the last two weeks they were in-country. Unlike the rest of the squad, they went with the University of South Carolina's team name instead of his home city. "Charleston" didn't fit him at all.

"The greatest trick the devil ever pulled was convincing the world he didn't exist.

Nashville rolls his eyes at Hollywood's quip. "Chicago, we buried him under that flag. You're not supposed to fly it."

"You know damn well that a flag that has been draped over a casket can be flown after the ceremony so long as you follow standard flag etiquette. This flag was folded and stored in that display case to honor the memory of our deceased brother. I can't think of a more meaningful tribute than to fly it here and now. Can you?"

Hollywood shrugs, and Nashville lowers his eyes. "You're right. In this case, Gamecock would probably be insulted if you didn't. But there is something else to consider. Even if you fly it from a makeshift pole, the yahoos that think they're in charge will just burn it again."

Emmit's lips crease into a smile as he spins the legal pad around and jabs his index finger at it. "They can try. I think they'll find this one a little harder to remove in the dead of night. Now, who wants to help me tactically reappropriate the neighbor's ladder?"

CHAPTER THIRTY-ONE
CHIEF VANESSA CAMPBELL

MPD TACTICAL COMMAND POST
MINNEAPOLIS, MINNESOTA

There are just shy of six hundred officers in the MPD, and just over half of them are watching the perimeter of the ADOZ. The other half are either patrolling the rest of the city or getting what little rest they can. This whole exercise is taxing her manpower to the brink.

Vanessa is getting support from outside agencies, but to call it minimal would be charitable. What she needs is the National Guard, but the mayor isn't going to ask for them anytime soon. This is her problem to solve, or so says the man who has axed their budget and slashed their numbers.

She had this command and control post set up for two main reasons. The first is that she didn't want to be near the mayor. The department's offices are in City Hall, and his constant presence only complicates things. Second, she needs to be close to the men who are manning the line…or, as the insurrectionists call it, the border.

The officers are calling this a "tactical command post." The name sounds more impressive than the reality. It's a series of pop-up tents, folding chairs and tables, and laptop computers. There is nothing tactical about it. But she can at least maintain some semblance of control from here.

The newest toys she has at her disposal are drones. They are nothing more than expensive civilian quadcopter models, but they get the job done. To avoid raising the alarm, she had the operator fly them in over the river from the west. He is keeping them low and away from the barricades where the insurrectionists have the majority of their manpower.

"What is this?" Inspector Sillyere asks after entering the command post.

"What does it look like? We're using a drone to check the district."

"You can't do that, Chief! Drones aren't allowed!"

"Says who?"

There is nothing she can say to refute that, not that such a little thing will stop her ambitious inspector. Vanessa read their little sheet of new laws. It didn't say anything about drones. At least, not yet.

"They can shoot the drones down."

The chief scoffs and shakes her head. "Let them try."

That should have been the end of the conversation. For most subordinates, it would have been. But Inspector Wilma Sillyere isn't just any subordinate. She's a pain in the ass and wants to be the person who, loudly and proudly, proclaims this to be a bad idea in case something bad happens. There is no better way to curry favor and gain a sought-after promotion than to be the person who shouted the first warning.

"It's provocative."

"It's necessary," Vanessa counters. "We need to know what's going on in the Arts District. Since we can't put boots on the ground, this is the next best thing."

Wilma shakes her head. "The mayor isn't going to like this."

"I'm sure," Vanessa moans, returning her attention to the monitor.

"He could *fire* you."

It's not the words that came out of her mouth – it's how she said them. The contempt in her voice is palpable, and the chief has had enough. She stands up straight and gets into Wilma's face, a pointed index finger the only thing bridging the distance between their noses.

"Then you're one step closer to getting my job, which is what you want, anyway. Until then, I am the chief of police for this city. As far as I'm concerned, the people in those neighborhoods are still under my protection. If you want to abdicate your responsibility to them, that's your decision. I will not, nor will I tolerate anybody who works for me siding with insurrectionists. So, get on board, or consider yourself relieved of duty!"

"I resent—"

"Whoa! What is that?" the officer at the table practically shouts.

Vanessa disengages to see what he's staring at. The video coming from the drone's onboard camera is a sight for sore eyes.

"You don't see that every day. Can you get closer or zoom in?"

"Yup. I can do both."

The officer guides the drone over a couple of houses and puts it in a hover near a tree. He zooms the camera in on the makeshift flagpole. The only thing that would warm Vanessa's heart more is to see Old Glory fluttering in the breeze. Unfortunately, there is no wind today.

There is a black flag underneath it. Vanessa can't make it out. It looks like it could be something ISIS would fly, but that doesn't make sense. MIA-POW, maybe? She doesn't think so.

"What is that other flag? Is that a cannon on it?"

The officer cocks his head before smiling. "The Gonzales Flag. It says, 'Come and Take It' beneath an image of a black cannon. The flag dates back to an 1835 confrontation between settlers and Mexican forces in Gonzales, Texas. Mexican troops attempted to retrieve a cannon they loaned to them. The settlers raised that flag in defiance. It became a symbol of Texan independence and resistance to tyranny."

Vanessa stares at the officer incredulously. "Do you moonlight as a professor at UM?"

He frowns sheepishly. "No, ma'am. I like history. The flag is fitting, considering what's going on."

"It is. We've been over this house before. Wasn't this…?"

"The house that they pulled the flag off and burned? I think so. That flagpole is definitely new construction. It wasn't there when we passed over this location a few hours ago."

The camera pans down to where the flagpole is affixed to the roof's peak. Whoever did this isn't a master carpenter, but the design ensures that the pole won't topple over in anything other than hurricane-force winds. It was a lot of effort to erect in such a short time frame.

"Find out who owns that house."

"I have it here, Chief. According to the city's property records…it was purchased three years ago by Clayton and Kenyala Brown."

"What else do we know about them?"

"Uh, not much…Clayton Brown…was killed in a construction accident a little over a year ago. His wife was the executor of the estate. Presumably, she got the house."

"Who else is living there?" Vanessa demands.

"Ma'am?"

"New husband? Boyfriend? There's no way a single woman erected a flagpole on her roof by herself. That was the work of two or three people, likely men, considering the strength required."

The officer leans back in his folding chair. "There's no way for us to know that."

"Then contact the FBI and have them do a background search. It'll give them the chance to do something useful. I want to know friends, family…you name it."

"Chief, it's a flag. Why are you making a big deal out of this?"

Vanessa turns to her insubordinate inspector. She should have dismissed the woman when she had the chance. "Do you need me to spell it out for you?"

"Clearly, you do."

This woman couldn't see the big picture if she were looking down at it from a satellite in low Earth orbit. Vanessa snatches a sheet of paper off the folding table and holds it in front of Wilma's face. The inspector steps back and quietly reads the sheet that has the new ADOZ laws printed on it.

"American flags are forbidden in their little fiefdom. I've been watching drone footage for over an hour and haven't seen a single one until now. And this one is affixed to the peak of the roof, so they can't get to it easily."

"So?"

"So, someone isn't playing by the rules. That means the president of this ADOZ has a choice to make – allow the flag to fly or take it down using violence. If he chooses the latter, I want to know about it."

CHAPTER THIRTY-TWO

KAI Z

GRAND STREET RENTAL HOUSE
MINNEAPOLIS ARTS DISTRICT OCCUPIED ZONE

Some people think being a YouTuber isn't a viable business. It's a laughable notion to any creator who approaches it professionally and puts in the work. Kai doesn't do sponsorships or other merchandising, but his channel is highly monetized, and he is on Patreon to generate subscription revenue.

Kai considers himself a journalist, but it's Babs who runs their little endeavor. She helps develop the schedule, promotes the channel on social media, manages the budget, and tracks the analytics to know what videos hit and which ones fall flat. He may have a knack for sniffing out stories and reporting the truth, but she is the reason he has over four million subscribers and makes almost $100,000 per month.

He may have captured the video of the flag burning, but her efforts introduced it to the world. The views have shot past the one million mark, and mainstream media is featuring the flag burning in almost every ADOZ story. For all that success, Babs is still not happy.

"What's wrong? I thought you would be over the moon on this video's performance."

"I am," she says, the tone in her voice not at all convincing.

"Yeah, it shows."

"The video is great, Kai. You're shining a light on what's happening on this side of the barricade. People need to see that."

He knows that she's setting him up. "But?"

"They know you're *here*, Kai."

He starts to say something and stops. That's a solid point. The video was clearly taken from inside the district, which means that's where he is. But, as with many things in life, size matters.

"Babs, the ADOZ isn't the CHAZ. This isn't six blocks – it's much, much bigger. They won't find me here."

"Sure. Because they don't seem at all like the type who'd go door-to-door and search houses looking for you."

"Wouldn't that footage be great!" It was a reflexive response that Babs doesn't appear to appreciate.

"Or they could search online for recently contracted rental houses and start there. How hard would it be to find this place?"

"Then we'll find a place to hide. Babs, they aren't going to find me. I promise."

It sounds good, but like most promises people utter to make people feel better, it's hollow. Events can spiral out of control. Life is unpredictable. There are a thousand reasons that promise can't be kept. Babs looks like she's about to argue one of them when they hear a commotion outside.

Kai moves to the side of the window and parts the blinds slightly. A man is yelling at men sitting in an SUV. The two in the back climb out, weapons slung across their chests. That isn't deterring the man at all. He launches into a tirade that features more expletives than a sailor could string together in a sentence.

"Are they looking for us?" Babs says in a near whisper from behind him.

"I...don't think so. I think it's just a patrol."

"What's he angry about?"

"I'm not sure. It sounds like...."

One of the goons unclips the rifle slung across his chest and cracks the belligerent citizen in the head with the stock. He collapses to a knee, looking up just in time to get punched in the face by the other armed man.

"Oh, my God!" Babs almost shouts, covering her mouth.

The man crumples to the ground and gets into the fetal position as he gets kicked by one sentry and butt-stroked with a rifle by the other. There are at least a dozen blows before a man in front calls them off.

"Kai, you need to—"

"Stop them? Weren't you talking about not being seen a minute ago?"

She purses her lips. He's got her there. Babs has a good heart, so it's natural that she'd want to help the man.

The man receives a final kick to the ribs as his wife comes out of the house. One of the men shouts a warning to her before the SUV drives off. She helps him to his feet, and he staggers back into the house.

Kai stares down at the screen and ends the recording. "I can't wait to post this!"

She knocks the phone out of his hand. "Are you stupid? Why don't you hang a banner outside that says, 'Kai is here,' and hire a marching band to ensure it gets their attention?"

Kai reaches down and retrieves the phone from the floor. "People need to see this. You know that."

"At what cost? Your life? Mine?"

"It won't come to that."

"Are you serious? You just watched them beat a man for shouting at them! What do you think they'll do to people exposing their crimes?"

"It's a risk, but that's what we do!"

"I'm not saying we don't post the video. I'm saying that we shouldn't be here when we do. Either we find a new home base, or we wait and post it when we aren't in danger of being exposed."

Damn her and her logic. She's right. They can use the video, but changes need to be made first. Kai's not willing to give this place up – at least, not right now. Maybe there will be a good time to release this to the world. Until then, he will have to search for other opportunities. The farther they are away from this base camp, the better.

"Okay."

She narrows her eyes at him. "Okay?"

"Yes. We'll post it once we've moved on. Until then, we should nap and get ready for tonight."

"Nap? Is that really what you want to do?"

He winks at her. "I'm not saying we shouldn't be exhausted from physical exertion first."

CHAPTER THIRTY-THREE

LANDON TAYSON

THE FIFTH STREET HOUSE
MINNEAPOLIS ARTS DISTRICT OCCUPIED ZONE

The drive from their makeshift command center to the problem house on Fifth Street isn't a long one, so Landon instructs the driver to take the scenic route. Their journey takes them a block north of the Broadway barricades and then up along the river. It's nice to get out of the confines of their shoebox and gives Landon a chance to address issues without distraction.

The streets are eerily quiet. Everyone is surprised at the absence of any real resistance in the district. There is a good chance that won't last. The first seed may be this flap over the American flag. That's why it needs to be stamped out and why Landon plans on handling it personally.

"There's one more thing," Muzzie says from the back seat. "I already told Raven, but our sentries are reporting drone sightings over the ADOZ."

"Drones?"

"Affirmative. Quadcopter types. It's likely the police are using them to conduct surveillance. I was hoping you'd tell them to cease and desist the activity."

"Backed up with what? Is there any way for us to bring the drones down?"

"Outside of a very lucky shot with a rifle, no."

"Then any threats would be immediately challenged, and we'd look like fools. Once they learn they can test us and win, they'll get bolder. I don't want them getting bolder. I don't want to give the weak-ass mayor of this city any easy wins. If they want to watch us with drones, let them."

"Roger that."

The vehicle stops outside the house, and Landon climbs out of the SUV. He stops and looks at the flag towering high from the roof. The makeshift pole is clearly made of wood, but they painted it dark gray and ran a rope through an eyelet at the top so they could raise and lower it. The attention to detail should be admired. The flag below it doesn't escape his attention. He's more familiar with the "Don't Tread on Me" Gadsden standard, but he knows about the significance of the Gonzales flag.

"Well, these guys are trying to make a helluva statement. There are three of them?"

Muzzie comes up alongside him. "At least. What are you going to do?"

"Politely tell them to take it down."

"And when they refuse?"

The corner of Landon's mouth curls. "Stop being polite."

Landon crosses the street and makes it to the sidewalk when the front door to the house opens, and two men step out onto the stoop. The black man is in front with the Hispanic guy slightly behind and to the right. At least he knows who the big dog is in this trio.

"That's far enough."

The ADOZ president looks around. He's fifteen or twenty feet away. That's far too far to have a civil conversation. "Really? I don't want to shout."

"I can hear your girly voice just fine."

The men don't like hearing their leader get insulted, and they raise their weapons. Muzzie turns and stops them. If there is a third guy, he has a shotgun, and it's probably pointed at Landon's head.

"Lower your weapons," the commander orders. The men do as instructed.

"Touchy, touchy," the black man says as the Spanish guy grins.

"It's been a long couple of days. My name is Landon Tayson. And you are…?"

"Chicago."

"Okay. Chicago. I'm the president of the ADOZ, and I wanted to personally inform you that you are in violation of several of our laws."

"President, eh?" Chicago says with a smile. He might as well put this on a silver platter for Hollywood. "Well, I didn't vote for you."

"The title was given to me."

"You can't expect to wield supreme executive power just 'cause some watery tart threw a sword at you! I mean, if I went around saying I was an emperor just because some moistened bint had lobbed a scimitar at me, they'd put me away!"

The British accent is terrible, but Landon has seen *Monty Python and the Holy Grail*. Muzzie clearly hasn't. That, and his commander doesn't have much of a sense of humor. The only time Landon has heard him laugh is after shooting at the range.

He nods in the Latino's direction. "Is he okay?"

"No…not really," the guy calling himself "Chicago" deadpans.

"All right. Listen, we don't want trouble with you, but that means you need to follow our laws. You will hand in your weapon and remove that American flag from your roof."

Chicago folds his arms. "And if I don't?"

"Then, the law will be enforced by any means necessary."

"Well, *Mr. President*, it sounds like you're looking for trouble, after all."

Landon scoffs. "You have a shotgun. We have an arsenal at our disposal and men who know how to use it. If you want to die for God and country, I'm happy to oblige. Just say the word."

A reminder of the situation and the odds against them is appropriate. This guy must realize that compliance is his only real option. Unless he's exceptionally brave or stupid because he doesn't exhibit any signs of being intimidated. If anything, he looks amused.

"Sounds like it's a date."

"My mama always said life was like a box of chocolates," the man standing next to Chicago says. "You never know what you're gonna get."

Confidence throws people off. Landon has used that tactic countless times in his life. Act like you're supposed to be someplace you aren't, and nine times out of ten, you won't draw any suspicion. Act like you know all the facts, and few people will challenge you for fear of looking like an uninformed dolt.

The tables have turned. A carload of armed men would cause most people to beg for forgiveness and become compliant. Not these men. They are daring Landon to take action. Why would they do that? Several possibilities race through his mind before one of Muzzie's lieutenants taps him on the shoulder.

"Sir, there's an ongoing incident on the east side of the ADOZ. It appears to be a house fire, and the residents need medical attention."

Alarm klaxons sound in Landon's head. "How close to the barricade?"

"A block. Maybe two."

"It could be a diversion. Captain Muzzie, send the patrols to reinforce the barricades to the north and south, and radio all others to be on high alert. Call Raven and tell her that I'm heading over there."

Landon isn't a big believer in coincidences. It may be just a fire. They happen in the city all the time. But this is the ADOZ, and it's near the barricade. He can't think of a better diversion. When you focus your attention to the east, you never see the SWAT team hitting the barricade in the north.

"Problem?"

"I have something that requires my attention. This is your last chance. If those flags are here when I return…well, it won't end well for you, Chicago…or whatever your real name is. You might want to tell me so I can have it engraved on your tombstone."

"Go ahead. Test us."

The man doesn't smirk. There is no emotion at all – anger, nervousness, or otherwise. He meant it as a direct challenge.

"A census taker once tried to test me. I ate his liver with some fava beans and a nice Chianti."

There's nothing more to be discussed here, as much as Landon wants to come up with a witty response to the Latino's *The Silence of the Lambs* quote.

"You have your warning."

CHAPTER THIRTY-FOUR

FIELD OFFICER DAVID BRASS

FOLGER PARK
WASHINGTON, D.C.

It's another venture in the lion's den of national politics, but at least this one won't include an uncomfortable meeting with a freshly chewed-out CIA director. The charming two-acre Folger Park is conveniently located near Capitol Hill. It's a peaceful spot with open lawns, mature trees for shade, walkways, and benches that's popular among families, walkers, and staffers looking for a quick escape from their rigorous schedules.

It's also Congresswoman Theresa Mazzala's favorite spot. The two-term representative from Minnesota still hasn't quite adjusted to how Washington works. She came here to pass laws to make people's lives better, and has been slow to realize that she is one of the few legislators in this city interested in doing so. That created an opportunity that Brass couldn't pass up.

The two met following a classified briefing to the Permanent Select Committee on Intelligence. How she landed a position there Brass will never know. The committee is composed of members from both major political parties and is tasked with monitoring the activities of the CIA, NSA, and the Department of Defense intelligence components. They play a critical role in ensuring that operations align with U.S. law and don't infringe on civil liberties. He assumes that's what the woman wants to discuss.

"Good morning, Congresswoman," David says, sitting on the bench next to her. "People are going to start talking about us."

"We're meeting on a park bench, not a room at the Hyatt Regency. Unless you plan on putting on a show for the tourists and doing me on this bench, I don't think anyone will talk."

Congresswoman Mazzala isn't a beauty queen, but she isn't unattractive either. Pushing forty-five, with medium-length auburn hair and a slender figure that still has some curves to it, he'd absolutely take her up on the suggestion. She's the married one, not him.

"You're not my type."

"Too smart?"

Brass grins. "Something like that. Is this about what's happening in your home state?"

"That's unpleasant business up there, and thankfully not in my district. The timing is curious, though. Imagine an insurrection movement popping up just as a domestic

CIA spying operation surfaces. You and your buddies in the apple export business must be pleased that it got pushed out of the media cycle."

This woman is too smart for this town.

"Not my monkey, not my zoo," Brass truthfully admits. "I had nothing to do with that particular Pandora's Box. Although Railspike wasn't a spying operation. It was counterespionage."

The congresswoman scoffs. "Sure it was."

"I have no reason to lie to you."

"David, I like you, but you have every reason to lie to me."

"Normally, I might agree with you. But not in this case. The CIA received actionable intelligence three years ago that foreign actors were looking to influence our political process. Our analysts thought that meant bribes to elected officials or high-ranking bureaucrats. They were wrong. Intelligence agents were placed in some of the country's most powerful political lobbies. You can appreciate better than most what that means."

"Are you suggesting I'm bought and paid for?"

The comment was meant to get under her skin a little. The tone of her voice lets Brass know that he hit the bullseye.

"I'm suggesting that you're a member of Congress."

"Isn't counterespionage the responsibility of the FBI on American soil?"

"Yeah, only I have it on good authority that they didn't take the information we shared with them seriously. That, and their agents aren't as...skilled as ours. Their disinterest worked out for the best. They would have been out of their depth."

"I wonder if they will agree with that sentiment when they appear before the Intelligence Committee."

Brass forces himself not to react. This was a danger when he arranged for the details to get leaked. He needed to apply pressure, but not so much that Congress was compelled to take an active interest. It's a dangerous game, but if he wanted safe, he would have chosen the life of a chess master and not become a CIA agent.

"Is there going to be hearings?"

"You work in the intelligence world. That means you know people. I'm sure one of them is the committee chairman. He's an opportunist who likes seeing his name in news articles. If he thinks hearings will raise his public profile, you can bank on it."

"What about you?"

"I represent good, honest Minnesotans. If I think the CIA or any other federal intelligence agency is abusing their authority and curtailing the rights of my constituents, you are making an enemy of me. Watch your lane."

Brass doesn't like threats, especially from public servants. Congresswoman Mazzala hasn't been completely corrupted by the system yet, but that doesn't mean she's above reproach. Everyone elected to serve in the marble halls of the Capitol has skeletons in their closets.

"When will Congress learn that we're not the bad guys?" David asks.

"I support the intelligence community and the role the agents play in keeping our country safe," she says, standing. "This meeting was a courtesy because of that. Don't force me to go on a headhunting mission. Keep Railspike out of the news. Have a good day, David."

He can't help but smile as she walks back toward the House office buildings. Keeping it out of the news is what he's planning to do. Fortunately, Pendulum is going extremely well. Now, he needs it to last. Since Nightshade is being obstinate, he needs a way to drive the point home. With that thought, he picks up his cell and makes a call.

CHAPTER THIRTY-FIVE
CHIEF VANESSA CAMPBELL

MPD TACTICAL COMMAND POST
MINNEAPOLIS, MINNESOTA

The command post has been anything but a hive of activity. Reports are received and orders relayed via radio, but it feels like a measured, business-as-usual operation. That has started to change. Two of the officers manning laptops at one of the folding tables are getting agitated. Vanessa is about to ask why when one of them turns to her.

"Chief, we are getting reports of multiple calls to 9-1-1 about a house fire and an injured man in the Arts District."

"What's the address?"

The officer looks at his screen. "Twenty-Second Avenue and Sixth Street."

The chief does some mental calculations. That isn't far from their barricade. For obvious defensive reasons, they used the elevated railroad tracks as the easternmost border of their occupied zone. Since she staged resources at a high school softball field a couple of blocks away, firemen and paramedics could get to the incident quickly.

"Get the mayor on the line," Vanessa orders.

"No need, he's already here. And, the answer is 'no.'"

Vanessa turns to see the mayor duck his head under the popup tent. Elliott Thurlow looks constipated on his best day. It doesn't take a swami to figure out what kind of day this is. He has bags under his bloodshot eyes you could put groceries in, and his hair looks like it hasn't been visited by a comb since the ADOZ was set up.

"You heard about the fire?"

"On the way here to see you. The protesters aren't going to permit EMS to enter the ADOZ. They've been very clear about that. I don't want to antagonize them by forcing the issue."

"Mr. Mayor, there is a *house* on fire there. If we don't send the fire department, and it spreads, it could burn down the entire district."

The mayor clasps his hands behind his back. "I understand. I am not sending those men into harm's way."

"Hundreds, if not thousands, of lives could be at risk."

"I'm aware of the danger, Chief Campbell. I'm not a moron!"

That's debatable under the best of circumstances, and Vanessa is hardly the only person to think so. "Then call the leader of the ADOZ and explain the situation. All we're looking to do is extinguish the fire and render first aid."

"President Tayson said in his press conference that they were equipped to handle emergencies. Let's watch them try."

Vanessa's jaw tightens, and her hands ball into fists. She can't believe he used that insurrectionist's faux title. That's going to be the mayor's approach to this crisis – he wants to wait around until they fail. But at what cost? Hope is not a tactic. In the meantime, there are citizens caught up in this tug-of-war in trouble, and he doesn't seem inclined to help…or even care.

"I'm going to state this plainly, Mr. Mayor – we need to send the fire department. If they turn us away, then we can say we tried."

"Unless they are willing to agree to a police escort, no fireman will set foot on the opposite side of that barricade. Is that understood?"

"Perhaps there is a happy medium," Otto Goldberg says from behind them. Vanessa didn't even know that he was here. "I'll go talk to them, Mr. Mayor. I think Landon Tayson is a reasonable man. I can convince him that allowing us to douse the fire and render medical aid is in his best interests."

"Except they have no interest in talking," Vanessa argues.

"To you, maybe," Otto says with a sneer. "They can be reasoned with. I know it."

The chief's face contorts as the mayor bites his lower lip. He's actually thinking about this now. What the hell?

"All right. It's worth a shot."

"EMS is standing by on the east side of the train tracks on Twenty-Second," Wilma says, upping her brown-nosing to the next level. "Their barricade under the overpass is smaller than most of the others. They should be able to quickly move it aside for emergency vehicles to pass."

The mayor nods. "You have my permission to negotiate with the protesters."

Frustrated is what you get when you don't have the grip strength to open a jar of pickles. The emotions Vanessa is feeling shoot way past that. He's not listening to her. He isn't considering her point of view. Just when she thought that their relationship was at rock bottom, the mayor started drilling through the bedrock to reach a new low. Worse, Otto and Wilma have grabbed shovels of their own.

"They're not going to move that barricade," she shouts at the mayor. "You just admitted that!"

"Then maybe we could use their vehicular access," Wilma says, causing the corner of Otto's mouth to curl. "This is how we should be handling this situation – with respect and grace."

"There is no point in arguing further. I've made my decision. Good luck, Otto. Come through for us."

There have been a couple of points during Vanessa's career when she wondered if her sacrifices were worth it. This can get added to the list. She would love to rip her shield off and toss it at the mayor, leaving this mess to him. But she can't bring herself to do that. The chief's first obligation has always been to the residents of this beautiful city. She isn't about to abandon them now, no matter how badly she wants to.

This is going to go well or very badly. Whichever way it breaks, she's going to be there. It's what duty demands. With that thought, she jumps into a squad car for the short trip up to the Twenty-Second Avenue barricade.

CHAPTER THIRTY-SIX
KAI Z

This was a bad idea. Babs was quick to point that out as he was making for the door. Now, he's finding himself agreeing with her, not that he'll ever admit it. A misstep like that would all but ensure he hears about it for the rest of his life.

The sun has dipped below the horizon, but there is still plenty of daylight. It's almost amazing that he got to this spot unnoticed. There aren't a lot of places to hide, but the base of this tree with some underbrush serves his purposes nicely. It's the best vantage point he can manage.

He has the advantage that nobody is looking for him. If this were a warzone, soldiers would have a good eye on this shady spot. But as militarized as the ADOZ pretends to be, the fighters, or whatever they call themselves, are not professionals. That doesn't mean they aren't well-armed. That's a fact that's been tugging at the back of his mind since he strolled past the barricade on the first day of this occupation.

Twenty-Second Avenue and the intersection with Monroe Street are swarming with Landon Tayson's toy soldiers. Men are fighting the fire on the first floor of the house. The rest are milling around without direction and wondering what they should be doing. Kai's out of sight and should be okay unless some guy needs to take a piss and chooses these bushes to do it.

But now he's stuck. If he suddenly stands up, he'll be noticed. He'll likely be challenged, and if anyone recognizes him, the trouble will compound exponentially. He needs to wait until it gets darker before he can leave this spot.

Fortunately, it is a good one. Kai has a direct line of sight to the Twenty-Second Avenue house that's on fire. The downside is that his needing to remain prone has made his body camera worthless. It's only recording darkness, the lens pushed into the ground and kept there by the weight of his body.

Kai keeps his small handheld camera pointed through the underbrush. The house fire is out, or at least appears to be contained. He wouldn't have guessed that fighting it with extinguishers and garden hoses would have worked, but it did. There's no sign of the fire department. Then again, with all the men here carrying rifles and assault weapons, no sane fireman would step foot on this street.

There is no indication of how it started, but the homeowners are on the small front lawn between the sidewalk and the front door. The man is on the ground in shorts with no shirt. Kai can't tell if he's bleeding, but his wife has been screaming that he needs immediate medical attention. The journalist smiles at the compelling footage. Her pleas have been falling on deaf ears, at least until a medic finally arrives. Well, Kai assumes he's a medic of some sort. It's not like anyone in the ADOZ wears a uniform or insignia that explains their function.

The response to the fire and the resulting medical emergency has been anemic. There is almost no leadership and little initiative. What little of either trait that exists amidst this chaos was focused on the blaze. Maybe with that under control, someone will step up and help the poor woman desperately screaming for help. It doesn't look that way.

She pulls out a cell phone and makes a call. She doesn't dial long, so this is either to a friend or, more likely, 9-1-1. Kai struggles to no avail to hear what she's saying. She starts speaking quickly, and her tone is urgent. That gets the attention of the men around her.

Two men grab her and struggle to rip the device from her hand. It's odd behavior that Kai can't begin to understand. Why does it matter? Her neighbors have absolutely called 9-1-1. Unless the leaders of this little rebellion plan to confiscate everyone's phones and laptops, there is no way to cut off communications with the outside world.

Ultimately, they succeed. Helpless, the woman returns to her husband and begins wailing. Kai watched Landon Tayson assure a crowd of reporters at the press conference that they could handle any emergency that arose in the occupied area. That is being put to the test, and they are failing miserably.

Speak of the devil. Landon Tayson arrives in an SUV and begins barking orders to the men around him. It's the first time many of his fighters look like they have a purpose. He walks over to the couple on the lawn and bends down to evaluate the man. The wife is still screaming at him despite his best efforts to calm her down. She rears her head back and spits in his face.

Kai has to suppress a chuckle. Tayson wipes his cheek and nose with his shirt as two of his fighters hook the woman under her arms and haul her away. Under Landon's direction, the man is loaded into the SUV, and it speeds off to who knows where. Maybe they have a medical clinic set up somewhere. If that was the case, why wasn't the man evacuated immediately? That would be a fun question to ask the president of the ADOZ.

Landon is approached by a sentry and turns his attention to the east, walking into the middle of Twenty-Second Avenue to stare down the road at the barricade. He has a quick conversation with another man decked out in all manner of military gear, and the pair set off on foot. He can't move yet, but he needs to see what's going on at that barricade if it's important enough to command the attention of the ADOZ's self-proclaimed president.

Kai looks at the slowly graying sky. "Come on, a little darker…I need you to be a little darker."

CHAPTER THIRTY-SEVEN
EMMIT "CHICAGO" HASKINS

THE FIFTH STREET HOUSE
MINNEAPOLIS ARTS DISTRICT OCCUPIED ZONE

They should have set up a watch yesterday. The problem is numbers. There are only three of them, and that can make for long days and nights. Emmit didn't expect the toy soldiers to return, and he was wrong. That was a mistake he's not keen to make again.

When Hollywood mused, "Well, here's another nice mess you've gotten me into," Chicago had to agree. One shotgun isn't going to hold them back, and they need to acquire more weapons tonight. Until then, he told the guys to prepare for the defense. What they've come up with is part *Home Alone*, part *A-Team*. It's a good start, but it won't deter a determined assault on the house. The robbers in the movie were bungling morons, and Hannibal's plans on the tv show only worked that well because that's what the script dictated.

After their flag-burning party, he expects someone to drop in to see if he got the message. They'll be waiting for them this time. Nashville is watching the back, while Chicago has the front. Hollywood has the shotgun and is resting on a bed upstairs. He's the quick reaction force if one is needed.

"Heads up, Chicago," Nashville announces from one of the second-floor bedrooms. "I see three assholes moving toward us through your neighbor's yard, loaded for bear."

"Guns?"

"Nothing visible, but all of them are wearing assault packs and carrying duffles. They may be the lead element of an assault."

That doesn't make any sense. An assault element would have long guns and wouldn't be carrying bulky items like duffles. It's unlikely they would even be carrying rucks. They would travel light, with only body armor and extra magazines. They would also have teams approaching from multiple vectors, but Chicago doesn't see any activity to the front of the house.

"Are they police?"

"Nope."

Chicago scowls. He said that conclusively.

"You got eyes on 'em, Hollywood?"

"Hello, gorgeous!"

He'll take that as a yes. Chicago isn't sure what movie that line is from, but he isn't going to waste time asking. "Let 'em know we're here before they get too close."

The Benelli belches, sending birdshot in the direction of the three yahoos sneaking into the back yard. They scatter immediately in separate directions. It's rare to see civilians move that tactically and communicate while doing it. Chicago braces for the inevitable response, but nothing happens. The yard goes eerily quiet.

"Jesus, Chicago! Did you give Hollywood the shotgun? You know that cat can't shoot for shit. Why do you think we made him the SAW gunner?"

"Nica?"

A guy steps out from the trees near the fence. "That's *Staff Sergeant* Nica now."

Sergeant Jose Centeno, now apparently promoted, was a team leader on Chicago's squad. His family legally immigrated to the U.S. from Nicaragua when he was ten, and he joined the military as a pathway to get his citizenship. While not the most physically gifted soldier in Chicago's squad, he was one of the smartest.

His fellow paratroopers called him "Common Cents." When asked about why, he said "Fifty Cent" was already taken. After going to Ranger School while serving in the airborne infantry, Nica reenlisted and joined the Regiment. Now, it looks like he's making a career out of it.

He begrudgingly went along with Chicago's edict of using home cities or states as nicknames, and "Nicaragua" quickly got shortened to "Nica." There were far worse names in the squad.

"I'll be damned. Stand down, guys."

"Come on out, boys," Nica announces. "Chicago let Hollywood have the boom stick, so we're safe unless he aims at something else."

"You guys are a sight for sore eyes," Emmit says, walking through the back yard and embracing his former team leader.

"You wouldn't know it. That's a hell of a welcoming party, buddy."

"Sorry about that. Things are a little tense around here."

"We gathered that from watching the news footage of the Stars and Stripes fluttering on top of your roof," Tulsa says, pointing at their makeshift flagpole.

Rob Hibbard was never cut out for the military. It's not that he wasn't a good soldier – he was an outstanding one. But he's a man who doesn't like playing by the rules, and the Army has a lot of them. That created friction with the company leadership, and Tulsa opted to take his DD214 and run back to Oklahoma when his enlistment was up.

"If you build it, he will come," Hollywood says as he and Nashville join the group in the back yard.

"I see this jackass hasn't changed any," Bronx says in a baritone voice that would almost make Barry White jealous.

Justus Coleman is a big, barrel-chested man who looks like he could lug a howitzer around on his own. Never a good runner, the New York City native was a liability in the Regiment. It made him perfect for Chicago's squad. He was reliable, was as tough as nails, and his slow foot speed made him the perfect guy to share a foxhole with. He was never going anywhere.

"Yeah, we're not making many friends around here since the circus came to town. How did you get here?"

"It wasn't that hard. The guys at the barricades have tunnel vision. They're only concerned about the police," Nica concludes.

"And the ones who aren't are distracted by a fire or something over that way," Tulsa says, pointing. "They seemed pretty concerned by it, and we slipped right past them."

"Makes you wonder why the police haven't done the same," Bronx says, shaking his head.

"We thought the same thing," Nashville confirms. "Let's get inside. We've seen drones flying around and don't want anyone to know our numbers."

The six men file inside with the three rucks and pair of duffles and gather around the dining room table.

"I thought you guys were in the field this weekend," Chicago says.

"There was a range incident at Benning, so the powers that be canceled our field exercise. Top owed me a favor, so he convinced the CO to sign off on our leave."

"And you came here."

Nica spreads his arms and twists his torso. "This is where the action is. We met up with this clown on the way."

Tulsa smiles. "Be fortunate they did. Tweedledee and Tweedledum here were content to bring knives to a gunfight. Fortunately, I'm Santa Claus and have a sack full of toys."

He opens one of the duffle bags. It's crammed full of rifles and other weapons, including a sniper rifle with top-of-the-line optics. Hollywood pulls out an M249 SAW and lights up like a kid on Christmas morning.

"Now I have a machine gun. Ho, ho, ho."

The M249 SAW Squad Automatic Weapon is a lightweight, belt-fed machine gun used by the U.S. military and other armed forces worldwide. It's a reliable and versatile bridge between M4 rifles and heavier machine guns. Hollywood is going to sleep with his tonight. He loved that thing.

The semi-automatic version is legal to own in most states, subject to federal and local regulations. This isn't a civilian model. The fully automatic M249 is only legal with ATF approval and if it was registered pre-1986. Of course, that only matters when the serial number isn't scratched off.

"Did you guys rob a gun store on the way here?"

"I run my grandfather's Army-Navy surplus shop. I told him where I was going, and he opened up the back room for me and told me to help myself. All these are untraceable, by the way."

Chicago whistles. "Must be one hell of a back room. Do you have Javelin missiles in there, too?"

"Sadly, no. Don't look so surprised, Sarge. It's Oklahoma. You know why our crime rate is so low? We don't report crimes so the po-po doesn't bother looking for the bodies."

"You guys are wearing civvies?" Nica asks, changing the subject as he takes in Hollywood's and Nashville's appearance. Both are wearing shorts and T-shirts.

"We dressed for a barbecue, not urban warfare."

"Well, hell, I'm glad we brought these."

Tulsa hefts a second large olive drab duffle bag onto the dining room table and opens it. He pulls out old battle dress uniform blouses and pants, along with black jungle boots that still have a shine. He even has a dozen old brown shirts soldiers used to wear underneath in there.

"Ah, the Lord's flannel. Nice!" Nashville exclaims.

The Battle Dress Uniform was the best camouflage pattern the Army ever designed. BDUs were the standard combat uniform of the armed forces from the early 1980s until the mid-2000s. Soldiers revered them, and the affection only grew when the Army began rolling out its worst camo pattern on the hated ACU. Emmit doesn't miss wearing that hot garbage.

"The sizes should be close. The jungle boots will fit. I even grabbed a women's pair for Hollywood's tiny-ass feet."

"You feelin' lucky, punk?" he asks in a terrible Clint Eastwood impression.

"What's the situation, Sarge?" Bronx asks, snickering at the faux-mad look on Hollywood's face.

"The short answer? We're the partisan resistance in our own country."

"Well, that's a change of pace," Bronx muses.

Outside of their experiences in Syria, all of these guys have done rotations at the Joint Readiness Training Center at Fort Polk, Louisiana. JRTC exists to prepare for the operational challenges of modern warfare by inserting soldiers, units, and leaders into realistic combat scenarios. Soldiers train in mock urban areas, dense forests, and open terrain with an emphasis on counterinsurgency, large-scale combat, and joint operations. It sucks, and the good guys are set up to lose. Units learn more that way.

"I appreciate you guys coming, but you shouldn't stay. This is serious stuff. These guys may only be playing soldier, but they're cocky and have an arsenal. It's us against more than a thousand. Those are long odds."

"Now it's six on a thousand. Thank God we're Rangers," Nica counters.

"If they add a few hundred more, it'll almost be a fair fight," Tulsa adds, sharing a high five with Hollywood.

Nica puts his hand on Chicago's shoulder. "Now, are you going to whine about your predicament or tell us how we can help?"

CHAPTER THIRTY-EIGHT

LANDON TAYSON

Whoever this guy is has a set of stones on him. The lone man walking up the street with an ambulance slowly rolling about thirty feet behind him looks like he walked out of a sales convention. He's the kind of guy who sells used cars or cut-rate auto insurance. Maybe he's going to ask Landon if he wants to buy an extended warranty for his Honda.

Muzzie doesn't look like he wants to wait to find out. He's tracking the man's every move through the sight mounted on his rifle. He isn't panicking. It's one guy, but Landon knows his military commander thinks this is the prelude to something bigger. He's about fifty feet from them when the challenge is issued.

"Stop where you are! One more step will be your last!" he shouts down at the man from their spot on the railroad bridge.

"My name is Otto Goldberg. I'm the Deputy Chief of Constitutional Policing for this city. Is there someone there I can negotiate with?"

"There is nothing to negotiate," Landon says into the megaphone he picks up off the ground from Muzzie's feet. "No outside assistance is required. Turn that ambulance around and walk back to your line."

The man turns and shakes his head at the driver. He makes a signal with his hand to turn around. Landon can't see the man's reaction, but there is a clear miscommunication. The signal grows more emphatic. Then, the ambulance's engine screams as the vehicle surges forward.

"Oh, hell."

Everyone's eyes are welded on the emergency vehicle as it careens past the man who tried to negotiate. He is forced to dive out of the way when flagging the driver down has no effect. Landon turns to see several sentries raise their rifles. The same must be happening at the barricade below them. These men know what to do.

The rifles don't fire simultaneously, but they begin barking within a few seconds of each other. The windshield explodes as rounds from AR-15s, hunting rifles, and even an AK-47 or two slam through the glass. The lightbar explodes, steam begins hissing from the radiator, and a tire goes flat as the staccato of gunfire reaches a feverish pace.

Police taking cover behind their vehicles at the intersection of Madison Street begin returning fire, mostly with their service weapons and a few rifles. Landon slides back a little and gets low to the tracks. It's not a comfortable position, but it beats getting shot. The concrete railing along the edge of the bridge provides some protection, but it isn't solid. A bullet that flies through one of the openings could easily find his head.

The ambulance slows and veers to the right before disappearing from his sightline. The driver is definitely incapacitated and likely dead. Landon feels the train overpass that he's on vibrate. The vehicle must have hit one of the concrete supports.

Landon lifts his head and peeks through an opening in the concrete wall. The man in the street is caught in a crossfire. Instead of staying low with his head down or running across the street to find cover in the apartment building, he stands, turns to face the police, and waves his arms frantically. Does he want them to stop shooting, or is he signaling them to commence breaching the ADOZ? If you have to ask the question…after all, they started this.

"I got him," Muzzie says, raising his rifle and staring at the red dot aimpoint. He exhales and squeezes the trigger once. It does the job. The bullet strikes the man right between his shoulder blades, and he crumples to the ground.

"I need a support team at the Twenty-Second Avenue barricade right now!" Landon screams into his radio. "We are under attack!"

"Wilco," the man says in response, meaning "will comply."

He changes the channel on the walkie-talkie and keys the microphone. "Raven!"

"Yeah?"

"We're in a firefight on Twenty-Second Ave. Issue orders to all barricades to shoot first and ask questions later. Nobody approaches. Challenge anyone who even tries crossing the street."

"Muzzie should give that order, not me," she protests.

Landon ducks when he hears snapping sounds over his head. Those bullets were too close for comfort. "He's busy. So am I."

Minneapolis sounds like Baghdad in 2003. Rifles bark, and handguns pop as men work the triggers. Muzzle flashes give away positions in the fading light of the day. Just when Landon thinks the final battle is about to begin, he can hear shouts coming from the police line. Within a few seconds, their guns fall silent. An eerie silence bathes the area when his men stop firing.

"Now what?"

"They gave a cease-fire order," Muzzie says, scanning the streets below.

"Yeah, but why?"

"This is Chief of Police Vanessa Campbell," a voice says over a loudspeaker.

"Maybe she knows," Muzzie playfully posits.

Landon shakes his head, not understanding soldier humor after just getting shot at. He brings a megaphone to his mouth. "Good for you."

"We need to retrieve the dead and wounded. Is there someone there who can make the decision to allow that without violent action? We don't want any more fire exchanged between us."

"I have already made the decision. Do not approach the barricade, or you will be fired upon. This is the only warning you'll receive."

"Fine," the woman says after a pause. "You can leave the bodies there so the television cameras get a good long look at the men you just gunned down."

"That was your fault!" Landon shouts.

"We didn't shoot them," the woman sings out.

"Shit."

"Don't let them near us, Mr. President," his captain warns. "They'll use the retrieval as a distraction. They aim to end this. That's what this is about."

Landon takes a cleansing breath. The difference between success and failure can usually be traced back to one or two key decisions. This is one of those moments. Muzzie could be right, but the optics of leaving a dead body in the street will undermine everything they are trying to do here. He needs to keep the populace on his side.

After taking another breath, he keys the megaphone's mic. "Send one ambulance without strobes or sirens. Paramedics only. If we see one gun or any attempt is made to infiltrate the ADOZ, we'll open fire, and the streets will run red with blood. Understood?"

"Understood, but I will not risk the lives of paramedics. Members of our SWAT team are willing to retrieve the dead and wounded, and they will be unarmed. I repeat, they will be unarmed. You can verify from your position before they proceed. Agreed?"

"This is a bad idea," Muzzie whines.

"It's the best of our bad options."

"Landon, come back," Raven says over the radio.

"Yeah?"

"The firefight has already hit the news. Broadcast networks have interrupted programming and cable news is all over this. Reporters will be flocking to the scene if they aren't already there. What happened?"

"I'll explain later. Out." Landon grimaces and hefts the megaphone. "Your terms are acceptable. We are watching."

"What are your orders?"

Muzzie is clearly not happy with this course of action, but they are surrounded by sentries, and he has enough military bearing to know not to question the president's orders in front of them.

"Break out the thermal and night vision and watch them like a hawk. If they try anything shady, drop all of them."

CHAPTER THIRTY-NINE
CHIEF VANESSA CAMPBELL

EAST OF THE TWENTY-SECOND AVENUE BARRICADE
MINNEAPOLIS ARTS DISTRICT OCCUPIED ZONE

Vanessa bites her lip and opens her eyes wide in surprise. She didn't think anyone manning the barricade would agree to any terms. They would lack the authority to make the decision that quickly. Unless, of course, she was talking to a decision-maker. Maybe it's even Landon Tayson himself. That would be the first time anyone from law enforcement or the government had any dialogue with him, even if it was shouting through megaphones and a PA system.

She tosses the mic into the squad car's passenger seat. She won't be needing it any longer. This isn't the time for further engagement. They need to retrieve the bodies of their fallen and hopefully render aid to the men in the ambulance. It doesn't look like Otto Goldberg can be saved. He hasn't moved since getting hit. That's not a good sign.

"Get on the radio and have an ambulance report to this location," she orders a sergeant who lowers his weapon and keys the mic attached to his shoulder.

Vanessa turns to Burke. "Can you find me three volunteers?"

"It will be me and two other guys. Watch our backs."

"We will. No guns, Burke. Now's not the time to do something reckless. I want you to go home to your family at the end of this, too. Play it straight."

He nods. Vanessa is fairly sure he will follow those instructions. They've already lost enough people today.

Time begins creeping by. Burke climbs into the ambulance and rolls forward slowly with the hazard lights on. Vanessa puts the binoculars up and scans the barricade. It's growing darker by the minute, but there's still enough light to make out the silhouettes. Men have their rifles at the ready, but none are actively aiming at her guys. Same for the sentries on the railroad overpass. That doesn't mean they don't have snipers with Burke in their crosshairs, though. The most dangerous foe is the one you can't see.

He stops the vehicle and exits with two other SWAT team members. They raise their hands and turn to show the sentries that they're unarmed. He orders the men to what's left of the first ambulance while he checks on Otto. He's dead. There is little doubt of that now.

Burke retrieves a gurney, and one of his men checking on the ambulance drivers hustles over to him to lift the deputy chief onto it. There is no sense of urgency to treat the two men in the ambulance. That's more bad news, even if Vanessa would have been surprised if they survived the barrage of gunfire.

It feels like it takes forever for the three bodies to be ferried and loaded into the back of the ambulance. Tension is still high. The media are filming everything for posterity. How much they are showing live on air is something the chief will find out later. Probably not much. It will be traumatizing for their families.

Burke doesn't turn around. He slowly reverses the ambulance to the police line. The squad car blocking the intersection moves back into place after he passes. The SWAT commander shifts the vehicle into drive and heads for the staging area at the high school softball field.

Medical professionals are tending to the bodies by the time Vanessa walks over there. This was a recovery, not a rescue. The medical kits on the ground aren't going to be needed.

Burke comes alongside her, the sullen look on his face evident in the flashing blue and red strobes bathing the area. "The two paramedics are dead. So is Otto Goldberg. From what I could see, two men at the barricade were wounded, and one may be dead."

"What was that ambulance driver thinking?"

"I wish I knew."

"What the hell happened?"

The mayor knows how to announce his arrival. He was barely out of the car when he bellowed the question. Paramedics and officers clear a path as he storms over to the ambulance.

"What the hell happened?" he asks again, almost as loudly as the first time.

Vanessa points at the overpass. "The ambulance gunned its engine and tried to run the barricade. Both of the EMTs are dead, as is Otto Goldberg. He was trying to negotiate with the ADOZ sentries when it happened, and they shot him. We had an officer closer to the overpass catch a bullet. He's being evacuated now. Three dead, one wounded on our side."

The mayor glares at her. "I told you not to challenge them!"

"And I followed the order."

"Then why did an ambulance try to run the barricade?"

"I don't know. I'd ask the driver, but I can't because he and his fellow EMT were just murdered in cold blood."

The mayor clenches his teeth and takes a deep breath through his nose. "This wasn't a part of an infiltration operation?"

"No."

He turns to Burke, who shakes his head.

"I don't believe you. Either of you. I'm holding you personally responsible for this!"

"You're holding me personally responsible for giving an order I didn't issue? Or are you holding me responsible for following your order that allowed insurgents to set up this occupied zone to begin with?"

"They are protesters, not insurgents!" the mayor shouts, pointing a finger in Vanessa's face.

"Protesters who just shot and killed three men and wounded a fourth. Your indecisiveness led to this."

"If you dare say their blood is on my hands, consider yourself fired."

Vanessa wants to take the bait but passes.

"There will be no further police action against anyone manning the barricades. Any calls to 9-1-1 from the ADOZ will go unanswered. They are responsible, not us. I will not antagonize them and give their movement the high ground by challenging their perimeter. If they murder and rape everyone in that district, it will still be better for us than storming the barricades. Ensure my order is followed to the letter, *Chief Campbell*."

The mayor storms off under the critical eyes of the men and women around them. She will issue the orders to the chain of command, but there is one order of business that needs attention first. Vanessa disappears around the side of the ambulance and opens her body camera unit. She looks around and pulls out the memory card. She swaps it with a spare she carries in a utility pouch and powers the device back on. You never know when some good footage will come in handy.

CHAPTER FORTY

KAI Z

TWENTY-SECOND AVENUE BARRICADE
MINNEAPOLIS ARTS DISTRICT OCCUPIED ZONE

Kai didn't join the military for a myriad of reasons. The first is that he abhors physical exercise. The second is that he doesn't like getting dirty. The low crawl out of underbrush along Twenty-Second Avenue and moving north through back yards resulted in plenty of both.

When he reached Twenty-Third, he should have turned north and west and returned to the rental house. Babs pleaded with him to do that when he radioed her. But something compelled him to get to the barricade. He moved east along Twenty-Third Avenue and cut through back yards between Seventh and Washington. He ducked in some overgrown brush, ironically in front of a tree care office. That's when all hell broke loose.

The sound of gunfire distracted everyone in the area. This isn't a round or two being fired off. This is a full-blown firefight. If the police are breaching, he needs to see it. Across the street is a triangular parking area for a squat, three-story apartment building. The residents huddling in there must be terrified.

The railroad bridge runs along the hypotenuse of that triangle. There is a wooden plank sound barrier in place on the west side of the tracks, so men on that overpass won't be able to see him. The problem is the barricade under Washington Street. If they spot him crossing, it's going to be a problem.

Kai says a quick prayer. With all the gunfire, they probably won't be looking this way. He hates the idea of relying on any assumption that uses the word "probably."

"No guts, no glory," he whispers before running across the street and ducking behind a car parked along the far curb.

So far, so good. Kai bolts into the parking lot, angling for a dumpster surrounded by a wood fence. He can only block line-of-sight from one direction. This was a bad idea.

"This is Chief of Police Vanessa Campbell," he hears a voice say over a loudspeaker.

"Good for you," another replies over a megaphone.

Kai looks in the direction of the overpass over Twenty-Second Avenue. "Tayson."

"We need to retrieve the dead and wounded. Is there someone there who can make the decision to allow that without violent action? We don't want any more fire exchanged between us."

Kai takes a deep breath and makes for an embankment that leads up to the tracks along the concrete bridge support. It's a narrow strip of tall grass, dirt, and rock between the abutment and the retaining wall for the tracks above. He makes quick work of it, taking a few deep breaths when he reaches the top. He only wishes he had heard Landon's response to law enforcement.

"I have already made the decision. Do not approach the barricade, or you will be fired upon. This is the only warning you'll receive."

"Fine," the woman says after a fairly significant pause. "You can leave the bodies there so the television cameras get a good long look at the men you just gunned down."

"That was your fault!" Landon shouts.

"We didn't shoot them," the woman sings out.

Kai chuckles. Score one for the police. He points his camera straight down the tracks. He's recording something but doesn't know what.

"Send one ambulance without strobes or sirens," Landon orders. "Paramedics only. If we see one gun or any attempt is made to infiltrate this ADOZ, we'll open fire, and the streets will run red with blood. Understood?"

"Understood, but I will not risk the lives of paramedics. Members of our SWAT team are willing to retrieve the dead and wounded, and they will be unarmed. I repeat, they will be unarmed. You can verify from your position before they proceed. Agreed?"

"Your terms are acceptable. We are watching."

It was a reasonable request, but Kai's still surprised the arrogant ADOZ leader acquiesced. It makes sense from a media perspective, and it doesn't take a genius to recognize that, but he doesn't give Landon that much credit.

"Hey! Who are you?"

Kai's head shoots around, and he makes eye contact with two men coming down the tracks from the north. They are staying low but moving quickly. The rifles they have slung on their shoulder are at the low ready.

"I know him! That's Kai Z!"

"Shit."

The last thing he needed was to run into a fan. They aren't going to be wanting selfies. That's evident when they raise their rifles at him. He slides back down the embankment, his feet intermittently making contact with the ground before sliding some more.

"We have an intruder!" he hears one of them shout from the railroad overpass.

Kai doesn't hazard a look back. He knows they are giving chase as he sprints across the parking lot and Washington Street. A couple of sentries break off from the closest barricade to join the pursuit. He blows through a back yard, gets to Sixth Street, and turns north. South is no good. He has to make it across Twenty-Third, or the game is over.

"Stop! Stop, or we'll fire!"

They don't give him long to react. He hears the sounds of bullets passing him. One strikes the ground near his feet. He zigs and zags and then turns down Fifth Street.

His lungs are burning, and his legs are aching. Worse, he's heading the wrong way. He needs to find a place to hide—

He feels the hit before he hears the shot. His right thigh explodes in pain, almost causing him to lose his balance. He turns hard right and heavily limps over to the side of a house before collapsing. He needs to warn Babs. He fumbles for his radio. The pain radiating from his leg won't allow him to think straight.

Two silhouettes emerge from the street, their weapons up. Kai takes a sharp breath and exhales. This is not good.

CHAPTER FORTY-ONE

EMMIT "CHICAGO" HASKINS

NORTHWEST OF THE TWENTY-SECOND AVENUE BARRICADE
MINNEAPOLIS ARTS DISTRICT OCCUPIED ZONE

Any war veteran will often talk about having their "head on a swivel." It's not a function of paranoia but of survival. It makes sense in a combat zone but is less important in the upper Midwest.

All three spot the man running toward them long before he can see them. The Rangers split up and take cover in the little foliage that adorns the front yards in this part of the city. Tulsa stays close to Chicago in the shrubs, while Hollywood settles in behind some boxwoods a house down.

"Run, Forrest, run!" he whispers into his tactical headset.

Tulsa watches the man scream past them at a dead sprint. "Why's he running—? Never mind."

A pair of sentries is in hot pursuit. One man has a hunting rifle, while the other is carrying an AR-15. Both men are wearing identical tactical vests but aren't wearing body armor. They have black baseball hats on instead of helmets. Chicago has seen better equipment at a paintball tournament.

The sentry with the hunting rifle slows to a trot before taking a knee. He's had enough. He raises his rifle and stares into the scope mounted on it. He draws a bead and then lucks out. The man they are pursuing stops and looks to his right. He makes it one step before the bullet from the hunting rifle puts him on the ground.

"Oh, and the quarterback is toast."

"Die Hard?" Chicago asks.

"I think so," Tulsa says, frowning.

The man must have been hit in the leg. He manages to climb to his feet and limp between two houses. His pursuers lose line of sight, but that won't last long. Running won't be on his itinerary with that leg wound.

"What do you want to do, Chicago?"

"The enemy of our enemy is our friend. Let's find out who this guy is before they decide to put him down for good."

Tulsa crosses the street first, followed by Hollywood and then Chicago. This is not the best way to traverse a linear danger area, but this isn't exactly a combat situation, and they aren't up against Spetznaz. In fact, this pair of yahoos has no situational awareness whatsoever. They have no rear security or awareness of anything happening around them. Tunnel vision is a killer, and their sole focus is on the wounded man propped up against the side of a house.

That makes this easy. The three Rangers approach the two men from different vectors. Even if one of the fake soldiers turns and fires, only one of the Rangers would be in peril. They converge with their weapons up and at the ready. The barrels of their weapons barely move with each step.

"Drop the weapons if you want to live," Chicago orders when they are fifteen feet away.

The two pursuers turn in alarm. They never expected anyone to get the jump on them, much less three men dressed in woodland camo BDUs and carrying rifles or a squad automatic weapon. Their reaction is instinct. They turn their bodies as they raise their rifles to bear on the three men.

Tulsa and Chicago fire with their ARs. Hollywood has no reason to let loose with the M249 SAW. The belt ammunition is harder to come by, and there is a house with an unknown number of occupants right in front of them.

Both sentries aren't wearing body armor and take the rounds center of mass. They drop to the ground instantly. Tulsa and Hollywood check for vitals. Neither is going to make it.

"Damn it," Chicago grumbles as his comrades relieve the two men of their weapons. He turns to the bleeding man holding his leg, wondering what he did to become the prey of this hunting party.

"Are…are…they dead?" the guy leaning against the house stammers, his eyes wide enough to almost mask his Asian heritage.

"No, just really sleepy," Tulsa says, getting a look from his former squad leader.

The man's eyes dart between the two soldiers standing over him. He's in pain, likely going into shock, and clearly scared about what happens next. "Is he kidding?"

"It's gallows humor. That's kinda Tulsa's thing. Who are you?"

"Kai Z. I'm a…I'm a photojournalist."

"Of course you are. Wait. You put the video up on YouTube of these asshats burning the flag." He nods slowly. "Hollywood, patch him up. Tulsa, keep an eye on our six."

Tulsa takes a knee with his weapon at the low ready and scans the street for threats. Hollywood puts the SAW down but keeps it close. More goons are bound to be coming. Even if nobody heard the gunshots, which is unlikely, they were clearly looking for this guy.

"Here's looking at you, kid," Hollywood says as he examines the wound in Kai's right leg.

The bullet went through and through. A man's thigh has the femur and the femoral artery. Damage to the former means crutches. Significant trauma to the latter almost certainly means death. Kai was lucky. The bullet only ripped apart flesh and muscle, and he doesn't need to go under the knife to get the fragments out.

"Who are you guys?" Kai says through clenched teeth as Hollywood cinches down on a pressure dressing to stop the bleeding.

"Army Rangers."

"Rangers? Here?"

"Let's just say we're not here in an official capacity," Chicago confesses. That's as much of the story as he's willing to tell for the moment.

Chicago and Tulsa look in the direction of some distant gunfire. Hollywood's eyes never come off the road to the north. There is no knowing what is going on. They need to get off the streets.

"Listen to them. Children of the night. What music they make," Hollywood says in his best Dracula voice, which wasn't that good but better than most of his imitations.

"Is he okay?" Kai asks.

"No," Tulsa and Chicago simultaneously answer.

"Can we get him back to the house?" Tulsa asks. "I don't want to sit here and listen to Hollywood run through AFI's top one hundred movie quotes all night."

"I need you to take me to my place."

"You're not in a position to make demands, buddy. Just because we saved your ass doesn't mean we're taking orders from you."

Chicago puts a hand on Tulsa's arm before looking down at Kai. "Where is it?"

"University Ave near Lowry."

"Too far and too close to their northern border. Our place is closer," Chicago says, shaking his head. "You'll be safe there until things calm down."

"There's no place like home," Hollywood muses.

"Then let me go."

"He can move, but he won't be going fast on that leg," Tulsa warns.

"I feel the need…the need for speed."

"Sure, you're free to go," Chicago says, ignoring Hollywood. "Just understand something. These clowns were aiming to kill you, probably because you're pissing them off with your videos. They're looking for you, and there's no chance you'll make it all the way to University Avenue. We'll be lucky to make it to Fifth Street, but at least we're armed. What are you going to do? Photograph them to death?"

Kai lowers his eyes. Tulsa has a different reaction. "I'm not carrying his ass."

"I can walk," the YouTuber says, gingerly climbing to his feet. "Sorta."

"We'll take it slow and move through yards. Street crossings will only happen when we know they're clear. Understood?"

"You know that neighbors could alert the sentries," Tulsa warns.

Chicago looks at the houses across the street. "I don't think these goons made any friends tonight. It's our only option. Radio Nica and give him a sitrep. Tell him we're RTB, and we'll approach the house from the east. Make sure he doesn't shoot us."

"Roger that."

Kai takes a few steps, fighting the pain that's probably shooting up his leg. Tulsa finishes up his advisory to Nica back at the house and nods. They're expecting them.

At least they can avoid friendly fire. It's the unfriendly kind they need to concern themselves with now.

"Chicago? What do we do if a patrol spots us?" Tulsa asks.

Both men look to their leader for guidance. This isn't a warzone. Chicago is willing to bet that a lot of these sentries don't understand what they got themselves involved in. He doesn't want to go around killing people. He also doesn't want to face the alternative of not defending themselves when they should.

"What we need to. Let's roll."

CHAPTER FORTY-TWO

LANDON TAYSON

UNIVERSITY AVENUE COMMAND CENTER
MINNEAPOLIS ARTS DISTRICT OCCUPIED ZONE

The coverage of the firefight at the barricade hasn't been kind. The media are often useful idiots, and they have more or less been sympathetic to Landon and his small army they continue to call "protesters." They are not openly supporting the establishment of the ADOZ, but they were inclined to outline the circumstances for its creation.

That has changed. The ambulance tried to ram the barricade, and somehow, it's being portrayed as Landon's fault. What were his men supposed to do? If they had let it pass, the police would only have become more emboldened to do the same. The casualties are regrettable, but it's the fault of the Minneapolis PD, not him. He wants to reach through the television and choke the smug anchor to death with his bare hands.

Muzzie enters the office without knocking, his trusted lieutenant Artie in tow. This is not good news. The look on their faces would almost lead Landon to think they had just tried kimchee for the first time. As if he doesn't have enough to deal with.

"What is it?" Landon proactively asks.

"Sir, we had a sighting of Kai Z near the Twenty-Second Avenue barricade. It's possible that he recorded the scene. Our men fired at him, and he fled. We gave chase."

"Where is he?"

Lieutenant Stein looks down at his shoes. "He escaped."

"Mr. President, two of our men had him pinned down but were somehow killed trying to take him into custody," Muzzie says, his tone dripping in anger. "Their weapons and ammunition were removed from their bodies."

"Captain, are you telling me that a prima donna YouTuber killed two heavily armed sentries?"

"No, sir. I'm saying that we lost two men. We're not sure how. I think we have to face the fact that the police or FBI may have personnel in the ADOZ. Kai Z got help from somebody. Even if he did manage to take down our men, which I doubt, he wouldn't have taken their arms. He would have run like hell."

That revelation poses a bigger problem. Landon thought the ADOZ was secure. The roving patrols are meant to keep the citizens in check, not root out a clandestine police force. And they killed two of his men. What does that mean? Only Kai can answer those questions.

"Find him, Muzzie. Find him fast. Double or triple the roving patrols if you need to. Have Raven start seeing if she can discern possible hiding places. He needs to eat and sleep. I want to know where."

"Yes, sir."

Landon nods at the sentry outside their command center and turns into the parking area. There are a few vehicles here, and the pop-up tents they had set up in Logan Park were relocated to better assist the badging process. Empty tables and unoccupied folding chairs are monuments to the small workforce that will man them in the morning.

There is still so much to do. Landon thought they would have progressed further than this once the ADOZ was established. Raven was less convinced before they began this journey, and she is proving to be correct. The shootout at the barricade will only slow things down.

The stress is starting to wear on him. The events of the day were bad enough, but it's the fallout that Landon is most concerned about. He needs the people on his side. Their support is the main contributor to police inaction. The feckless fools who run this city have no backbone. The only way they will take action is when the vast majority of the public demands it. Even Raven agrees with that conclusion.

Landon strolls along the side of the building toward the far end of the fenced-in parking area. The movement feels good, and the cooler night air is almost soothing. It allows him to think more clearly.

Maybe that's what the police planned? Would they be so callous as to have innocent paramedics purposely run the barricade, knowing their possible fate? It's not inconceivable. The government has done far worse than that to its citizens. They use people all the time.

The thought causes Landon to smile. The government of the people, by the people, for the—

A hand clamps onto his chin and forces his mouth closed. Landon immediately tries to lunge when a figure in a blank ski mask materializes in front of him. He doesn't say anything other than with his fist. The strike hits Landon in the solar plexus, causing his diaphragm to convulse and knock the air out of his lungs. He'd scream if he could…but he can't.

The man behind him lets go of his face, and his jaw opens to allow more air in. With lightning speed, a gag is placed into his mouth and pulled tight. The man in front of him sidesteps and kicks his foot in a sweeping action. His shins explode in pain as he's pushed forward and planted on the ground. His wrists are bound, the plastic clicking sound of zip ties piercing the quiet night.

Landon strains to see his attackers. He lifts his head higher, mistakenly making it easier to put a nylon bag over it. The bottom is cinched, and he's hauled off the ground by men with a vise grip on each of his arms. They push him forward.

He hasn't regained his wind, and screaming with a gag in his mouth is pointless. Fear seizes him, but there is no fighting against the two guys who have a hold on him.

He's walked forward. *Please, please…somebody needs to have seen this.* There are always people around the command center. Only he hears no shouts or sounds of alarm.

Despite the gag and bag over his head, it's the absence of conversation that's the most unnerving. These men know what their mission is. Maybe they're using hand signals, which would still imply confidence. Whoever these guys are, they're professionals.

The acoustics change, and his foot hits what may be a small step or threshold. He's indoors, still in the ADOZ, and not far from the command post. *Have the police been there the whole time spying on them?* A hundred scenarios run through his mind, fighting with his panic for attention.

He hears the scraping of metal against the floor before he's pushed down into a chair. One of the men keeps his hand on Landon's shoulder, and not in a gentle, reassuring way. He's making sure there is no attempt to get up.

Landon can hear men shuffling around the room. Finally, he hears a whisper. The energy changes. Someone of authority must have walked in. *They aren't going to hurt him,* he convinces himself. *They're law enforcement. He may be placed under arrest, but he won't be tortured.*

"Well, if it isn't the great leader of the ADOZ. You're not so untouchable after all, are you, Mr. President?"

Landon would respond if he could. It's not the black fabric bag over his head but the gag in his mouth that keeps him from responding. When the bag is unceremoniously pulled off, his eyes are greeted with bright white light that washes his vision out. He squints and turns his head to fight the brightness searing his retinas.

He feels a tug on the gag and fingers brushing the back of his neck as the knot is undone. When the material falls from his mouth, Landon exercises his jaw. As his eyes adjust to the light and focus, he expects to see a phalanx of Minnesota law enforcement or maybe even the FBI. Instead, he sees the one man he never expected.

CHAPTER FORTY-THREE
FIELD OFFICER DAVID BRASS

Brass waits for the man's eyes to adjust. The lighting in this storeroom is beyond bright. At some point, the owner of this retail shop switched out the incandescent or compact fluorescent lighting for 1250-lumen 6500K daylight LEDs. Nobody is taking a nap during work hours in this room when the light is on.

Most of the storefronts in the Arts District have been closed since the takeover. This location had two things going for it – the absence of an alarm system and the proximity to Landon's "command center." The owner may figure out that someone was here when he or she returns, but nothing will be taken from the shelves. No harm, no foul. They only need to borrow the space for a bit.

"David? Wh-what are you doing here?"

"You aren't returning my messages, Landon."

"I've been busy."

Brass half scoffs and half chuckles. "That's not how this works."

"How did you get here?"

"I run a very capable organization. What you know only scratches the surface of the truth. And your perimeter isn't as solid as you think it is. It wasn't difficult."

Brass has been cagey with Landon about who he works for, and with good reason. The man despises the government and wouldn't react well if he found out he was being supported by the CIA, of all agencies. So far as the young leader of the ADOZ is concerned, Brass works for a private military contractor. Or he runs a PMC. The details aren't important.

"It's dangerous for you to be here."

"More dangerous for you, I think," Brass says, gesturing at the imposing masked men gathered around him. "To answer your next question, I'm here because I'm contemplating a change in leadership. Considering you are calling yourself a president, that would make this a coup."

"A coup? Why? You're the one supporting me!"

"I support you because our interests align," Brass counters. "My corporate concern supports you because I told them to. What do you think happens when they don't?"

Landon's nostrils flare as he presses his lips together. "We have an arrangement."

"We do, and part of it is you not being an insufferable idiot. I've given you everything you asked for. You have an arsenal at your disposal and mindless automatons who will follow your every order."

"And I created the ADOZ, just as I promised."

Brass moves over to a shelf and picks up a bottle of liquid cleanser. He inspects it, not because he's actually interested in its contents. He wants young Landon to think about what he plans on doing with it.

"You don't get it. This isn't about seizing a chunk of Minneapolis. It's about creating a movement that will endure. Nothing you've done here is inspiring anybody to fill your ranks."

"And yet, reinforcements are on their way. Thousands of people from across the country are joining our revolution."

"Are they? I can stop those convoys with one call."

"You wouldn't. You said you support me."

Brass rolls his eyes and pulls a weapon out of one of his men's holsters. "I support the cause. *You* are expendable."

To make his point, he holds the gun to Landon's head. He doesn't really want to kill him, but intentions are known only if you publicize them. The kid cocks his head to one side, trying to move it away from the Glock. As if that would make any difference.

"Everyone in this ADOZ serves you. And you serve me. I am the man behind the curtain. I can replace you before your dead body hits the ground. Do you need me to demonstrate?"

"No."

"Good," Brass says, removing the weapon from the man's head. "Then get things under control."

"They *are* under control."

Brass claps his hands once in excitement. "Excellent! Then you've found and neutralized Kai Z."

Landon Tayson has a big mouth and likes to use it. Most of their interactions were over the phone on SMS messages, but he did nothing but talk the few times they spoke, and the couple of times they met face-to-face. It's almost bizarre seeing him speechless.

The corner of Brass's mouth curls. "What? You don't think I watch YouTube? I admittedly don't spend much time on it, but considering every news outlet in the country showed you burning an American flag, it was hard to miss."

"It's unfortunate that got out."

"I'd say."

There's a long pause in the conversation. Brass's men don't move an inch, making the silence in the crowded storeroom that much creepier. Landon doesn't want to admit the truth. He screwed up, and he's not the kind of man that easily admits his mistakes. Finally, David's patience wears thin.

"Well?"

"I have patrols looking for him. We'll find him."

Brass bites his top lip. "Are there any other issues I should know about? Anything that will derail this movement?"

"Nothing that can't be handled."

"Good. Start demonstrating your worth by getting that homeowner to take his flag down. People are taking notice of his defiance, and we can't have that. You have an army at your disposal. It shouldn't be that difficult. Unless there is a reason for your inaction."

"No. We were handling it when the house fire broke out. That was the priority."

"Make this the new one. The ADOZ isn't a place. It's an idea – a movement that will inspire others. That's the goal. Understood?"

"Yes."

"Don't let me down, Landon. You know I'll be watching. The next time it comes to this, you won't be walking out of the room."

A guard moves behind Landon and cuts the zip ties binding his wrists. The kid rubs his wrists and nods, slowly rising from his metal folding chair and exiting the storeroom. Brass doesn't say anything until he hears him use the front door.

"Let's move out."

Brass doesn't think the president of the ADOZ would be stupid enough to send a patrol here, but that's not a chance worth taking. They will leave the area the way they came in – the only one Landon and his minions forgot to guard. He wonders if the kid will figure it out. Not that it matters. Brass got what he wanted out of this meeting.

CHAPTER FORTY-FOUR

CHIEF VANESSA CAMPBELL

CITY HALL CONFERENCE ROOM
MINNEAPOLIS, MINNESOTA

Sleep is a luxury none of them can afford. Exhaustion has set in with a majority of the Minneapolis police force, and Vanessa is acutely feeling its effects. She glances at the clock on the wall. It's just after midnight, and today is bound to be longer than yesterday was.

"Well, this is a mess," Governor St. James decries, entering the room and taking his seat at the head of the conference table. "What happened at the barricade?"

Fresh in from St. Paul, he looks more rested and less stressed than she, Burke, and Thurlow do. The mayor gestures to Vanessa. She briefs the governor on the events leading up to the firefight, what transpired when Otto Goldberg began his negotiation, and the aftermath of the deadly exchange of gunfire. The governor listens intently, asking only two very specific questions during the monologue. He nods after she finishes.

"Your bravery in retrieving our fallen first responders under such difficult circumstances is commendable," St. James says to Burke, who nods in appreciation. "And the ambulance driver did this on his own?"

"So the chief says," Mayor Thurlow spews.

She purses her lips slightly. "No orders were given to the contrary."

"If we were planning a breach of the barricade, it would have been my men in that ambulance, not EMTs," Burke says.

The governor again nods before turning to the mayor. "What are your plans to deal with this?"

"We're going to wait them out. We figure there are only about eight hundred of them. Many were protesters at City Hall who fled that way after the tear gas was deployed. They're going to get tired and bored…once their numbers dwindle, there will be cracks in the perimeter. Then we go in."

"Chief, do you concur with this course of action?"

She's done running interference between these two elected officials. They are in the middle of a crisis, so politics be damned. Both need to step up and exhibit some leadership. She only needs to stay as professional as possible while telling them that.

"First, I believe they have more than a thousand fighters. Second, that plan is based on a lot of assumptions."

"Chief Campbell wants direct action," Thurlow interjects, "which I think could result in a bloodbath."

"That is a risk," Vanessa admits. "However, I believe that the ADOZ is more manageable now than it could be in a week or a month. The assumption is that they will grow weary. What if they don't?"

Thurlow crosses his arms and leans back in his chair. "They will. It's human nature."

Governor St. James rubs his chin. "What if you're wrong, Elliott? What if they don't get tired and go home?"

"They will. I'm certain of it."

Vanessa isn't so sure. She shakes her head just enough that the governor catches her body language. She may not like the man, but he's the lesser of two evils in this room.

"Mr. Mayor, the FBI has remained on the sidelines, but I have been personally briefed by them. There is an interstate component to the ADOZ. The feds believe that the guns, along with many of the men wielding them, crossed state lines to get there. Have you discussed this with them?"

Thurlow shifts in his chair. "No, I haven't."

"I see. Well, between the feds' information and what other governors have relayed to me, five large convoys are heading to Minneapolis as we speak. The closest is two days away, and there are at least four hundred people in it. Two others are larger." The governor leans forward. "Manpower isn't going to be a problem for them much longer."

Vanessa doesn't outwardly react. She didn't know about the convoys but isn't surprised at the governor's revelation either. There is an unhealthy percentage of people in this country who believe in what Landon Tayson is doing. Too many are eager to join his cause.

"They shouldn't be allowed to come here."

"We are not under martial law, Mr. Mayor. Unless they are breaking laws, I have no authority to stop them."

"Then we will stop them at our perimeter around the ADOZ."

"Under what auspices?" Vanessa asks. "We have the same issue. Our perimeter can keep civilians out for their safety, but we can't physically stop anyone from coming or going, per your orders."

The mayor likely doesn't remember issuing that. He's been shooting from the hip since this started. He doesn't have a plan other than waiting and hoping the problem goes away so he can get back to cutting her budget.

"The governor can declare a state of emergency."

"Why would I do that, Elliott? You said you would handle it and haven't asked for one. I distinctly remember telling you to ensure I didn't need to get involved. Are you saying you can no longer manage this crisis? Just say the words."

He's not going to say them. The two men glare at each other across the table, mired in a contest of wills defined by stubbornness and stupidity. Ego will prevent either from doing the right thing unless she acts. This may cost her job, but Vanessa is beyond caring at this point.

"Governor, we need you to declare a state of emergency in Minneapolis and order a National Guard mobilization to support law enforcement. I would also appreciate any state resources you can spare to help police my city and keep its citizens safe."

The governor nods. "Okay. I will act upon your request at once, Chief Campbell."

This is going to cause a media frenzy. Everyone will wonder why Thurlow didn't ask for this earlier. The governor is going to crucify him. Vanessa doesn't really care about any of that. She's worried about the people behind enemy lines.

CHAPTER FORTY-FIVE
KAI Z

THE FIFTH STREET HOUSE
MINNEAPOLIS ARTS DISTRICT OCCUPIED ZONE

The coast was clear, so the three men took the risk of moving straight down Fifth Street to the house. If it were just them, they could have covered the distance very quickly. They are or were Rangers. Physical fitness is a big thing in the Regiment.

But they had baggage. Kai Z is ambulatory, but a gunshot wound to the leg is bound to slow anyone down. Still, it's faster than moving through back yards. Nica was waiting at the door when they reached it and entered.

"More house guests?" he chides. "Are you turning this place into an Airbnb?"

"No, but you know I'm a sucker for strays. Bronx, you're a combat lifesaver. This hero was shot in the thigh. Can you take a look at it?"

The big man moves to their casualty after they plop him on the recliner and elevate his legs. Bronx peeks at the bandage. "Damn, Chicago, who patched him up?"

"Hollywood."

"Did you forget everything about first aid when you left the Army?"

"It's just a flesh wound," he says in his best British accent, offering a little shrug before accepting the beer Tulsa hands him.

"Monty Python. Nice," Kai says.

"Don't encourage him. Please," Nashville pleads as Tulsa hands their guest a rain grenade.

"All right. You wanna tell us why the sentries were chasing you?"

Kai looks at Chicago and smirks as he cracks open his beer. "I'm not well-liked."

"Clearly."

"I'm a YouTuber. I shoot—"

"We know who you are," Nica interrupts, putting his hands on his hips.

"Did you see the big flag on the roof?" Nashville asks.

"It was tough to miss."

"We had to help Chicago build it because I showed him your video of them burning the first one."

"Chicago?" Kai asks.

"Yeah. We go by the geographic names of where we're from. The big guy working on your leg is Bronx. Mr. movie quote here is Hollywood. That's Nica, Tulsa, and Nashville."

"Nica?"

"As in Nicaragua," the staff sergeant clarifies.

"Got it. I'm Kai, but you can call me Inazawa. It's my Japanese hometown."

"We'll stick with Kai," Chicago concludes as all six men shake their heads. "What do you know about what's going on here?"

"Probably about as much as you do. But I'll tell you this…there's more to it than we know."

"What do you mean?" Tulsa asks before anyone else can.

"You guys were military. You know how to conduct complex operations. Setting up the ADOZ had a level of organization that I've never seen. It was being established even before the protest went to hell near City Hall. And the guns…I was at the Seattle CHAZ in 2020. They were armed there, but it was nothing like this. No, this was planned, and I mean planned long in advance."

"By who? Landon Tayson?"

Kai shrugs. "I have no idea, but I doubt it. He's a figurehead. Is there anything he's done that's impressed you?"

"Not really," a couple of Rangers simultaneously mutter.

"Me neither. That means someone in a foreign government or a well-financed private interest has a hand in this. My first guess is that it's someone in our government."

Chicago looks at the man like he has three heads. "Did you hit your head after you were shot? The government wouldn't support something like this."

Kai lets out a breath. "The one thing you learn in my line of work is that the conspiracy theories everyone likes to mock are closer to the truth than you think. MK-ULTRA was a real program testing LSD on soldiers. The CIA was peddling drugs to Americans. The FBI did spy on John Lennon. The COVID-19 virus did start in a Chinese lab using gain of function research funded by our own government."

"9/11 was an inside job?" Nashville mocks.

"I'm not willing to say that…yet. What I am saying is that, under the right circumstances, the government could absolutely somehow be involved in this. Look, I know you guys are DoD. It's hard for you to have the perspective I have."

"These guys do have a lot of guns."

"Yeah, news flash, it's America, Nashville," Tulsa argues.

"I know, but all AR-15s? I could see if these yahoos were toting six-shooters and hunting rifles, but c'mon, man. They brought an arsenal to this party. I'm not ready to wear my tin foil hat, but you have to admit that it's fishy."

Kai stares at the beer in his hands. The more he talks about this, the more he's convincing himself that it's the part of the story he never considered. His reporting focused on the events in the ADOZ but not the *point* of its creation. Maybe that's what he really needs to be doing – uncovering the dark truth behind who is backing Landon and his band of marauding insurgents. If there is a link to the government he can uncover, his channel will make social media history.

"Why would the government be involved in this?" Nica asks, walking over to the front window and peering out.

"People think the government is this big monolith," Kai explains. "It isn't. Most of the time, one arm doesn't know what the rest of the body is doing. There is no great federal hive mind where they're all on the same page."

"We are the Borg. Lower your shields and surrender your ships. We will add your biological and technological distinctiveness to our own. Your culture will adapt to service us. Resistance is futile."

Kai narrows his eyes before appealing to Chicago. "Is he okay?"

"No," they all answer.

"Anyway, I'm not saying this was sanctioned by the Oval Office. But a splinter group of some three-letter agency? Yeah, I'd almost bet on it at this point."

"Why? Why do you believe the government is involved?"

Kai takes a long swig from his beer and wipes his mouth. "I've come to know how the CIA and these clandestine organizations work. Trust me, to borrow from the movie *The Skulls*, 'If it's secret and elite, it can't be good.'

"I've been to dozens of protests. I know many of the players. They're ideologically driven and very motivated. What they aren't is proficient in tactics or administration. This ADOZ came together too perfectly. I watched them unloading a van full of guns. Someone is helping them, and I want to know who and why."

Bronx finishes dressing Kai's leg wound. He should go to a hospital, but there is no time for that right now. They would never let him out of the ADOZ. If he did manage to sneak out, he could never get back in. He has a new mission, and that is more important.

"Is that why you were poking around the barricades?" Bronx asks.

"Not exactly. I heard about the fire and wanted footage for my channel."

"So, you're a grifter?" Nica says with a sneer.

Kai's face turns red, and he takes a deep breath. He hates being called that. A grifter is a con man who uses deception or fraud to swindle people. That's not what his channel or his reporting is about.

"I report the news from a perspective nobody else has. I've been in the middle of riots, confronted Antifa demonstrators, and gotten my ass kicked a few times in the process. And, yeah, I make a few bucks off my channel being monetized. If you want to call me a grifter for earning a living, fine. But the mainstream media doesn't have reporters in the ADOZ. Only I can bring the truth of what's really happening here to the world."

"Only you? That sounds a little conceited."

"It's a fact. No reporter for ABC or CNN is going to risk their lives for a story."

"You'll have to forgive my friends," Nashville says. "Serving in Uncle Sam's Army tends to bring out someone's cynical side."

"Whatever. I appreciate the rescue more than you know, but can you get me back to the place I'm staying? I need to review this footage with my colleague and then package it for upload."

"We have to wait for things to calm down a little. The sentries are amped up, and the roving patrols are no doubt looking for you. Once the dust settles, a couple of my guys will sneak you up there. Fair?"

Kai nods. "Fair."

"Good. Now, tell us everything you know about Landon Tayson."

"Yeah, it looks like you can ask him yourself, Chicago," Nica says, peering through the blinds out the front window.

"What do you mean?"

He gives his friend a grave look. "I mean that he just pulled up outside with half a platoon of men."

CHAPTER FORTY-SIX

LANDON TAYSON

He has already been to this house too many times. This time, Landon brought twenty other guys. One way or another, that flag on the roof is coming down before lunch. Yesterday's firefight at the barricade was a revelation. He has to show everyone that he's serious. That was the first step. This is the next.

He only wishes that Muzzie were here. In the wake of the firefight, he's been personally visiting every point on the perimeter to ensure his men are alert, doing the right thing, and have an understanding of their orders. It's also to keep up morale. They took their first casualties yesterday, courtesy of the MPD. They need to ensure that it doesn't have an adverse impact on the men manning the perimeter.

Landon takes two steps forward and stares at the house. It's quiet on the street, so he isn't going to bother with his trusty megaphone for this.

"Chicago? That was your name, right? You in there?"

"Yeah, I'm here," a voice says from one of the upstairs windows.

"Come out and talk to me."

"Nah, I'm good."

Landon shakes his head. This guy has a set of balls on him.

"I see you didn't heed my warning," he calls out.

"No, it's more like I ignored your empty threat."

"Well, you're about to find out that it's not so empty. That flag is coming down. It's either going to be you willingly taking it down or us doing it by force."

"Come and take it."

If that's what he wants, that's what he'll get. Landon nods at Artie, who orders three men to break down the front door. They stroll up, their rifles at the low ready but not pointed at the house. There's no point in being overly antagonistic.

A shotgun blast from a different upstairs window shatters the peaceful quiet of the street. A tuft of grass pops up ten feet away from the trio, causing them to freeze.

"That was your only warning, Landon," Chicago says. "If anyone approaches this house, we will defend ourselves."

At least two of the three guys in the house are watching the front from the second floor. Landon assumes the third guy is probably behind the door. He should send guys around back, but they'll be observed. Chicago and his buddies will adjust positions inside if they're smart. He needs to convince these guys that fighting is hopeless.

"Be sensible, Chicago. There are three of you and twenty of us, with a whole lot more I can call."

The man laughs. "Then I suggest you make that call to help you even the odds."

"He's bluffing," Lieutenant Stein offers.

Artie may be right. He may be wrong. There is only one way to find out. Landon signals the three fighters standing in the street forward. This time, they raise their rifles and point them at the house before running toward the small stoop at the front door.

A shot rings out, and one of them drops. It wasn't a shotgun blast. That came from a rifle. A second shot catches a second fighter in the leg. The third man immediately retreats.

The men around Landon scurry behind the vehicles. He wastes no time doing the same. Nobody returns fire. They are all waiting for instructions from their leaders.

"We should light them up and storm into that house," the lieutenant says.

Another rifle reports, and Landon hears a window in one of the vehicles behind him shatter. They have the numbers, but the guys in the house have the high ground, and there is no element of surprise. They can't do much about the former, but they can about the latter.

"No. I have a better idea. Order everyone to mount up."

"Sir! We can't give up!"

"We're not," Landon says, peeking over the hood at the house. "Just using a different tactic."

"What about my men?" the lieutenant asks.

Landon catches movement out of the corner of his eye. A drone is hovering over the road about six houses down. He doesn't know how long it's been there, but its presence could be to their benefit this time.

"Order some of your men to disarm and retrieve them."

"What if they get shot?"

He points at the quadcopter lingering down the street. "Then our use of excessive force will be more than justified, and the world will understand why we leveled this house with everything we have."

Artie relays the order to four of his men, none of whom look enthusiastic about the task. After some prompting, they do what they're told and move out to the other side of the street to collect the casualties. Landon holds his breath as he awaits a reaction from the men in the house. Nothing happens.

The two wounded men are loaded in the rearmost SUV, and the men climb into the vehicles. Landon is the last to move. He opens the door and turns to the house.

"This isn't over, Chicago!"

"I didn't expect it to be. But you should reconsider that, for your sake."

Landon takes a hard last look. "This guy just signed his death warrant," he mumbles to himself as he climbs in the vehicle and slams the door.

First the fire, then the ambulance trying to run the barricade, the visit from his benefactor, and now this. It's been a rough fourteen hours. If this isn't taken care of quickly, the next fourteen could be just as bad. The thought has just given Landon an idea.

"Go around the block," he orders the driver.

"Why?"

"I have an idea that solves this problem."

The driver goes south, cuts over to Sixth Street, and then heads north, stopping at the intersection of Twentieth Avenue. They have vehicles they can use. They have materials. They have the manpower. This should work, even if it isn't the most elegant solution.

"What's the plan, Mr. President?"

"It's time for you to command your first mission, Lieutenant Stein. You're going to get the chance for some payback for what happened to your men."

Artie's chest fills with pride. It's what Landon wants to see. The young lieutenant can handle this. Best of all, if it goes wrong, he has someone to pin the blame on. Either way, Chicago and his friends are about to die.

CHAPTER FORTY-SEVEN
EMMIT "CHICAGO" HASKINS

THE FIFTH STREET HOUSE
MINNEAPOLIS ARTS DISTRICT OCCUPIED ZONE

He did what he had to do. That's what Chicago keeps telling himself as he takes his eyes away from the ACOG on his rifle and watches the convoy pull out. They had bad intentions. It was an imminent threat, and the men were a real danger to him and his friends. He wonders if a prosecutor will see it that way.

"They're retreating," Tulsa says over the headset.

"Received a coded retreat message we have."

"Thank you, Master Yoda," Nashville says, mocking Hollywood. "But not for long. We drew first blood. Only a fool would think they aren't going to be back."

"My money's after sunset," Bronx says from his position on the back side of the house.

"Let's circle up," Chicago says, leading the men down the stairs and into the living room. They are greeted with knowing nods from Tulsa and Bronx, who were watching the front and back doors while Nica babysat their guest.

"Nice shooting, Brother. You okay?"

Chicago shakes his head. "There's no telling what they would have done once they came through that door, Nica."

"You shot them?" Kai asks, probably wishing his guardian had allowed him to shoot a video of it. That's why he was keeping the journalist close. "Are they dead?"

"Yeah. I don't do home invasions."

"They were Americans!"

An unpleasant thought seeps into Chicago's mind. When he was a teenager, some neighbors down the street were victims of a home invasion. It was South Chicago, so crime wasn't unheard of in his neighborhood. This one was brutal. Two assailants shot a man in cold blood in his kitchen and repeatedly raped his thirteen-year-old daughter. The guys were eventually caught, but the damage was done. She committed suicide a year later. They were Americans, too.

"So were the two guys who shot you, buddy," Tulsa says, dragging Chicago from that nasty stroll down memory lane.

"You gave them fair warning," Nashville adds. "They had it coming."

"You should have shot Landon so we could end this, Chicago," Bronx surmises.

That's a favorite hypothetical in the military. When soldiers have too much downtime, the craziest subjects come up. He spent a couple of hours musing whether they would have shot Hitler before he started World War II if they had the chance. The answer was a resounding "yes," but that comes with the benefit of hindsight. Who could know what would have happened had Hitler not risen to power? Maybe Stalin would have taken his place, like in the *Red Alert* video games. That war likely wouldn't have been any better.

He could have killed the president of the ADOZ very easily. But, despite his takeover of part of an American city, he isn't Hitler. He wasn't the one with the weapons heading toward Chicago's front door. He wasn't the threat. In combat, there is a difference between doing one's duty and committing murder. Chicago knows that if he lined his sights up on Landon Tayson and pulled the trigger, he would have wandered into morally ambiguous territory.

"I'm not gonna make his ass a martyr."

"I'm glad you're drawing a line somewhere," Kai moans.

"Ideals are peaceful. History is violent," Hollywood says, quoting Wardaddy from *Fury*.

"As much as it pains me to admit it, he's right," Nica says.

"I've watched your videos, Kai," Nashville adds. "You know a thing or two about violence. Chicago didn't pick this fight – they did. We told them multiple times to leave us alone. They made a choice not to let it go. They reaped the consequences. It's that simple."

It's not that simple, but the YouTuber doesn't look like he's willing to challenge them. He would likely be dead or worse had they not intervened when he was pinned against a house and bleeding out.

"Were they looking for me?" Kai asks.

"Nah," Chicago says, crashing into the sofa and putting his feet up on the coffee table. "This was about us and the flagpole on my roof. They don't know you're here."

"Speaking of which…."

"Yeah, I hear ya, Nashville. We need to get Kai out of here before the toy soldiers take another run at us."

"Now, I want you to remember that no bastard ever won a war by dying for his country. He won it by making the other poor dumb bastard die for his country."

"Hollywood's *Patton* impression sucks, but he ain't completely wrong," Bronx says. "Three of us can handle twenty of them. If they come with more, it's gonna take all of us to defend this place."

Chicago sits up and looks around the house. It's a wooden structure with a number of approach avenues from two sides, with neighbors blocking the north and south. That's two men each, and that would be the bare minimum to mount a resistance against a determined assault. Even with proper fortifications and the weapons they have, it would take a staunch defense will all hands on deck to deter.

"He's not going to risk a frontal assault after that demonstration," Nica argues.

"He also ain't going to go away quietly, either," Nashville counters.

"Nica, Nashville…we'll wait until EENT, then can you guys get Kai where he needs to go?"

The end of evening nautical twilight, known in the military as EENT, is the point at which the center of the evening sun is twelve degrees below the horizon. It marks the end of nautical twilight and the beginning of astronomical twilight. It's also the time when the horizon becomes difficult to distinguish, but there is too much light for night vision. The Army considers it prime time for possible enemy attacks.

"Yeah, we'll get him there."

"Good. We'll rotate watches until then. The rest of us will stand to once you leave. While you're out there, do some recon. I'm betting they're planning something after nightfall. That means they'll stage somewhere in the area. Drop Kai off and then find out what they are up to and report."

CHAPTER FORTY-EIGHT
FIELD OFFICER DAVID BRASS

CARRIAGE HOUSE RENTAL
MINNEAPOLIS, MINNESOTA

This is more space than Brass needs, but he isn't paying the bill. Instead of opting for a hotel, he wanted the privacy that comes with an online rental that still has easy access to the downtown and the airport. He also wanted a place he could check in under an alias without much fuss.

The carriage house is in Loring Park, a few blocks from the Walker Art Center and a short walk to the downtown area. David has full use of the kitchen, entertainment area, and bedrooms. As a bonus, it has dedicated off-street parking and is only seven miles from Minneapolis-St. Paul International Airport.

After releasing the ops team back to whatever assignment they were working on, he told them to keep their phone on. He hopes their services won't be needed again, but they are a good card to keep in his hand in case a problem should arise. And one likely will.

Brass checks his watch. It's nearly three in the afternoon. He missed lunch, which would explain why his stomach is growling. It's a little early for dinner, but any hunger pains he feels tonight is why the midnight snack was invented.

His phone dings, and he checks the display.

> **Nightshade**
> *Mission to remove the flag failed.*

> **Brass**
> *Failed?*

> **Nightshade**
> *Two men killed. Trying again tonight with a different tactic.*

Brass shakes his head and types. The fist is clenching, but at least his pep talk had the desired effect.

> **Brass**
> *Keep me informed. I expect results. Keep it off the television.*

Nightshade
Will do. You will get results.

He doubts that and tosses the phone on the sofa cushion next to him. There is a decided difference between being an agitator and a leader. Mobilizing people is a different skill set than running a city…or part of one. The ADOZ is falling apart, and the lack of good leadership is hastening its demise.

Brass would love to milk this for a few weeks, but the occupation won't last that long. They're so inept that they can't even manage to take a flag down. Sooner or later, a weakness will be exploited, the police will finally act, and the whole thing will come crashing down. That's fine, so long as there are fireworks at the end. Pendulum's success doesn't necessarily hinge on the ADOZ's longevity – only its ability to churn stories in the media covering it. That can be accomplished in its life and even its death. In some respects, the latter may be even more desirable.

David picks the phone up off the cushion and places a call. The key to success in any endeavor is thinking ahead. Planning isn't about what you want to happen, but ensuring you're in a position to act for anything that *does* happen. The best part of his job is he can shape the events that transpire.

"I don't have an answer for you, Brass," Remsen says after accepting the call.

"Oh, well, I'm glad I didn't ask a question."

"You were going to ask about the Railspike leak."

Brass smirks. Matt thinks he's so smart. "Not this time. A bigger problem just landed on my desk that I could use your expertise with."

"Anything I can do to help," the fed says, his voice an octave or two higher. "What's up?"

"We got some HUMINT about that Minneapolis ADOZ."

Human intelligence is the gathering of information from actual people through debriefing, interrogation, surveillance, and recruitment of informants. Unlike its signals or open-source counterparts, it can be messy and difficult to cultivate. The risks and efforts are worth the rewards. It is often the most valuable source because the information derived typically cannot be gleaned using other methods.

"Who's the source?"

Brass scowls. "That's highly classified, Matt. Let's simply say he's well-placed, considered reliable, and in a position to know."

"A state actor?"

That question would usually go unanswered. Classified means classified, even if the information is being shared with a sister intelligence agency and a man with an appropriate security clearance. Not that any of this matters. Brass is lying his ass off, so it's not like there is an actual source to protect.

"Yeah."

"FBI counterintelligence concluded that this ADOZ is a domestic problem."

"I know. I think that's an erroneous finding, but I can't prove it…yet."

"And you need my help?" Matt asks.

"I think I know how we can start making connections. Several convoys are heading to Minnesota from other states."

"Yeah, the FBI is tracking them. We don't have cause to stop any of them. No laws are being broken."

"What if I was to tell you that I have it on good authority that they are carrying guns across state lines with the intent of participating in an insurrection?"

"Nobody has labeled it that yet."

"The governor is about to. He's mobilizing the Guard."

That's probably news to Remsen. It's likely not common knowledge outside the governor's office. Fortunately, people like to talk, and others like to listen to what they say. Be in the right place at the right time, and there's almost nothing you can't learn. Brass doesn't much care if the governor calls in the National Guard. Knowing that he's about to issue that order is what he needs.

"All right. I don't know if the Hoover Building will listen to me, but I'll see if I can get them to intercept a convoy. Which one do you want us to stop?"

"All of them."

"You don't ask for much," Matt says sarcastically. "Do you have any idea what shitstorm this will cause if they aren't armed?"

"They will be. If they aren't, then tell the agents on the scene to get imaginative. I know the FBI has rules, and I know that you all know how to bend them. These guys are planning to actively support an insurrection. Some could call it a terrorist action. Those convoys cannot make it to the state line."

"I'll make some calls."

Brass disconnects and leans back into the sofa. Without reinforcements, Landon will get desperate. He will feel his grip on power slipping and tighten his fist. Now, the only thing left to decide is how to give the action thriller lovers in this country the climax to the ADOZ they are tuning into the news for.

CHAPTER FORTY-NINE
EMMIT "CHICAGO" HASKINS

THE FIFTH STREET HOUSE
MINNEAPOLIS ARTS DISTRICT OCCUPIED ZONE

"Stand-to" is a military term that refers to a heightened state of combat readiness at dawn and dusk. These periods of reduced visibility are historically considered times when defenders are vulnerable, providing a tactical advantage to attacking forces. Units are typically at one hundred percent security to guard against such a threat. Soldiers are in full battle rattle and in their defensive positions, scanning sectors of fire for suspicious movement or activity.

The practice of stand-to dates back to World War I when dawn and dusk were common times for attacks against opposing trenches. Old habits die hard. Stand-to is now a standard military practice in defensive positions, like forward operating bases. Now, it applies to a little single-family home on Fifth Street in Minneapolis.

"Chicago, we may have a problem," he hears Nica say over the comms.

"What is it?"

"We're just to the north and west of you. The orcs are up to something. They're gathered around an F-150 about three hundred meters from our AO. We may be looking at a VBIED."

Chicago assumes the area of operations is their block. A vehicle-borne improvised explosive device would be a significant change in tactic but one that makes sense against a fortified defender. Or, in their case, a wooden house.

"Do you see explosives?"

"Negative. It looks like they're loading the truck up with fuel cans."

"They're going to ram it into the house and try to burn us out," Bronx concludes.

"I concur. That will thrill my sister."

"It's a bold strategy, Cotton. Let's see if it pays off for them," Hollywood mumbles, causing Chicago to grin at the *Dodgeball: A True Underdog Story* reference.

"We're about to find out," Nica confirms. "The driver looks like he's sixteen. He just fired the truck up. Twenty or so assholes are doing weapons checks."

"They're going to drive it up to the house? That's a death wish," Bronx muses. "How much do you want to bet that kid is the low man on the totem pole?"

"We were all privates once," Nashville says over the radio. "We've been there. Maybe the driver will bail when he gets close."

"Yeah, nothing could possibly go wrong with that," Tulsa moans.

"You know what I've noticed? Nobody panics when things go 'according to plan.' Even if the plan is horrifying!"

"I'm not comfortable with Hollywood mimicking the Joker from *The Dark Knight*. Nobody ever said these guys were bright, guys, but the quote machine is right. Let's make things not go according to plan. Nica, can you stop that truck?"

"We ain't gonna disable that thing with ARs. The best we can hope for is to punch some holes in the radiator or take out the driver."

"I knew I should have grabbed the two-forty bravo," Tulsa laments, forcing Chicago to wonder where his uncle got all that firepower for his rural Oklahoma shop.

"I wasn't carrying that pig," Bronx argues. "You know you would have made me."

His complaint isn't without merit. The machine gun delivers long-range stopping power and would be more than effective against an unarmored pickup truck. Unfortunately, at nearly thirty pounds, it's heavier than some other machine guns, and that's not counting the weight of the one- or two-hundred-round linked ammunition belts they would need to bring with them.

It would come in handy. The AR-15s Nica and Nashville are toting are the closest thing available to the M4s they used in the Regiment. That caliber of ammunition isn't typically designed for destroying engines or disabling vehicles. The round lacks the mass and kinetic energy needed to penetrate and destroy an engine block. However, at close range, it *might* cause enough damage to disable a vehicle. A few well-placed shots in the radiator could cause overheating, and a lucky hit to the fuel line or electronics could make the truck undrivable. Chicago has a better idea.

"He's rolling, Chicago. It's now or never."

"Take out the tires before he starts to turn onto Fifth."

"That isn't going to stop him!"

"No, but it'll slow them down. The driver's a kid. I'm willing to bet he stops the truck to figure out what to do next."

Army Rangers are highly trained special operations soldiers. Marksmanship is absolutely one of the core competencies. Their mission requires effectively engaging targets while under stress and in the worst of conditions, including limited visibility and extreme ranges. This is a cakewalk by comparison.

Chicago hears the AR-15 open fire. They are single shots. It takes only four or five rounds to achieve the desired result. He looks through his scope. The pickup truck is just east of the intersection, turned at a forty-five-degree angle and at a dead stop.

"Did you become a psychic in your off-time or something, buddy?"

The victory is short-lived. A man starts yelling at the driver to get moving. He closes the truck door and hits the gas. The pickup lurches forward.

Chicago pauses his breath and fires his sniper rifle at the engine. And again. And again. None of the bullets have the velocity or mass to stop the vehicle.

"I'd kill for a Barrett right now."

The Barrett .50 caliber sniper rifle is one of the world's most iconic and powerful long-range sniper systems. The Rangers use it for a variety of missions where extreme precision and stopping power are absolute requirements. It's capable of taking out any civilian vehicle and even most lightly armored targets.

The vehicle turns the corner. Chicago has a decision to make. Life or death. Them or us. The classic dilemma faced in every dire struggle. He takes a breath and looks through his scope. He pauses his breathing just long enough to squeeze the trigger.

The driver is hit in the shoulder, but it's not fatal so long as he gets medical attention. Chicago is happy for once that his aim was off. Men shout and start firing at the house from the rear of the vehicle. There goes the paint job.

Nica and Nashville begin laying down suppressive fire. It commands their aggressors' immediate attention. As they begin to advance, Hollywood unleashes with the SAW. The "infantrymen" seek cover, and he switches targets to the back of the pickup. The rounds punch holes in the fuel containers, and a spark from one of the bullets hitting the aluminum bed causes the vapor to ignite. The whole back of the truck erupts in a fireball.

Some of the fighters were too close. Three or four men catch fire, causing others to drop their weapons to try to extinguish the flames. They are easy pickings, but all the Rangers hold their fire. In Syria, they would be dispatching targets without prejudice. This isn't Syria. At least, not yet.

The man shouting orders moves out in front of the truck. He levels his weapon and fires in the direction of Nica and Nashville. It doesn't sound like single shots. He either has a bump stock, or his weapon was modified to shoot full auto. As a result, he blows through his thirty-round magazine in a matter of seconds.

"Stay down, guys. I got him."

The angle is extreme, but Chicago has just enough line-of-sight to take the shot. Aim. Breathe. Squeeze. The recoil jolts his shoulder as the round hits its mark. The guy never has a chance to finish reloading. He crumples to the ground in front of the fifteen or so remaining men who have no idea what to do.

"Nica? Tulsa? You guys okay?"

"Yeah, we took cover before Captain Pampers decided to go all Jesse Ventura in *Predator* on us."

"Get to the choppa'!" Hollywood says in a passable Schwarzenegger voice.

"Get back here, guys. Come in from the rear. Bronx has you covered."

"Roger that. Out."

Chicago watches out the window. In the Army, there is a chain of command. Every soldier knows who is in charge when a leader falls, all the way down to the lowly private. Their job is the mission, and that is to be executed regardless of losses. These men don't have that training. They literally look like they're about to cry.

Someone will show up and take charge. Until that happens, all they can do is sit back and watch…and wait. This won't be the end of it. If anything, Chicago just escalated things. He said he was willing to take on their "army." Now, he realizes he may get his wish.

CHAPTER FIFTY

LANDON TAYSON

Landon slams his hand on the desk out of frustration. Raven jumps, but Muzzie shows no reaction at all. Maybe he has nerves of steel. More likely, he knew the outburst was coming after delivering the bad news.

The house on Fifth Street is still standing. Worse, the owner, or whoever the guy is, scored yet another victory. Two of his men are dead, and four more are in the clinic with gunshot wounds or severe burns. What amazes him most is the tactics they used to thwart the plan. That wasn't something Landon expected to hear.

"What did they shoot the tires out with?"

"According to one of the fighters, AR-15s."

Landon looks at his captain suspiciously. "Is he reliable?"

"He's ex-military, so yeah, he would know. The shot from the house that killed Artie was a single-shot rifle. It could be a hunting rifle, but we can't discount it being a sniper rifle."

"I thought this guy and his two friends only had a shotgun."

"Apparently not."

So, they have more than a shotgun. Landon wonders if they are wrong about other things, as well. They assume there are three guys. Are there more? According to what was reported to Muzzie, there was one at the house and two who assaulted the truck. It makes sense that there are only three. Unfortunately, at this point, he can't be certain of anything.

"Do we know anything about the owner?"

"No, but I'm beginning to think he may be ex-military. His buddies probably are, too. They're comfortable with firearms, can fire accurately, and they display tactical proficiency. These aren't guys who play paintball or go to Airsoft tournaments. They've had real training. And then there's the flag."

"A soldier would defend it with his life."

"Some of them would, yes," Muzzie says with a smirk.

Landon rubs his forehead. "Was the incident observed?"

"Observed?"

"Watched by a drone. We know the police are flying them over the ADOZ. Did any of your men spot one before or after they came under fire?"

"Not that was reported. That doesn't mean there isn't footage of it. Everyone has a cell phone camera. One of the neighbors may have videoed it. Hell, that prick Kai could have been lurking in the bushes."

Landon turns to his paramour. "Raven?"

She shrugs. "I haven't seen anything on the news. Kai Z's social media channels have been eerily quiet."

"He's probably still running for his life," Muzzie mumbles.

He may think it's somewhat funny, but Landon isn't amused. He stares hard at his commander. "We should have caught him by now."

"We're looking."

Landon shakes his head. "Raven, get on social media and see if anything is trending about what happened. If there is a video of this, that's where it will end up."

"I'm on it."

Raven opens her laptop and stares at the camera so that the operating system's facial recognition will grant her login access. Landon turns to his commander and rubs the growing stubble on his chin.

"Thoughts on our next move, Muzzie?"

"There are only three of them in that house. There are hundreds of us. Even if they fortified it, how much ammunition could they have? Do the math."

"That's a terrible idea, Muzzie," Raven says without looking up from her laptop's screen.

"Did anyone ask for your opinion?"

"No, but I was going to," Landon snaps. "Go ahead, Raven."

She leans back in her chair and takes a breath. "Set aside the PR nightmare and the casualties of a full-out assault. Everyone is going to wonder what the big deal is."

"They are flying a flag…an American flag!"

"So?"

Muzzie's face contorts as he takes a threatening step toward her. "It's against our laws…the same ones you drafted."

"Yeah, it is," Raven admits. "But if you think storming that house like it's a D-Day beach is going to win over any hearts and minds, you're sorely mistaken. We're going to have issues keeping our morale up after the botched firebombing."

"It wasn't botched. We were attacked! My men are resilient!"

"Are they, Captain?" she challenges. "I already have three reports from barricades of defections. More are going to follow. We are losing men, and the rest are starting to lose the stomach to fight on if they think we're comfortable wasting their lives."

"Let the cowards go," Muzzie says, flicking his hand away from him for effect.

"I thought they were resilient. And, besides, we don't have the personnel for that."

"Reinforcements are on the way, Raven," Landon says, his voice quiet and even to help alleviate some of the tension between his two most trusted advisors. "The first should arrive tomorrow. That will give us the manpower we need. The flag *has* to come down. Leaving it flying isn't an option."

"That's what I like to hear!" Muzzie exclaims, violently clapping his hands together.

Raven remains silent. She doesn't even look at Landon. He knows what that means, and he will no doubt hear about it later. At least he doesn't need to be worried about sleeping on the couch. That's where he's been since this began. That is when he can find time to catch some shut-eye.

"Muzzie, start putting together a roster. It needs to include our best men. I'm done playing with these fools."

"Yes, sir, Mr. President!"

Muzzie strides out. There is so much bounce to his step that he almost looks like he's skipping. He has never been vocal about wanting action. He likely knew it would happen sooner or later. They all assumed that but expected it to be directed against law enforcement.

Raven looks up from her laptop and eyes Landon. The woman knows how to speak with her eyes. Without her uttering a word, he knows that her opinion about this mission hasn't changed. She wants a reason.

"There are forces at play here that you don't understand. This needs to be done."

CHAPTER FIFTY-ONE
CHIEF VANESSA CAMPBELL

MPD TACTICAL COMMAND POST
MINNEAPOLIS, MINNESOTA

Somebody brought a television. It may never be known whether it was for police business or because one of the officers here wanted to have a trapping of home in the tent they spend hours under. Vanessa also isn't sure if it came from the 2nd Precinct, City Hall, or someone's house. It's not what she would want to watch a Superbowl on, but the thirty-two-inch, 1080p smart TV on the table the officer is screencasting to is far better than looking at a laptop screen.

The video was emailed to the department as an attachment. That they aren't watching this on YouTube or other video-sharing services is a near miracle in the modern age. It will end up there eventually, or a censored version of it will.

Vanessa watches the tires get shot out, and the back of the truck erupt in a fireball before the video moves around. Whoever shot this must have ducked in fear. When the camera is refocused on the scene, men are burning as their comrades try to douse them. Another man points his rifle and opens up in what almost sounds like automatic fire. He is dropped with a single shot. The video ends moments later.

"This is right around the corner from the Fifth Street house with the flag on it. That may be meaningless, but it'd be a hell of a coincidence," Lieutenant Burke admits.

"And this video hasn't been posted online?"

"Negative, Chief. At least, not yet. It was emailed to us by an older couple who lives here," an officer says, pointing to a digital map pulled up on the laptop. "They may not know how to post online."

"Well, they know how to use a cameraphone. Who was shooting at the ADOZ fighters from the street? I find it hard to believe that the owners of that house with the flag would leave it."

The officer shrugs.

"Could there be some dissension within the ranks of Landon Tayson's little army?"

"It's possible," another officer admits. "But more likely, whoever is in that house has friends."

"Friends with AR-15s who actually know how to use them?"

"I may be able to answer that," Lieutenant Burke says. "I have some friends who are 42-Alphas and still work in Army Human Resources. One of them did me a favor in return for wiping out an old poker debt. We already learned that Kenyala Brown has an older brother…Emmit Haskins. What we didn't know is that he's a former Army Ranger."

"Helllloooo," the officer at the laptop says.

"That explains a few things," Vanessa confirms.

"Wait until you hear what's on the back of his baseball card," Burke says, opening the file.

"Infantry Advance Individual Training Course and airborne school graduate. He attended the Fort Benning. Ranger Assessment and Selection Program and went on to complete Ranger School. Was assigned to the 2nd Battalion, 75th Ranger Regiment. Went to the Basic Leader Course and was promoted to sergeant. He reenlisted and attended the Advanced Leader Course and was promoted to staff sergeant.

"A staff sergeant. That makes him an infantry squad leader," Vanessa mumbles. She knows a thing or two about the service.

"It gets better. Staff Sergeant Haskins attended the Regimental Pre-Sniper and Combat Marksmanship Training courses."

"Of course he did. Enough about his training. Tell me about the man."

"Uh, he had all the makings of a lifer," Burke says, staring at the folder as he flips a few pages. "Haskins had great NCO evaluation reports, at least until his last one. I'll get to that in a minute. He has multiple decorations, including an Army Commendation Medal, three Army Achievement Medals, a Good Conduct Medal, and a few others…he earned a Silver Star with a 'V' device for valor on his Syria deployment and a Purple Heart for wounds sustained in combat action against ISIS insurgents."

"This guy is Captain America. Why did he get out?"

Burke scowls. "That's where things get a little weird. It looks like a voluntary discharge, but there is a note in the file from the company C.O. that he was being forced out due to disobeying a direct order. Apparently, he ignored his commander during an ISIS ambush in Syria. According to statements from his team leaders, Haskins rushed out under withering fire to drag two wounded squad members back to safety. He got himself wounded in the process and didn't know it until he got back to the base."

Vanessa shakes her head. "Thus the Purple Heart. That's the kind of leader you want to have in combat."

"The officers in his unit didn't think so. Apparently, he was given a choice to accept a Silver Star and leave the service voluntarily or face a court-martial. The good news is, one of the men he dragged back to the convoy survived."

The chief uses her thumb to crack the knuckles of each of her fingers in sequence as she processes that information. "So, fresh out of the military, a jaded Emmit Haskins returns home with a chip on his shoulder and moves in with his sister in Minneapolis. We've confirmed she isn't there, which means she either left right before or just after this went down. Who are the other guys with him?"

"I don't have information on that. I'm betting whoever these guys with Haskins are served with him in the Rangers."

It's a safe bet. He was a squad leader. The military is a brotherhood, and the Rangers even more so. More importantly, to save his men, he chose to disobey a direct order from his commander to retreat. That act likely made him a legend in that unit. It'd be surprising to Vanessa if a plea for help didn't result in every soldier he served with showing up here.

"Is it possible we have at least three highly trained Army Rangers in the middle of the ADOZ?"

"Possibly. What are you thinking, Chief?"

She grins. "Did you ever see *Die Hard*?"

Burke returns the smile. "It's my favorite Christmas movie."

Vanessa sees movement outside the tent. She bends down and sees Inspector Sillyere lurking near the CP. Her brash and slightly insubordinate underling has been running a low profile since Otto Goldberg's death. Most likely, she's busy currying favor with the mayor. That's fine. So long as she stays away from Vanessa, the ambitious little shit can have this job when this incident is over. Those two clowns deserve each other.

"Keep this information between us, guys. Things are already too tense around here. Nobody else needs to know," the chief says, turning to the officer seated at the table. "I want you to find out if there is a landline in that house. If there isn't, see if Staff Sergeant Haskins has a cell phone and try to track down a number."

"And if he does?"

Vanessa smirks. "I'm going to call it."

CHAPTER FIFTY-TWO
KAI Z

Kai is looking out the window and listening. Noise travels farther at night due to atmospheric and environmental conditions that affect the propagation of sound waves. During the day, air near the ground is warmer than the air above, creating a temperature gradient that causes sound waves to bend upward and quickly dissipate. At night, the ground cools faster than the air above, creating a temperature inversion that bends sound waves downward, allowing them to travel farther horizontally.

Add lower levels of background noise from reduced human activity, calmer winds, and higher humidity. Kai can't remember how or why he learned that. It may have been during a trek down the YouTube rabbit hole. He wanted to know if there was an explainable reason someone could hear noise from farther away. In this case, the racket was coming in the direction of the Rangers' Fifth Street house.

"It got quiet," Babs says, handing him a steaming cup of coffee.

He takes a sip. "Yeah. It's almost midnight."

"Do you think the Rangers are okay?"

Kai nods. "I think Tayson will need his whole army to take them out."

He moves away from the front window and into the living area. He sets the mug on the end table, swings his damaged leg in the air, and flops onto the sofa. He ignores the stabbing pain radiating from the wound but is happy it subsides quickly. He can't sleep. The amount of caffeine he's ingested has made that an impossibility. But he does need to rest his eyes.

"But you're worried about them," Babs surmises, sliding gracefully into a chair.

He's not overly worried about the soldiers. They are more capable than any men he's ever met. The fighters in this ADOZ can't begin to compare, and bad things are going to happen if they face off. The fighters have superior numbers and may eventually overwhelm them, and nobody is unkillable. But the Rangers won't go quietly. A ten-to-one or greater kill ratio wouldn't be remotely surprising.

No, it's not the Rangers that he's concerned about. It's something else. Landon Tayson isn't a leader, administrator, or politician. He doesn't care about the people in this district, nor does he pretend to. Nothing he does is on their behalf. Kai isn't certain what his true agenda is, but it isn't for the betterment of the community. No amount of rhetoric coming out of the man's mouth can hide that.

"I'm worried about everybody here. We watched a man get beaten in the street in broad daylight. I watched a woman get dragged away from her burning house because her husband wasn't getting the medical care he needed. Then, an ambulance got shot to pieces," Kai says, pointing at the television.

"You couldn't do anything about any of that."

"I know."

Babs isn't reassured. "But?"

He doesn't answer. It's not out of fear of what she'll think. He already knows what she's going to say or, at least, thinks he knows. It's that the thoughts in his head are an unorganized mess. Listening to the gunfire to the south did little to help him organize them. He simply doesn't know how to articulate any of it in a meaningful way.

"Kai, talk to me."

He sits up on the couch, propping his leg under a throw pillow. "What do you think about the ADOZ?"

"Other than they're setting up a pseudo-fascist state?"

"Yeah. Other than that."

Babs is a critical thinker. She doesn't like to delve into the speculative realm. She deals with facts and then forms opinions from them. There isn't enough information for her to be comfortable offering a judgment.

"I don't know. Why?"

"When I was talking to the Rangers, some of what I was saying came out of my ass. I mentioned off the cuff that it felt like someone powerful was behind this and that my first choice was the government."

Babs narrows her eyes. "Kai, the government isn't behind this."

"How can you be so sure?" he asks, reaching back for his mug of coffee. "I know it sounds insane, and I can't think of a good reason they would be, but think about the setup here. Remember how perfect their timing was. Look at all the guns they have. You can't tell me it *isn't* a possibility."

Conspiracy theories arise and evolve because of a lack of information. It's the same reason they are nearly impossible to disprove. Nobody can say for certain there wasn't a second shooter on the grassy knoll during the Kennedy assassination. Nobody can definitely say that someone in the U.S. government didn't know about the terrorist attacks on 9/11.

Even if any of that could be confirmed, not everyone would believe it. The world is round. There is more than enough evidence to prove that. Still, thousands of people belong to various flat-earth societies.

"And you can't prove it is a possibility."

Kai's lips crease. "I can try."

"The hell you can!" Babs screeches, catapulting out of her chair. "You were shot! I should be taking you out of here and straight to a hospital."

"I'm where I need to be. My leg is fine, and even if it wasn't, this is more important. Someone is funding this, and it could be the scandal of the century."

Babs folds her arms across her chest. Sometimes, she does that to rest them. Not this time. Her forearms are tense.

"No! We're not going down that road this time. I've watched you do a lot of stupid things over the years. I bit my tongue each time because that's who you are. But this is different. It's way more dangerous than anything we've ever faced, and you're not leaving this house to search for information that probably doesn't exist."

"Babs—"

"No! Promise me you won't do something reckless."

"The people need to know the truth about the ADOZ."

"Then someone else will tell them when this is all over. Promise me, or you are on your own from now on."

Kai closes his eyes. That's not an idle threat. She has stood by him through everything. Babs nursed him back to health after he was assaulted in a riot. She has always had his back. That she has chosen this moment to draw a line in the sand....

"I promise."

CHAPTER FIFTY-THREE
EMMIT "CHICAGO" HASKINS

THE FIFTH STREET HOUSE
MINNEAPOLIS ARTS DISTRICT OCCUPIED ZONE

The duty roster has them working in shifts. Two guys stand guard upstairs, one facing the rear and the other the front. There are blind spots, but Chicago doesn't think the ADOZ fighters are tactically proficient enough to exploit them. Two more guys are on the quick reaction force, meaning they are ready to go should the pair on watch need support. The final two guys get to rest and sleep.

That's what Chicago is supposed to be doing. The sofa is comfortable, but he isn't tired. His mind is racing. He has killed men, and even for a soldier, there is a mental toll that must be paid. He can justify his actions, but that doesn't make things any easier.

He stares at the ceiling, and only one thought comes to mind. Keeping his voice low, he begins reciting one of the first things he learned as he readied himself to join the Regiment.

"Recognizing that I volunteered as a Ranger, fully knowing the hazards of my chosen profession, I will always endeavor to uphold the prestige, honor, and high esprit de corps of the Rangers.

"Acknowledging the fact that a Ranger is a more elite soldier who arrives at the cutting edge of battle by land, sea, or air, I accept the fact that as a Ranger my country expects me to move further, faster, and fight harder than any other soldier.

"Never shall I fail my comrades. I will always keep myself mentally alert, physically strong, and morally straight, and I will shoulder more than my share of the task, whatever it may be, one hundred percent and then some.

"Gallantly will I show the world that I am a specially selected and well-trained soldier. My courtesy to superior officers, neatness of dress, and care of equipment shall set the example for others to follow.

"Energetically will I meet the enemies of my country. I shall defeat them on the field of battle, for I am better trained and will fight with all my might. Surrender is not a Ranger word. I will never leave a fallen comrade to fall into the hands of the enemy, and under no circumstances will I ever embarrass my country.

"Readily will I display the intestinal fortitude required to fight on to the Ranger objective and complete the mission, though I be the lone survivor. Rangers lead the way!"

Nica starts slowly clapping as he cuts through the living room to the kitchen and begins rummaging through the fridge. He pulls out a can of soda and slams the door shut.

"It's well after midnight. You're supposed to be resting, not indoctrinating yourself by reciting the Ranger Creed."

Chicago sits up on the couch and rubs his eyes. "I know. I can't sleep. Nica, you're not gonna like what I'm about to say."

"Aw, hell…then let me sit down first." Nica parks himself in the chair across from Chicago and sips his cola. "All right. What's up?"

"I need you and the other guys to leave."

Nica speaks fluent Spanish in addition to English. But what he heard must sound like Swahili to him because he cocks his head and furrows his brow. "What?"

"You had the best ears in the squad, Brother. I know you heard me."

"I heard the words. I just don't believe they came out of your mouth."

"This is my fight, not yours. I should never have asked you guys to come here."

Nica presses his lips together and shakes his head. "That's where you're wrong. It's not *your* fight. It's *ours*."

"How do you figure?"

Nica rests his arms on his knees and interlaces his fingers as he bends slightly forward. He hangs his head, but he's wearing an amused smile. Chicago thought it was a serious question. His friend is acting like he can't believe it was asked.

"When you were our squad leader in the Regiment, you were always looking out for us. It didn't matter if we were in trouble or needed personal guidance…whatever the problem was, we could always count on you to help. Now, it's our turn to return the favor."

"It's not worth the price."

"The price? Really? We salute the flag not just because it's what the military demands. It's because that gesture means something. We pledged to defend this nation against all enemies, foreign and domestic. The idiots running this ADOZ, or whatever they call it, are domestic enemies. If we ignore that threat now, it makes that courtesy meaningless. I could never stand in formation again and salute without thinking I'm a fraud."

Chicago tightens his jaw. "Nica, you're still on active duty. So are Tulsa and Bronx. Do you have any idea what will happen if the Army learns you are here?"

"Yeah, I do. The guys understand, too. There may be consequences, but that's a risk we all agreed to take. You're gonna need to hit each of us in the head and drag our unconscious asses out of this house. Short story? We ain't leaving."

"I'm probably going to jail for murder when this is over. I can accept the consequences of what I've done because I believe it was the right thing to do. I can't accept your sharing a cell block with me because I roped you into this."

"Well, you ain't gonna fight off the mindless horde without us. Besides, there is nobody we would rather be with during a fight. You're damn near our lucky charm."

Chicago scoffs. "Lucky charm? I couldn't save Gamecock."

"Nothing would have saved him, Chicago. Men die in combat. It doesn't matter how good their leaders are. We honor their sacrifice and fight on. Before you start feeling sorry for yourself, why don't you ask Missoula? You disobeyed a direct order and charged into automatic weapons fire to save his ass. It may have gotten you kicked out of the Army, but he's a husband who's about to become a father because of you."

He's never thought of it that way. He did a lot of soul-searching after losing Gamecock. The loss haunted him. It doesn't matter that Missoula survived or that he would have met the same fate had Chicago followed his captain's orders. His biggest fear is losing one or more of these guys.

He stares at Nica, who holds his gaze. The man is determined, as most Army Rangers are.

"There's no way to get you to leave?"

"Well, we could do the democracy thing and put it to a vote, but you'd lose five-one. And then you get to hear Hollywood quote political movies we've never watched."

"I'll pass on that. I could order you to leave."

"You could, but even if you had the authority to order us to do shit, we'd disobey it. Remember, we learned from the best."

He almost wants to slap that smile off Nica's face. He wasn't forced out of the Rangers just because he disobeyed an order in the heat of battle. He was made an example of so that others wouldn't follow in his footsteps.

"All right. Is there any way to get you out of this house?"

"Yeah, sure. We'll leave when we win."

CHAPTER FIFTY-FOUR

KAI Z

GRAND STREET RENTAL HOUSE
MINNEAPOLIS ARTS DISTRICT OCCUPIED ZONE

Kai has gotten very good at this. He isn't as skilled as Babs is, but he can give her a run for her money. His eyes are tired from staring at the laptop screen, and he is feeling the lethargy and brain fog that come with a lack of sleep. This needed to be done.

Video editing isn't a science – it's an art. Sure, there are technical skills behind manipulating and rearranging video footage, but the look and feel of a work is up to the creator. The best use the montages they splice together and set to music to convey a message, tell a story, or induce an emotion. It's similar to how advertising executives make television commercials appeal to prospective buyers.

Babs had already done much of the hard work. She chopped most of his footage into clips and labeled the files for easy access. Since Kai already knew what he was looking to do, it was a matter of trimming unnecessary parts of each video segment and arranging them in a timeline to tell the story he wanted. Then, he used fades and dissolves, along with some overlapping stock imagery, to smooth changes between scenes.

Content that the video hits all the marks he wants, Kai chooses the resolution, format, and settings for each of the platforms he plans on uploading it to. All he has to do is click upload. He pauses and takes a deep breath as his cursor hovers over the button.

Babs is going to be livid that he created this video and posted it without her. He has faced her wrath before, and it didn't go well. He can almost imagine the little angel and devil sitting on opposite shoulders, whispering in his ear. The devil wins. Kai presses the key and waits for the upload to finish. This will capture some attention.

He closes the laptop and checks his watch. It's almost six a.m. If he's going to do this, it needs to be now. It's not about moving in darkness or during the first rays of the morning sun. This is the time when the roving patrols in the ADOZ change shifts, or whatever Landon and his minions call them. That means there is about an hour when he doesn't need to worry too much about dodging SUVs filled with armed morons.

Fortunately, he planned this out. The note he's leaving has already been drafted. Babs will see it in the morning and most likely ignore the instructions it contains. Kai needs to remember to turn his phone off. Even a phone on vibrate can be heard, and that's not something he's going to want to deal with an hour or two from now.

This mission is going to require him to travel light. The walking will be hard enough on his wounded leg. He grabs some energy bars and a bottle of water and stuffs it all into a small knapsack with his bodycam, the walkie-talkie switched off, and some extra batteries. He has one chance to make this work.

Con artists exploit human psychology, trust, and vulnerabilities to get cooperation. He's met enough of them in his travels to know. They're skilled manipulators who use natural charm and deception tactics to achieve their goals. It's not as hard as it sounds. Humans are naturally inclined to trust others and reciprocate kindness. In the ADOZ, Kai only needs to pretend to be one of them. At least, that's the plan.

He ensures the envelope is left where Babs can find it and takes a last look at the place. The next time he comes back here, it will be with the story of the century. Kai is going to blow the lid off this conspiracy and expose everyone involved. With that thought, he quietly opens the front door and eases out of it.

CHAPTER FIFTY-FIVE
CHIEF VANESSA CAMPBELL

A slip of paper. That's what Vanessa was handed by the officer at the table. She expected a printout or even several sheets that comprise a call log. In almost every investigation that required cell phone records to be retrieved, that was the case. Not this time. Then again, this wasn't an official investigation. She supposes that's why the ten digits are handwritten on what was once the bottom of a sheet of paper on a legal pad.

The chief looks around. There are several officers standing under the tent and countless more in earshot. Inspector Sillyere has been coming and going all morning. If this conversation gets leaked….

She needs to make this call in private. After advising an officer that she needs to go for a walk, Vanessa wanders away from the command tent. The area is swarming with police and other first responders, but that doesn't mean every inch of ground is covered. She finds a quiet spot alongside a building and leans her back up against it.

Vanessa pulls the slip out of her pocket and unlocks the phone. She brings up the keypad and dials number. It rings, and she holds it up to her ear, contemplating the odds that he will—

"Hello?"

"Emmit Haskins?" she asks, getting greeted with nothing but silence on the other end of the line. "I'm partly surprised you took this call. I'm Vanessa Campbell…the chief of the Minneapolis Police Department."

"How can I help you, ma'am?"

Vanessa panics a little. "Nice flag."

"I don't know what you're talking about. I need to—"

"Please don't hang up on me, Staff Sergeant. I know all about your sister, your house, and why you built a flagpole on your roof. I'm an ally, not an enemy."

"So you say."

She closes her eyes. "Yeah, if our roles were reversed, I probably wouldn't believe me, either."

"What can I do for you, Chief Campbell?"

It's a good question that Vanessa doesn't really have an answer to. It would have been time well spent to think about what she wanted to say on the off-chance Staff

Sergeant Haskins, U.S. Army Ranger, actually answered the phone. Now, she has to wing it.

"Nothing, really. We've been watching your house for a while now. I just felt the need to talk to you."

"Watching?"

"We've been flying drones over the self-proclaimed ADOZ almost since the beginning of the takeover. It's the only way we can get any intelligence about what's happening in there. That, and whatever gets uploaded to YouTube."

"Kai Z," the Ranger says.

"You know him."

"Yes, ma'am. It's a long story. It's good to hear the police are doing something. We're not seeing much else."

Vanessa wants to argue, but he's right. They haven't shown any support to the people trapped within the ADOZ. The words may hurt, and the acidic tone of his voice may cause them to sting that much worse, but he has every right to utter them.

"Our inaction…let's just say that it isn't by choice. You were in the Rangers. You know a thing or two about taking orders. I have the same burden."

"You seem to know a lot about me, Chief Campbell. Then you also probably know why I'm not in the Army anymore."

"I know about the circumstances of your discharge. The reports in your file read like complete bullshit."

He chuckles. "That's one way of putting it. I had to act in Syria. The lives of my men depended on it. You have a lot of terrified citizens here. Why haven't you disobeyed orders and acted?"

It's another good question. The better question is, why isn't this guy on her police force? He reminds her of Lieutenant Burke, and she wishes she had a few hundred more officers just like him. There is no appropriate answer except the truth.

"I don't have the courage to do what you did."

"Fair enough. Ma'am, I'll give you one last chance to answer. Why are you calling me?"

"You're in grave danger."

"All danger is grave. We already figured that out. These clowns have already tried to burn the house down with me in it."

"We know. The incident was captured on video and sent to us. I know you have at least a couple of friends with you. No, I don't want you to confirm that or tell me their names. It's better if I don't know who they are."

Vanessa hopes that helps establish some trust between them. She also means it.

"So, you know what we did?"

"I know you defended yourselves. You're going to need to do it again. A guy named Seth Muzzebach is the commander of all the fighters in the ADOZ. He goes by 'Muzzie' and is a disgruntled veteran who aligned himself with Antifa after leaving the military."

"We've met."

"I bet. We keep tabs on him the best we can. Muzzie has been very busy visiting the barricades and talking to their roving patrols. Each time he does, their manpower decreases by one or two. The head of my SWAT team is convinced that they're assembling a force."

"And you think we're the target."

Vanessa grins. "Don't you?"

"Do you plan on doing something about that?"

If it were up to her, she would. "My hands are tied, Sergeant. I'm giving you the information so you and your guys can be prepared."

Not that she thinks they aren't. Haskins is a Ranger. His friends are probably Rangers. While they aren't invincible, they are among the most formidable infantry units in the world. If Landon Tayson knew what he was up against, he wouldn't go within three blocks of that house. Unless he really is as dumb as everyone thinks he is.

"You know what that means."

"I do. That's why I'm calling from my personal phone, and this conversation never officially happened. Whether you know it or not, you're inspiring the country. I can tell you definitively that every officer here knows about the flag. Most know about the firebombing they planned. Everybody is pulling for you."

"Anything else, ma'am?"

"No. Just stay safe, Sergeant. If you need anything, you have this number. Don't be afraid to use it."

"One last question, Chief. How long do the mayor and governor plan on sitting on their asses?"

"Longer than they should. Stay in touch."

Vanessa ends the call and looks around. That could have gone worse. It also could have gone better. She isn't sure if she accomplished anything other than confirming there is active resistance in the ADOZ by men who know what they are doing. If Landon attacks, she'll be rooting for them. If things go her way, she can even support them when the time comes.

CHAPTER FIFTY-SIX

LANDON TAYSON

The video is pure propaganda. Landon was too young to remember much about the terrorist attacks on 9/11. But the feeling of the country was memorialized in memes and videos uploaded to sharing services. That was before either was as ubiquitous as they are today.

This newest opus is reminiscent of them. Those videos were meant to seize on the country's anger and stoke the fires of revenge. This one feeds on emotions by showing the darkest side of the ADOZ. He didn't know about the beating. He was there for the house fire, and he obviously knows about the flag burning and subsequent reconstruction. Splice all those together and add some patriotic music, and the little prick managed to paint an unflattering picture of what everyone is trying to do here.

The video ends, and Raven lifts her eyes to gauge Landon's reaction. He doesn't have one. The video was bad but unsurprising. Kai Z isn't exactly an unbiased voice in the chorus of talking heads.

Landon moves to his desk and uncaps a warehouse store-sized bottle of antacids. He pours four of them into his hand and pitches them into his mouth. The indigestion could be caused by stress or the acid from all the coffee he's been drinking. It's likely a little of both.

"It's propaganda," he concludes, moving to his desk to stare at the map of the ADOZ stretched out on it.

"It's effective."

"Not on the people who are dedicated to this cause."

Raven sets her phone down on the table she uses as a desk in his office. "We had ten more defections from the barricades last night. From what I read, they laid down their guns and walked across the street."

"Who left?" Landon asks after stretching his jaw. "Our people or the protestors who joined us?"

"They were protestors," Raven confirms.

He snaps his hand at the wrist, whisking the concern away. "We knew that would happen. Reinforcements should arrive today. After that, the whole lot of them can leave for all I care."

"You're not weighing the impact that will have on the morale of the people who stay."

Landon glares at Raven. "The lion doesn't care to listen to the bleating of the sheep."

"I see," Raven says after scoffing. "You think you're above it all. You haven't *earned* that yet, Landon. You used to speak about needing the people behind you. Then you had them in lockstep behind the cause. Now you don't. The protests that popped up to support us are dwindling in numbers. Some have completely disappeared. Everyone is turning against you, just like I warned before we created the ADOZ."

"Is this your way of saying 'I told you so?'"

"Yes, because you aren't listening…to me or yourself."

Landon's shoulders sag, and his head rolls to his right shoulder. "I am listening."

"Sure…to Muzzie."

"Seriously? Are you saying I shouldn't listen to my commander, Raven? Because last I checked, he was instrumental in getting the ADOZ set up in the first place."

She sighs heavily. "I'm saying Muzzie is a blunt instrument. He can handle the fighters, but he isn't an administrator. He isn't a politician. He doesn't realize that everyone here doesn't share his level of zealotry."

"People are with us or against us. It's that simple."

"Well, the ones who live here are making their decision. They're leaving."

"What do you mean?"

Raven grimaces. "You don't read the ops reports, do you? You should pay more attention to the area you're running. The residents in the district are beginning to leave in droves. They've had enough."

Landon has to fight the surge of anger. His teeth clench and grind against each other as he struggles to stifle the rage-filled response that pops into his mind. That's not how leaders are supposed to act. It's also the reaction that Raven is expecting so she can make her point. She never likes being wrong, and he's not going to give her the satisfaction that comes with getting under her skin.

"Close the borders. Send word out to the barricades immediately. Nobody leaves, and nobody enters except for our reinforcements."

"That's going to create another set of problems."

"Issue the order, Raven."

"*Ja, mein Führer.*"

Landon's head cranks in her direction. He's about to go off on her when Muzzie comes barging through the door, out of breath and gasping for air. He's a former soldier. Landon would have thought he'd be in better shape than he is. Thank God he's here for his leadership and not physicality.

"We…we have a problem," Muzzie breathes, hanging on the edge of the door as he bends forward.

"Add it to the list."

"This one's serious, Mr. President."

"They're all serious. Catch your breath and get a grip on yourself. What is it?"

Muzzie takes a deep breath and forces himself upright. "I just got a call. One of the convoys with our reinforcements was stopped at the state line. They were all arrested."

Landon feels the blood drain from his face. Then it returns with a vengeance as he flushes with anger, his hands balling in fists. Now he knows why his commander is out of breath. This unwelcome news needed to be delivered immediately.

"For what?"

"Gun charges and…."

"And what?"

Muzzie's face turns grave. "Domestic terrorism."

CHAPTER FIFTY-SEVEN
EMMIT "CHICAGO" HASKINS

THE FIFTH STREET HOUSE
MINNEAPOLIS ARTS DISTRICT OCCUPIED ZONE

Chicago stares at his phone, wondering if that just happened. He didn't recognize Vanessa Campbell's name when it popped up on the caller ID, and he can't explain why his finger immediately slid down to the green icon to accept the call. How would he know she was the chief of police? He pays very little attention to the local news, at least until a week ago.

"Hey, Chicago, have you seen our buddy's newest video?" Nashville calls out from the living room. "Get down here, man. You need to see this. It's fire."

"I approve of his soundtrack," Bronx says.

"I bet he gets a copyright strike for that," Nica adds, pointing to the screen.

"I don't think he cares," Tulsa argues. "I know I wouldn't if half the country watched one of my videos."

"What's wrong, Bro?" Nica asks when Chicago reaches the bottom of the stairs. "You look like you just laid a girl who told you she has herpes."

Three of them are on the living room furniture. Tulsa is watching out the front window while Hollywood scans the back yard. Even without being told, these guys always maintain security.

"I just got off the phone…with the chief of the Minneapolis Police Department."

"All right, I didn't have that on my ADOZ bingo card. What the hell did she want?"

Chicago looks stone-faced at Nashville. "To give me a pep talk, apparently."

"Wait! She knows who you are?"

"The police aren't stupid," he concludes.

"Inept, maybe," Tulsa mumbles.

"Not according to her. She said their hands are tied, and I believe her. She had someone dig up the property records for this place," Chicago says, looking around. "My sister's name will pop up DEERS, and that will point to my records jacket."

The Defense Enrollment Eligibility Reporting System is a centralized database the Department of Defense administers to manage benefits and entitlements information on service members, veterans, and dependents. One of the steps Chicago had to endure while out-processing from the military was to update that record. He knows that Kenyala's name and address are in there.

"The police don't know what's going on here."

"They have video of the attempted firebombing, Tulsa. They obviously know about the flag. The good news is that she doesn't seem to know about you guys."

It's a half-truth, but Chicago isn't in the mood to explain nuances.

"So, what was the point? Provide notice that you're going to be arrested?"

"No. Chief Campbell wanted to warn me that Tayson and his military commander are apparently rounding up fighters from the barricades."

The Rangers in the living room all come to the same conclusion, but Bronx is the one who articulates it. "They plan on coming in force."

Chicago nods. "It sounds that way."

"Well, once Landon sees this video, he'll definitely be gunning for us. Whether he meant to or not, Kai basically made us the symbol of the ADOZ resistance."

"Big symbols make big targets."

Tulsa cocks his head. "Bro, did you just quote *G.I. Jane?*"

Hollywood shrugs.

"Last chance, guys. This is about to get ugly. I don't expect you to fight this battle. It's been all fun and games until now, but these are real bullets coming from guns aimed by who knows how many of these asshats. Shit is about to get real."

"I ain't goin' anywhere," Bronx says, welding his beefy forearms across his ridiculously large chest.

"Me neither," Nica says, not referencing their earlier conversation. *"Molon labe."*

The Greek expression is used among soldiers and veterans all the time. It is famously attributed to King Leonidas of Sparta's response to Persian king Xerxes's demand to surrender their weapons during the Battle of Thermopylae in 480 BCE. It translates to "Come and take them."

The badass phrase symbolizes defiance and resistance against oppression. Its modern usage is by individuals committed to liberty, self-defense, and a refusal to yield to tyranny. Very fitting for this crowd, and it ties in nicely with the second flag on the makeshift pole on the roof.

"Nashville?"

"What? I told you I would follow you to hell and back. Nothing's changed."

Chicago nods. "Tulsa?"

"To borrow one of Hollywood's lines, 'Beam me up, Scotty.'"

Everyone turns to Hollywood, who is still manning the back door. "Spartans! Ready your breakfast and eat hearty... For tonight, we dine in hell!"

Chicago smirks at the line from *300*. He doesn't share his comrade's enthusiasm but appreciates the message.

"Okay. Then we have work to do. They'll wait at least until EENT, if not until nightfall or early morning. So, that gives us about nine-and-a-half-hours, minimum."

"To do what?"

"Turn my sister's house into a fortress and warn the neighbors that all hell is about to break loose on Fifth Street."

CHAPTER FIFTY-EIGHT

FIELD OFFICER DAVID BRASS

CARRIAGE HOUSE RENTAL
MINNEAPOLIS, MINNESOTA

Most of the men and women who work in the intelligence community have little use for the media. Sure, some useful idiots are used to advance elements of the national agenda, but that is rare. The same applies to what is colloquially called "the new media." Podcasters and citizen journalists are every bit as insufferable as their mainstream counterparts.

Kai Z is no exception. Most agents in the CIA and other three-letter agencies view him as a grifter who uses civil strife and national division to fatten his wallet. He's not reporting the news; he's exploiting it. Despite his misgivings about the kid and his motives, David has to admit that he can put together an effective video. This is going to turn a lot of people against Landon and the ADOZ.

A knock on the door prevents Brass from contemplating the consequences of what he just watched. Someone must be lost. He isn't expecting guests, and he absolutely doesn't expect to see the woman standing outside his door.

"Fancy meeting you here, Londynn. How did you find me?"

"You're not that slick, David. It wasn't difficult."

He nods and gestures her in, closing the door behind her. It's an unwelcome visit. David prides himself in his ability to stay below the radar. He doesn't work at Langley and rarely engages with agents or assets who aren't directly working with him. That the CIA watchdog showed up at his rental house in Minneapolis only demonstrates that he isn't as invisible as he thought.

"You want coffee?"

"No, thank you. I don't plan on staying long."

The offer was made out of politeness, and he assumed she wouldn't take him up on it. Had she, this visit would be far more cause for concern. That doesn't mean he doesn't want some, and he pours a cup for himself out of the decanter.

It gives him a moment to figure out how he wants to play this. Londynn Knight is assigned to a group that monitors CIA activity directly for the deputy director of operations. She is young but is considered an up-and-coming talent in the ranks of the Agency.

What she needs to make it to the next level is a scalp or two. It is well-known that the CIA engages in off-the-books operations that are of questionable legality. The DDO wants to clamp down on agents abusing their power. Londynn is his bloodhound, and she is on the scent of something that literally led her straight to Brass's door.

"To what do I owe the pleasure of this unannounced visit?"

"I was in the neighborhood," she says, her smug grin conveying that is definitely not the case. "I couldn't help but wonder why *you're* in this neighborhood."

Brass offers a theatric shrug. "Do I need a reason?"

"For the CIA to be operating on American soil? Yeah, you had better have a good one for violating the National Security Act of 1947."

The corner of Brass's mouth twitches. The act established the CIA and limited its powers to foreign intelligence operations. Along with Executive Order 12333, signed by President Ronald Reagan in 1981, the agency is barred from directly engaging in domestic activities, except in specific circumstances that require coordination with domestic agencies like the FBI.

"I'm not operating here. The CIA has no involvement in what's happening in the ADOZ."

"I would hope not. Railspike was bad enough."

She's fishing. There is little doubt in David's mind that Londynn knows about the Railspike operation, but she doesn't know the details. She certainly doesn't know about his connection and is trying to goad him into divulging something he shouldn't know. It's a solid plan, but he understands the tactic for what it is.

Londynn is more than a pretty face. A petite, fit, youngish black woman with a good head on her shoulders is bound to have a good career in the Agency, given the current sociocultural climate. He's not about to let the ambitious twat notch her next promotion at his expense.

"Ah, I see. You're here to curry favor with your boss. Hey, if that's what it takes to make people believe you aren't an affirmative-action project."

The comment was meant to get under her skin. It doesn't. "Is that what you think I am?"

"That's what everyone thinks."

"Then there is no point in trying to convince them otherwise. So, let's assume I'm here because I actually have a job to do. Why are you in Minneapolis, David?"

The woman is unflappable. Brass is actually impressed. An accusation like that rattles most people.

"You're not cleared to know."

"The DDO would disagree."

"I don't work for him."

"I do. You can tell me now, or I can give him a call. He'll contact the director, and you're going to be forced to tell me anyway."

David closes his eyes and nods. "I received information about foreign influence in the ADOZ. This wasn't a random takeover like what happened in Seattle or even the Occupy Wall Street movement in Manhattan. It was organized and well-funded. My asset confirmed that it's a state-sponsored operation and that at least one and possibly more leaders of this insurrection are foreign agents."

"I haven't seen any report on that. Who is your source? And don't say something tedious like you can't tell me."

"I can't give you a name outside of a SCIF," David argues, knowing that information that's above top secret shouldn't be discussed outside a Sensitive Compartmented Information Facility. "Do you remember Operation Shadow Whisper?"

Londynn cocks her head. "It was a Russian penetration mission. The CIA was tasked with gaining assets in the highest ranks of their government. The Russians found out and went public with it, causing the State Department to have a stroke. The bosses shut it down because it was a colossal failure."

"It was actually a resounding success," David says, sipping his coffee. "We made it look like a failure. A lot of those assets are still in place. One of them passed me information that the Russians are looking to destabilize our country by undermining faith in our municipal and state governments."

"To what end?" Londynn presses.

"We're a republic, Londynn. Not a democracy. If you destroy faith in one level of government, you impair it for all of them."

"What does that have to do with the ADOZ?"

"We're fairly certain Landon Tayson isn't a Russian operative. His girlfriend, however, may be. Her name is Raven Crusoe. She has a checkered past with countless gaps."

Londynn narrows her eyes. "You think it's a cover?"

"That's what I'm here to find out. Satisfied?"

He doesn't know how much of that she bought. People who work in the intelligence community are groomed to be skeptical. They are a suspicious bunch and often become jaded, completely untrusting, and downright neurotic as their careers advance.

"For now. I'll see you around, David."

"I can't wait."

Londynn leaves, and Brass locks the door behind her. He needs to move some pieces on the board. Self-preservation is a thing in the CIA, and David ensured that he's fairly well protected. After all, the director himself gave the go-ahead for Pendulum. But the idea of Londynn Knight sniffing around this could cause problems. With one phone call, he could force the DDO to warn her off, but that would likely lead to more headaches.

No, he told his lies, and now he needs to make them truths. Or, at least, make them appear that way. That's going to require some legwork. He initially wanted the ADOZ to last a while. Now, he's thinking that it needs to end sooner rather than later so loose ends can be tied.

CHAPTER FIFTY-NINE

KAI Z

This hasn't gone quite as he envisioned it would. Kai was planning on sneaking down to the building the ADOZ leaders commandeered and are using as their *de facto* city hall. Or their capital building. Or White House. Whatever they want to call the main building for this illegal takeover.

For most of the week, there has been nobody in the streets. The residents in the Arts District have huddled in their homes like COVID-19 hostages. That seems to have changed this morning. What started off as a couple of people heading south turned to five, and the number has only grown from there.

Kai joined them, preferring not to try to sneak through people's yards while residents were walking down the middle of the street. There are a couple of dozen of them by the time they reach the street just north of the barricade. They don't seem intent on stopping.

That doesn't mean he won't. Kai peels off and watches from afar. There are two reasons for that. The residents may not know who he is, but he can't risk the men at the barricade recognizing him. The last time that happened, he got shot. And that's the second reason. His leg is absolutely killing him. This is way too much walking for someone shot in the upper thigh, even if it was only technically a "flesh wound."

The group reaches the barricade as another dozen or so pass him and head in that direction. Kai raises his camera, not content to rely on the bodycam to catch this. Men guarding the makeshift barrier greet the residents cordially. There is no hostility at all as they let the first group through while their leader has a conversation on his walkie-talkie. Orders are orders. They are probably there to keep cops out, not people in.

The leader drops the small device to his side and barks orders that Kai can't make out. The second group is stopped in their tracks. Something changed. The people start shouting, and the sentries on either side of the barrier ready their weapons. A man pushes one of the guards and gets a shove in return. Then, weapons get raised, causing a woman to scream and the rest of the group to step back.

They are ordered to leave. One of the men protests, and the shouting gets loud enough for Kai to hear.

"Leave now! Return to your home."

"That's not gonna happen!"

Two of the sentries train their guns on the man. "It's not a suggestion. All crossings are closed. If you have a problem with that, take it up with the president."

"Maybe I will."

The group reverses direction with urgency and determination in their strides. They are captives in this ADOZ, after all, and it isn't sitting well with them. Kai joins the group as it heads up to the building on University Avenue. When they arrive, they are quickly joined by other small groups who had similar run-ins at the barricades.

Kai talks with a few of them, knowing his bodycam is catching the conversations. They are in the middle of University Avenue, but there is no real need to worry about traffic in the ADOZ. Cars are banned here, except those used by patrols.

Gunfire erupts to the north. A few of the now close to one hundred residents gathered here turn their heads, but most are desensitized to the reports of semi-automatic weapons. It is way too common to command attention since the creation of the occupied zone.

The man next to Kai picks up his cell phone when it rings. He listens intently, asks a few questions, and hangs up.

"Those shots we heard?" he asks, commanding the attention of the people around him. "It was people trying to leave in their car. A friend of mine was at the barricade. They just shot and killed a family of four!"

Landon walks out of his headquarters with a complement of security to augment the ones trying to conduct crowd control. The anger is ratcheted up with news of the deaths. Kai doesn't know if it's true, but it doesn't matter to these people. Anger is turning to rage, and there will be little that Landon or his guards can do to pacify them. Now is the time to make his move.

He weaves through the irate crowd and sneaks past a guard to the north side of the L-shaped structure. A concrete driveway belonging to the house next door abuts the building, and Kai hobbles as quickly as he can down it. He reaches a rusting steel staircase that leads to a door on the second floor, and he climbs it, pain radiating from his left leg with each step.

Fortunately, the door is unlocked. The journalist peeks in and scans the hallway. It's clear. He moves into the corridor and pokes his head around the corner, checking the hall leading back toward the street. It's also clear.

Kai walks quietly, listening for voices or other telltale signs of movement. He can't imagine that this place is completely unoccupied, but that appears to be the case. Everyone here must be outside dealing with the enraged crowd. His timing is perfect.

At the end of the corridor is a large office. Kai pokes his head in to ensure it's empty, and he slides into the room. Landon must be using this one. A large map of the city is spread out on the desk. A thick red line denotes the border of the ADOZ. Blue dots look like they depict known police staging areas. Some have small Post-it notes with the function. One is labeled "CP," and another reads "SWAT."

He's not here for a map. He catches a glimpse of the phone on the table. Bingo. He walks over and picks it up, causing the screen to come to life. Kai doesn't know the lock code but has friends who can help with that. This was easier than he expected.

"I don't believe that's yours," a female voice announces from behind him.

Kai spins to find a woman standing in the doorway. She slides a pistol out of its holster but doesn't immediately point it at him. She stares hard at him until realization flashes on her face. Then the gun comes up, and its muzzle is trained on his chest. This just got bad… really bad.

"Well, if it isn't Kai Z," she says in a tone that, to Kai, almost sounds amused. "We've been looking for you."

CHAPTER SIXTY

LANDON TAYSON

Landon tries to simmer the angry crowd. They listen to his words…sort of. But every sentence is greeted with profanities and calls for him to have improper relations with his mother. Nobody said politics was easy.

He launches into a monologue about their safety and tries to explain that the ADOZ border was closed for their protection. That is met with an equal amount of consternation and vitriol. These people want to leave, and words are not going to dissuade them. At least, that's the message he's getting in response.

It's worth one more try. Landon promises to arrange safe passage out when the security threat diminishes. Until then, he asks them to return to their homes. That only makes them more agitated.

"Sir, I have an urgent message from Raven," a young guard says, coming up alongside him. "She needs to see you immediately."

"Uh, can't she see that I'm a little busy?"

"She says it's of the utmost importance."

"So is this," the ADOZ president says, gesturing at the angry crowd of his citizens.

"Alas, Babylon."

Landon's head shoots around to the man. *Alas, Babylon* is a post-apocalyptic novel published in the late 1950s that tells the story of a small town in Florida struggling to survive after a nuclear war devastated the United States. The title comes from a biblical reference in the Book of Revelation, symbolizing doom and destruction. The main character's brother in the story, a colonel with the U.S. Air Force's Strategic Air Command outside of Omaha, uses that phrase to warn him of an imminent disaster.

Raven and Landon bonded over the book when they first met. Both loved it and agreed that if there was ever dire trouble the other needed to know about, that phrase would be uttered. She had never once used it…until now.

"I've said what I need to say," Landon says to Muzzie after tugging on his body armor to get his attention. "They aren't interested in listening. Let them scream and have their temper tantrums. When they simmer down, order them to disperse. If they don't, make them."

"You got it, Mr. President."

Landon heads back into the building and upstairs to his office. Whatever has Raven spooked must be important. When he reaches the door, he sees why and freezes in place. This is not what he expected, and his face probably betrays that.

"We have a visitor, Mr. President," Raven sweetly says as she holds their guest at gunpoint.

Landon stares at the man for a long moment. He isn't sure what to say. Uttering something witty would be epic, but nothing that isn't cliché comes to mind. He settles for crossing his arms and appreciating this small yet important victory.

"Kai Z…I'd say I'm a fan, but I'm really not. What are you doing here?"

He thrusts his chin out. "Getting the other side of the story."

"Since when do you care about that?" Landon asks after a scoff.

"I'm a journalist."

"You're a provocateur," Raven interjects. "I caught him snooping around. He was about to walk off with my cell phone."

"I picked it up to figure out whose it was."

"What were you looking for up here?" Landon asks, ignoring the lie for what it likely is.

"You."

"You could have made an appointment."

Kai lets out a short snicker and points to his leg. "Two of your men shot and tried to kill me. I wasn't going to take that chance."

Landon cocks his head. "What makes you think I won't shoot you right now?"

"You're the president of the ADOZ, and you already have a serious image problem."

"No thanks to you," Raven decrees, the seething contempt in her voice causing the YouTuber to turn to face her.

"Yes, I contributed to that. I'm doing my job, and I make no apologies," Kai says, shifting his eyes to Landon. "It's why you should let me interview you. Think of the power of that optic."

Raven raises her eyebrows. Landon has been with her long enough to read her body language. She doesn't think that's a half-bad idea. He isn't so sure but is willing to tease it a little.

"Take your video down, and we'll talk."

Kai presses his lips together and shakes off the suggestion. "I can't do that. Even if I scrubbed it from my channel, it's out there now. That will make it go even more viral, and I'm pretty certain you don't want that."

Raven nods, but was it because of the reason for not taking it down or the second part about it going viral? Landon isn't sure, but it's irrelevant. He wants this guy to take a long dirt nap, as Muzzie likes to call it. Soldiers have the best metaphors for death.

"I already gave a press briefing."

"I know. I was there. You told the country and world that you set up this ADOZ. You didn't say *why*. Here's your chance, and I can promise that what you say won't be carved into ten-second sound bites. You'll have an entire long-form video to explain your actions and goals. It's more than you'll get from anyone else."

"All right," Landon says, exhaling loudly. "Assume I say yes to your request. When do you want to do this?"

Kai's face softens. "How about right now?"

CHAPTER SIXTY-ONE
CHIEF VANESSA CAMPBELL

The scenic Boom Island Park, located along the Mississippi River, offers an almost unparalleled view of the downtown Minneapolis skyline. While it will never compare to Manhattan or Chicago, it is still very serene. Vanessa has lived in this city for decades and doesn't recall ever coming up here.

There are walking and biking trails that are connected to the extensive Minneapolis trail system, a small, nonfunctioning lighthouse, picnic tables and open spaces for gatherings, and even a boat dock. She can imagine this being a busy place in the summer during normal times. Thanks to the ADOZ, this isn't a normal time.

After hours of staring at video from a drone flying over the Arts District, Vanessa needed to step away. She hasn't gotten much sleep since this started, and it's starting to catch up to her. Despite desperately needing the rest, she can't bring herself to be away for more than an hour or two. Some would label that as her having trust issues with her subordinates. She calls it a sensible precaution.

"Extended lunch break?" Lieutenant Burke asks. He may be the only subordinate she does trust. "Or do you not want to be found?"

"Both, but I'm clearly failing at the latter since you're here. Speaking of which, how did you find me?"

"I was a detective before I transferred into SWAT," he says with a wry grin before sitting at the picnic table. "You left Sillyere in charge, so I figured you didn't go too far."

Vanessa offers a half grumble, half moan. "Has she surrendered yet?"

"No, but we hid every white cloth within three miles of the command post just in case."

"Good call."

"Do you want me to leave you to your thoughts?"

There is a part of Vanessa that wants to say yes. She came here for solace so she could do some quiet reflection. However, Burke is a sympathetic ear, and she also feels the need to talk. Maybe using her words might help put order to the chaos of the random thoughts clouding her mind.

"Have you ever wondered how we got here?"

"I walked. I'm not sure how you did."

"I meant how we got into this situation," Vanessa clarifies after giving her SWAT commander a disapproving look.

"I know what you meant. I haven't had any time to think about it."

"I just did. We let a bunch of protestors seize an entire area of our city."

"We didn't. You wanted to immediately go in, if memory serves. That was the mayor's decision."

"Yeah, it was. What consequences do you think Thurlow will face for that?"

"He'll lose reelection."

"You think so? In this city? I doubt it."

Minneapolis is a progressive city with political leaders and voters who generally support very liberal policies. That's not an inherently bad thing if it's what the people want. What it also means is that if he decides to run again for mayor, there is little chance of his not winning. Blame will be deflected. Excuses will be made. And, most likely, she will be scapegoated to preserve his political career. It's not an original story.

"Are you really in this park lamenting the mayor's fate?"

"No," Vanessa says, turning her head to take in the sweeping view of the city across the river. "I'm lamenting the people's future. We implemented a lot of measures to get better after 2020. Some were good. Some were absolute disasters."

"Otto Goldberg."

"I don't have a problem with creating a position that ensures our officers are following proper police procedures and respecting our citizens' constitutionally protected rights. I had a big problem with his siding with criminals."

Burke takes his hat off, sets it on the table, and runs his hand through his close-cropped black hair. "And his affinity for armed thugs got him killed."

"Our failure to protect the people of this city got him killed. There are plenty of people to blame for that, including me. I've been too permissive in allowing this nonsense to continue."

"What do you think you could have done?"

"Fight," Vanessa immediately answers. "Not *against* the mayor but *for* the people. There are thousands of citizens on the other side of those barricades. We've done absolutely nothing to help them."

"What do you want to do?"

"End this."

Vanessa turns her head to gauge Burke's reaction. He knows what they are up against better than anyone. The men guarding the ADOZ barricades aren't armed with squirt guns. They are toting assault rifles and have demonstrated a willingness to use them. Ending this likely means a confrontation that will quickly turn deadly if mishandled. SWAT members are trained. They aren't invincible.

"I don't see that happening anytime soon, even with the National Guard beginning to arrive. You know the governor won't give them the order to intervene in any meaningful way. He's using them as political cover."

Vanessa lowers her eyes. He's right. Their presence is for show. The extra manpower will allow her to rotate her people for rest, but when push comes to shove, she doesn't expect the military to act. Ironically, the 1st Battalion, 194th Armor Regiment, headquartered in Brainerd, could provide the heavy armor and mechanized infantry ground combat power that would end this occupation in ten minutes. Shooting at tanks with an AR-15 wouldn't have much impact. Instead, the governor mobilized support units.

"Are Landon and his commander still pulling men from the barricades?"

"It looks like he stopped and returned to their command center. We've seen people taking to the streets in the ADOZ, so it may be because of that."

"They need to act. Tayson is losing control. I don't know what he'll do to regain it, but I'd bet he'll start with the house on Fifth Street. If he makes a move on it, we need to be ready to capitalize."

"The mayor won't give that order," Burke counters. He isn't wrong.

"You don't take orders from him, Godroy. I will give it, and I'm asking you to follow it. Trust me, I'm not going to put you in a position where it's a suicide mission. But I need you and your guys ready to act at a moment's notice."

Burke puts his hat back on. "Okay. We'll be ready. I'm trusting you, Chief. Please don't make me regret that."

"I won't."

CHAPTER SIXTY-TWO

KAI Z

UNIVERSITY AVENUE COMMAND CENTER
MINNEAPOLIS ARTS DISTRICT OCCUPIED ZONE

He isn't prepared for this. The request to do an interview was a Hail Mary to save his ass. He doesn't have the right cameras and has only limited sound equipment and no lighting. Even podcasters who post online have that equipment as a bare minimum. But Landon agreed, so now he needs to make this work.

The office Landon is squatting in is dark, even with the overhead light on. He dispatched people to find some equipment, and they returned with LED stand lights, some microphones, and even two extra cameras. Kai wonders if they left some money at the electronics store they raided or just looted the place. Most likely, the latter.

Kai arranges two chairs with the wood-paneled wall behind them as a young woman with jet-black hair watches his every move. She was the one who taped the map that was on the desk to the area behind the chairs. It's the best backdrop he's going to get. The lights are set up, as are the cameras that will give three angles – him, Landon, and a wide shot of both of them. It's actually pretty good for a hasty setup.

Bryce Cronkite provides him instructions on the interview after the microphone check is completed. It's the first time Kai has seen or heard from him since the press conference. He would have expected regular online updates from the wanna-be journalist, but the man is apparently camera-shy. Despite his name evoking one of journalism's legends, he's a lightweight. His crappy channel has about ten subscribers, and they're likely his immediate family who don't even watch him.

Kai nonchalantly puts his earpiece in. The two men may be speaking in hushed voices out in the hall, but that doesn't mean they should have an expectation of privacy. He adjusts a light one final time while he listens.

"Did you give Kai any instructions?"

"Yep. You're damn right I did."

"Will he listen to them?"

Bryce rewards the question with an apprehensive look. "Don't hold your breath. He made a name for himself by being edgy. I don't expect that to change for the first sit-down interview with the leader of the ADOZ."

"What does that mean for us?" Landon asks.

"Just mind your tongue."

Kai smiles. Landon forgot that he's already mic'd up. It's a forgivable sin that even professional politicians fall victim to. Ronald Reagan joked during a mic test that he was outlawing Russia, and they were going to begin bombing in five minutes. George W. Bush and Dick Cheney were caught disparaging a *New York Times* reporter, and Barack Obama was overheard striking a deal with the Russian president, Dmitry Medvedev.

"I'm ready for you, sir," Kai says, poking his head out of the office.

He thought adding the "sir" was a nice touch. Too bad Landon doesn't look overly impressed. Kai doesn't respect anyone in the ADOZ, and they likely know it. If he shows a little deference, he may be able to get out of this mess in one piece.

The ADOZ president sits in his chair and patiently waits. Kai ensures the cameras are recording, and he opens the interview by describing the takeover of the Minneapolis Arts District. It's a brief recap. News networks have already done in-depth pieces on it.

"Joining me now is the president of the ADOZ, Landon Tayson. Thank you for agreeing to this interview."

"Thank you for giving me the opportunity to speak the truth."

Kai wants to say, "The truth is relative," but he keeps his mouth shut. Instead, he asks about Landon's background, and they talk about his activism. It leads nicely to the events that have transpired.

"Where did you get the idea for the ADOZ?"

"I was outside City Hall when the police shot tear gas and fired at us without provocation. We needed a safe place to go. This was as good as any."

"It must have been challenging to get all the barricades set up so quickly."

"The people here are passionate. They believe in the cause. I gave them a mission, and they executed it."

Kai nods. "What is your cause?"

"Justice."

Landon launches into a long monologue about the misdeeds of the police and the repression rampant in America. He makes a few good points, but like most rabid ideologues, they are buried in anger and extremism. To him, the police are evil, the politicians are fascists, and the people are brainwashed. It's almost ironic that the same characterization can be applied to the fighters in the ADOZ.

They move on to the challenges the group has faced, excluding anything about the shooting at the barricade per Bryce Cronkite's instructions. Kai would love to get some answers about that, but he wants to walk out of here alive. The interview is beginning to drag, but this isn't meant to be one in the first place. Besides, he can cut it in post-production if there is anything worth releasing. His only goal is to get out of here.

Landon begins discussing the logistics behind their effort, ostensively to impress people with his planning skills. The information is vague and innocuous, but it also provides an opening. Kai smiles as he tees up the question.

"What support have you gotten from outside the ADOZ?"

Landon cocks his head. "What do you mean?"

Kai knows he shouldn't ask this. The idea of the interview was nothing more than a cover story he conjured up after getting caught in this building. He shouldn't press his luck.

"There are people who believe that you are getting outside support. It could be anarchist groups, our government, or even foreign governments. Is that true?"

"No."

"Mr. President, those weapons your fighters have at the barricades didn't come from the local Walmart. Who is supporting you?"

Landon shifts in his chair. "The people."

"There was a report I read that you were getting foreign support…possibly from a terrorist group or rogue government."

"It's a lie. Don't be a party in spreading misinformation, Kai," Landon says in warning. The podcaster nods, heeding it.

"What does success look like for you? Reform? Firings? An apology? How does this end?"

"It is too late for those measures. The answer to your question is, 'Who says it will end?'"

The grin that creeps across Landon's face is enough to make Kai's skin crawl. He believes in his heart that this occupation is going to last forever. A five-year-old would know that isn't the case. This district isn't self-sustainable. Most states couldn't secede from the Union and survive as an independent entity. California and Texas may be able to pull it off, but that's it. The rest would struggle mightily, and they are a lot larger than a few neighborhoods in the heart of a major city.

Kai ends the interview with the two men shaking hands. He rises and shuts the cameras off.

"You were awfully interested in who's supporting us in the ADOZ," Landon says from his seat.

"It's a question most people have. It's the one I have. I thought you handled it brilliantly."

Landon presses his lips together. It seems like he accepts that explanation.

"Did you get what you need?"

Kai nods. "I think this is going to go a long way for your cause. Millions of people will see this online. They'll have a greater understanding as to what you're doing here and why."

"I wish that was the case. Unfortunately, nobody will ever see it."

"What do you mean? I have almost five million subscribers on my channel. Mainstream media will absolutely run segments. Everyone is going to see it."

"Not if it doesn't get uploaded."

"Why wouldn't it?"

Kai is legitimately confused. He's responsible for videos. There is no need for him to answer to producers or executives because there are none. That's the beauty of being independent. So, it will absolutely get uploaded unless he means….

"Because you won't be alive to post it."

He watches Landon pull out a weapon from its holster. His eyes clearly see what's happening, but his mind simply refuses to believe them. Then it registers. Kai feels a sharp pang in his chest as his heart jumps. His mouth hangs open, and his eyes grow wide as he stares into the muzzle of the gun and watches Landon's finger move to the trigger. He hears the brief sound of a shot before…nothing.

CHAPTER SIXTY-THREE

LANDON TAYSON

UNIVERSITY AVENUE COMMAND CENTER
MINNEAPOLIS ARTS DISTRICT OCCUPIED ZONE

Landon holds the gun out for a few beats before holstering it. He glances at Raven, who is standing against the wall with her hand over her mouth. It's one thing to see someone killed on video. It's another when it happens right in front of you.

"He should have seen that coming," Bryce mumbles, the first to enter the office and see Kai's dead body lying on the floor.

Two guards rush in, their weapons drawn. It's not the best response time. The gunshot was nearly thirty seconds ago. If it had been Kai with the gun, he would have had time to kill all of them and enjoy coffee before these guys showed up. Fortunately, it didn't happen that way, so Landon chooses not to make an issue out of it.

"It's okay, guys," he assures them, causing them to relax, if only a little.

"Why did you do that?" Raven says from along the wall, having recovered from the shock.

"Because it had to be done."

"Bryce?"

"I agree with Landon. Kai waded into waters that he didn't belong in."

"Get someone to take this piece of trash out of my office," Landon orders the guards. "And one of you call Captain Muzzie. Tell him I need to see him."

They exit the office and get on the radio. Landon does a circle around Kai's body. He knows what he's done. The poker term for it is "going all in." All his chips are in the pot. They only need to wait for the turn and river cards to see who wins.

"He could have helped us!" Raven screeches, pointing at the dead YouTuber.

"He had no interest in helping us," Bryce says. "You heard his questions. He was on a fishing expedition."

"He's right," Landon confirms. "Kai wanted to know who was supporting us. He knew we had a benefactor and was trying to sniff out who it was."

"You don't know that."

"It's a safe assumption," Bryce confirms. "He knew something, and his questions were crafted to confirm his source's information. He could have exposed everything. I think that was his goal in wanting this interview."

"And why he was about to walk off with your phone, Raven."

"He just picked it up from the table. There's no proof that he was going to steal it."

"If you say so. Either way, it's not worth the risk of exposing our supporters. I made that pledge to them, and I'm keeping it."

Muzzie storms into the room. His eyes shift from Landon to Raven to Bryce and then down to Kai on the floor. "Damn! I wanted to shoot him."

"See what you miss when you're not here?"

The commander pouts. "What's the word, Mr. President?"

"Do you have the attack force identified?"

"Yes, sir."

"Good. Tell the men to rest up and assemble in the parking lot late this afternoon. We take the house on Fifth Avenue right after sundown."

"You're going to storm it?" Raven asks.

Landon looks at the body. "No more half-measures. Our reinforcements are stalled, and the natives are getting restless. The time has come to consolidate our power. It starts with that infernal flag coming down."

"I'll see to it," Muzzie says, doing an about-face and marching out of the office.

Bryce collects the cameras. "I'm going to go through Kai's footage."

He leaves, and three men come to collect Kai's body. Landon doesn't feel compelled to give them instructions about what to do with it. Muzzie will take care of that.

Raven grabs his arm. "Are you sure you want to do this, Landon?"

"I've never been more sure of anything in my life. That flag comes down, or we all die trying to take it down. It's us against them. Someone dies tonight, and I plan on it being them."

CHAPTER SIXTY-FOUR
EMMIT "CHICAGO" HASKINS

FIFTH STREET
MINNEAPOLIS ARTS DISTRICT OCCUPIED ZONE

Urban warfare is easily one of the most complex and dangerous forms of combat. Cities are three-dimensional arenas complete with limited visibility, noncombatants, and plenty of places to hide. Engagements happen at close range, leaving precious little reaction time to events.

The American Army has always played offense in urban areas on the modern battlefield. Soldiers are trained to look for improvised explosive devices hidden under the rubble, booby traps, snipers, and enemies posing as civilians. The brutality, pace, and unpredictability of urban warfare require tactical precision, discipline, and adaptability to overcome. Rangers have it. ADOZ fighters don't.

Best of all, Chicago and his men are defending instead of attacking for once. Threats can come from anywhere in a built-up area, and Chicago will leverage that advantage. A single high-rise building can take hours or even days to properly clear. This may only be a single-family home, but Landon Tayson is about to discover how hard and costly taking even a small house can be.

A man walks out his front door and stares at Chicago for a long moment. One of the eeriest things about this occupation is how few residents have been outside. Neighbors may meet, but it's likely in their homes or across the fences in their small back yards. Almost nobody is on the streets.

The man is dressed in jeans and a T-shirt. He idles over, taking in the uniform without patches and the rifle slung across Chicago's chest. He may wonder if he's an ADOZ fighter. The former Ranger can only hope he doesn't look that pathetic.

"You live across the street there. I think I've seen ya before. Expectin' trouble?"

Chicago turns and looks over his shoulder up at the flag. "Yeah, I'm afraid it's coming."

The man nods his approval. "Give 'em hell."

"Do you have a place you can go, sir? It's likely to get ugly out here."

"Yeah, I'd go to Virginia, but they ain't letting anyone past the barricades."

"Can you shelter somewhere else in the district?"

The man gestures back at his house. "This place is all I have."

Chicago smiles. "I know what you mean. If you hear them outside, go down to the basement. If bullets start flying, you'll be safer there."

"You got it."

"One more thing, sir. Spread the word if you're willing. We're trying to warn people that danger is coming, but some of our neighbors aren't answering the door. I'm not sure who is here and who left."

"I gotcha. You look like Rambo. I wouldn't answer for ya, either. I've lived here for thirty years. They'll answer for me. When do you think they're coming?"

"I'm guessing tonight."

"You take care of yourself, Soldier."

He nods and moves off to talk to the people next door. Chicago sees his five men coming up the street, looking every bit the badass an Army Ranger should. BDUs were the greatest uniform the Army ever had. They had switched away from it long before he joined, but now he sees why the veterans he knows spoke so poetically about it.

"Yo, Chicago…your house may be the least defensible structure I have ever seen."

"It wasn't meant to be Mont Saint-Michel."

Mont Saint-Michel is one of the most impregnable fortresses in the world. Located in Normandy, France, the medieval stronghold sits on a rocky island surrounded by treacherous tidal waters. It has thick stone walls and clear lines of sight to identify approaching enemies. It was impossible to effectively besiege.

"Fixed fortifications are monuments to the stupidity of man. If mountain ranges and oceans can be overcome, then anything built by man can be overcome."

"I hate to agree with good ol' Georgie Patton here, but Hollywood is right," Tulsa says. "The Alamo is a cool bit of history until you remember that everyone *died* defending it."

"Shut your pie hole, Hollywood," Nashville advises, getting a sly look from the quote machine. At least he took the warning to heart and spared them another line.

"God, I hate to agree, but they're right," Nica says. "We're Rangers. We hit hard and fast, overwhelming enemies using hit-and-run tactics, ambushes, and infiltration."

"Preach!" Tulsa seconds.

He isn't wrong. The scroll they wear on their uniforms identifies them as an elite infantry unit. There are plenty of other outfits the Army can use to hold ground. When you want it broken, dead, or pregnant, you call the Rangers. It's the most Alpha-male unit in the military. They run on caffeine, testosterone, patriotism, and hatred.

"I know, guys. Static defense isn't our thing. But that house is our FOB. It's also my *home*. I'm not about to let these asshats take it from me…from my sister. That doesn't mean I plan on fighting fair while we defend it."

"What do you have in mind?" Tulsa asks. "I didn't have room for drones, air support, or tanks in my duffle bags."

"We have company."

Everyone's heads turn in the direction Bronx is staring. They spot a woman walking down the street toward them. Her strides are determined, as is the look on her face. His men spread apart and bring their weapons up to the low ready. She stops when she's about ten feet away.

"Nice camo. You must be Chicago."

CHAPTER SIXTY-FIVE
CHIEF VANESSA CAMPBELL

CITY HALL CONFERENCE ROOM
MINNEAPOLIS, MINNESOTA

The word "suffering" comes from the Latin *"sufferre,"* a combination of "sub-," meaning under, and *"ferre,"* meaning to bear, carry, or endure. The term entered Old French as *suffrir* and later Middle English as *suffren* before evolving into modern English. It is generally defined as the experience of pain or distress caused by physical, emotional, existential, or social hardship. Vanessa is experiencing all of those in this meeting.

The news coming from the perimeter around the ADOZ is good, except for all the reasons that it isn't. Morale among the fighters at the barricades is low. The adrenaline has worn off, and boredom has set in. They are tired, hungry, and beginning to question why they are there.

And that's what leads to the bad news. Mayor Thurlow thinks his plan is working. To a degree, it is, as much as Vanessa hates to admit it. Their united front against repression and persecution is showing some cracks. There are defections, and Landon's behavior is becoming more erratic if their infrequent social media posts are any indication.

"It's all because of your superb leadership during this crisis, Mr. Mayor," Wilma Sillyere says from the opposite side of the table. "There is no doubt in my mind that this movement will collapse soon without any bloodshed."

Vanessa doesn't react. She already knew that her lipstick was all over Thurlow's ass. She can't be sure how she manages to get around his shoulders, though. They must be blocking the way. He has his head shoved so far up his own ass that he could give a proctologist a detailed report of what he sees.

"Does the FBI have anything to report?" the governor asks.

"Over the past forty-eight hours, we intercepted convoys heading for the ADOZ based on actionable intelligence from a different agency. In addition to identifying convoy members with outstanding federal warrants, we seized hundreds of firearms, most with serial numbers removed and likely obtained illegally."

"Are they being charged?" Vanessa asks.

"For now, we are only indicting them on the gun-related charges. The DOJ is considering labeling them domestic terrorists."

"That may be a little brash, don't you think?" the governor asks.

"I'm just the messenger."

"The good news is that no reinforcements are heading for the ADOZ," the mayor concludes. "What about police presence, Chief Campbell?"

She begins her briefing, referencing the notes she wrote out on a yellow legal pad about an hour ago. Not much has changed in the situation on the ground, so she focuses on resources and personnel matters. She concludes with the arrival of National Guard units, which are taking up positions opposite some of the larger barricades. There's nothing like the sight of a HMMWV with an M240B machine gun mounted on the turret to send a message. Not that she thinks the fighters in the ADOZ are remotely intimidated. They know the military won't move in.

"For the record," Governor St. James interjects, "they are not to be used in operations or any law enforcement capacity."

Vanessa's thought of driving an M2 Bradley through one of the barricades is nothing more than a pipe dream. The National Guard's role is limited by law. The governor activated it under Title 32 state active duty status, a provision that allows them to assist in natural disasters, riots, civil unrest, and emergencies. This qualifies, and the Guard may help local police but cannot make arrests themselves unless authorized by the governor. He's not going to give that order.

That means they are only there for show. It's a PR stunt, with the only added benefit of allowing her to better rotate her people to keep them fresh. She wonders if Landon Tayson knows that. Probably. She'd bet her salary that the governor would announce it at a press conference the first time a reporter asks what their mission is. She's surprised it hasn't happened already.

"Nobody enters the ADOZ, Chief," the mayor orders. Even if a barricade is unmanned, not a single officer is to cross Broadway or the other surrounding streets. Understood?"

"What if there's violence?" Vanessa asks, the edge in her voice sharp and accusatory.

The mayor draws a breath. "There won't be."

It's an insane response that nearly everyone at this table seems willing to accept. It's not a statement of fact – it's wishful thinking. There has already been violence in the ADOZ, and she is certain more is coming.

"You don't know that, sir."

"Okay, Chief Campbell, you seem to have some conviction about this. Explain to us why you think there will be?"

"If they are on the verge of collapsing, as you suggest, why wouldn't they act rashly? What if they attack the house with the flag?"

"Then that will accelerate the end for them. The public will learn the truth."

Vanessa shakes her head. That won't be much solace to the victims.

"If there is nothing else, this meeting is adjourned," St. James announces.

It was an abrupt end to the meeting, but the governor didn't really want to be here to begin with. The men and women who crammed into the conference room scatter, leaving a clear path for the mayor to beeline to his embattled police chief. A sinister grin paints itself on his face as he leans in.

"I'm right, and you're wrong, Vanessa. You need to come to terms with that. When the people learn that my plan succeeded when yours would have led to more bloodshed, you'll be begging for me to accept your resignation."

His face doesn't change as he leans back, stares hard at her, and turns for the door. The only thing more condescending he could have done is wink at her. Burke comes to her side just as Sillyere struts over, her head bobbing like a peacock.

"See what happens when you're on the wrong side of history, Chief?"

"Wilma, the Arts District is in your precinct. Aren't you the least bit concerned about the people trapped in there?"

"I was relieved of those duties when Tayson took over."

Vanessa shakes her head. "What about if their lives are in danger?"

"Again, it's not my problem."

"You have a duty to them."

"No. As of now, they're in a foreign country. The mayor agrees, and you should, too. Get with the program, Vanessa. For your sake."

She leaves, her gait and posture reflecting the confidence of someone who thinks she's winning. Vanessa glances at Burke's chest. He is still geared up, having come directly from the perimeter to attend this meeting.

"Godroy? Please tell me you've had your body camera on the whole time during that meeting."

"Are you kidding? It's more dangerous in here than it is out on the streets. You're damn straight that I have it on."

CHAPTER SIXTY-SIX
FIELD OFFICER DAVID BRASS

FBI MINNEAPOLIS FIELD OFFICE
BROOKLYN CENTER, MINNESOTA

There is a time to sit back and be an administrator, and there's a time to get your hands dirty. If that's what this can be called. Brass backed himself into a corner when he squared off against Londynn Knight. He managed to satisfy the aggressive bitch for now, but he needs some cover. He told her that there was foreign influence in the ADOZ, and now it needs to be true. There is one group of useful idiots he can use to turn fiction into fact.

The FBI's Minneapolis Field Office is actually located in Brooklyn Center, roughly ten miles northwest of downtown. The office covers the states of Minnesota, North Dakota, and South Dakota, investigating domestic and international security threats, cybercrime like hacking and ransomware, organized and white-collar crime, and civil rights enforcement. Brass isn't here for any of that.

This meeting is with the special agent in charge of counterintelligence. Since the CIA isn't technically allowed to operate on American soil, identifying and removing threats within our borders falls to the Bureau. On paper, the two entities cooperate on those matters. The reality is a touch different.

After 9/11, the intelligence sharing between the CIA and FBI did improve. The National Counterterrorism Center is an information clearinghouse that allows coordination of efforts. Additionally, the FBI's Joint Terrorism Task Forces often include CIA analysts providing international intelligence. Despite appearances, there are still jurisdictional and personality conflicts.

That's the primary reason behind Watchtower. Brass knows that real information sharing across the eighteen agencies that make up the United States intelligence community can lead to real results. Capability isn't the issue. The complete lack of coordination and desire to leverage it is.

So contentious is the current relationship, it took Matt Remsen making a call to set up this meeting. The cranky bastard across the desk from him wasn't thrilled about taking it. Fortunately, he's a crusty old agent from a bygone era who still believes in professional courtesy.

"What is Langley's interest in the ADOZ? And don't give me the 'it's classified' BS."

"I wouldn't dream of it, Special Agent Grimaldi."

"Right. Because the CIA is always quick to offer up information."

Grimaldi clearly predates 9/11. He's probably been in the Bureau for longer than Brass has been alive. He's jaded, war-weary, and not in the mood to spar with anyone from other agencies. It wouldn't matter if Brass were carrying an olive branch the size of Kansas to make amends.

"Matt and I have managed to find a way to cooperate outside of channels. I'm more interested in results than hoarding information. Sharing is the only way to get things done."

Grimaldi pouts and looks like he's chewing on his lip. It must be a nervous tic. "Okay. So, why are you talking to me?"

"Because we believe that foreign agents are behind the Minneapolis ADOZ."

"Based on what information?"

"Human intelligence."

"I suppose that's classified," Agent Grimaldi says, shifting in his seat.

Brass leans forward. "I suppose you wouldn't be brazen enough to ask me to divulge sources. In the spirit of cooperation, the source was part of a Russian penetration operation called Shadow Whisper. Langley was directed to gain assets in the highest ranks of the Russian government. I'll leave it at that."

"Fair enough. What was the information?"

"That the Russians are looking to destabilize our country by undermining American faith in our municipal and state governments. I know you've been working up profiles on the ADOZ leaders. Do you have information on Raven Crusoe?"

The agent pulls out a file. Shockingly, it's printed in hard copy. This guy is nothing if not old school.

"There was no information we could find on her until two years ago. She's likely using an alias, which means without prints or DNA to run against the database, she's a ghost."

The FBI maintains the Combined DNA Index System to assist with criminal investigations. The database allows law enforcement agencies to compare DNA profiles from crime scenes, convicted offenders, and missing persons to help solve cases.

"She won't be in CODIS because she's a Russian agent."

There's a long pause while the agent processes that. Part of it is a measurement against what he knows to identify deception. The other part is wondering what he can do with the information. Or if he should do anything with it.

"You know the FBI isn't officially involved in the ADOZ. It's considered a state and local issue."

"I do. It's politically toxic. But we both know the difference between 'officially' and 'unofficially.' You became involved when counterintelligence stopped the caravans en route to Minnesota."

Grimaldi folds his arms across his chest. "I'm assuming you had a hand in that?"

"Did you trace the guns?" Brass asks without answering his question.

"The serial numbers were filed off."

"That doesn't mean they're untraceable. Raven Crusoe arranged for an arms transfer from a shell company to one of the men you have in custody. We traced that company back to a Russian oligarch who was murdered last year by the FSB."

"Why?"

"Because he was a double agent. Well, triple agent. He was also feeding information to MI6."

MI6, formally the Secret Intelligence Service, is the United Kingdom's foreign intelligence agency. It gathers intelligence outside the UK to counter threats and protect national security. It was only publicly acknowledged to exist in 1994, despite being formed just after the turn of the last century. It's best known by its most prolific agent…James Bond.

"Why are you giving up *that* source?"

"He's dead. He can't be killed again," Brass can't resist saying.

"So, you're saying the Russians are behind the ADOZ?"

"No, this is Landon Tayson's brainchild. The Russians are supporting him with funding and weapons. In this file are details of an off-shore account Tayson used to procure what he needed. It's a steep climb, but it's enough to start building a case against him when this is over."

Brass hands Grimaldi the file and stands. His work here is done.

"That's it?" the jaded agent asks.

"That's it. Other than if you connect all the dots, remember my name and speak kindly of me to your superiors."

Brass flashes the curmudgeonly man a toothy smile and shows himself out of his office. That was almost too easy. The FBI will spend months tracing that information only to run into the mother of black holes. Sooner or later, someone will leak the information about Russian involvement. They will deny it, but the world stopped taking their denials seriously decades ago.

All that matters is how many fingers point in that direction. The media will latch on to it, and that's good for another few news cycles once the fervor around the ADOZ dies down. That's why Brass loves this job. It's all in a day's work.

CHAPTER SIXTY-SEVEN
EMMIT "CHICAGO" HASKINS

FIFTH STREET HOUSE
MINNEAPOLIS ARTS DISTRICT OCCUPIED ZONE

The offers of tea and coffee were politely refused. When Nashville poured a glass of bourbon, the woman's attitude changed. That was music to the ears of Chicago's fellow Rangers. There is nothing more enticing on the planet than the combination of a blonde and alcohol. Their tongues are practically dragging on the ground behind them.

Babs O'Leary is, well, gorgeous. She's way too attractive to be hanging around with the likes of Kai Z. At least, that's a reason the guys implored Chicago to take her in. Now, it's a matter of understanding what she's doing here. That's the question he's about to ask before she takes three large gulps of the whiskey and wipes her mouth.

"A woman after my own heart," Nashville muses.

"Sorry. It's already been a long day."

"Love means never having to say you're sorry."

"Hollywood, Tulsa…you guys take watch just in case the party starts early."

They nod, but they aren't happy about it. Everyone wants to be in close enough proximity to flirt. They move upstairs to watch the street and back yard.

"Your friend just quoted *Love Story*," Babs says. "Is he okay?"

"No," they all answer.

"What happened with Kai?" Chicago asks, cutting to the chase. "Why did you come here?"

Babs takes another long sip of her drink. "I went to bed. Kai was still pretty wired after getting shot and rescued by you guys, so he stayed up to work on some things. He cut and uploaded a video and then left before I woke up. He left me this note."

She pulls it out of her pocket and hands it to Chicago.

> The evolution of wisdom is first not knowing what you
> don't know. Then you know what you don't know. I'm
> not content with not knowing. I hope you'll forgive me,
> but I need answers. It's what I do.
>
> --Kai

Chicago passes the note to Nica, who frowns. It's not because of the profound words about wisdom. It's what they implied. He went to dig for dirt on Landon Tayson. That he hasn't checked in since leaving is not a good sign.

"All right. Kai's injured, and there are armed men basically everywhere in this neighborhood. Why would he be reckless enough to search for information in the lion's den, assuming that's where he went?"

"Because he's dedicated," Chicago concludes.

"More like a fanatic," Babs corrects. "I've been with Kai for a while, and he's been that way since before we met."

"You must love him," Nashville says, sounding disappointed. "And he must love you."

Babs eyes him coolly. "Kai loves his work. I'm a mistress, at best. I should have known he would try something like this. I thought maybe his leg wound would deter him. I was wrong."

"He's probably fine," Nica offers. "If he got caught, they probably have him tied up in a closet or something. We'll find him when this is over."

"I don't think so," Babs says, fighting tears forming in the corners of her eyes.

"Why not?" Bronx asks.

"They were ready to burn this house down because of a flag. What do you think they'll do to a guy who is undermining them?"

That's a fair point. But it's different when you're face-to-face. It makes the act far more personal, and not everyone can handle that.

"It'd be cold-blooded murder."

"You watch the news, Chicago. These guys shot and killed a policeman in the middle of the street."

"That likely wasn't Landon," Nica argues.

"I saw Kai's video from that day. He was right there before they spotted him. That's where he was running from when he got shot, and you guys found him. Landon was on that overpass. I'd bet it was him."

There's no point in arguing with her. It's irrelevant either way. Either he pulled the trigger himself, or the men under his command did. Landon is still responsible. It's the burden of leadership.

"What do you expect us to do?" Bronx asks. "We can't go looking for him."

"I'm not asking you to," Babs snaps, her eyes appealing to Chicago. "When this is over, I want you to sneak me out of here."

"You're not going to stick around to look for your boyfriend?" Nica asks.

"No," she says, crossing her arms and welding them to her chest. "I'm going to pretend I was never here. I'm done with Kai. Our relationship ended the moment he snuck out of the house and closed the door this morning. He abandoned me in that rental house. I can't forgive that."

"I'll get her out of here," Nashville volunteers, his voice dripping with enthusiasm. It may be the first time in memory he ever volunteered for anything. Pretty girls make men do stupid things.

"Stand in line, buddy," Bronx adds.

The sound of a big engine in front of the house causes their heads to turn. It can mean only one thing.

"They're heeeeere!" Hollywood sings out from upstairs in his best *Poltergeist* voice.

CHAPTER SIXTY-EIGHT

LANDON TAYSON

OUTSIDE THE FIFTH STREET HOUSE
MINNEAPOLIS ARTS DISTRICT OCCUPIED ZONE

Landon slams the vehicle in park and kills its engine. This isn't the dumbest idea he's ever had. It's not the smartest, either. This guy is responsible for several deaths already. He wants vengeance, but he also doesn't want to be added to the casualty list. That means negotiating, and if he can accomplish his goal without further bloodshed, that's the win he desperately needs.

"Chicago! Come on out, man," Landon bellows after exiting the vehicle and leaning against the passenger side door. "I just wanna talk. I'm alone and unarmed."

Muzzie warned him that Artie was likely killed by a sniper. It was one of a litany of reasons he thought this was a bad idea. The president of the United States doesn't travel without a security detail. The president of the ADOZ shouldn't either.

It's sound logic, but Landon doesn't think this guy will kill an unarmed man. Artie was leading a contingent that was planning on burning Chicago's house down. The circumstances are completely different. At least, he hopes they are. Now, it's just a matter of whether the man will show his face. He didn't last time.

To his surprise, the door opens. Chicago strolls out like he doesn't have a care in the world. He's also unarmed. Both are interesting revelations. It means the guy is confident, and it also means that Landon is probably lined up in a set of crosshairs from one of those windows.

The two men meet in the middle of the street but don't bother shaking hands. "I have to be honest. Part of me is surprised you showed your face. I could have a sniper lying in wait in the bushes."

The corner of the man's mouth curls. "You could. But the moment he fires, you know you will die next. Something tells me that you're not willing to trade my life for yours. Go ahead – tell me I'm wrong."

"You're not wrong."

"Then, in a shocking first, we agree on something. You called for this parlay, Landon. What do you want?"

"Peace."

"Become a Buddhist monk."

It's the same witty retort he would have expected from Muzzie. This guy is definitely military. He wants to ask but decides to wait. Business first. Background later.

"Hmm, maybe in my next life. We got off on the wrong foot, Chicago. I don't want any harm to come to you, the two guys with you, or your house."

"Interesting words from a man who tried to burn it down."

"And my men paid the price for it. Lieutenant Artie Stein was only twenty-four."

"Give me his parents' address. I'll send flowers."

Another "Muzzie" response. This guy is all testosterone and no brains. He also has no remorse. Landon has met plenty of people he thought were sociopaths. Now, he knows he met one.

"You don't seem upset. You killed a man, after all."

"People die. It happens every day. I'd feel more guilty about it if he wasn't set on killing me."

Landon smirks. "You must be a soldier."

"I was in the Air Force, actually – a loadmaster on a C-17 Globemaster III in the 437th Airlift Wing out of Joint Base Charleston."

Landon has no way to check that information. What he can do is read people. If it's a lie, it's a good one delivered effortlessly. But it likely isn't a lie, meaning the man only has limited weapons training and no real tactical knowledge. That will make Muzzie happy and their lives easier tonight.

"What exactly does a loadmaster do?"

"We ensured the proper loading, securing, and unloading of cargo, personnel, and equipment. I was responsible for properly balancing and distributing the weight in the aircraft so we didn't crash during takeoff or landing."

"Interesting," Landon muses.

"Not really. That's why I got out."

His eyes shift up to the roof and the makeshift flagpole with the Star-Spangled Banner on it and a black flag with a cannon below it. "It explains why you are flying the flag."

Chicago chuckles. "Is this where you order me again to take it down?"

"You're not in the United States of America anymore. This is the ADOZ."

"Ah. Yes, of course. So, where's your flag?"

Landon doesn't want to admit they don't have one. He has been lamenting that oversight since taking over the building on University Avenue and finding an office. Once this problem is solved, he needs to get Raven to commission the design and manufacture of one. It'd be great to see it flying over every barricade and a huge one over their headquarters.

"I'm here to extend an olive branch. My men want retribution for the deaths of their fellow warriors. Take your flag down, and we'll call it a draw. We will leave you alone so long as you don't interfere with our operations or activities."

"Or else?"

Landon's eyes narrow. "We get our retribution, and the flag comes down anyway. I'm generously offering you a way out of this, Chicago. I urge you to take it."

Chicago takes a deep breath and shifts his eyes skyward. Landon feels a surge of optimism. It looks like he's pondering it. Maybe the man is smarter than he thought. Or, at least, not as suicidal.

"Thank you for your offer."

"So, you accept?"

His lips crease into something that looks like the "expressionless face" emoji.

"Not a chance in hell."

Landon nods. "I'll give you until sundown to change your mind. If you don't…well, what happens next is on you."

"And all the men who die trying to storm this house will be on you."

Chicago spins and stomps back up the sidewalk, climbing the stairs and disappearing through the front door. Landon moves around the front of the SUV and climbs into the driver's seat. He starts the engine and drives down Fifth Street until he's out of sight of Chicago's house before making the call.

"Yes, Mr. President?"

"Get the men ready, Muzzie. He isn't going to budge. We take the house tonight."

CHAPTER SIXTY-NINE

EMMIT "CHICAGO" HASKINS

THE FIFTH STREET HOUSE
MINNEAPOLIS ARTS DISTRICT OCCUPIED ZONE

All eyes are on Chicago when he enters the house. Tulsa is watching through the living room window, and Nashville bounds down the stairs to join the rest of the boys and Babs O'Leary. He looks at each of them.

"The party is on for tonight."

"Toga! Toga! Toga!" Hollywood starts shouting, pumping his fists up and down like John Belushi as he tries to rev up his fellow Rangers. They aren't impressed. It's mission time, and things are going to start getting serious.

"What are we facing?"

"I don't know, Nashville. It could be ten guys. It could be two hundred."

Bronx shakes his head. "They ain't gonna pull that many guys off those barricades. They need to show strength to the police."

"He's right," Tulsa says, "but it's best to hope for the best and plan for the worst."

Nica rubs his chin. "Speaking of which…how do you want to tackle this?"

Chicago moves to the coffee table. He sets a tissue box up as the house and grabs various knick-knacks, setting them up to look like the neighborhood. It's a decent impromptu 3-D map that they can use to visualize movements.

"Divide and conquer. Three of us hold the house," Chicago says, tapping the tissue box. "Hollywood will have the SAW, and I'll switch between the AR and the sniper rifle. We'll protect the front as it's the most likely avenue of approach. Nashville can cover the back.

"You, Tulsa, and Bronx will take positions here, here, and here," he continues, pointing at areas to the south, north, and east. Harass their flanks or hit them from the rear if they try to surround us. Use hit-and-run tactics. Try to stay in position to support each other in a pinch since you'll be operating solo."

"I don't like the idea of not working in teams," Tulsa says.

Like other elite units, U.S. Army Rangers often operate in "buddy fire teams" for efficiency, survivability, and when it creates a tactical advantage. Pairs are small enough to stay stealthy while still being lethal enough to handle threats. They can effectively split combat roles, provide 360-degree security while on the move, suppress and bound in a quick ambush, and share resources like ammo and medical supplies. Few soldiers like acting alone.

"I don't like it either," Chicago admits, "but this is the mission and there are only six of us to accomplish it. Without intel on their movements, these are the likely approaches, and they all need to be covered while we secure the house."

Tulsa nods. "Okay."

"There's a bigger problem," Nashville says. "We'll have concealment but no cover in this house. Their rounds will tear through the exterior walls."

"I know. We can dig up the patio and use the stone to reinforce positions in the front and back. We can also cut firing ports so we aren't always shooting from windows."

"Your sister's gonna love that," Bronx points out.

Chicago presses his lips together and exhales. "Don't remind me."

"I have some flares and smoke grenades in my goody bag," Tulsa adds. "We can set them up in the back to cover the rear and give Nashville some advance warning."

He nods. "I appreciate that."

"We'll have most of our firepower massed facing east. You think the orcs are gonna try another mass assault?"

Chicago stands a little straighter as he stares at the replica of his street and the cross street. "I'm willing to bet that's the first tactic they try. Landon thinks there are only three of us and that we'll melt against his numbers."

"Still…we're Rangers."

"I told Landon I was in the Air Force."

They all laugh. Babs doesn't join them, not in on the joke. Most civilians aren't.

"That explains it," Bronx says between chuckles.

"What's wrong with the Air Force?" Babs asks.

"Nothing," Chicago says with a shrug. "Military branches like to pick on each other, and the Air Force is an easy target."

"Why?"

"They have a different mission set," Nica interjects. "We're ground pounders. We get up close to the enemy and kill them. The flyboys drop bombs from ten thousand feet unless they're flying a Warthog."

"Brrrrrrrrrrrrrrrrrrrt!" Nashville screeches, mimicking the sound of its cannon.

"It doesn't mean we don't appreciate them," Bronx says. "When it hits the fan, air support is usually the difference between living a long life and your corpse rotting away six feet in the ground at Arlington."

"All right. We have our mission profile."

Nashville clears his throat and jerks his head at Babs a few times. Chicago almost forgot about her.

"It's too late to get you out of here. We can hide you in the cellar until this is over."

"I can help," Babs offers, her head bouncing between the six men in the room.

"Our mission is to defend this house and sneak you out," Nica says. "We can't do that if you're no longer alive. You can help us by not becoming a casualty."

"We only have a few hours. Let's do this."

CHAPTER SEVENTY

FIELD OFFICER DAVID BRASS

GRAND STREET RENTAL HOUSE
MINNEAPOLIS ARTS DISTRICT OCCUPIED ZONE

Brass isn't sure why he's still watching the news. They haven't reported anything different in a day or two, and most are still showing old images or videos of the house with the flag. All that serves to do is raise his ire. He can't believe it isn't down yet. Did Landon not take his threats seriously?

His cell ringing grants him a reprieve from the torture. He checks the caller ID and sneers. This had better be good. If the kid is calling again to tell him that he hasn't found anything, he's going to choke the life out of him upon returning to Virginia.

"Wesley? I'm assuming you have something useful for me this time."

"That depends. When are you getting me out of this ridiculous cubicle?"

This isn't the first time he's leaned on Wesley for information. The last was getting Chris Byrnes's contact information after the analyst managed to identify him as part of Railspike without having the proper clearance to know. As a result of that discovery, he promised the kid greener pastures at Watchtower once it's established…provided he keeps delivering.

"Once you prove you're worthy. This group I'm standing up is the big leagues. There's no room for an A-baller."

The kid probably doesn't understand the baseball reference. He doesn't strike Brass as the sports type. He doesn't need to be.

Wesley may be a junior analyst, but he knows how to get things done. He has skills but would never be considered elite at any of them. He improvises, utilizes resources, adopts strategies, and leverages situations to get results. Best of all, he understands the power of favors.

"Let's start with this – Kai Z is missing."

"The YouTuber? What do you mean by 'missing?'"

"I mean that he hasn't posted in a while."

Wesley doesn't know about Brass's relationship with Landon Tayson and will never be permitted to find out. Maybe the worthless, self-proclaimed president finally got himself a win. It'd be a first, outside of managing to take over the district without getting himself killed.

"Maybe Kai is taking a break."

"From inside the ADOZ? Unlikely. He's the only journalist there. Everything he previously posted earned him millions in ad revenue."

"Millions?"

"Yeah. It's a brave new world. I may have missed my calling."

Brass misses the 1980s. Everything was great about that decade. The best was the lack of reliance on computers and the absence of cell phones. Sure, the latter is useful, but both of those things have made the world more stressful…and complicated. How anyone gets paid for posting videos is beyond him.

Brass rolls his eyes. "Is that it?"

"No. I did some digging on that house with the Star-Spangled Banner atop it. No red flags with the owner. The husband died in an accident a while back, and the wife works at a downtown law firm."

"She doesn't sound like someone who would climb on the roof and erect a twenty-foot flagpole."

"No, but her brother would. Staff Sergeant Emmit Haskins, 11B infantry, airborne qualified, Ranger School graduate and, until eight months ago, a squad leader assigned to 2nd Battalion, 75th Ranger Regiment out of Hunter Army Airfield in Savannah, Georgia."

Brass pushes deeper into his sofa. That explains a lot. "He sounds like he's career Army."

"That was his trajectory until the end of his Syrian deployment," Wesley informs him.

The analyst goes on to explain the convoy attack, Haskins's actions, the award he won, and his subsequent discharge. The guy has balls of solid rock. Nine times out of ten, anyone trying that would have only succeeded in getting himself killed. Earning a discharge for his heroism must be burning him up inside.

"Okay, so he's a guy with a deep love of country who's bitter about authority figures."

"That sounds about right."

"He's not doing this by himself," Brass concludes. "He has friends there."

"How do you know that?"

"Because he's a Ranger, not Superman. I don't care what he scored on his physical fitness test. Putting up that flagpole is more than a one-man job, and his sister didn't help."

"No, she didn't. She's in a hotel just outside the city."

"All right. Find out who's hanging out with Haskins. Start with his old unit and then branch out to anyone recently discharged. I'd bet my salary they all served with him."

"I already know where to start. What do I get if I find this?"

Favors. The kid knows how to negotiate them. Brass relents. He's already decided that he wants the kid on the team, but he doesn't need to know that.

"The position you want. I'll even have a nameplate made up for you."

"Consider it done. There's one more thing – I searched Haskins's cell records. There was nothing out of the ordinary except one number that stuck out. It was a local Minneapolis cell."

"He does live there, Wesley," David moans.

"Yeah, but why would he be having a conversation with the chief of police after the ADOZ was established? She initiated a five-minute, forty-three-second call with him. Curious, right?"

Too curious. "Focus on the Rangers and get back to me when you have names."

He ends the call and leans his head back on the sofa. The police chief talked to the Ranger. That could pose a problem. He's not exposed…or is he? What if she uncovered information she shouldn't know and is using the Ranger to investigate? It sounds far-fetched, but it is possible.

Brass can't imagine that she knows anything useful. But leaving that thread dangling is how an operation gets unwoven. He needs to find out why she placed the call. If she's a threat, it's something he needs to deal with. With that, he places another call.

"Matt? I need you to do me a favor."

CHAPTER SEVENTY-ONE

CHIEF VANESSA CAMPBELL

LOWRY AVENUE BARRICADE
MINNEAPOLIS, MINNESOTA

It's the calm before the storm. At least, that's what Vanessa senses. She doesn't know it for sure, but she has been in law enforcement her entire adult life. She sensed what would happen in 2020. She predicted the fallout from those events with great efficacy. Now, she's getting a similar feeling. Something is about to happen.

Vanessa is also powerless to stop it. Her orders are clear, and a violation of them will end her career – not just with the Minneapolis Police Department, but anywhere. No police force in the country will hire a senior cop who can't follow orders. It's too much of a risk, even if the media doesn't turn her into a pariah, which they likely will. So, she waits, just like everyone else.

Without much to do, the chief decides to check the perimeter. National Guard troops have taken up positions in the South on Broadway and East along the railroad bridge. There is still a police presence there, but many of the officers not rotated for rest have repositioned in the north opposite Lowry Avenue.

After exchanging some pleasantries with a couple of bored officers monitoring a cross street, she stares across the road and sees a barricade manned by only one person toting a rifle like he's never carried a firearm before. He's young and seemingly unsure of himself.

"How long has that guy been alone?" Vanessa asks, pointing.

"An hour," the sergeant advises. "Maybe two. Why?"

"Just asking."

"Don't even think about it, Chief. You know we have strict orders not to try to breach. That applies even if the barricade was unmanned."

That's true. Orders are orders. As explicit as they are, they aren't detailed. When a fellow officer arrives with a tray filled with steaming hot coffee, she gets an idea.

"I know, Sergeant," she says, pulling the cup he was just given out of his hand and returning it to the paper drink tray. "We don't have orders not to talk. I'll get you a fresh cup when I'm done."

"Done with what?"

Vanessa doesn't bother answering the question and moves around the car and across the street. The movement immediately gets the kid's attention, and he unslings his weapon, pointing it at her.

"Halt!" he shouts, earning immediate compliance. "What do you want?"

"I'm bringing you coffee."

"I don't want it!"

Vanessa scoffs. "Yes, you do."

She slowly walks forward, twisting so he can see her gun belt and empty holster. The kid starts getting agitated, but he issues no other commands and lowers his rifle.

"Don't worry. I'm not armed, and the officers over there are under orders from the mayor to hold their positions. So long as you don't shoot me, they ain't moving."

Vanessa stops opposite the barrier. The young man eyes her hard before gesturing at the paper tray with the two cups.

"How do I know that isn't laced with something?"

Vanessa pops the plastic tab on the lid, withdraws the cup from its carrier, and takes a sip. The fluid is hot, and while not the best coffee she has ever tasted, it's still pretty good. She holds it out, meeting him at the left side of the barricade. He accepts the drink and backs off a few steps.

"I'm Vanessa Campbell."

"Zachary Baumann. I go by Zach."

Vanessa looks around. "Why are you here alone, Zach?"

"Who says I'm alone?" he fires back.

She gestures around the area. "Most of the barricades have at least three or four fighters. This is a smaller one and has only had two since it was erected. You've been manning it by yourself for a couple of hours now."

"I'm capable," Zach argues.

"I'm sure you are. Nobody is questioning that, but even the military uses the buddy system. Two men to watch each other's backs."

"One of the guys was pulled off the line."

"Yeah, we know," Vanessa confesses. "What about the other? The relief, since you guys work in shifts."

"He quit."

She nods her understanding. Desertions are becoming a thing in the ADOZ, and Landon Tayson likely has no idea what to do about them. He was probably counting on those reinforcements the FBI intercepted. He needs every man now.

"What about you?"

"I'm no quitter!"

"Well, Zach," Vanessa says, pulling out the second coffee and taking a sip, "we may be on opposite sides of this, but we have that much in common. Enjoy your coffee. I haven't seen your food supply come through in a while, and it doesn't look like anyone is getting rotated off the barricades. If you get hungry, wave down the sergeant across the street. He'll get me, and I'll bring you an MRE."

MREs, or "meals ready-to-eat," are field rations primarily used by the military, emergency responders, and survivalists. They are lightweight, durable, and nutritionally balanced for sustaining individuals in the field. Despite having come a long way since their introduction, they still aren't the tastiest of things that will ever hit your tongue.

"Why are you doing this?" Zach asks, his voice more somber than accusatory.

"Because your leaders aren't, and that's not fair to you. My job is to look after everyone in this city, and that includes you. Take care of yourself, Zach."

Vanessa marches back across the street without hazarding a glance over her shoulder. That was where she wanted the short conversation to end. It gives him something to ponder while he waits for absolutely nothing to happen.

The chief explains to the sergeant and the other officer what she told the kid. They don't look amused. Staring across the street at the barricades, anyone on that side is now viewed as the enemy. It's an understandable emotional reaction, if not an entirely correct one.

"All right. We get you, but what was the point of even talking to any of them? They're fanatical insurgents who just took over part of our city. What did you hope to gain?"

"Nothing," Vanessa admits. "I'm just making friends."

CHAPTER SEVENTY-TWO

LANDON TAYSON

OUTSIDE THE FIFTH STREET HOUSE
MINNEAPOLIS ARTS DISTRICT OCCUPIED ZONE

Landon has never been much into meditation. Anybody walking up to his office would think that's what he's doing. It would be an easy conclusion to draw when seeing him sitting in the brown, high-back leather chair with his eyes closed and hands folded on his chest. He doesn't need to clear his mind – just unclutter it.

The last week has been a whirlwind of emotions. The highs of success battle against the lows of unfortunate incidents, making for a rollercoaster that Landon needed to stop, even for a short period. No man can be expected to handle this level of pressure in perpetuity.

He's tired and is half surprised he hasn't dozed off. Opportunities to rest are few and far between. When sleep comes, it's too often been interrupted, and the lack of it is beginning to take its toll. Maybe after tonight's mission, he can try again.

Almost on cue, Muzzie knocks on the door jamb and enters the office. Landon opens his eyes to see his military commander standing before him, all geared up and ready to go. He's looking forward to this fight.

"The men are assembled outside and awaiting your orders."

Landon doesn't say anything. Words will only get in the way. He stands and holsters his sidearm in his hip rig. He grabs his rifle and follows Muzzie into the corridor. Raven is there waiting for him. She stares at him apprehensively.

"It will be okay. You hold down the fort until I get back."

"Landon," she says, grabbing his arm and holding it. "Don't be reckless with your life."

"It's not my life you need to worry about," he says, the corner of his mouth curling. "It's theirs."

He passes by Raven and heads downstairs and out the front of the building. His jaw slacks at the impressive sight. The men are dressed in neat lines in the parking lot, much like a military formation. There must be over a hundred here, broken into four large groups with a few paces between them. Each is wearing the best equipment Landon could provide. They are standing tall, silent, and waiting for their next orders. Muzzie has trained this lot well.

The president of the ADOZ assumes his post in front of the small army. He stares at them for a few long moments, pride filling up his chest. Seeing this sight, how could he not be optimistic about the future? These men are the best of the best.

"Did you ever think you would see this day? For years, we talked about creating an area that we could call our own. One free from the persecution of politicians. One free from the oppression of a police state. Until a week ago, that's all it was – talk. Then we acted. We threw off the yoke of our oppressors and created this ADOZ.

"Now comes our greatest challenge. We must fight for its survival – not against the police, but from a resident who has shunned our embrace and clutches to a bankrupt ideology. Our laws were not harsh. Our demands were not excessive. All we requested is that they be followed. Apparently, for some, it was too much to ask.

"The house on Fifth Street has flaunted their disobedience. The flag they fly no longer has value to us or this neighborhood. This district is ours now. It's our home, and we will defend it!"

The men begin hooting and hollering. Landon doesn't know if that's military protocol. It's probably against the rules in the military, but this is the ADOZ. These are his rules, and he is feeding off their enthusiasm. It's energizing.

"You men have been with me from the beginning. You are closer to me than my own family. Tonight, I call upon you now to finish what we started. This cancer must be excised from our midst, or it will grow and consume us until we're dead. We don't fight for honor or glory. We fight for our freedom. We fight for the ADOZ!"

Another cacophony of loud cheers erupts from the men. They are amped up, which is what he and Muzzie need them to be. There is no telling what awaits them at the house, but how can any one man or three resist these determined fighters?

"We will do our duty, and when the sun comes up in the morning, it will be more than a new day. It will be a new reality. Long live the ADOZ!"

Muzzie gets them moving out after another round of guttural shouts. It wasn't President Whitmore's speech from *Independence Day*, but it was good enough for these purposes. Landon doesn't have scriptwriters, and he also isn't acting. That gives his words more authenticity.

The men file out of the parking lot and load up in vehicles procured for this task. Landon doesn't know where his commander got them, but it doesn't matter. The rest set out for their rally point on foot. It's not far. All the teams should reach their assigned positions at approximately the same time.

After making last-minute preparations, Muzzie and Landon climb into their SUV to meet up with the troops. They pull up to the designated point a half block to the north of the intersection of Fifth Street and block the road with the vehicle. He has line-of-sight to the house at an oblique angle. If they are going to shoot at him from a window, he's not going to make it easy.

Muzzie barks orders into his radio and receives reports from the teams. They divided up into three action groups. They will storm the front from two directions and push the occupants right into the guys in the back. Nobody is going to stay in that house once the assault begins. It would be suicide.

"It's showtime," Muzzie says when he's confident everyone is ready. "Remember, they may have a scoped rifle in the house."

He could have done without that warning. The two men climb out of the vehicle, and Landon moves around the engine so he can take cover behind the SUV if it becomes necessary. He watches his guys scramble into a loose arc, some on a knee and others lying prone on the ground.

"Chicago?" he announces through his megaphone. "I'm sure you can hear me. The time for talk is over."

CHAPTER SEVENTY-THREE
EMMIT "CHICAGO" HASKINS

THE FIFTH STREET HOUSE
MINNEAPOLIS ARTS DISTRICT OCCUPIED ZONE

The entire neighborhood hears the ultimatum Tayson is bellowing from up the street. Hopefully, they will heed the advice the Rangers offered and find a safe spot in their homes. Shit is about to get real.

For his team's part, they are ready. The radio checks have long been completed, weapons maintained, and fighting positions readied. Everyone is in place for the show to begin.

"What is with this guy and his megaphone?" Bronx moans over the radio.

"I'll give you sixty seconds to come out of the house. If you don't, we're coming in!"

Chicago shouldn't say anything, but he can't resist. "Go ahead. Make my day."

"Son of a bitch. He stole my line," Hollywood muses.

The *Good Will Hunting* line is almost an appropriate metaphor. Hunting is precisely what they are about to start doing. He may not have wanted this fight, but it's now come to them. One way or another, this ends tonight.

"Spartan Six, this is Havoc Six. Fifteen guys moving into position to your two o'clock."

They didn't want to use even their nicknames over the radio on the off-chance that anyone is listening. Team names were chosen, and designations were assigned. The Spartans are the defenders of the house in honor of the Battle of Thermopylae. The "six" element of any unit is the commander, so Chicago responds to "Spartan Six" despite not being an officer. He has two one-man platoons, so Hollywood is Spartan One, and Nashville is Spartan Two.

"This is Havoc Two. I have twice that at five o'clock."

The Havoc team are the three active-duty Rangers hiding in the neighborhood. Nica is the "Six" element and is behind the neighbor's house to the front. Bronx is oriented to the south, taking the "Two" designation, while Tulsa is "One" and is just to the north and west of the cross street to keep an eye on their rear.

They had a fairly heated argument over how to align the clock. Half wanted twelve o'clock to be the direction the front of the house faces, in this case, east, while the others wanted to orient it to the compass rose. The latter won. North is twelve o'clock, east three, and so on.

"Havoc One? Anything?"

"I have a plus-sized squad dismounting two blocks to the west. They look like a reserve or a blocking force, but they could be planning on hitting from the rear."

"This is Six. It sounds like they're going to come to the citadel from the north and south on Fifth. The guys at nine o'clock are probably there to ensure we don't slip out the back."

The "citadel" is the code name for the house. Chicago wanted to use "Thermopylae" to designate his sister's house, but he was quickly overruled by the entire team. Too many syllables, as if the one extra was a big deal.

"Time's up, Chicago!" Landon warns.

Men open fire from the north, causing Chicago to withdraw deeper into the room. With men holding observation points in the neighborhood, he doesn't need to monitor movements. That means there is no reason to be near a window unless he's engaging targets. Why get your ass blasted off in the first ten seconds for no reason?

The windows all shatter. Much of the fire is aimed at the first floor, but there is a shooter or two actively suppressing the bedrooms on the second. That should be reversed, considering the high ground is more important, but nobody ever said these guys were tactical geniuses.

"The north is the base of fire," Nica concludes. "South must be maneuvering."

"This is Havoc Two. I have a squad element sprinting toward the house."

"Hollywood?" Chicago shouts.

"All right, Mr. DeMille, I'm ready for my close-up."

From the southeast bedroom window, Hollywood has a decent view down the street. The suppressive fire is aimed at the window, but it's coming in at a forty-five-degree angle. He's in no immediate danger as he opens up with the SAW.

The men charging the house are bunched up. They aren't maintaining separation at all. Seven of them fall in the first two bursts. The third and fourth score three more. The remaining two men move to the house two doors down from the citadel, out of Hollywood's field of fire. That won't help them.

"Havoc Two engaging."

Bronx emerges from his position and drops them in their hiding spot before ducking back into cover. The support element to the south probably saw him but had no time to react. Like the havoc his team chose as a name, he was there, raised hell, and was gone just as quickly.

The remaining assault force never saw it coming. Hollywood immediately ceases fire to conserve his ammunition. Chicago doesn't bother engaging the fire support team suppressing the front of the house. They aren't hurting anything except the wood clapboard siding. He may send them scurrying, but he likely won't hit any of them. Not that he needed to.

One by one, their rifles fall silent.

CHAPTER SEVENTY-FOUR

LANDON TAYSON

OUTSIDE THE FIFTH STREET HOUSE
MINNEAPOLIS ARTS DISTRICT OCCUPIED ZONE

This is unexpected. Landon expected to hear a rifle and a shotgun. Maybe throw in a handgun for good measure. Not in his wildest dreams would he hear the rhythmic firing that sounds like something out of a World War II documentary.

It didn't last long. He thought maybe his men silenced the guy firing it. When the screaming starts over the radio, he knows that isn't the case. Something bad just happened.

"They're dead! They're all dead!"

"Who's dead?" the captain asks over the rifle fire around them.

"The assault team. They're all gone! They aren't moving!"

Muzzie looks sick to his stomach. "Cease fire! Cease fire!"

The shouts over the staccato of firing rifles aren't as effective as the hand signal. Muzzie shows the palm of his hand as he waves his arm up and down through his field of vision. Men begin repeating the gesture and shouting to their comrades. Slowly, the shooting comes to a stop.

"What the hell happened? What was that?" Landon bellows. They weren't so much questions as a reaction to the shock. He heard the urgent report over Muzzie's headset.

"Who are these guys?" Muzzie demands.

Landon recoils at the force of the question. "Chicago said he was a loadmaster in the Air Force."

"Air Force, my ass! These guys have infantry training. That sounded like a SAW."

"A saw? Like, for wood?"

The captain stares at the ADOZ leader like he's a moron. "M249 Squad Automatic Weapon. It's a light machine gun!"

"Where the hell did they get one of those?"

He shrugs. "How the hell would I know? We need to pull back and reevaluate."

Landon shakes his head emphatically. "No! We're committed. If we pull back now, it will be worse than the firebombing. We'll look weak. I need you to take that thing out and storm the house."

Captain Muzzie stares at the pale blue home. It's riddled with bullet holes in the front. The windows are all shattered, but the structure is dark…and quiet. They aren't firing indiscriminately or taking potshots. Landon would have ordered his men to. It's a show of force.

"Whoever those guys are have serious firepower and are fighting from an elevated position. We can't storm the house without getting mowed down."

Landon points at the structure, his other hand balling into a fist. "There are only three of them, and they don't have a good line of sight. Use the neighboring houses to sneak up on them, Captain!"

His commander grimaces. Landon doesn't think he should have to explain tactics to the man. He's here because of his military experience. It's not doing much good at the moment. There is no reality where a guy who never served a second in uniform should be explaining tactics to someone who spent years in the armed forces.

"Berserker Three, this is Berserker Six Actual. Send a five-man team to the rear of the house with an additional five men in fire support. Report when in position."

"Roger."

Muzzie frowns and turns to Landon. "The correct response is 'wilco,' but whatever."

"Wilco" stands for "will comply." It acknowledges that a message was received and that the instructions will be followed. At least they didn't pair it with "roger," which means "message received." That would be redundant. Landon may not know much about the military, but he does know that.

"Berserker One, Berserker Two. On my order, I want suppressing fire placed on the front of the house. Target the windows, focusing on the second floor."

"Roger."

Muzzie scowls again. "Berserker One, Two has taken heavy casualties. Ready a ten-man team to head for the corner of the house. Nobody moves until I give the word."

"I thought you said we aren't storming it?" Landon says over the response on the radio.

"We aren't. The team to the west will engage from their back yard. The guys inside will panic and shift their focus to protecting their rear. Then, we'll hit them from the front with overwhelming force."

Landon takes a hard look down the street. That makes sense. But it is still based on an assumption.

"How do you know they'll shift?"

"Because they'll think our suppressing fire is a distraction, and that the real attack is coming from their rear. When they change positions in the house to engage it, we'll sneak up without their noticing. Once we enter the house, it's all over."

Landon almost lets out a sigh of relief. Finally, they have another plan.

"Make it happen."

CHAPTER SEVENTY-FIVE

FIELD OFFICER DAVID BRASS

GRAND STREET RENTAL HOUSE
MINNEAPOLIS ARTS DISTRICT OCCUPIED ZONE

Brass stuffs the last of his things into his bag. His time here is up. While he gets a lot of latitude at his Department of Agriculture office, he still has official duties to perform along with the unofficial ones. It's part of his cover, and he isn't in a position to ruin that just yet.

More importantly, he doesn't want to be around when the FBI and law enforcement begin picking up the pieces. Nearly every station has broken into normal programming to bring the nation the developments in the ADOZ. They don't have footage of the action, but reporters are outside the perimeter, prattling on about what they are hearing. If the sounds are any indication, it's quite the gunfight.

"What do you have for me, Remsen?" he asks after answering the call.

"Your friendly neighborhood police chief wasn't overly friendly."

Brass rolls his eyes. "Would you be if FBI counterintelligence started asking you questions?"

"I wouldn't be as cagey as she was."

David doubts that. Remsen's point of view is from the opposite side of the equation. If he were a civilian, he'd be peeing his pants if the feds rang his cell phone.

"She didn't admit to anything?"

"Not a thing. Campbell claimed she never made such a call and that it had to be spoofed."

"Right."

Cell phone calls can be spoofed, but Brass has never heard of anyone having the capability to hack into a device and place a call from it. Maybe someday. But if the cellular carrier has a record of that call, it's because the police chief placed it.

"It's her story and she stuck to it. Unfortunately for her, Chief Campbell is a terrible liar. She likely knows who's now laying waste to Landon's men in the ADOZ."

"Have your people heard anything from the governor or mayor?"

"Nope. From the looks of it, everyone has orders to stand fast, and neither of those two worthless politicians plans on changing that."

It's a fine example of modern political leadership. All these rich people do is fight to get elected so they can build their wealth. Once in a while, they do something for the people to get reelected. It's sickening.

"You're telling me that the neighborhood is seeing more combat than Iraq, and the governor isn't sending in the Guard?"

"Radio silence from Saint Paul. Ditto from City Hall. The military isn't going to intervene unless the president federalizes them, which he won't, or the mayor sends in the police. Which he won't do, either."

"One way or another, someone needs to end this. Do you know if the police or military have any drone assets watching the ADOZ?"

"The police have one. That's some of the footage you see of the ADOZ on television. I don't know if it's up now."

"Oh, I'm sure it is. Thanks, Matt. I'll be in touch."

Brass grabs his bag and takes one last look around to ensure he isn't forgetting anything. He packed light but never takes chances. Now, there's one more thing to do before he heads for the airport and leaves the Land of 10,000 Lakes.

CHAPTER SEVENTY-SIX

CHIEF VANESSA CAMPBELL

LOWRY AVENUE BARRICADE
MINNEAPOLIS, MINNESOTA

Zach didn't take her up on her offer of food. Maybe Vanessa shouldn't be surprised. It's not like she offered him a surf and turf entrée with filet mignon and a lobster tail. Most soldiers don't eat MREs unless they absolutely have to. It might have been different had Landon launched his attack closer to midnight.

Since that wasn't the case, she decided to cross the street without even telling any of her officers. The distance is covered quickly and without any warning cries this time. The kid isn't paying any mind to the street. His undivided attention is on the battle that is starting to rage somewhere to the south. The brief lull ended, and now the constant sound of gunfire is unmistakable.

"It sounds like a war in there," she says from the opposite side of the barrier.

The sound of her voice startles the kid. He turns and points his gun at her head. Vanessa slowly raises her arms.

"I'm not armed."

"You snuck up on me!"

"I'm not a ninja. I just walked across the street. Remember when I told you that the military uses a buddy system. That's why. Nobody is here watching your back."

"The guys manning the other barricades would respond."

Vanessa nods. "Sure, but you'd still be dead."

Zach turns to face the sound of the gunfire. This isn't a random shot or two being fired. It's the clap of dozens of rifles and the occasional staccato of something heavier piercing the darkening night sky. It's the sound of war, and it's unnerving.

"What's going on?"

Vanessa moves around the barricade and leans up against it next to Zach. He's not remotely bothered by the move. "Landon Tayson and your commander are attacking the house with the flag on Fifth Street."

"How do you know that?"

"We have our methods," she replies as the volume of gunfire suddenly increases. "It sounds bad, doesn't it?"

"I'm sure we're winning," the kid argues.

Vanessa doubts that. Despite the lopsided numbers, training evens the odds. If Staff Sergeant Haskins has comparable weapons, this fight is fifty-fifty for Landon, at best. From the sound of it, they do. This would have been over in minutes if that weren't the case.

"They pulled almost a hundred guys off the barricades to attack that house, and that doesn't count the manpower from the patrols. There are, what? Three guys in that house? That's a hell of a fight when you're outnumbered more than thirty to one. My guess is that your compatriots are getting massacred."

Zach shifts his weight. "Why aren't you doing something about it?"

"Because I have orders."

"To do nothing?"

"Acting would require coming through this barricade," Vanessa says, slapping at a wood table that makes up part of the barrier. "You have orders to stop us. That means you would shoot at us, and we would shoot at you. You would die. My men would die. Nobody wins."

There's a simple beauty in honesty. In a world where seemingly everyone lies, most people express shock at hearing the truth. They also respond better to it. At a near-unconscious level, people can tell the difference. When issues arise, it's because of conscious rationalization. It also helps when logic is on your side. If the police storm the ADOZ, the outcome will be the same. The only difference will be the body count.

"I'm not letting you in."

"I'm not asking you to."

That's another truth. Vanessa can't convince Zach. He was devoted enough to come here and support Landon Tayson. Like most ideologues, he needs to recognize the truth for himself and make his own decisions without interference. Fortunately, that's the path he's on if his tortured facial expressions are any indication.

"The ADOZ is gonna collapse without Landon."

"Probably." Vanessa doesn't disagree with that conclusion.

"What will happen to us?"

The chief shrugs. "I don't know. Sooner or later, we'll be given an order to storm the barricades. Some of you will fight and die, most likely. A bunch will quit. Anyone taken into custody will be charged with…well, the list starts with domestic terrorism."

"We're not terrorists!" Zach shouts, taking a step away from her.

"I know you're not, but the mayor and governor likely don't agree. Neither does the FBI or Department of Justice. The president is starting to get involved in this mess. Once this thing goes federal, all bets are off."

Zach reassumes his position next to her. "I don't want to go to jail."

"I don't blame you. Jail sucks."

"What the hell is this?" a voice shouts from Vanessa's left.

Of all the crappy timing…. Zach was about to crack. She's been in enough interrogations to know when someone is looking to make a deal. That was just undone by the man walking toward them with his rifle aimed at her chest.

CHAPTER SEVENTY-SEVEN
EMMIT "CHICAGO" HASKINS

Suppressive fire is used to limit the ability to move or return fire. Continuously firing in the direction of the enemy stymies their ability to effectively operate. The goal isn't to eliminate a foe but to keep them pinned down. Sustained, rapid fire is required at the expense of precise shots that slow things down and reduce the effectiveness. But this is ridiculous.

They aren't just firing at the windows, which would make the most sense. They are targeting the entire front of the house. Their inaccurate fire is wrecking the exterior, and bullets are starting to find holes and travel through the bedrooms.

"Jesus! You okay, Hollywood?"

"The Almighty tells me he can get me out of this mess, but he's pretty sure you're f–k'd."

Somehow, in some way, his Irish accent is worse than his British one. It may be worse than the ones the actors used in *Braveheart*. If he's going to spend the rest of his days quoting movies, he needs to start nailing those.

"Do you think we can wait until they run out of ammo?" Nashville asks.

He's half serious. It's also not the worst tactic. Logistics is crucial to combat operations and often determines the success or failure of a mission. Competent generals like to say, "*Amateurs talk strategy; professionals talk logistics.*" Soldiers require food, water, medical supplies, and, in this case, ammunition to continue fighting. Without bullets, even the best-trained troops falter. And ADOZ fighters aren't the best-trained.

That presents an opportunity. They may or may not run out of ammunition, but they are guaranteed to have tunnel vision. It's why he deployed half of his guys outside the house. The fighters are going to get tunnel vision. They'll be so focused on their target that they won't be paying any attention to what's happening around them.

"Havoc team, engage their fire support."

"Wilco," they say in response.

Chicago's hearing is already shot, but the whistling and popping sound in the back is distinctive. Units that secure their positions with concertina wire will often rig visual and audio booby-trap devices to alert them to possible intrusion. They set the ones Tulsa brought in the small treeline behind the back yard that separates them from the neighbor's house. Someone just tripped one.

"This is Spartan Two – our countermeasures just popped in the rear of the citadel."

That radio announcement was informational. Nashville knows what he needs to do. He engages targets with his rifle, pausing to change firing positions. The tactic makes return fire ineffective while possibly making the aggressors think there are more men in the house than there are.

"A team-sized element just moved into the treeline in the back…Whoa!"

Gunfire erupts from the rear. The support team must have gotten into place to lay down suppressive fire while the maneuver team prepares to kick down the back door. Chicago can hear the rounds hitting the house. He closes his eyes and exhales. That's a lot more siding his sister will need to fix.

"Havoc Two, shift position and try to flank that fire support. Havoc Six, engage the guys in the south."

Chicago switches positions by high-crawling across the bedroom floor. One of the preparations he made was to use his reciprocating saw to carve a firing port into the sheetrock and the exterior siding. He disguised it by shaving the sides down so he could replace it until needed. Now's the time. He uses the muzzle of the rifle to punch out the siding and opens fire.

On the other side of the house, Hollywood lets loose with the SAW. Chicago hopes he is using one of his firing ports. Both were reinforced with pavers from the patio, so they have some protection from return fire as well.

"These guys need to learn a thing or two about concealment and cover," Nashville says. "They aren't the same thing."

That's the truth. Concealment keeps you unseen, while cover keeps you safe. Ideally, a soldier wants both. Bushes and darkness are good, but when bullets start flying, a concrete wall or vehicle will provide you the protection you're going to need.

"Cover" is a foreign concept to the men in the north, as well. Some are firing from prone positions on the ground. Others are running around. All of them are easy to hit.

Smoke erupts from the neighbor's yard across the street. Tulsa brought a few canisters of white smoke in his goody duffles. Nica is moving out, shifting to help Hollywood deal with the guys in the south.

The smoke is freaking out the guys in the north. Chicago decides to add to the chaos as he loads a fresh mag and engages with his AR-15. He misses "burst" on his M4. A single trigger pull fired off three rounds when the selector switch was set to that mode. Fully automatic fire was a waste of ammunition and reduced accuracy. Burst fixed those problems while still allowing for a high rate of fire.

"This is Six," Nica says, winded. "Two large elements are forming. I almost ran into the one to the south."

"Confirmed," Tulsa adds. "I can see the guys to the north getting ready to move. Heavy squad-sized."

"They're going to storm the front. They must think we shifted to protect the rear."

Deception has always been a key component of warfare. The less an enemy knows about your capabilities, the better. That's why he lied about being in the Air Force. The plan makes sense if you are going up against amateurs. Panic would compel defenders to reinforce the rear in the face of an attack. Fortunately, none of the men here are amateurs. Quite the contrary. Rangers are infantry experts, as Landon Tayson is learning the hard way.

"This is Spartan Two; the support team pulled back. The assault team followed. Well…what's left of them."

"Not for long," Bronx says.

Chicago can hear his rifle reports. Only their SAW is capable of automatic fire, but he's quick on the trigger. It sounds like Bronx emptied the entire magazine in just a few seconds.

"Both teams are down. Rear threat neutralized."

"That was fast," Chicago says.

"Yeah. They were standing in a group on Sixth Street like a bunch of dolts. Fish in a barrel."

"This is Havoc One. Save your victory lap, boys. The assault teams are moving.

"Hollywood?" Chicago shouts. "You see them?"

"Say hello to my little friend!"

Hollywood opens up with the SAW. Anyone standing in the open will regret that life choice. He's got the south handled. Chicago takes aim and starts picking off the guys sprinting across the street. There is no shortage of targets. He does another reload and fires a few more times before the men duck into the neighbor's yard.

"Havoc One, I have no angle. I need the window. Take out that northern support element so I don't get my ass shot off."

"Wilco. Stand by…."

He can see them turn their heads and point at the new threat from a direction they didn't expect. Some of them don't get the chance to fire, and they drop where they're standing. Chicago seizes the opportunity to move to the window and continues firing at the men trying to cross through the intersection.

About half of them make it to the safety of the house on the corner. He struggles to get an angle on them and doesn't really want to risk the neighbors' lives by taking unaimed shots. It doesn't matter. They aren't going anywhere. Between Tulsa and Chicago, they are effectively pinned down.

He closes his eyes and takes a moment to catch his breath.

CHAPTER SEVENTY-EIGHT

LANDON TAYSON

OUTSIDE THE FIFTH STREET HOUSE
MINNEAPOLIS ARTS DISTRICT OCCUPIED ZONE

Something has gone seriously wrong. Landon looks down the sights of his rifle at the house but doesn't shoot. There are plenty of others doing that for him. He's more concerned with Muzzie's urgent radio calls directed at the team they posted behind the house. It's his seventh or eighth attempt, and he hasn't gotten a response.

They were supposed to report when they were in place for this plan to work. Instead, everyone could hear them open fire. Did they jump the gun, or is it something else? He doesn't know, and apparently, neither does his commander. This must be what they mean by "the fog of war."

Muzzie removes the radio from his face and leans hard against the side of their SUV. "We should pull back."

"It's too late! The only path is forward. We've invested this much. We can take them!"

Retreat is not an option. Landon has the manpower assembled now. Ignoring the effect that pulling back would have on morale after so many losses, there will never be a better opportunity to take this house. The men have already sacrificed so much. Failing to complete this mission would dishonor them all. No, this house must be taken, and its occupants' bodies dragged through the streets as a warning.

"Sir, we are—"

"Send the assault team in. They can't stop them from breaching the house."

Muzzie inhales deeply and keys the microphone. "Commence the assault."

It takes about ten seconds for the command to have the desired result. About twenty guys rise from their positions and begin sprinting forward. It's an impressive sight.

"Covering fire!" the captain shouts as he raises his rifle and begins firing.

Landon does the same, taking aim at the house and rapidly squeezing the trigger in as the assault team scrambles across the intersection. He watches as they fall one by one. The fire coming from the target isn't intense, but it is accurate. He can hear the machine gun and sees its muzzle flash in the other window. The other team probably isn't faring much better.

About half the team reaches the house two doors down from Chicago's little fortress. They stay close to the front, hunkering down and afraid to move. They are pinned down.

"Push forward!" Muzzie screams, waving at them. "You can't stay there! Move!"

"Damn it!"

"Cover me. I'm going to lead them in."

Landon starts to protest, but his commander is already sprinting toward his men. He can see bullets pelting the asphalt as Muzzie streaks toward them. Other than providing some cover fire and holding his breath, there's nothing more that can be done.

Muzzie reaches the team. He barks out instructions and stands, compelling two men to rise and join him in the charge. The captain takes a single step before his head explodes and his body crumples to the ground. There is no need for someone to check his pulse. Landon's commander is dead.

"Nooooooo!"

Landon moves around the front of the vehicle and slaps a fresh magazine into the well of his rifle. He fires as fast as he can, letting out a deep roar as it barks each time he pulls back on the trigger. The bolt locks to the rear, and he is reaching to replace the bag when he feels a sharp pain in his thigh. His leg gives out, and he collapses to the ground. Struggling to sit up, he slides across the pavement and leans against the fender of the SUV.

They are running out of people. The volume of fire has slowed to a few shots here and there. The assault teams are gone. The fire support elements lie dead or wounded all around him.

One of the guys near him cries in anguish. He reaches out toward Landon as the asphalt under his chest turns bright crimson. Landon wants to help, but he's wounded, too. Not only does his leg wound negate his moving, but trying to reach the man would only draw more fire from the house.

Landon ignores his pleas. After a few moments, his arm drops to the ground, and he stops moving. Most of the men around him aren't, either.

He sees muzzle flashes in the house. Then, another across the street. It feels like the enemy is all around him. An unsettling thought pops into Landon's mind – there had to be more of them than he thought. He has a new respect for the Air Force. They played him. He walked into a trap.

That doesn't mean he can't still get out of here. If he can get around the SUV and make it to Muzzie's radio set, he can call for Raven to pick him up. They can leave this area and find a place to hide when the police come through the barricades. Or they can try to sneak out, maybe even slipping into Canada to lie low. From there, arrangements can be made to relocate to a warm, non-extradition country. There's still money left in the account from his benefactor.

Three men in the south make a break for the house from the neighbor's porch. They have no fire support, but the angle prevents anyone inside from shooting at them. That was the approach they should have used all along. Instead, the trio are the first fighters to reach the front door.

They open up on the door with one of their rifles. The sound of the shots is almost deafening now that the rest of the area has fallen silent. They force their way into the house. Maybe there's hope.

"Get 'em, boys!"

The three men disappear inside. More shots are fired. Maybe they caught Chicago and the other occupants by surprise and introduced them to the afterlife. He wants nothing more than to see that man knocking on the gates of Hell.

Everything falls silent. Landon stares at the door, waiting for one of them to come out and wave, giving them the "all clear." Nothing happens. Landon pulls his sidearm. He tries to climb to his feet, but the pain in his leg is too much. Resigned to his fate, he sets the gun down beside him. It's over.

He should have taken Raven's advice. None of this was worth it. Landon has lost men he had known for years. He lost Muzzie. But what's done is done. All that's left to do now is wait and hope for a miracle.

CHAPTER SEVENTY-NINE

CHIEF VANESSA CAMPBELL

This isn't the first time Vanessa has had a gun pointed at her. The first time was when she was a rookie. The most recent incident was when she approached the barricade in the early hours of the ADOZ. She doesn't count the time she first met Zachary Baumann. He only had his rifle aimed in her general direction.

Every instinct she has is to reach for the gun that is absent from her holster. She fights to play it cool. If this guy wanted her dead, she'd already be bleeding out on the ground.

"Were you left alone at your barricade, too?" Vanessa asks, barely flinching.

The man walks closer, almost gliding as the business end of his rifle remains trained on her chest. "I asked you a question."

"I heard you. I'm Chief of Police Vanessa Campbell. This is a conversation."

He eyes Zach coolly before returning his gaze to her. "You're on the wrong side of the street."

"I know. I'm just listening to the show playing down south, same as you."

"Did you leave your post?" Zach asks.

Alarm flashes on his face as he lowers his rifle. Her guess was correct. This guy was alone at his barricade, too. She wonders how many other ones up here only have one or two men manning them.

"Don't worry about it. My guys aren't crossing the street unless I give the order, and I've been ordered not to. You could all leave your posts along this street and go to Applebee's and we still wouldn't move."

"Why not?"

"The mayor won't permit it," Zach interjects, his tone a cross between disgust and satisfaction.

"He's an ass."

Apparently, the kid she's been talking to isn't the only person manning these barricades who is a good judge of character. "No argument there."

Another two guys join them from the west. The size of her little confab is growing. At least these guys didn't point their guns at her. The four men chat briefly with each other before a sudden rash of gunfire causes them to face south.

"This sounds bad," one of them observes.

"Do you want to see how bad?" Vanessa asks, prompting them all to turn and look at her. "We have a drone up. No doubt it's watching the action."

They nod. She radios for the drone operator to patch into a mobile device and come unarmed to bring it to her at the barricade. Three minutes later, he strides across the avenue. None of the four men she's with point their rifles at him. The trust is growing.

"Here ya go, Chief," he says, handing her a tablet.

"Thanks. You can go."

Everyone gathers around as he scurries back to the perimeter. The drone is a distance away, using the zoom feature on the camera to check the situation. There are bodies everywhere in the streets. She can see muzzle flashes in the neighborhood and some coming from the house. Just as Vanessa thought. The Rangers are handling their business.

"Oh…my…God," Zach mutters. He articulates what they all are thinking.

"Three guys are doing this?" his buddy from the barricade next door asks.

"There could be more than three. I don't have an exact count. My people don't think it's more than six or eight, though. We're pretty certain about that."

"Who are they?"

"They put a flag up on their roof. It's a very patriotic thing to do, so we assume military veterans. My guess? They're ex-Special Forces. Or, maybe Army Rangers, paratroopers, or even Marines. Regardless of what unit they were in, they're nobody I'd want to screw with."

The ADOZ fighters look at each other. That's not what they want to hear. If their leader is up against that, what are the odds of him winning? Or even surviving? And if he does, could he even maintain control?

"I know what you guys are thinking. Yeah, it's over for the ADOZ, one way or another."

"What happens if we surrender?" Zach asks, looking at his feet as he poses the question.

She expects at least one of these guys to object to that. Or even all three of them. Instead, they all look at her and wait for an answer. Morale here is even lower than she thought. If the mayor had any foresight, he would have exploited that earlier, and maybe they could have avoided the bloodbath happening on Fifth Street.

"You mean right now? Well, so far as I'm concerned, I'll let you go home."

"No charges?"

She looks at one of the guys who joined their gaggle late. "If you're not here when we start making arrests, there's nothing I can do, right?"

"You know my name," Zach says.

Vanessa presses her lips together. "You know, I forgot to document our first chat in a report. I need to write things like that down. I seem to have forgotten it."

Zach can see the slight smile on her face. He gets the point. Without much hesitation, he unslings his rifle and hands it to her. The others do the same.

"Come on. Let's get you guys out of here before things get ugly."

Vanessa slings the four rifles and crosses the avenue. Her men lower their weapons. She didn't cuff any of the men, which is completely against procedure. It also would have been counterproductive. Her officers watch her lead them past the squad car blocking the intersection. She stops, keying the radio mic fastened to her shoulder.

"Burke, you have my location, right?"

"Roger, Chief."

"There are three barricades vacated on Lowry. Open the door and march the troops through."

"Wilco."

"You guys are free to go. Good luck to you, and stay out of trouble."

Zach hands her his radio. "Channel three will get you in touch with everyone on the barricades. Maybe you can make them the same offer you made us before any more shooting starts."

She nods and signals an officer over. "Escort these men out of our AO and let them go. Don't take any information from them."

"Ma'am?"

"You heard me," Vanessa says before turning to Zach and shaking his hand. "Promises made. Promises kept."

CHAPTER EIGHTY
FIELD OFFICER DAVID BRASS

CIA COVERT TEAM SAFEHOUSE
HOPKINS, MINNESOTA

Men around the table look at him through apprehensive eyes. Brass is more than willing to wait until one of them speaks, although none of them are. This is quickly becoming a battle of wills, and whoever opens their mouth first loses.

He knew this was a big ask and wargamed how to do it on the way to the safehouse, if one could call this that. A safehouse is technically a covert location used for intelligence operations, surveillance, or protection of assets and operatives. They can be used for debriefings, hiding high-value targets, or as a staging site.

They are mostly apartments in urban areas, luxury homes, or abandoned buildings. The difference is that operatives usually employ counter-surveillance and defensive measures to prevent discovery. Those range from CCTV cameras and geofencing alerts to reinforced walls and bulletproof glass to escape tunnels and Faraday cages.

This online rental is within walking distance to downtown Hopkins and its plentiful dining options. The town itself is just fifteen minutes from Minneapolis and just over twenty to the airport. At about a thousand square feet, it has comfy vibes and convenience to go with its separate entrance. It's perfect for this team to lie low in.

"You want us to do what?" the team leader asks.

Brass smiles at winning the battle of wills. "You heard me."

"It's one thing to operate in hostile territory," one of the other men says, "but you're asking us to snatch the target off the street."

"You didn't sign up for easy. I already gave you a cakewalk when you grabbed Landon so we could scare the bejesus out of him. Now it's time to earn your paychecks."

CIA Tactical Teams are paramilitary units within the CIA's Special Activities Center. As a part of the Special Operations Group, these guys conduct covert operations, engage in unconventional warfare, and execute high-risk missions in hostile environments. Most operatives are recruited from elite military units like Delta Force, SEAL Team Six, Marine Raiders, and Green Berets. These guys are no exception. They can handle it.

"You realize that the target is bound to be surrounded by cops, right?"

"Yeah."

The commander shrugs theatrically. "Most people at Langley would be bothered by that. They wouldn't assume the risk."

Brass crosses his arms. "That's why I don't work in that infernal building. Chance favors the bold."

"All right. Left and right limits?" the second man asks as the team looks at Brass.

In the military, "left and right limits" are the boundaries of a unit's area of responsibility. They are crucial for ensuring coordinated operations, preventing friendly fire, and maintaining situational awareness. In this context, they want to know what they can and can't do.

"Just take the target alive and make as small a scene as possible."

"Timing?" one of the other men asks.

"Yesterday," Brass says, meaning as soon as possible.

"Exfil?"

"Grab the target, get out of Minnesota, and head east. I will arrange for a transfer to a secure facility. I'll let you know the details once you're en route."

The men shift their weight and clench their jaws. Operators are planners, and planners don't like not having those specifics ironed out in advance. Despite their misgivings, they hold their tongues.

"There is going to be fallout," the team leader warns. "We can't make this target disappear into thin air."

"Leave that for me to handle," Brass says, handing him a sheet of notepaper with a number scrawled on it. "Here's a contact you can get SIGINT and IMINT from. I'll leave you to the planning and execution."

Operators don't like to be micromanaged, and Brass doesn't feel compelled to look over their shoulders. They will complete the mission. They're also right about the outcome. This is a risk, but one with a potentially huge payout. What happens next will make the difference. With that thought, he fires up his rental car for the drive to the airport.

CHAPTER EIGHTY-ONE

EMMIT "CHICAGO" HASKINS

There is a critical point in any firefight when a decision needs to be made. In combat, the difference between success and failure is making the right call at the right time. In this fight, the ADOZ fighters should have withdrawn after their initial attack was mowed down. Yes, they had numbers, but that was their only advantage.

Instead, Landon pressed the attack. Their deception was obvious, and it was clear that they had no understanding of what they were up against. Every battle is won before it's ever fought, and this was no exception to Sun Tzu's axiom.

Now, the men trying to storm the citadel are realizing that it's a lost cause. They should be running away. Instead, they are uncertain, hesitating, and making themselves easy targets. The remaining fighters are going down like bowling pins.

Chicago has moved to sniping the fire support team to the north. He can see that Tulsa is doing his part. Nica is focusing on the south, filling in for Bronx, who moved west to flank the guys Nashville had pinned down out back. They have given up on challenging Hollywood and his SAW.

"Spartan Six, this is Two. Three assholes just moved up along the houses to the south. They got through. You're about to have uninvited guests."

"Heads up, guys," Chicago says as he moves to the top of the stairs. "Company is coming."

One of the men outside opens up with his rifle. Bullets crash into and then through the solid wood front door. That will make breaching easier, but that's when their problems will really begin. They are about to learn the hard way why entering a structure that way is a bad idea.

A doorway creates a bottleneck for attackers. In military lingo, it's known as a "fatal funnel." It's a tactical term used in close-quarters battle to denote any narrow, confined space from doorways and hallways to stairwells. Movement in these areas is predictable, and cover is limited, making anyone who ventures into one a prime target.

Soldiers try to avoid doors when possible, but when it is necessary, a breach is preceded by tossing in a fragmentary grenade. He doubts these ADOZ fighters have grenades, and even if they do, would they even know how to properly clear a room?

Sure enough, a man kicks in the shattered door, and the three men charge into the small foyer. Nashville greets them with accurate fire, taking out the lead guy. The man behind him doesn't fare any better, catching three rounds to the chest before he drops.

The third guy tries to take cover behind the small table against the wall in the entry. It may protect him from Nashville. It won't help him against Chicago as he hustles halfway down the stairs.

The man barely has time to realize his mistake. His eyes grow wide as he sees the Ranger on the stairs with the rifle pointed at him. He tries to swing his weapon in Chicago's direction, but it's way too little, too late. Chicago fires several times, eliminating the threat.

Battles end. Regardless of the size and scale of the conflict, the guns eventually fall silent. That's what's happening now. There is a shot or two still ringing out around the house, but this fight is all but over.

"You okay?"

"Never better," Nashville sarcastically mumbles.

"Hollywood, you good?" Chicago calls up to him from the stairs.

"Looks like I picked the wrong week to quit sniffing glue."

Chicago smiles. He loves that movie. "Havoc team, give me a quick ACE report."

"Havoc One, two mags, and an arm wound that I'm bandaging. It's not serious."

"This is Havoc Two. Full hit points. I moved closer to the street. No tangos in sight. I'm down to my last magazine."

"Havoc Six, three mags, and I'm fine."

"This is One. There's a ton of wounded out here, and I have eyes on Tayson. It looks like he's down."

The report surprises Chicago. Landon strikes him as the kind of guy who would stay far to the rear when the bullets started flying. How was he in any position to get himself shot? Not that it matters.

"Down, as in dead?"

"Stand by…Negative, he's still moving. It looks like he caught a leg wound."

"Do you have a shot?"

"Kinda. Tayson's on the west side of the vehicle facing the house. I don't have a good angle."

"This is Havoc Six. I'm moving north toward you."

"Stand fast, Six. Keep an eye on our three o'clock in case anyone left gets frisky. I'm gonna get back on the sniper rifle."

Chicago moves back upstairs. The room is a disaster, and the window is completely shot out. He picks up the rifle and rests it on the makeshift support. It takes him only about ten seconds of sweeping to find the man on the ground leaning against the front fender.

"This is Spartan Six. Target acquired."

"You gonna take him out?" Nica asks.

It's a valid question. Landon's death will end this right now. Without his leadership, the fighters at the barricades would have nobody left to fight for. They may believe in the cause, but he doubts it's with the fanaticism that the leadership does.

He lines the man's head up in his crosshairs. The ADOZ leader is out of the fight. This isn't combat. It's murder. Chicago closes his eyes and lets out the breath he was holding. Some lines shouldn't be crossed.

"Negative. Hold fire. I want Tayson to surrender. We can—"

"Hold that thought, Gents," Nica interrupts. "I have a vehicle pulling up from the east with hazard lights flashing."

"I have it," Tulsa confirms. "What's this all about?"

"One occupant. Female," Nica relays. "She just exited the vehicle. She may have a sidearm in a hip holster."

"Aw, man!" Tulsa exclaims a few seconds later. "That's one cold-hearted bitch. She just stepped over some dude's body. She's walking toward Landon."

"Target acquired," Chicago whispers into his headset. He saw her do it, too.

Chicago puts the crosshairs of his scope on her head. One wrong move, and whoever this woman is will join the rest of her friends in the afterlife.

CHAPTER EIGHTY-TWO

LANDON TAYSON

OUTSIDE THE FIFTH STREET HOUSE
MINNEAPOLIS ARTS DISTRICT OCCUPIED ZONE

Raven climbs out of the vehicle and slams the door. Landon's jaw hangs slack as he peeks around the fender to watch her casually stroll over to him like she just parked at a supermarket to buy groceries. This is anything but that. Is she crazy? She just drove into the middle of a warzone.

"What the hell are you doing? You're going to get yourself killed! Take cover!"

Raven looks up at the house. Landon follows her eyes, expecting to see a muzzle flash from one of the windows any second. One second goes by…then another…and another. His heart is firing in his chest, probably awkwardly close to its maximum rate. The shot he's waiting for – the one he fears – never comes.

She stares a few beats longer before raising her arms and showing her hands to the house. Is that a signal? Is it an indication of surrender? Why aren't they shooting at her? She holds the pose for a few long seconds before walking over to Landon.

"What is this?' he apprehensively asks.

"I'm not looking to kill the guys in that house. I think they know that."

"Do you know who they are?"

Raven shakes her head. "It doesn't matter."

It matters to him. He lost over a hundred of his best men. These weren't protestors enlisted in the cause or vagrants who meandered up to the ADOZ, thinking it would be cool to join their ranks. Landon knew many of these guys for a couple of years. Some of them helped plan this. All of them were invaluable.

Now, most of them are dead. The wails of a few wounded only serve as a warning that not all perished in the slaughter. But the fight is over. They were eradicated by a few men who were far better armed than any of them knew. He absolutely wants to know who they are. He wants to live to find out.

"Help me behind the car before they finish me," Landon orders, shifting slightly from his position against the car.

"That doesn't matter either," Raven deadpans.

He stares at her and blinks. "What are you talking about?"

She doesn't bother explaining. Sliding to her left, she steps on the handgun Landon dropped beside him and kicks it away. He watches it skitter across the asphalt.

"I think you know."

A surge of electricity jolts his spine. Raven's tone is different. So is her attitude. This is not the woman he has known for two years. She was efficient and supportive.

The woman hovering above him is cold and calculating. It's like a switch has been flipped.

"What…? You're betraying me?"

Raven sighs heavily and frowns. "You know a thing or two about betrayal. You betrayed your own country. And for what?"

"We could have built a better life in the ADOZ!"

Landon watches the smile that crosses her lips. It's not joyous – it's evil.

"That was never going to happen. This is America. It's a country that shows a great deal of patience, but that particular resource isn't inexhaustible. You're a fool if you think this takeover was going to last a month, much less be permanent."

"The government is filled with tyrants!"

"Yes, that's true. And you assaulted a house for the sin of flying a flag. Unsuccessfully, from the looks of it. You were going to kill these men for…flying…a…flag. Who, exactly, is the tyrant, Landon?"

"You work for them, don't you?"

Raven grimaces, her head almost imperceptibly moving left and right. "It's not that simple."

He doesn't believe her. She's a fed, probably from the FBI. It explains her reaction to Kai's death. She has been here the whole time, gathering evidence to use against him. The only question is why she didn't stop him sooner. She had hundreds of chances.

"So, are you going to take me into custody?"

"I'm not a cop."

Yeah, right. "Then what are you?"

"A ghost. A figment of your imagination. Someone who was never here, Landon."

"Oh, you were here. I'm going to burn everyone, including *you*. I know where all the bodies are buried. I have the names of everyone who helped me – every company that supplied us. I will tell them everything! You think you're a ghost? Let's see how well you hide! Otherwise, you'll be in a cell right next to me."

She shakes her head. "Neither of us is going to prison."

Raven pulls her gun out and points it at Landon's forehead. His face freezes in surprise and horror.

"Alas, Babylon."

CHAPTER EIGHTY-THREE
CHIEF VANESSA CAMPBELL

Burke isn't wasting any time. The Minneapolis Police Department acquired military-style equipment through the 1033 Program. Following the George Floyd riots, they decided not to advertise their inventory. Not that it's a secret that they have a couple of armored vehicles.

The Ballistic Engineered Armored Response Counter Attack Truck is better known as the BearCat. The armored vehicle is designed for tactical law enforcement use. It features military-grade steel plating to protect against small arms fire, can operate in rough terrain and urban environments, and is used by the department's SWAT team.

The vehicles have firing ports, which she sincerely hopes the team doesn't need to use. What will come in handy is the ram attachment at the front. Vanessa watches the beast bolt across the avenue and slam into the small barricade. It makes quick work of it before backing up, moving to its right, and doing the same at the one she was standing at with Zach.

She doesn't need to issue orders. She developed a plan with Lieutenant Burke, who is now executing it. The officers were briefed on their responsibilities and they begin steering their squad cars into the ADOZ after the two barricades are removed. It's now a matter of coordinating movements. They agreed that they would clear all the Lowry Avenue barricades before progressing south and east. The outlooks that Landon posted to watch the river won't be a problem.

Vanessa is about to get on the radio when an irate Wilma Sillyere storms over and begins shouting. "What the hell do you think you're doing?"

"My job."

"You have orders not to breach!"

"I heard them."

"I have the mayor on the phone," she says, holding her cell out to her. "He wants to talk to you."

"And people in hell want ice water. I'm busy. I'll talk to him when the operation is completed."

Vanessa has learned a thing or two about de-escalation during her time in law enforcement. That usually applies to criminals and suspects and not subordinates, but the tactic is just as applicable. She is turning to walk away when Inspector Sillyere grabs her.

The chief stares at her hands and looks Wilma in the eyes. "You have three seconds to remove your hands. Don't make me count."

She does as ordered.

"Now, get out of my way.

Wilma places her hand against the chief's chest to stop her again. She changes the device over to its speaker and holds it out. "Go ahead, Mr. Mayor."

"End this incursion, now, Chief, or consider yourself relieved of your position. I will have your badge. You will never work in law enforcement again."

"Mayor Thurlow, I'm not sure if you're paying attention, but there is a war going on inside the ADOZ. Our citizens are in grave danger."

"I told you that's not *our* problem."

"I'm not abandoning our citizens. The barricades were breached without a shot being fired. It's time to end this. So, if you're done with your threats, I have work to do."

"Inspector Sillyere, you are now acting chief. Remove your predecessor from the area."

She grabs at Vanessa again. That's the last straw. The chief has never considered herself much of a fighter. There is a big difference between wrestling a criminal to the ground, which she did in her youth, and punching someone in the face.

Vanessa brings her right arm back and lets it fly, landing her fist squarely on the unexpecting inspector's jaw. There is power behind the punch. A week of frustration and irritation is channeled into her arm.

Sillyere's head snaps to the side, and the torque corkscrews her to the ground. It almost looks like something from a comedy movie. She's conscious but seeing stars. The best part is that her mouth is shut for a change.

"Did you guys hear the mayor?"

The pair of officers look at each other briefly before turning back to her. "Hear what?"

"His voice was garbled," the other lies. "I couldn't make out what he was saying."

"Good answers. Consider yourself relieved of duty," she turns and tells Wilma, who is starting to recover from the blow. "Get her out of my sight."

Vanessa picks up Zach's radio and ensures it is set to channel three. She keys the mic. Here goes nothing.

"Attention, all ADOZ fighters. This is Chief of Police Captain Vanessa Campbell. We have entered the ADOZ to quell the violence taking place on Fifth Street. Anyone who surrenders now to law enforcement or military personnel will face minimal charges, if any. Any fighter who resists will face domestic terrorism charges, and the list will grow from there. Anybody who fires at law enforcement will be charged with attempted murder.

"You have made your point with this takeover. Your voices have been heard, but now the occupied zone will cease to exist. Order will be restored. What happens next is up to you. Put down your weapons and surrender, and you will be treated fairly. Don't, and you may not survive to see the sunrise. You must comply immediately."

CHAPTER EIGHTY-FOUR
EMMIT "CHICAGO" HASKINS

THE FIFTH STREET HOUSE
MINNEAPOLIS ARTS DISTRICT OCCUPIED ZONE

The shot pierces the relative stillness that has blanketed the neighborhood. There are still wails of agony from the wounded, but the sharp crack of the round being fired easily drowns that out for a moment. Chicago removes his eye from the scope and stares at the entire scene, half not believing what his eyes just saw.

"Whoa! Did you guys see that?" Tulsa says over the radio.

"See what?" Nashville asks, still watching the back of the house in case there is a group of Landon's fighters that they missed.

"Some chick just shot the ADOZ honcho in the head," Tulsa summarizes.

Bronx whistles. "Bye-bye, buddy."

"Oh, no, it wasn't the airplanes. It was Beauty killed the Beast," Hollywood belts out. Chicago wonders how long he has been waiting to use that particular *King Kong* quote. There aren't a lot of opportunities.

The woman looks off to the side before training her eyes up at the house. Chicago shakes his head as he nestles his cheek against the stock and stares back through the scope. She has to know she has at least a couple of guns trained on her. That would make most people nervous. Instead, she grins as she types something into her phone. It's a cold-blooded smile se would expect from an assassin, not a hippie Antifa chick.

"I have her in my sights," Tulsa says. "She looks like she's phoning a friend. What do you want me to do? I can drop her like third-period French."

Whoever this woman is had to be in Landon's inner circle. There was no resistance from him as she approached. They had a conversation while he was on the ground. Why would she shoot him? Does it really matter? What's done is done.

"She did us a solid. Let her go."

The woman takes one final look at the house and turns to head back to the vehicle. Her back is turned to Chicago, and he lines the crosshairs right in the center of it. He doesn't bother moving his finger to the trigger. She isn't aggressive toward them, so there is no reason not to let her live. The police can hunt her down. Less than a minute later, the SUV turns in the street and heads back the way it came.

"Let's rally in front of the house."

Chicago lowers the rifle to the floor and hustles out of the room and down the stairs. He emerges from the front door and stops in the street. The moaning from wounded fighters hasn't ceased. He would render aid, but help is coming.

The havoc team converges on him. Tulsa nods and heads into the house. He and Hollywood share a quick hug, and Nashville does the same in the foyer. The former stops at Chicago's side and inhales deeply.

"I love the smell of napalm in the morning. It smells like…victory."

"You're bleeding," Chicago says, seeing the red splotch on Hollywood's tricep.

"There will be blood tonight!" Hollywood exclaims as he checks his arm.

"*The Princess Bride*? Really? Been waiting a while to use that line, haven't you?" He beams as Chicago turns toward the house and runs his hand through his hair. "Oh, my sister's gonna be pissed."

"I don't know," Nashville says, coming up from the side of the house and draping his arm around his former squad leader. "Some wood putty, a little paint…."

"Won't put a dent in that damage, Brother," Bronx concludes as he arrives at their gaggle. "I hope you have good homeowner's insurance."

"Let's see if they cover armed assault," Nica adds, clearing his rifle.

The sirens to the north grow louder. Then, they begin erupting to the south. The police are making their move on the barricades. There is one notable absence – the sound of gunfire. The ADOZ sentinels watching the perimeter may have no fight in them.

"Police are going to start swarming this area. You guys need to bounce. Do you have an exfil plan?"

"Sure," Nica says. "We'll just blend in."

Chicago scoffs. "You're dressed in camo and toting duffle bags full of weapons. Is that your idea of blending in?"

"Yeah," Bronx says, his voice an octave or two higher. "All the police activity will make it even easier."

Plans for slipping out of the area when this was over were discussed but never settled on. The more urgent task was survival. But these guys are seasoned warriors trained to slip past sentries and move stealthily to accomplish their missions.

"We'll be fine, Chicago," Nashville says. "What about you?"

"Don't tell us you're going to stay here to face the music," Bronx warns. "There are like a hundred bodies on the ground. You don't want to listen to that orchestra."

"Naw. I need to grab a few things, and then I'll be right behind you."

"What about her?" Nica asks, nodding behind Chicago.

The Rangers in front of her are dirty and reek of gunpowder. They must be a sight. Her eyes shift to her left and right as she sees the bodies in the street. Finally, they settle on Chicago for a long moment before she lowers them to the ground.

"I have no place to go," Babs says in a near whisper.

"You can stay with me in Tennessee," Nashville offers. "We already share a last name. My place isn't much, but I have a spare bedroom you can crash in until you figure things out."

Babs looks at him and beams, her eyes immediately brightening. "Thank you."

Tulsa packs the last of the weapons as hugs and handshakes are shared. The end is bittersweet. These men are Chicago's brothers. They have fought and shed blood together. They share a bond that no civilian could ever understand or appreciate. He is going to miss all of them.

The hug with Nica is the longest. "Thank you, Brother. For everything."

The man grins when they finally let go. "You know, if this is your idea of a summer barbecue, I can't wait to see what the Christmas party looks like."

"All the weapons are packed," Tulsa advises. "I'll take care of them. Let's hope the police and feds don't pull any prints off all the brass we're leaving behind."

Fingerprints aren't their only concern. The cops could have drone footage of the battle. Neighbors absolutely saw these guys and may provide descriptions to the police. Even if his guys successfully get out of Minnesota, it would take a miracle for their identities to remain a mystery.

Hollywood and Nashville will get visits from the FBI. The three guys still in the Regiment will face an uncomfortable conversation with the MPs. They won the battle, but the legal war is only beginning. They are all going to get hemmed up for this. That's the reality.

The police chief already knows he's here, even if his men may not be as easy to place on the scene. His cell phone has been pinging off the local tower from the beginning. There will be no hiding that. Can he live as a fugitive? Is it worth trying? That's something to figure out after a shower, some sleep, and a hot meal.

"Can't do much about that," Bronx advises. "What happens, happens. I made my choice. I'd do it again."

"No ragrets!" Hollywood says, quoting *We're the Millers*.

"Thanks," Chicago says. "To all of you. Now get the hell out of here."

Hollywood shakes his hand one last time. "We'll always have Paris."

"In case I don't see you, good afternoon, good evening, and goodnight." The quip gets the desired smile.

Chicago watches the men range-walk up Fifth before passing the carnage and disappearing with Babs into the night. Chicago needs to do the same. All he needs to do is retrieve the go-bag he packed and slip out of the Arts District. There's one thing that must happen first. He comes to the position of attention and snaps a crisp salute to the flag on top of the house.

CHAPTER EIGHTY-FIVE
CHIEF VANESSA CAMPBELL

NORTH OF THE FIFTH STREET HOUSE
THE FORMER MINNEAPOLIS ARTS DISTRICT OCCUPIED ZONE

Luck hasn't been on her side during this ordeal. At least, that's how it feels. There was no reason to believe this would work. It's like throwing a dart at a board blindfolded. The chances of hitting the bullseye aren't zero, but they aren't high, either.

But that's what happened. Vanessa sees the camouflaged figure moving up the street with a purpose. She slowly and quietly moves closer to the house, ensuring she's deep in the shadows. There is no upside to spooking him until she's ready. She slides her gun out of its holster with one hand and retrieves her cell with the other.

Vanessa presses the green icon, and the phone begins to ring. She can actually hear the muted chime, causing him to stop in his tracks. To her surprise, he connects the call. He doesn't speak, but the line is open.

"Don't go that way, Chicago. The police have breached the barricades on Lowry. They are filtering south to the warzone you just left behind while the Broadway barriers are being dismantled by the National Guard."

He takes a sharp breath. "How did you know I was heading north?"

"Turn to your left."

He spots Vanessa standing on someone's porch. She removes her phone from her ear, and the screen illuminates her face for a moment as she hangs up. Pocketing the phone, she descends the three stairs with her gun drawn. The chief walks over to him with it at the low ready until confirming that the soldier is unarmed. Content, she holsters her weapon and extends her hand.

"It's nice to meet you in person, Sergeant."

"I wish I could say the same, Chief Campbell. Why aren't you with your fellow officers?" he asks, shaking her hand before looking around.

"They are all capable men and women. They don't need a bureaucrat like me looking over their shoulders. I was more interested in finding you."

"How did you know I was heading this way?"

"Call it a hunch. Where are your men?"

"In the wind."

Vanessa is thrilled that there was no additional information. She doesn't want names, numbers, or direction of travel. If this conversation is ever discovered, and she gets questioned, she won't have to lie.

"Good. Did you take any casualties?"

"Nothing consequential. Landon's people, on the other hand? Well...."

"From the sound of it, we're going to have a mess to clean up, and forensics is going to be busy for a while. And Landon Tayson?"

"He was shot in the head by some woman who was with him."

Vanessa cocks her head. "And you know this, how?"

"I watched it through my scope," Chicago says, getting a nod. "Am I under arrest?"

"You should be. Even if it was self-defense, that's for a court to decide, and the number of other laws you broke...phew. Fortunately for you, I've been advised by elected officials that the ADOZ isn't technically in my jurisdiction after the takeover. Besides, I've been technically relieved of my position by the mayor. So, I guess I can't *legally* arrest you."

"That sounds like malicious compliance."

Vanessa lets out a sharp chuckle. "It's a story for an Internet post someday. I'm certain there's a Reddit thread that will get a kick out of it."

"Thank you, Chief Campbell."

"No need to thank me. I'm glad you're okay. I'm glad your guys are okay. But you need to understand something. After this, there's nothing I can do to protect you or the men who were with you. What's going to happen next will be outside of my control."

"I understand."

"Good. Now, get going. Head to the river and move north from there. Most of our manpower will be here or at the main barricades to clear them for emergency vehicles to enter. We won't have units over that way for some time."

He starts heading east down the avenue. Vanessa can't help but admire him. That's the best of America right there. He's everything she would ever want in a soldier defending this nation. Honor, duty, and courage still mean something to him. It clearly meant something to his comrades, whoever they were.

"Chicago? There's one more thing. That flag you flew...it's funeral size. I'm guessing it draped the casket of one of your fellow Rangers. It's going to be in our evidence locker for a while, but at some point, it may mysteriously disappear. If you ever want it back, look me up. It will be folded and stored in a place of honor on my mantel until you claim it."

He nods. "Thank you, ma'am."

The sergeant moves off at a light jog, or what a paratrooper might call an "Airborne shuffle." Vanessa returns to her car and fires it up. She heads south and reaches the house a split-second behind a small convoy of police and paramedics. They immediately go to work treating the wounded as her men sweep the area, weapons drawn.

"My God," is all she can manage to say.

CHAPTER EIGHTY-SIX
FIELD OFFICER DAVID BRASS

MINNEAPOLIS-SAINT PAUL INTERNATIONAL AIRPORT
ST. PAUL, MINNESOTA

The Minneapolis-Saint Paul International Airport isn't the busiest in the nation, but it's hardly quiet, either. It typically ranks in the top twenty, handling more traffic than Portland and Nashville but far less than Chicago's O'Hare or Atlanta. As a major hub for Delta Air Lines, it has a high number of daily departures for domestic flights while lacking international routes.

That doesn't matter. Brass is heading back to Virginia on the last nonstop flight there for the day. The terminal was easy to navigate, and the security line was mercifully short. He finds his gate and checks his watch. Whatever Landon has planned in the ADOZ is likely going down. That is confirmed when he checks his phone and sees the news alert about all the gunfire in the district.

Airports are simultaneously among the most monitored and most anonymous places on Earth. For security reasons, they have thousands of cameras and hundreds of vigilant guards. His identification was checked multiple times to get to this point. Every move he makes is being captured on video that gets stored on hard drives somewhere.

At the same time, nobody knows or cares who he is. Fellow passengers never remember whom they see at an airport unless they meet a celebrity, sports star, or someone doing something way outside the norm. If you look like a traveler and act like a traveler, then nobody pays any attention to you.

Brass has made a living fitting in. He's dressed in a suit and is wheeling a standard carry-on behind him. He looks like a businessman on a sales trip. So, when he stops to check the text message on his phone, nobody would think twice about it. Little do they know who the contact is or why he is receiving the text.

Nightshade
Mission accomplished.

Brass
Good work.

Nightshade
Instructions?

Brass
Exfil and lie low. I'll contact you.

Nightshade
Okay.

Brass pockets his phone. Landon is dead. His commander has likely joined him in the afterlife. That's all that was needed. There is nobody else who could remotely track anything in that ADOZ to Brass. The corporate cutouts that he created to transfer the arms have been dissolved. Nothing can be tracked back to the CIA, even if conspiracy theorists push that narrative. Landon was the last of the loose ends. Nightshade proved the adage that "dead men tell no tales," and as of tonight, Raven Crusoe becomes a ghost.

Now, for the coup de grâce. Brass hadn't anticipated this development when he set out on this operation. The more he's learned about the ADOZ, the more he thought this particular wrinkle was too enticing not to explore.

He punches a contact in his phone and waits for it to ring. There are a thousand things that could go wrong with this, but intelligence operations are often high-risk, high-reward endeavors. He has leverage. Now he's going to use it.

"Yeah?"

"The ADOZ has fallen. It will be complete chaos there. You're a go."

"You're sure?"

Brass scowls before pressing his lips together to suppress it. He hates having his orders questioned. These guys are operators. Their job is to follow his directives, not question them.

"You have your instructions. Make it happen."

"Understood."

The line disconnects, and Brass pockets his phone as he looks at the activity behind the gate counter. The attendant has the phone in her hand and is ready to make an initial boarding call announcement. Everything's on track for an on-time departure. There's a first for everything.

It's about a two-and-a-half-hour flight to Dulles. He doesn't think his team will complete their assignment by the time he lands. He didn't hand this assignment to them with a promise that it would be easy. Few worthwhile things in this world are.

The delay suits him fine. Brass has preparations to make in advance and needs to be in Virginia to make them. All-in-all, everything is working out nicely. The grin marching across his face may stand out among all the dour faces waiting to board, but he can't stifle it. The Minneapolis Police Department will never see this coming.

CHAPTER EIGHTY-SEVEN

EMMIT "CHICAGO" HASKINS

There may be no worker more indifferent to what goes on around them than the desk clerk of a cheap motel. They've seen pretty much everything and turned a blind eye to all of it. So, Chicago showing up fresh from combat didn't even cause the grizzled man to raise an eyebrow. He changed clothes, but he's filthy and reeks of gunpowder.

He caught a rideshare when he was well north of the Arts District and took it to a few blocks away from some decrepit lodging off I-694. He gave the driver a fat tip after getting dropped off at a fast food joint and walked the rest of the way to this no-tell motel. He had to use a card linked to his rideshare app, but this rathole takes cash, and not much of it.

Brooklyn Center is a suburban city located just northwest of Minneapolis. It has a diverse population and is known for its parks, shopping centers, and proximity to the Twin Cities. It also is home to a few cheap hotels he can flop in.

The room is what he expected to see. Cheap furniture, a small television on the desk, a lamp, a phone, and a bed with a comforter that looks like it was purchased in the 1970s. It doesn't need to be fancy. It just needs to be discreet.

Chicago desperately needs a shower, but he needs the rest more. Sleep has been elusive for a week, and now that the adrenaline from the fight has worn off, his body is shifting hard from his heightened "fight or flight" state back to something more normal. The worst of the after-effects is fatigue. He feels like he could sleep for days.

He crashes face-down on the bed before rolling on his back and staring at the ceiling. There has been no word from his guys. Chicago doesn't know if that's a good or bad thing. He'd be more likely to hear from them if something had gone wrong with their escape. But he does have a nagging thought – if the police chief can find him, then the MPD could have found the rest of them, especially with Babs in tow.

All they have to do is get to Tulsa's truck, wherever they left it. Chicago has a more complicated exit strategy. He has no car and doesn't want to ask his sister for help. They have been in contact, and he told her that he was okay following the firefight. She was relieved, for now. No sane person would look forward to a conversation about the condition of her house. That, and he doesn't want to implicate her in anything that went down there. She is going to face enough questioning from law enforcement once they haul all the bodies away.

Fortunately, he has an idea about how to get out of Minnesota. Crystal Airport is a general aviation hub primarily serving private and corporate aircraft, flight training, and recreational flying. There is no commercial airline traffic there, meaning it won't be monitored by any law enforcement or federal agencies hunting him. He may be able to charter a small plane to take him…somewhere.

His eyes get heavy. The where can wait. He can figure it out in….

* * *

Something clamps down on his jaw. Chicago can't open his mouth, and that's enough to rouse him from a deep sleep. His eyes open to see three men in black masks standing over him. Then, the adrenaline dump hits his bloodstream.

He starts to struggle, but one of the men has a vise grip on his arms. Chicago switches to plan B. He kicks but hits nothing but air. They were ready for that. He tries to twist his torso to break free before feeling a prick in his upper arm.

Chicago manages to turn his head enough to see a syringe. What the hell is this?

"It's time to atone for your sins, Sergeant Haskins. Nite-nite."

He tries to fight the drowsiness, but it's a losing battle. These drugs are used for a reason – they're effective. He's losing the fight to keep his eyes open. They get heavier and heavier before closing for good.

CHAPTER EIGHTY-EIGHT
CHIEF VANESSA CAMPBELL

OUTSIDE CITY HALL
MINNEAPOLIS, MINNESOTA

Two Days Later

The speed at which modern society moves never ceases to amaze her. It's not just information that can circle the globe in minutes thanks to satellites and the Internet. In two days, the official story has been articulated, challenged, and reformulated. In its place, new narratives formed, perceptions changed again, and all that translated into a set of unexpected actions.

For starters, Vanessa has gone from pariah to unsung hero as the political winds shifted. Her actions, lambasted by the mayor and Inspector Sillyere, were heralded by the media, who were quick to assert that her decisive actions saved a lot of bloodshed. When her absence at the initial press conferences was noted and challenged, the mayor stammered as he concocted excuses.

The mayor relieved her of command. Or did he? He made it clear during the takedown of the ADOZ and immediately afterward, but that's not what he told the press at the first press conference. To the world, he announced that she was still on duty and evaluating the impact of the takeover on the police force and community.

When the men and women manning the barricades started giving interviews, her radio message was given as the reason for their surrender. The instructions she gave officers to avoid rough behavior with the fighters helped secure the quick surrender. She made good on her promise that anyone associated with the ADOZ would be treated fairly.

The result was nearly bloodless. Most of the fighters at the barricades surrendered, but one group on the railroad tracks decided to fight it out. Vanessa assumes they may have been the ones involved in the murder of Otto Goldberg, and they didn't want to go down without a fight. They got one. Five were wounded, and two died. But that was the exception, not the rule.

The whole incident has garnered massive national media attention. The battle on Fifth Street is big news that continues to dominate the headlines. Reporting on cable news networks shifts between her heroics and speculation over what happened on Fifth Street that led to the carnage. Theories are emerging, but nobody in law enforcement has provided any concrete facts. It's an interesting development, and the "it's still being investigated" excuse won't hold much longer.

Her absence could no longer be explained, either. So, here Vanessa is, standing on this dais in City Hall as the mayor gushes over her quick thinking and brilliant policing to end the crisis. What a change a few days makes. Now, it's her turn to address the masses as he yields the podium to her.

"I know there are a lot of questions about what happened two nights ago. The actions during the breach of the barricades are fairly well understood, but there is a lot of mystery surrounding what happened on Fifth Street. Nearly a hundred people are dead, and that would make this among the largest mass murders in American history.

"That's why little information has been released as we investigate. You will get the results of that investigation. The mayor has made it clear that he believes in transparency. After what happened in this city, you deserve that. I believe it, too."

The mayor beams at the explanation. He asked Vanessa to use her newfound media celebrity status to tamp down the criticism and stifle the emergence of conspiracy theories surrounding the massacre. He probably expected her to argue, but she did his bidding. Thurlow is clearly overjoyed at the remarks.

"In the interest of transparency, there is another angle to this story that I believe you should all hear. This crisis was a test of our mettle. It required sober analysis and tough decisions. The mayor led the charge in countless meetings held during this emergency, and he was backed up by members of the police force, including Inspector Wilma Sillyere, whose precinct is responsible for the Arts District."

"I firmly believe that she is my heir apparent when I retire," Vanessa adds, getting a warm, appreciative nod from her inspector, "so I think the citizens of Minneapolis should know what to expect."

Vanessa signals the man on the side of the room running the media presentation. For the mayor's briefing, slides were shown on large-screen televisions on each side of the dais. Now, they are about to show something else. The man pulls up a video clip from Burke's body camera and turns up the sound.

"See what happens when you're on the wrong side of history, Chief?"

"Wilma, the Arts District is in your precinct. Aren't you the least bit concerned about the people trapped in there?"

"I was relieved of those duties when Tayson took over."

Vanessa is seen shaking her head. "What about if their lives are in danger?"

"Again, it's not my problem."

"You have a duty to them."

"No. As of now, they're in a foreign country. The mayor agrees, and you should, too. Get with the program, Vanessa. For your sake."

The press mumbles as they turn to each other in disbelief. Vanessa steals a glance at Wilma. A picture of her face should be in the dictionary next to the term "nauseated." The mayor turns white as a sheet. His "chosen one" has just been eviscerated, and he knows it.

"I wish I could tell you that this was induced by stress, but it wasn't. I wish I could assure you that Inspector Sillyere was the only one to display apathy for our citizens trapped in the Arts District. Mayor Thurlow has maintained that the safety of the people in the ADOZ was his primary concern throughout this crisis. But that isn't true, is it, Mr. Mayor?"

"Of course it is!" he argues from his position behind her.

"Let the people decide," Vanessa says, nodding at the tech. He brings up the second video and presses play.

"They are protesters, not insurgents!" the mayor shouts, pointing a finger in Vanessa's face outside the area of one of the barricades.

"Protesters who just shot and killed three men and wounded a fourth. Your indecisiveness led to this."

"If you dare say their blood is on my hands, consider yourself fired. There will be no further police action against anyone manning the barricades. Any calls to 9-1-1 from the ADOZ will go unanswered. They are responsible, not us. I will not antagonize them and give their movement the high ground by challenging their perimeter. If they murder and rape everyone in that district, it will still be better for us than storming the barricades. Ensure my order is followed to the letter, *Chief Campbell.*"

Disbelief from the journalists in the room quickly begins to morph into simmering outrage. Vanessa arranged for an email with the full body camera footage to be sent to major news outlets and YouTube channels. She showed only clips that could be taken out of context. That argument doesn't hold when they see the full length of the raw footage.

The chief turns back to the mayor. He has daggers in his eyes. She half expects him to tackle her and order some minions to drag her out of the room. The only reason he isn't is optics. That footage would be memorialized on the Internet. It's the one thing that it's good at – saving embarrassing clips for posterity.

"I've dedicated my life to law enforcement. This city has always been my home, and I came to work every day with the people's interests in mind. My officers do the same. We are not perfect. We have made mistakes in the past. We will make mistakes in the future, but they won't be because we don't care.

"This crisis has taken a toll on us all. But the hardest part is my realization that the real enemy wasn't the men and women who took over the Arts District – it was our own government. I cannot continue to serve under such poor and thoughtless leadership. As a result, effective immediately, I am resigning as chief of the Minneapolis Police Department."

The press corps in this briefing room goes batshit crazy. The reporters all surge out of their seats and shout questions at the cyclic rate of a machine gun. The noise grows so deafening that it would drown out the engine noise of a Boeing 747.

Vanessa nods at Burke, who offers her a wry grin as she turns and walks off the dais. The last thing she hears before leaving the room is the mayor trying to restore order over all the questions being shouted at him. He has his problems, and Vanessa has hers. She needs to decide which Caribbean island beach she wants to lie on for the next two weeks.

CHAPTER EIGHTY-NINE
FIELD OFFICER DAVID BRASS

THE WASHINGTON MONUMENT
WASHINGTON, D.C.

Six Days after the Fall of the ADOZ

The Washington Monument is one of the capital's most iconic landmarks. It should be since it honors the first president of the United States. The height of the marble and granite obelisk at five hundred and fifty-five feet and its prominent location on the National Mall near the White House makes it one of the most recognizable symbols of the nation.

Brass thinks it's uninspired and boring. He's likely in the minority with that opinion. The Washington Monument is a popular attraction. Visitor traffic varies with the season, but it's an ideal space for sightseeing. That is absolutely not why he's here. He'd rather get picked up and have this meeting in a car.

He's here because his mission was a resounding success. Nearly a week after the collapse of the Minneapolis ADOZ, it's all the press is talking about. Cable news is fixated on it. Podcasts churn out videos about it. Online sites can't post their articles fast enough. There are too many interesting aspects of the story to tell. Of course, that doesn't mean the head of the CIA won't find something to bitch about.

"You said Pendulum could be bloody," Director Lancaster says, coming up alongside him, "but I never expected to hear it resulted in a warzone and a mountain of dead bodies."

"I don't control events. I only influence them."

"Yeah, well, the result was a massacre."

Brass nods. "And that's what the media will spend the next three months talking about. It's what you wanted to happen."

"You got those people killed, David."

Career bureaucrats are the worst. Brass can say that with confidence because he is one. The only three groups of people he despises more are lawyers, politicians, and political appointees. It just so happens that Alistair Lancaster is all three wrapped up in a gaunt, lanky package and tied with a bow of arrogance. It's a present nobody wants to open.

"I did no such thing. Landon Tayson attracted people into his orbit. They agreed to participate in his illegal activities. They fired on law enforcement at the barricade and followed his order to storm a house defended by military veterans. They paid the price for those decisions. I had nothing to do with any of that."

"Tayson's dead," the director confirms, moving the conversation along. "Is there anything that happened up there that can get linked back to you or the Agency?"

"No. The shell corporations we used to fund and arm his little takeover have been folded, and my agent on the inside successfully exfiltrated. She will be ready for her next assignment in a couple of months."

"What about the guys in that house? Any exposure?"

"We have several cover stories ready to go. Which one we go with will depend."

"On?"

Brass grins. "Circumstances and choices."

If there is one advantage in dealing with the head of the Central Intelligence Agency, it's that the man knows when to stop asking questions. As someone subject to congressional oversight and constantly being handed subpoenas to testify, sometimes it's better not to know the particulars. Lying to Congress is perjury. While he isn't above doing that, pleading ignorance is a far better course of action.

"All right. Button it up, and we'll never speak of this again."

"There is one more order of business," Brass says before his boss can walk away. "I kept my part of the bargain. Now, it's time to keep yours."

Alistair likely hoped this wouldn't come up. That dream is dashed.

"What do you plan to do with this pet project of yours?"

"Redefine intelligence gathering and sharing in our government. I'm tired of fighting ourselves as much as our enemies. This will help solve that problem."

"By creating a group that operates outside the chain of command?"

"I still report to you, Alistair. They'll report to me. You have plausible deniability, and I have a team that can perform the actual mission our intelligence agencies were designed for. It's a win-win."

The director sighs heavily. "So you say."

"Well?"

"You have the green light for Watchtower. I'll arrange the funding."

There's an old adage in sales that preaches, "Once you get the answer you are looking for, leave." Brass has never been a salesman, but he took the lesson to heart. The conversation is finished, so he turns to start the trek back to his office. The director grabs his arm before he makes it more than a half step.

"David? Don't make me regret this."

"I wouldn't dream of it," Brass says as he stifles a smirk and heads for the metro station to take him back to Virginia.

EPILOGUE

EMMIT "CHICAGO" HASKINS

UNDISCLOSED CIA FACILITY

Seven Days after the Fall of the ADOZ

Six days. Well, almost six days. That's how long it's been since his escape was interrupted and he was moved to this…facility. If one can call it that.

Chicago has a room that locks from the outside. There is no such thing as freedom of movement here. Meals are brought to him. He has a television with nothing else to look at in this windowless room made of painted cinder blocks. It's an infuriating existence that has been mercifully interrupted.

He's brought to another sterile room with a table and two chairs. Chicago is surprised that he wasn't shackled. Then again, he's not even sure if he's under arrest. Nobody has read him his rights. He was plucked off a street and "disappeared." Even his sister has no idea of his whereabouts. Not that he could tell her if a call was permitted.

A half-hour after being seated in a chair and left to occupy his time in the most boring room on the planet, a man with a file enters the room and sits down. He's clearly not one for idle chit-chat or even a perfunctory greeting. Chicago watches him open the file and scan its contents. Finally, the silence becomes overbearing.

"Am I under arrest?" Chicago asks, his voice betraying his annoyance and frustration. "Because I've been here just shy of a week, and nobody has read me my rights."

The slightly portly man across from him shakes his head. "I'm not in law enforcement."

"What is this?"

"I've read through your military record, Staff Sergeant Haskins. Your service in the Rangers was exemplary."

Chicago leans back in his stiff-back metal chair. "The officers in my unit didn't think so."

"No, I can imagine they didn't. In some respects, the civilian sector, government, and even the military are the same. People in positions of power are more worried about their next promotion than the men who serve them or their mission. Career ladders are designed to be climbed. Too many feel that it's at any cost."

"Who are you?"

He lifts his eyes to make eye contact with Chicago. "My name is David Brass."

"Of?"

The question isn't rewarded with an answer. Mr. David Brass of whatever agency he's with goes back to reading the file. It's theater. He wants Chicago to be left with questions for some reason. It's not a game the former Ranger feels like playing.

"Look, if you're going to charge me with something, do it. Otherwise, let me go."

"Do you want to be charged? Ninety-seven men died storming your house. Another dozen or so are being treated for gunshot wounds in a Minneapolis hospital. That's a lot of murder and attempted murder counts. And that's what we know about. I'm betting there are some others from your time behind the lines in the ADOZ. Then there are the gun charges and everything else in the book that prosecutors will throw at you."

"So be it," Chicago says. "It was self-defense."

"I agree. I'm not sure a jury will. Fortunately, there is an alternative that makes this problem disappear."

He lifts his eyes to study Chicago's reaction. If he is wearing anything on his face, it's disbelief. He had to almost climb over the bodies to get off his street. Even the mighty federal government can't Houdini that.

"Can…make…this…problem…disappear. Bold words. How? It's a little hard to cover up what happened that night."

"You're right. People know about the event and the carnage. What they don't know and are waiting to hear is the story behind it. It turns out there was a civil war among members of the ADOZ. Landon Tayson's military commander went rogue and tried to overthrow him. When the coup failed, he barricaded himself in an empty house and raised a flag in protest of his leader's actions. Tayson got upset at his insubordination and tried to storm the residence, and they were both unfortunately killed. That will make for some flashy headlines, right? Emmit…may I call you that? It's not hard to cover up who was involved. It happens all the time."

"Nobody will believe that."

David Brass offers a smug grin. "Are you sure?"

He isn't sure. Not at all. "The police know the truth."

"Some of them do," Brass concedes. "Narratives are powerful. The MPD knows that better than anyone, and we are among the best at creating them. Vanessa Campbell resigned from her position as chief of police. The mayor is on the political hot seat with the good people of Minneapolis. The governor is livid. They will fall in line. There are methods to ensure that in the event they don't."

"What do you want in return?"

Nothing comes for free in this world. Chicago had to earn his airborne wings at Fort Benning and shed blood, sweat, and tears to earn his Ranger tab. What is the going price for a "Get out of jail free" card? It's likely more than he is willing to pay.

"I'm impressed by you, Emmit. Not too many people could pull off what you did. They sent over a hundred men armed with assault rifles after you, and you emerged from the firefight without a scratch. Hell, you almost escaped altogether."

"Almost. Also, for the record, I had plenty of scratches, and there is technically no such thing as an assault rifle. It's a made-up term. And you didn't answer my question."

Brass nods. "You're a sharp guy. That's why I want you to work for me."

Chicago crosses his arms and leans back. "You're offering me a job?"

"Yes."

A simple one-word response. No other sales pitch is forthcoming. It's like making a Faustian deal when you ask if the devil gets your soul at the end.

"Maybe I would consider it if I knew who you work for."

Brass nods. "That's fair. Officially, we gather, analyze, and act on information related to national security."

"You're with the CIA," Chicago concludes, getting a nod from the man across from him. "Not interested."

He smirks. "Even if it means safeguarding your future?"

"I'm a soldier, not a spook."

"You *were* a soldier. Now, you're a fugitive who will soon be a felon guilty of mass murder and facing the death penalty, self-defense or not. You may have escaped immediate arrest, but nobody can protect you from the approaching storm. Right or wrong, you had a Fallujah-style firefight in the middle of Minneapolis. Politicians will want their pound of flesh to save their skins, and ambitious prosecutors will line up to make a name for themselves in getting it for them."

"I told you. I'm willing to face those charges."

"What about your friends?" Brass asks, causing a jolt of electricity to shoot up Chicago's spine. "I know you weren't in that house alone. Maybe you should ask Specialist Justus Coleman, Specialist Rob Hibbard, or Staff Sergeant Jose Centeno. Bronx, Tulsa, and Nica, I believe you call them."

Chicago's mouth hangs open after hearing their names. "How did you know?"

"It wasn't hard to track down. The three of them were in your squad, and all took leave at the same time. Then, there are your buddies who were discharged. Felix Ramone flew to Chicago from California, and Buddy O'Leary took an emergency vacation. When you take interstates, it makes it easy to track vehicles. We will continue to develop the evidence against Hollywood and Nashville, and they will join you and the others in courtrooms for the next few years."

"And if I agree to join the CIA?"

"That all goes away. I will ensure that none of their names are ever associated with this incident. Yours won't be, either."

"What's the catch?"

"There is no catch. That's the deal. Take it or leave it. Not that I think you have much of a choice. By all accounts, you were a great squad leader. I highly doubt you'd be willing to subject your men to what you know is coming when there's an easy way to protect them."

He's right. Chicago knows he is willing to face the music, but his men don't deserve that. None of those guys needed to be there, and they were anyway. He owes them, and that includes protection from prosecution. It doesn't matter if they feel like they did the right thing.

"There is one condition."

Brass chuckles. "I don't do conditions, and you're really not in a position to demand one."

"You'll do this one. I want you to restore my sister's home and ensure she is shielded from any responsibility for what happened. Every bit of damage to the house will be fixed, and you will pay for all of it. The CIA spends countless millions on its operations. You can afford the hundred grand or so that it will take to make her whole."

"She has insurance," Brass argues.

"No adjustor will be eager to pay that claim. The company will likely label it *force majeure* since the area was taken over by insurgents. That's my one condition, and I don't think it's a big ask. What'll it be?"

Brass rubs his chin. It's more theater. He's already made up his mind.

"Done. Welcome to the CIA."

If you enjoyed this Watchtower Prequel,
please consider leaving a review.

CONTINUE THE JOURNEY!

THE EYES OF OTHERS
THE WATCHTOWER THRILLERS, BOOK 1

A sample chapter has been included for your enjoyment!

PROLOGUE

"BOSTON" HOLLINGER

U.S. FORWARD OPERATING BASE
DEIR EZ-ZOR GOVERNORATE, SYRIA

I hate this place. The "graveyard of empires" was hardly a garden spot, but I would take Afghanistan over this hellhole any day. Satan would be eager to return to hell after spending seven months in this Godforsaken place. Syria is always under threat from the government regime, pissed-off rebels, the remnants of ISIS, the Russians, and groups allied with them. It's a mess, and the reason American troops are stuck protecting large oilfields and the potential revenues they could bring in.

None of that matters to me. It's my exhausting, often thankless job that brought me to a desert four hundred fifty miles from Damascus and over five thousand miles from home. As an intelligence analyst, I turn raw data collected from various sources into useful products that help keep the men and women here safe. Commanders here make life and death decisions every week. It's the information that I provide that they base them on.

I pull the small towel out of my cargo pocket as I walk and mop the sweat off the back of my neck as I make my way back to the tent. The temperatures here are already unbearable, and it's only the middle of June. My military deployments have taught me to hate insufferably hot places void of vegetation. The only respite to the misery I manage to enjoy is the time I spend with some of the other soldiers on the base. Some of them have quickly become close friends.

"So, we're haulin' ass across the desert in the MRAP like we stole the thing, and these two Apaches drop down on us from the sun. I swear, man, we never saw 'em," Mexico says, his arms flailing as he acts out every single word in front of the soldiers lounging outside the tent.

"Remind me never to travel anywhere with you in the turret," Colombia says, not bothering to look up as he adjusts the plate in his body armor carrier.

"You can't shoot for shit, anyway," Georgia says, lounging back in her chair as if she's working on her tan.

"I'm an expert marksman, thank you very much."

"Hold on, hold on, I'm not finished," Mexico admonishes. "These pilots must have been bored or something because sneaking up on us wasn't good enough. No, these asshats start practicing their attack runs on us. My driver panics like he's being chased by a hive of hornets or something. He starts dodging and weaving the truck like he's gonna get away from them."

"How long has this story been going on?" I lean over and ask Maryland, who's trying to read a book and pretending not to pay attention to the grunt.

"Twenty minutes or so. Mex is on his third story."

Maryland is the only other guy in this gaggle of unlikely friends who is also in military intelligence. He's the most mission-oriented soldier in my unit. All he wants to do is get the mission done and get home, or so he whines to us almost every day.

"The driver screams at me, 'Find us a place to hide!'" Mexico continues. "So I yell back at him, 'make for the tree line.' Don't you know, he shouted back, 'What tree line?' like we weren't in the middle of the damn desert."

The group roars like it's the funniest thing they've ever heard. Soldiers have a sort of dark humor, and it's something they carry with them when they no longer don the uniform. Mexico has a bright future doing comedy someday, although civilians aren't likely to get most of his jokes.

"He stops us on this little rise, and one of the Apaches comes at us head-on and flies over the MRAP, like ten feet over our turret. I swear, I could smell the pilot's aftershave. The other Apache flares up right next to us. He looks at my driver, and the gun points wherever he looks. My driver looks like he's about to shit his pants, so the guy starts shaking his head, and the cannon moves left and right like he's waving at us."

"Your tall tales are getting taller," Georgia moans from her makeshift lounge chair.

"I'm with her. I can't take it anymore. Which one of you dumbasses gave Mexico caffeine this morning?" I ask the group, knowing the cause of his hyperactivity all too well.

Everyone looks at Louisiana, who's smoking a cigarette as he listens to the story. Maryland points without looking up. Realizing his friends just ratted him out, he puts on a face of mock surprise. The prankster combat engineer of the group, Louisiana would have been my first choice as instigator anyway. What he lacks in stature and athletic ability, he makes up in attitude and intelligence.

"Maryland, why you always blamin' me, bro?" he protests in his Cajun-tinged accent.

"Because you're the one always doing stupid crap," Maryland says, only half-joking.

"Like what? Name one time I've done anythin' stupid." He left that wide open.

"The story about the strip club in Augusta," Maryland deadpans.

"The ATM at the PX in Kuwait," Colombia adds with a grin on his face.

"Something about the flight attendant on the plane to Kuwait," Mexico adds.

"I haven't heard that story yet," Arkansas says, getting nods from his buddies Kansas and Indiana.

The motley group is made up of different military occupational specialties. We have infantrymen, combat engineers, military intelligence, military police, and even a cook who stays quiet for obvious reasons. The food here is also terrible, and he hates us reminding him of that.

After seven months on this deployment, we've become a tight-knit group. It's why we stopped calling each other by our rank and last name, and use our home state or country instead. Most are states and countries like Maryland, Louisiana, Mexico, and Colombia. I got named after a city because Boston sounds slicker than Massachusetts. Together, we're a walking geography lesson.

"How 'bout you, Boston? You wanna add to the list of my transgressions?" Louisiana asks. I don't have to think about it for long.

"Did anyone mention about how you almost burned down the general's house at Lewis-McChord?" I say, smiling. It's funny to me, but not for his commander, who ended up standing in front of a furious colonel for a serious ass-chewing.

"Hold on, wait a sec!" Louisiana shouts before grinning broadly. "I had accomplices for that one."

"Yeah, Sergeant Jack Daniels, Specialist Johnnie Walker, and Private Jim Beam," Colombia announces in his typical cool, James Dean manner.

"The three wise men that manage to turn Louisiana into a complete idiot," Maryland needles.

"Wow. There's a whole lotta sell-outery goin' on here," Louisiana decrees, eliciting snickers from the group.

"What's new in the world, Boston?" Arkansas asks. "We win the war yet?"

"I'm in the SCIF staring at field reports all day. I'd be the last to know."

In intelligence parlance, the "skiff," as it is pronounced, is the Sensitive Compartmented Information Facility where we analyze classified material. It's an enclosed structure with stringent access controls and is restricted solely to personnel who have passed a thorough background check and have been granted clearance to enter. We just think of it as our office.

"Guys, we need to take the fobbits on a field trip one of these days," Indiana says, doing a function check on his M4 carbine.
"Fobbit" is a derogatory word used to shame soldiers afraid to head outside of the base. Just as most hobbits from *Lord of the Rings* never left the Shire, most fobbits never leave the forward operating base. Technically, this isn't a FOB, but the term carried over from the Iraq War.

"Shut up, dude, before you get some unlicensed dental work," Maryland threatens. He likes to talk tough, but the guys know that the dog has no bite.

"Bro, you don't have the strength to open a can of Coke, so what are ya goin' to do?" Louisiana retorts.

For most road warriors trekking to work in the U.S., the biggest concern they have is not to rear-end someone when they cut you off. The only mental energy they expend is listening to the local radio station's traffic report to figure out how to get out of the bumper-to-bumper traffic. A tragedy back home is spilling coffee on your work clothes.

"I'm going to beat you senseless tonight," Maryland says.

"Promise?" he responds, blowing his rival a kiss.

"You guys need therapy. Did anyone—"

A blinding light precedes a deafening blast, and a wall of dust blows over us like a tsunami as I try to keep my balance. Seconds later, the telltale barking of a pair of M240B machine guns rips through the desert air.

"Shit. That was the gate. Let's go!" Kansas says, rallying his fellow infantrymen. They start grabbing their gear when the whistling of falling mortar rounds grows louder.

"Incoming!"

There's no time to react. The round hits the tent, and I feel myself hurtling through the air before crashing on the ground. My ears are ringing… What's going on?

A sharp pain stabs at my head. It feels like it's…split open. I try to move but can't. My body has gone limp.

I see movement above me…everything's hazy. Muffled voices…who is that? Maryland? The infantry guys? Their shouting barely registers…I can't understand.

Hands grab at me…I'm not where I was. There's a piercing pain in my shoulder. I feel like I'm being dragged into… Another bright light destroys my vision and makes me wince. My head is pounding, and it's getting worse. The pain is so bad.

I hear popping sounds. I search the sky above me and see streaks of light…smoke… Another jolt of pain goes through my body as I'm jerked along the ground. I feel dirt kick up into my face as a soldier drops next to me. I try to move my left arm, but nothing happens. I touch my face with my right hand and feel it sticky and wet. Is that blood? My blood?

"Hang in there, pal. We'll get you out of here," a muffled voice reassures me.

There are popping sounds everywhere. They sound like firecrackers. I can't hear or see anything well. My head is swimming. I can't stay awake.

Another small explosion erupts next to me. I can taste the sand kicked up as everything grows dim. I need to get up and try to make my legs move, but nothing happens. Everything sounds more distant now as my world grows darker…and darker.

A NOTE FROM THE AUTHOR

While the events of this story are completely fictional, they were heavily inspired by real-world happenings. The first one is easy enough to discern. The CHOP, or CHAZ as it later became known, was a self-declared autonomous protest zone in Seattle's Capitol Hill neighborhood in June 2020. It emerged amid the George Floyd protests after the Seattle Police Department abandoned the East Precinct following clashes with demonstrators. The zone in this novel is much larger in size, encompassing much of the Minneapolis Arts District.

They are also better armed. While the Seattle CHOP was more akin to the result of a spontaneous protest, this clearly had some organization and someone powerful to finance it. In this instance, my first "what if" question arises: What if a massive social protest was planned, organized, and executed by the CIA?

As surprising as this may be, Rangers squaring off in a major city against thugs actually happened. In 1989, Sgt. Bill Foulk purchased a cheap house in a rough Tacoma neighborhood as an investment. Foulk grew concerned that a house on his block was an epicenter of gang activity and began to videotape the people who visited the suspected drug house.

The occupants were members of the Crips, the violent street gang that was spreading from California to Washington. Foulk told *The Associated Press* that gang members threatened him when they noticed he was filming their movements. Fearing that the gang would escalate to direct action against him, he called friends from the 2nd Ranger Battalion to his house for a barbecue. Not long after the Rangers arrived, fifteen to twenty gang members began to shoot up the house. It didn't end well for them.

The concept of this novel was born during the COVID-19 pandemic, and I married that first "what if" with the second: What if Army Rangers were in the Seattle CHOP? How would they respond?

When I introduced Chicago as a character in *The Eyes of Addicts*, I knew he needed a backstory. I was in the middle of writing that novel when I realized that this tale was it. It gives him depth as a character, and this was a story I really wanted to tell. It also explains how Chicago came to work for David Brass and the CIA. If you haven't read the Watchtower Thrillers, you should check them out.

ACKNOWLEDGMENTS

This was a really fun novel to construct. As I mentioned, the inspiration for it came long ago, and I'm glad I could finally bring it to you. As always, my sincere thanks go to you, the reader. There are thousands of other books you could have picked up to read, and I am sincerely honored that you chose this one. I hope you decide to check out my other works as well.

Thank you to my lovely and supportive wife, Michele, my family, and my friends for always being by my side and having my back. Every protagonist has a strong supporting cast of characters. They are mine.

Michael Waitz at Sticks and Stones Editing, a man who must get giddy in correcting my many mistakes, is as much a friend as he is an editor. It's thanks to his diligence that I didn't completely botch the spelling of the main character's name. Please don't ask how that happens. Let's just call it the creative process.

People absolutely judge books by their covers, whether on Amazon or in a bookstore. I want to thank Dave and his team at JD&J for their amazing work in creating the cover for this novel.

A lot of research went into community policing and the effects of the unrest in 2020. I promised to leave their names out, but thank you to those who helped with their insights.

The first video I saw about the Rangers taking on a gang was made by Popo Medic. I can't speak to how accurate the information in the video is, but I will include the link here for you to check out for yourselves. It's not a long one and well worth the watch: https://youtu.be/Z4iQxpwYhAg?si=nUAFtZCsGoMkE5gd

ABOUT THE AUTHOR

Mikael Carlson is the award-winning author of *The iCandidate* and the Michael Bennit Series of political dramas. He also wrote the Tierra Campos Series, the dystopian America, Inc. Saga, and the Santa and Dancing Trilogies. The Watchtower Thrillers is his fourth series, and this prequel is his twentieth novel.

A retired veteran of the Rhode Island Army National Guard and United States Army, he deployed twice to support military operations during the Global War on Terror. Mikael has served in the field artillery, infantry, and in support of special operations units during his active duty career at Fort Bragg and in the Army National Guard.

A proud U.S. Army Paratrooper, he conducted over fifty airborne operations following the completion of jump school at Fort Benning in 1998. Since then, he has trained with the militaries of countless foreign nations.

Academically, Mikael earned a Master of Arts in American History and graduated with a B.S. in International Business from Marist College in 1996.

He was raised in New Milford, Connecticut, and lives in nearby Danbury.